WINTER RIDE

"Wh-what are you doing, Mr. Drayton?"

He reached over to remove her goggles and Polly stiffened. "I'm making you listen to reason."

After the goggles, he began working on her next layer of defense: the big motoring scarf tied over her hat. It took every ounce of her resolve to keep from twining her fingers through his and drawing his hand to her lips. She wanted to kiss him so badly she ached.

Quick as lightning, Polly snatched her hand away and hid it in her lap. She wasn't sure whether she was more afraid of what he planned to do to her or of what she wished she could do to him.

Then James cupped her cheeks in his big hands and Polly realized what she really feared was the pleasure she took from his touch. She couldn't afford to feel this pleasure.

"Please, Polly, what can I do to make you see us as a man and a woman rather than an employer and employee? There must be something I can do."

Polly opened her mouth to speak, but nothing emerged. She felt her eyes widen as James's face came closer and still closer to hers. Her gaze fastened on his full lips until she could no longer see them; then she felt them, and reason fled.

Other *Leisure* Books by Emma Craig:
ROSAMUNDA'S REVENGE

Christmas Pie

EMMA CRAIG

LEISURE BOOKS NEW YORK CITY

A LEISURE BOOK®

December 1997

Published by

Dorchester Publishing Co., Inc.
276 Fifth Avenue
New York, NY 10001

ISBN 0-8439-4331-9

The name "Leisure Books" and the stylized "L" with design are
trademarks of Dorchester Publishing Co., Inc.

Printed in the United States of America.

This one's for my daughters, Anni and Robin. Robin's the one who found the poem ("Let Us Sing Our Roundelays" by George Wither, 1588-1667) and copied it in calligraphy onto one of her beautifully crafted Christmas cards. Anni adored Edgar Eager's books when she was a child, and so did I. This book was inspired equally by Wither's poem and Eager's *Half Magic*.

LET US SING OUR ROUNDELAYS
by George Wither (1588-1667)

So now is come our joyful'st feast;
Let every man be jolly.
Each room with ivy-leaves is dressed,
And every post with holly.
> Though some churls at our mirth repine
> Round your foreheads garlands twine,
> Drown sorrw in a cup of wine,
And let us all be merry.

Now all our neighbours' chimneys smoke,
And Christmas blocks are burning;
The ovens they with baked meats choke,
And all their spits are turning.
> Without the door let sorrow lie,
> And if for cold it hap to die,
> We'll bury't in a Christmas pie,
And evermore be merry.

Now every lad is wondrous trim,
And no man minds his labour;
Our lasses have provided them
A bagpipe and a tabor.
> Young men, and maids, and girls and boys,
> Give life to one another's joys,
> And you anon shall by their noise
Perceive that they are merry.

Then wherefore in these merry days
Should we, I pray, be duller?
No; let us sing our roundelays
To make our mirth the fuller.
> And, whilst thus inspired we sing,
> Let all the streets with echoes ring;
> Woods, and hills, and everything,
Bear witness we are merry.

Chapter One

San Francisco, California, November 1899

Polly MacNamara rushed along the narrow street, cluttered with stalls and teeming with merchants hurrying to move their wares indoors. She didn't blame them. The weather was as cold as the inside of her mother's icebox and it looked like rain. Taking a peek at the pea-soup sky, she wished she'd been able to afford that pair of galoshes she'd seen in the window at I. Magnin.

Perhaps next season, she thought, more to keep her mind off her frozen toes than from any true hope.

At least, thanks to the typewriting class she'd taken at the Young Women's Christian Association four summers earlier, Polly possessed a real skill and could earn an honest wage, unlike so many poor woman who were forced into lives of wretched dependence or servitude. The thought warmed her heart, even if her nose stung and her cheeks were chapped from the frigid wind doing its best to whip the scarf from her head. Perhaps the MacNamara ladies were not able to live elegantly; still, Polly took a good deal of pride in her independence. Not many other women her age could honestly be said to support their families.

Although her gaze seldom strayed from the walkway in front of her this foggy afternoon—staring into shop windows only led to idle wishfulness—an ivory gleam caught the edge of her preoccupied attention as she hurried by a window. When she turned to look, she stopped in her tracks, enchanted.

"Oh, how lovely."

It cost her a good deal of warmth, but Polly withdrew her unmittened hand from the nest she had created in her coat pocket, fisted up her fingers, and rubbed a bare circle on the frosty glass to better see inside the shop. Sure enough, her initial impression had not deceived her. There, nestled on a piece of exquisitely embroidered Chinese silk, lay two carved ivory combs. They were beautiful—the very thing to give her mother for Christmas.

Since expense was always Polly's first consideration, no matter what the occasion, she wondered how much they cost. If she priced them and found them too dear, she'd feel very bad. Of course, she might be able to lay them away and pay something each week until Christmas. After deliberating for a moment or two, Polly gave herself a little shake and stepped up to the door.

Fog swirled around her shoes and trailed her heels inside the shop. She noticed it tagging after her like a friendly puppy and her whimsical impression amused her. A little bell hanging from the door tinkled invitingly, and the warmth of the room felt like heaven after the wintry out-of-doors. A pleasant scent of sandalwood hung in the air, as though incense were as much a part of the shop's decor as its furniture.

When the bell stopped tinkling, Polly expected to see a shopkeeper appear from behind the beaded curtain separating the shop from the living quarters in back. Nobody emerged, so she decided to take a look around the fascinating shop.

It was a pleasantly cluttered place. There were so many pretty things to look at; to want. *Perhaps one day,* she thought as she ran her fingers over a length of patterned silk draped over a carved teakwood stand.

"Good evening, lady."

Startled, Polly swirled around to behold a very tiny woman, wrinkled with age, her face creased into a smile owing little to the presence of teeth. The old woman bobbed her head, and Polly smiled back. "Good evening."

"May I help you, lady?"

As the old woman hobbled toward her, Polly noticed her hands, dry and papery as old parchment, clasped in front of her. She was dressed in the typical Chinese manner, in dark blue pajamas. A faint scent of pungent cooking seemed to have entered the room with the shopkeeper, and it blended surprisingly well with the sandalwood.

"I saw those ivory combs in the window and came in to price them. If they aren't too expensive, I would like to purchase them for my mother. For Christmas."

Polly's circumstances had been distressed for a good deal of her life and she always asked prices. She did so now, firmly, secure in her judgment that a person's wealth did not determine her worth. Besides, she couldn't afford not to.

"Two dollar," the old lady said, and gave a pleased cackle.

"Two dollars."

My goodness. Two dollars was two days' wages. Two dollars could buy groceries for a week or more. Two dollars was a handsome price, indeed.

Polly eyed the combs pensively. She caressed the smooth ivory with her fingers and thought how pretty they would be in her mother's hair. Her hair was her mother's pride and joy. She had so little else in which to take pleasure. She enjoyed fixing her hair for church on Sunday and when Mrs. Plimsole came over for tea on an afternoon.

Still, two dollars was a lot of money.

"But, who else do I have to buy for?" Answering her own question with, "Not a soul," she turned to offer the tiny shopkeeper a smile. "I'll take them."

The little old lady had a very sharp way about her. Polly got the feeling she was being scrutinized with great care. Oddly enough, the woman's examination did not make Polly, who was quite reserved, uncomfortable.

After their business with the combs was transacted, the old woman put a shriveled, clawlike hand on Polly's arm. "Minute, lady. Wait minute. I got something for you.'' With that, she vanished behind the beaded screen.

''Oh!'' Polly wasn't sure what to do, so she merely stood still, waited for the woman to return, and fretted. She hoped her mother wouldn't be worried about her. Intrigue overcame worry, though, and held her fast for several minutes.

Just as she came to the conclusion that she had misunderstood the shopkeeper and was getting ready to leave the store, the beads rattled again and the woman reappeared.

''This for you.'' The old lady thrust a trinket into Polly's hand and closed her fingers around it.

Surprised, Polly exclaimed, ''Oh, please, no! I can't accept anything from you. Truly, I—''

When she lifted her gaze, it was to find the old woman, arms resting atop one another across her chest, hands buried in the sleeves of her coat, nodding at her. A happy smile lit the ancient face, giving it a gnomelike appearance, bringing to Polly's mind thoughts of elves and fairies. The elderly lady looked so benign and cheerful that Polly couldn't find it in her heart to protest further.

At last she said simply, ''Thank you very much.''

Then she opened her hand to see what she had been given. It looked like a coin. Holding it up to the one lamp casting its antique amber glow through the shop, Polly decided the trinket was indeed a coin, but of so old a vintage and so foreign a mint that she couldn't place its age or its origin.

It looked very worn, as though it had lived an interesting life. The coin seemed almost to glow in the faint light of the lamp. A small hole had been drilled in it once upon a time, and Polly thought it would look pretty suspended from a ribbon—a nice bauble to wear on Christmas Eve if she had the proper evening dress to go with it. She wished she did.

The strange coin charmed her. She turned to thank the shopkeeper for the small treasure, but the old woman was gone. Polly scanned the shop for her, thinking to find her among the shadows, but didn't see her anywhere.

I guess she went back to her cooking. Polly wondered why she hadn't heard the beads clacking together, then decided to come back another day and thank her properly.

On that cheerful resolution, she put the coin in her pocket and once again braved the chilly out-of-doors. The weather, unusually foggy and cold for this time of year, had not become any friendlier as she'd whiled away precious minutes in the shop. The wind had picked up and nearly tore the parcel of combs out of her hands. Fat drops of rain began to find their way through the soupy fog, and Polly heard them splat on the paving stones and felt them pelt her old black hat.

"Oh, bother. I wish I were home already," she muttered as she pulled her scarf more tightly to her throat. Almost at once, she was taken up short by a shout.

"Miss MacNamara! I say, Miss MacNamara, is that you?"

Surprised by the hearty male voice, Polly turned and discovered to her amazement that a shiny black horseless carriage, complete with a canvas cover, was being driven across the dirty street. It came to rest next to the sidewalk. Unused to seeing such luxury on the skinny, crowded streets of Chinatown, Polly mistrusted it.

When the door of the fine vehicle burst open and James Drayton stepped out, her alarm increased. Owner of the law firm for which Polly industriously typed away each day, the brusque and imperious Mr. Drayton made her nervous just walking past her workroom. Here, on a public street, away from the comfortable trappings of the office, the thought of having to speak to him made her nerves jump.

"What are you doing out on such a foul night, walking alone in this neighborhood?" He sounded irritated.

Although his show of temper sparked her own, Polly didn't voice her annoyance. It would be unwise to do so, and she was not unwise. He was, after all, her employer.

She did not have to grovel, however. Rather rigidly, she said, "I live at the end of Market and Powell, Mr. Drayton."

"Well, you'd best get in the carriage. I'll drive you home. It's not fit for man nor beast out tonight. Why, they say it's going to snow, for heaven's sake." His tone conveyed the surprise appropriate to his news. Snow was almost unheard of in San Francisco.

Startled by his offer, Polly only stared at him for a second. She'd never been inside a horseless carriage in her life. The lure of such a novel experience drew her even as uncertainty held her motionless. After a moment's hesitation, during which long-held notions of propriety did battle with fascination and the fierce weather, Polly stepped forward. She was so cold her fingers hurt when she unwrapped them from her parcel and reached for the door handle.

"I'll do that." James whipped open the door, then took her hand and assisted her into the car.

"Good Lord, why aren't you wearing gloves, Miss MacNamara?" It sounded as though he considered Polly no better than a fool to be walking about in a November rain bare-handed.

She pretended not to hear him. "Thank you, Mr. Drayton," she said punctiliously.

In truth, she'd almost rather have walked than to have been discovered by this man. Being in a closed vehicle with him unnerved her. She had to stifle a gasp when he leaned across her lap to rifle around in a small leather satchel on the floor.

"Here, put these on." It was not a request. He flipped a pair of fur-lined gloves onto her lap.

Polly stared at the gloves for several seconds before she decided that to protest would be worse than to obey. Slipping on the warm gloves, she said, "Thank you," and was glad it was dark. He couldn't tell her cheeks blazed with embarrassment if he couldn't see her.

"Don't know why you didn't take the cable car. It's too damned cold and wet to walk these days."

Polly recoiled at his language. She might be poor, and she might feel intimidated by James Drayton's wealth and privilege, but she was a young lady of firm principles. "Cable cars cost money, Mr. Drayton," she said stiffly. "The sidewalks are free."

He shot her a piercing look she chose to ignore. Then she lifted her head to a regal angle and wished he wouldn't be so abrupt with her.

Damn. James slanted another look at Polly, sitting as straight and inflexible as a fireplace poker. No. That was too warm a description for his passenger. An icicle was more like it.

Too bad, he thought, as he maneuvered easily through the twisting, cramped streets of Chinatown. She was quite a good-looking girl. He guessed she didn't like his prying. But, for God's sake, cable cars only cost a nickel. Who couldn't afford a nickel these days? Another look at the pretty typist made him think perhaps she couldn't. He bet she'd never seen the inside of a horseless carriage, either.

Well, as long as she was here, he might as well put on a show. With a flair that seemed to go with the motorcar, he pressed the rubber horn, startling not merely people on the street but his companion as well. She jumped a foot.

"Sorry, Miss MacNamara," he said sheepishly.

"Oh! It's all right. I—I've just never been in a motorcar before."

She looked so unnerved that James felt boorish and more than a little silly about his bravura display. With uncharacter-istic candor he said, "Well, I do love motorcars. This is a Benz Landaulet-Coupé. I imported it from Germany, but since I'm convinced motorcars are the investment of the future, I'm putting my money on the Americans. We're more innovative and daring than any of the European manufacturers."

"Really?"

It was a rather perfunctory *really,* and James wasn't sure Polly truly cared much about horseless carriages. Nevertheless, an unfamiliar compunction to be friendly nudged him and he forged ahead.

"I'm sure of it. I've gone into partnership with an Ameri-can, Ransom Eli Olds. In fact, I have an experimental model of the Olds Curved-Dash Runabout in my stable at home. It's not as luxurious as the Benz, but it's quite a fine motorcar."

Polly uttered a tiny, tinny, "Oh," and James guessed he was right about her level of interest. Somewhat annoyed, he cleared his throat and asked, "You live with your family, Miss MacNamara?"

"My mother." She did not elaborate.

James sighed, irked that she was going to make him pry. Usually girls opened up and spilled their lives all over his lap during the first three minutes or so of his acquaintance. He'd never had to work at it before.

17

All at once, he decided to try another tack. Take some time. Perhaps it would be amusing to expend a little effort on this one. He'd noticed Polly before. In fact, he noticed her every time he walked past the typewriting room in his place of business.

Always well-groomed in simple dark skirts and prim white shirtwaists, she was the only typist in his law firm's employ who didn't giggle and simper every time he braved the gauntlet of typists to fetch a brief or relay an assignment. She possessed a dignity and an air of self-possession that captured his attention at work and did so now as well.

Trying on politeness as he might try on a new hat, James smiled, cocked his head, and asked, "And do you have any siblings, Miss MacNamara, or is it just the two of you ladies?"

He saw Polly gulp, and smiled. Although he seldom had need to, James Drayton could slather on the charm when he chose to.

"I—I have an older brother, Mr. Drayton. He is at present in the United States Navy."

James wondered why she wouldn't look at him. As a rule, ladies were fluttering their lashes at him by this time. Not Polly. At the moment, she sat like a queen, her attention firmly fixed outside. Giving another push to open her up, he said, "A seafaring man, is he? And does he enjoy life at sea?"

Polly swallowed again, the only sign she gave that his presence affected her at all. James had the impression of sadness when her shoulders slumped, but she straightened again immediately, and he experienced a reaction he'd never felt to a woman before. All at once he wanted to lighten her burden, whatever it was. How odd.

"My brother Stephen's present assignment is as chief petty officer on the U.S.S. *China Seas*."

"Oh. Oh, my goodness."

Now James understood the fleeting moment of dejection that had weighted Polly's shoulders. The U.S.S. *China Seas,* after having participated heroically in the glorious Battle of Manila Bay last year, had been on its way home to port when it seemed to have vanished from the ocean. The ship had been reported missing last month. Although the war with Spain was officially over and had been for some time, rumors abounded that a rogue Spanish vessel was to blame for the noble *China Sea*'s disappearance.

James had read all about it in the *Chronicle*. He paid attention to such things because his father's business, the Pacific-Orient Freight Shipping Lines, often crossed sea lanes with naval vessels.

A grim smile twitched his mouth when he thought about his father. The old man would be perfectly astounded if he ever discovered that James kept track of the family business, if only via the newspaper.

"I'm very sorry, Miss MacNamara."

"Thank you." Her voice was strong, but James detected an undercurrent of pain.

Glancing over, he discovered Polly sitting with her hands stuffed into her coat pockets, as though she'd hidden her courage in there and was now groping for it. She looked pensive and awfully appealing. That seemed strange to him, too.

She was different from the other women in his orbit. James had no illusions about himself. He knew he was good-looking, and he knew he possessed enough wealth to attract designing women. In truth, designing women were the only ones he knew. They threw themselves at his feet so often, he'd become quite cynical about the fair sex. Polly, with her aspect of cool indifference, was a mystery. James loved a mystery.

The heavy San Francisco air had changed in the last couple of minutes. Instead of spitting raindrops, the sky began to disgorge small wet snowflakes. They swirled in windy eddies and shone in the light of the gas street lamps like ribbons of tiny, glittering pearls. The thick weather seemed to capture light from his new Benz Landaulet-Coupé's carriage lamps and fling it back into the motorcar.

"By God, they were right. Look at that, Miss MacNamara. It's truly snowing." James leaned forward so he could view the phenomenon more clearly. When he peeked at Polly, he saw her watching, too, her eyes as bright as stars.

"I believe you're right, Mr. Drayton. How unusual. Why, it looks almost magical."

Filtered buttery lamplight played glancing, dancing games

with Polly's features and, watching her, James thought *she* looked almost magical. He felt something in his chest soften.

She was such a pretty thing, and possessed a grace at seeming at odds with her employment as a typist. Suddenly it seemed a shame she had to work so hard at such a tedious occupation.

"Do you miss your brother, Miss MacNamara?"

She turned, and James realized that she was surprised he'd ask such a question. He felt his mouth quirk again. He'd worked hard for his reputation as a devil-may-care ladies' man. This was the first time he'd had occasion to rue his success. However, he discovered he didn't want this lovely creature to fear him.

After a pause, Polly said, "Yes, I do, Mr. Drayton. Stephen is very dear to both Mother and me, and we miss him. I wish he were here in San Francisco with us, particularly as the holidays approach."

James had a feeling she wanted to say more, but he saw her full lower lip tremble slightly as she closed her mouth in a hurry and turned away. With a pang, he realized she didn't want him to witness her sorrow.

Sifting through the empty social clichés one could use in situations like this, James ultimately settled on one he deemed the least offensive. "Well, I certainly hope you'll both see him soon, Miss MacNamara."

"Thank you."

"Maybe he'll be home for Christmas."

As though she appreciated his trite words, she shot him the tiniest of smiles. "I hope so. I wish for it every day."

Struggling to think of something else to say to prolong the conversation, James said, "Isn't chief petty officer a high rank for someone your brother's age? At least, what his age must be." He felt silly.

For the first time since she entered his carriage, though, Polly's smile seemed genuine, and James guessed he hadn't been silly after all. "Oh, yes. Stephen is a very hard-working young man. He had planned to go to Annapolis until . . ." Her voice trailed off and she looked flustered.

"Until what, Miss MacNamara?" James was surprised to hear the gentleness in his voice.

Polly took a deep breath and said, "Until the accident that took our father's life and left our mother an invalid. He was unable to support the family and attend school, too, I'm afraid."

"I'm sorry."

As though to ward off his sympathy, Polly said quickly, "He still longed to go to sea, however, so he enlisted. He does love the life. And he supported us quite well until . . ."

She stopped speaking and James entertained the notion that she believed she'd said too much. It took less imagination than he possessed to understand that she felt uncomfortable talking about her personal life with her employer. Especially an employer who'd gone to such lengths to create an image of himself as authoritative and unapproachable. And wicked.

Silence settled between them, broken by the splatter of wet snowdrops against the carriage hood and the motorcar's loud engine. James shot peeks at Polly from time to time, always to find her staring out the window to her right. She didn't seem to want to look at him, a circumstance he thought both charming and unfortunate.

"What kind of accident was it, Miss MacNamara?"

She didn't answer for a moment, then heaved a deep sigh. "A shipping accident, Mr. Drayton. My father was an importer of Oriental silks and porcelains. Mother and Father had gone to China and were on their way back home with a shipment of goods my father planned to market in the United States. A boiler blew up as the ship neared the dock. My father was not the only person to lose his life. My mother, fortunately, was not killed, but she has been in a wheelchair ever since."

James shook his head, dismayed. Polly's recitation stirred a faint memory, but he couldn't put his finger on it. "That's a real tragedy for your family, Miss MacNamara. I'm sorry."

"Thank you."

"Er, what about insurance? Was your father's shipment not insured?"

"I'm afraid I don't know, Mr. Drayton. My mother doesn't like to talk about it."

"I see." Although James was far from satisfied, he guessed

he wasn't going to wring any further information out of his companion this evening.

"We're approaching my house, Mr. Drayton. It's the one with the light in the window."

"I'll see you to the door, Miss MacNamara."

"Oh! Please. You don't have to do that. It's just up the sidewalk."

James pulled his horseless carriage across the muddy street and up to the sidewalk. It was an expert maneuver, but Polly would have appreciated it more if he'd not threatened to see her to her door. Not that there was anything wrong with her door—or her entire house, if it came to that. But this was James Drayton, her employer, and she found it unsettling that he should be showing her courtesies.

"Don't be ridiculous, Miss MacNamara." James hopped out of his side and slogged to Polly's door, opened it and took her hand to help her out.

Oh, dear. Although she was somewhat reticent, Polly was generally self-confident. Right now, however, she felt completely inadequate. She said, "Thank you," and didn't mean it.

As they walked up the sidewalk, she stuffed her package of combs into her pocket and tugged off the gloves he'd given her. "Here, Mr. Drayton. Thank you for lending these to me."

"Don't be silly, Miss MacNamara. Keep them. You'll need them again tomorrow."

But Polly, who had never taken charity in her life, had no intention of starting now. "No, Mr. Drayton. Thank you, but I can't accept them."

Although he didn't look happy about it, James took back his gloves. Polly was glad. It was embarrassing enough, having him drive her home and then walk her up to the door of her inelegant, albeit trim abode.

One of a long block of tall, thin wood-frame structures, the MacNamara residence stood cheek-by-jowl with neighbors on either side. The area had been elegant once, but that was long before Polly and her mother came to live here. Now it existed in the shriveled heart of San Francisco, a reminder of the city's bygone, booming youth.

22

Before she got to the front porch, the door swung open and Polly saw her mother outlined against the warm background of the gas lighting inside. As always happened when she glimpsed her mother, Polly felt a mingling of love and sadness well up inside her. She hurried the last several feet and ran up the steep steps to the small porch.

"I'm sorry, Mother. Were you worried about me?"

Mrs. MacNamara smiled indulgently at her daughter. "Why, no, Polly. You're right on time. I only thought I heard a motorcar and wanted to see it."

Of course. Such a conveyance was a luxury seldom seen in this neighborhood. Fingering the coin in her pocket, Polly wished for her mother's sake that their life wasn't quite so hard. The odd old coin felt warm to her touch and she experienced a surge of unexpected comfort.

"You were right, Mother. Mr. Drayton happened to drive by as I was walking down Grant, and he offered me a ride home."

"Mr. Drayton?" Polly's mother sounded every bit as surprised as Polly had been by James's timely arrival.

"Yes. I'm sorry. I don't suppose you can even see him with me in the way."

Polly stepped aside, revealing James standing at the foot of the narrow staircase, smiling up at the two of them. Her breath caught when she looked at him. Oh, my, he was a handsome man. This evening he appeared different than he did in the office; why, he looked almost friendly.

James took the six steps quickly. "How do you do, Mrs. MacNamara?" In spite of the weather, he removed his hat and extended a hand.

Polly, who had never seen James Drayton be polite until tonight, was taken aback by the gracious, easy manner he exhibited with her mother.

"I'm quite well, Mr. Drayton. Thank you very much for seeing to my daughter's welfare this evening. I don't like to have her out walking in Chinatown these dark chilly evenings."

Her mother's hand looked awfully delicate as it grasped James's large, firm palm. As she watched, Polly wished again that things could be different. If only they knew Stephen was safe. If only their circumstances weren't quite so straitened. Polly was proud that she could earn her keep, but she couldn't help wishing her mother could be better off. Her mother had once been accustomed to luxury. It had been very hard on Mrs. MacNamara when their fortunes plummeted.

"It was my pleasure, Mrs. MacNamara. I often have business in Chinatown in the evenings. Perhaps your daughter would consent to allow me to see her home more often."

He didn't look at Polly until she cried, "Oh, no!" Then she felt like a fool when he turned his exquisite smile upon her. "Oh—I mean—oh, please, Mr. Drayton. You don't have to do that."

With a deep, slow laugh that sent hot shivers rioting up her spine, James said, "Of course I don't have to, Miss Mac-Namara. It would be my pleasure."

Before Polly could utter another idiotic disclaimer, her mother broke in. "How very kind of you, Mr. Drayton. We owe you two debts now."

Polly frowned and felt a lick of annoyance. She worked hard for her wages and didn't appreciate being made to feel indebted.

James lifted a brow. "Two debts, ma'am?"

"Yes. We owe you thanks for bringing Polly home, and we owe you our eternal gratitude for allowing her to work at your law firm. Her income is most handy."

Handy? Polly stared at her mother. Her income might well be all they had if Stephen did not return.

"That's no debt at all, Mrs. MacNamara. Miss MacNamara earns her income at the law firm. She's the best typist we have in our employ."

He gave Polly another warm smile, making her cheeks catch fire. Although she appreciated his acknowledgment of her superior skills—and they *were* superior—she wished he'd go away.

"Won't you come inside and take tea with us, Mr. Drayton?" Lillian waved an elegant hand in the direction of the doorway. Polly wanted to die.

For the space of a heartbeat, it looked as though James was

going to take her mother up on the invitation. But all at once he paused, pulled out a handsome gold pocket watch, and frowned at it.

At last he said, "Although nothing would give me greater pleasure, ladies, I'm afraid I almost forgot an appointment. I'm late now. But I would be happy to take tea with you another day if you'll have me."

Another devastating smile nearly made Polly want to faint dead away on her mother's front porch.

"Well, good night, then, Mr. Drayton. Thank you again for bringing my Polly home to me."

"Yes. Thank you, Mr. Drayton." Polly discovered her vocal chords weren't happy about being called upon to work. Her voice sounded shaky. Small wonder. She *felt* shaky.

She held out her hand, once again bare, for James to shake. To her utter horror, he not only shook it but lifted her fingers to his lips and placed a demure kiss upon them. It was all she could do to keep from snatching her hand away and hiding it behind her back.

"Good night, Mr. Drayton."

"Good night, Miss MacNamara." James smiled warmly, and looked supremely confident as he turned and strode back to his motorcar.

Polly's heart had taken to swooping like a disoriented sparrow in her rib cage when she pushed her mother's wheelchair back through the door of their home. Good heavens.

"My, what a nice man your employer is, Polly. And you never told me how handsome he is, either."

Polly had to take a deep, steadying breath before she could speak without stammering. "I really don't have much to do with him, Mother. I just type legal briefs for the associates."

"Well, he appeared to be a very nice man, at any rate."

"Yes. Yes, he did."

And that fact astounded Polly, who had never seen James Drayton be anything but cold and businesslike. She'd heard he had a reputation as quite a rake among the upper echelons of San Francisco's society, too. Small wonder, she decided, if he was as charming to the rich and pampered as he had been to her.

Wrenching her thoughts from James Drayton, she observed, "You seem quite chipper this evening, Mother. Are you feeling better? This morning your poor legs were predicting rain, and they were right."

"Oh, I feel much more the thing now, thank you. Mrs. Plimsole brought me a dose of salicylic powders, and my legs don't ache nearly as much as they did earlier in the day."

"I'm glad."

"Yes. One doesn't like to be dependent on medicines, but they certainly do help one on occasion." Mrs. MacNamara patted Polly's hand and said, "Now, wheel me into the parlor, Polly darling. There's a surprise for you there."

"A surprise?" Mercy. Polly couldn't recall the last time she'd received a happy surprise. Most of the surprises in her life had not occasioned the pleased lilt she detected in her mother's voice this evening.

When Polly stepped into the parlor and saw her mother's surprise, a smile lit her up inside.

"Oh, my! Wherever did that come from?"

James felt an odd combination of pleasure and discomposure as he drove back to Chinatown to meet Raymond Sing, his friend and translator. The weather had turned once more and instead of snow, rain slashed through the darkness. He drove slowly, not merely for safety's sake, but because he wanted to do some thinking.

Oh, it was true he'd noticed Polly MacNamara in the office before. He couldn't help it. She would stand out in any company. Particularly in the society of her fellow typists, her special quality shone.

Not only was she a remarkably lovely girl, with gleaming auburn hair and lustrous, cinnamon-colored eyes, but she possessed a grace, an elegance, unusual in a person of a typist's social standing. Yet she never appeared to consider herself superior to her fellows; far from it. She exhibited a charming reserve and seemed to shrink from putting herself forward. Indeed, she was endowed with a rare quality, unique to herself.

He understood her air a little better, now that he'd heard her story, and wondered why he hadn't suspected something of the sort sooner. So her family's fortunes had once been much larger, had they? It was a pity, that. And to have one's assets lost in such a dreadful accident must have been especially hard on her and her mother.

James's thoughts took an abrupt turn as he neared his destination. There was Raymond, punctual as ever. James smiled to see Raymond's slight figure hunched against the driving rain, his hat pulled low over his forehead. James leaned over and opened the door as he pulled up to the boardwalk.

" 'Evening, James," the young Chinese fellow said as he climbed into the vehicle. "Sorry I'm dripping on your fine new upholstery."

"Don't worry about the seats, Raymond. Did you manage to find a suitable institution?"

"Sure did. It's an orphanage run by the Order of the Sisters of Benevolence, on the corner of Grant and Rampart. Through your Businessmen's Trust, you've been supporting them for years, although you probably haven't been there or anything."

"No, I haven't."

"Well, they've been around for fifty years or more. The orphanage was established first. Now they run a soup kitchen for derelicts next to the orphanage, and another one on the docks. Get a lot of riffraff from the wharf, I understand."

With a big, satisfied sigh, James shot a conspiratorial grin at his companion. "Sounds like just my kind of place, Raymond. Just exactly my kind of place."

Raymond grinned back and gave his head a little shake, scattering sparkling water droplets over the carriage seat. "Nobody would ever guess, James. You know that, don't you?"

With a wink, James said, "And that's exactly the way I intend to keep it, too."

Chapter Two

"Oh, Mother, where on earth did this come from?" Polly stared, delighted, at the huge steamer trunk sitting open on the parlor floor. The trunk's contents lay folded in intriguing stacks of undiscovered mystery, a treasure waiting to be exposed. Polly couldn't wait to dip into those tidy piles.

"George brought it over. One of the wealthy ladies on his milk route gave it to her maid to give to him."

"Good old Cousin George."

Long gone were the days when Polly and her mother would shrink from taking gifts from George. Although neither lady would dream of accepting charity from anybody else on earth, they felt no such qualms with Cousin George. His milk route encompassed the most elegant neighborhoods in San Francisco, and his cheerful disposition and honest good heart had earned him friends everywhere.

This was not the first time George had been given something by a wealthy society lady through her household staff, nor was it the first of those gifts he'd shared with Lillian and Polly. The people on George's route knew he'd find a worthy home for their discards. If one *had* to endure poverty, Polly

28

often thought, it was nice to have relatives who possessed kind hearts.

"He dropped it by this afternoon, dear. I haven't looked inside, but saved it until you came home."

"Oh, how fun." Polly grinned at her mother. "Let's eat first, and then bring our tea in here. We can savor the trunk's contents without our stomachs getting in our way."

"That sounds like a fine scheme, Polly," her mother said in a voice Polly knew was meant to sound cheerful.

In spite of her happy tone, a look of great sadness passed over her mother's face. Polly saw it and was disheartened. Oh, how she wished things could be different.

For some reason, Polly thought of her strange new trinket and pulled it out of her coat pocket. It felt warm between her fingers; she liked touching it. Quickly, she bent and kissed her mother's troubled brow.

"I'll just run and change, Mother, then we can eat and go through the trunk." As she dashed off toward the stairs, she called back, "And I was given something today, too. I'll show it to you over supper."

Lillian MacNamara held the coin up to the flickering light of the candle separating her from Polly as they sat at their small dining-room table. They had just finished the soup course, prepared earlier in the day by their cook, Mrs. Ragsdale.

Although the cook would have been an expense they could ill afford, Mrs. Ragsdale insisted on working for Polly and Lillian half time, for no wage. Over and over again she declared she wouldn't allow Polly to earn her bread and cook it too. After all, Mrs. Ragsdale said, she had worked for the MacNamaras for decades; she wasn't about to leave them just because they'd fallen on hard times.

"I'm retired now, young lady, and can do as I please. If I please to cook for you and your sainted mother, who are *you* to deny me the pleasure?"

Polly had argued as much as she dared, but Mrs. Ragsdale was inflexible on the point.

"My goodness, what strange designs," Lillian murmured as she peered at the coin.

Polly thought it looked dull and lusterless in the older woman's fingers. Funny; before when she'd inspected it, the coin had seemed to possess a luminescence of its own. She shrugged. "I can't tell whether the designs are Chinese or not, although I suspect they are. A Chinese lady gave it to me."

A quizzical look from her mother made Polly, who never thought to dissimulate, wish she'd remembered to make up a good story to explain the coin. She couldn't very well say she'd been buying her mother a Christmas present.

"I—I stopped into a shop in Chinatown on my way home, looking for—for some gloves." There. It wasn't a deft lie, but it would do. Her mother seemed satisfied.

"It's a cold little thing, too, isn't it?"

Surprised, Polly looked up from her empty soup bowl. Cold? It had felt warm to her. Maybe that was because it had been in her pocket.

"I wonder what kind of metal it's made of." Lillian squinted hard at the coin.

"I don't know."

"Well, it's a curiosity, at any rate. It's actually quite lovely." Lillian handed the coin back to her daughter.

Polly took it and rubbed it between her thumb and forefinger. She liked feeling it; liked having it. "I'm glad the lady gave it to me."

"Well, Mr. Drayton, there's no doubt we can use the help, but I'm not altogether certain criminals are the answer."

Mother Francis Mary's voice was dry as chalk dust and her dark eyes glittered with amusement as she stared across her cluttered desk at James. The Mother Superior's face was an interesting map of wrinkles, and James suspected each one of them could tell its own story.

He placed a sheaf of papers back into his leather satchel and smiled at the nun. She was a first-rate lady, Mother Francis Mary, he decided as he took note of her twinkle.

"These people aren't lawbreakers, ma'am. They're Chinese boys who haven't been given justice by our criminal system.

Basically, there is no justice for the Chinese in our country. For the most part, these boys are barely more than children, used by the Tongs for their own felonious purposes and picked up by our law to be prosecuted and deported as though they were hardened hatchet men.''

"And you're telling me they're not hardened anything, is that right?''

"That's right.'' James took out one of the papers he'd just shoved away. "Just take another look at this one. Soong Lee. Why, he's only sixteen years old. Barely speaks English. His only crime was to take a quarter and a message from a *boo-how-doy* to Charley Fong. The poor boy can't even read. He had no idea what the message said or that Charley Fong is a hired killer. Why, he—''

James realized that the Mother Superior was holding up her hand. He stopped his impassioned plea, faintly embarrassed. The long-remembered and -resented voice of his father rose up in his brain and chanted, "Strays and misfits! Why the devil are you so interested in strays and misfits when you don't even care about your own family?''

"Sorry, Mother Francis Mary,'' he mumbled.

Raymond Sing, sitting stiff and straight in the chair beside James, said, "It took a good deal of persuasion on Mr. Drayton's part before the judge would agree to this proposal, Mother. He said that only if a suitable institution could be found would he allow the experiment to continue.''

A look from James silenced Raymond.

"These boys want to work, Mother,'' James said, feeling the need to fight this battle on his own. "They didn't come to the United States with the idea in mind that they would be used for criminal activity. With the help of Raymond here, I've interviewed each one of them. I only took the ones I trusted implicitly.''

Mother Francis Mary's smile contained what looked very much like maternal affection. James felt his embarrassment rise and heat his cheeks.

"Tell me, Mr. Drayton, what is your interest in downtrodden Chinese immigrants? I can't quite fathom the connection.'' She folded her hands on a stack of papers and sat up straight in her big chair. She looked as though she had all the time in the world.

She was a small woman, one who looked as though her many years had shrunk her, and her head barely showed over the pile. In her stark black-and-white habit, she gave James the impression of a celestial judge, and he had the feeling he was being examined shrewdly.

He cleared his throat. "Let's just say I have a personal interest in the damage done children shipped to the United States to be used as chattel by greedy businessmen."

A smile played on Mother Francis Mary's wrinkled lips and the sparkle in her eyes became more marked. "Your father is J. P. Drayton, owner of the Pacific-Orient Shipping Lines, isn't he, Mr. Drayton?"

James looked up, surprised. The Mother Superior's clear, glittering eyes betrayed only benevolent amusement. James guessed it wouldn't do to fib to a holy sister, so he nodded and murmured, "Yes."

"And was it by way of your father's shipping business that your personal interest in these exploited children arose, Mr. Drayton?"

"Yes."

"And is your father a philanthropist, as well, Mr. Drayton?"

Stiffening, James said, "No, Mother Francis Mary, he is not."

The Mother Superior gave James a benign smile. "Ah, I begin to understand."

James eyed her hard. Every time he thought about his father and his father's shipping business, he felt his guts tighten into a hot, strangling knot. He hated talking about the old man. But tonight, caught in the sharp, knowing gaze of this little nun, he suddenly found himself telling the truth.

"My father is a brilliant businessman. His shipping business is fabulously successful. The fact that his success has been built on the broken backs of thousands of people like this boy, Soong Lee, doesn't seem to matter to him at all."

James paused to suck in a breath. His voice held a sharp edge when he continued. "I, on the other hand, care a great deal. I'm not as wealthy as my father but have risen in my profession—on my own and by my own efforts—so that I now possess a tidy fortune. In my own way, I'm trying to help; to rectify in some small manner the evil he's done through the years."

"Evil is a very strong word, Mr. Drayton," Mother Francis Mary said gently.

James suddenly felt like a little boy again, trying to grab his father's attention and make him care. "Puling about the yellow devils," his father would have called it. James's gaze dropped in spite of his determination. He didn't know what to say.

"I've noticed," the nun continued in a dreamy tone, "that a person's background often predicts his future behavior. You grew up with plenty, no doubt."

"Yes, I did. My father provided well for his household, financially."

He didn't add that when he was a little boy, his father's presence was so rare in the home, James used to dread J. P. Drayton's infrequent appearances. Such appearances were invariably accompanied by much fussing and bothering and dressing up of a boy who felt more like an ornament than a child. Little James was infinitely more comfortable with his sweet Chinese nanny than his dynamic, overbearing parent. James didn't even remember his mother, who had died shortly after giving him life.

"Yes." The Mother Superior's twinkle softened. "Well, you see, it's always been of interest to me, as one whose entire adult life has been spent among the underprivileged, to observe how children of rich folks go on in the world. So many children who grow up surrounded by great wealth become listless and idle as adults. They spend money like water in frivolous pursuits, and fritter their time away, caring for nothing but their own amusements. Yet others, people such as yourself for example, feel compelled by guilt to try to rectify the disparity between the rich and the poor."

James had to make an effort not to frown. "Compelled by guilt?"

The nun nodded. "Your father, as I understand it, came here from Ireland and made his own fortune?"

"Yes."

Hours of James's adolescence had been spent in his father's study, listening to lectures about how John Philip Drayton had arrived in the United States with nothing but the shirt on his back and had made his own way. The little boy who could have used a father's attention became a young man who hated the very thought of those lectures.

"I see. And am I correct in believing you chose the law over your father's shipping business?"

"Yes."

James could have sworn the holy Mother gave him a wink before she said, "And your father didn't approve, did he?"

"No. No, he did not."

"So you've made it a practice to work for the rights of the very people your father ground under his high-handed boot heels. If you'll pardon a badly mixed metaphor."

James narrowed his eyes and looked keenly at the Mother Superior. He couldn't say he much liked the way she had of phrasing things. Nevertheless, he gave her a stiff, "Yes."

The wrinkles on Mother Francis Mary's face folded up as she bestowed another smile on him. "Ah, guilt. Such a useful emotion from time to time."

Stuffing the story of Soong Lee back into his satchel, James stood. He held out a steady hand to the nun.

"Well, Mother Francis Mary, if we can't do business, I guess I'll take my leave."

Raymond, unsettled by the odd turn of the conversation and James's obvious discomposure, rose too. His gaze darted between the Mother Superior and his employer. Strange emotional currents rode the air in the nun's stuffy office. Raymond seemed every bit as affected by them as James.

The nun's smile broadened. She did not take James's fingers, but rather waved her own wrinkled hand at him.

"I'm not trying to be offensive, Mr. Drayton, although I seem to be doing a very good job of it. And I'm not refusing your offer, either. I think your plan is well thought out. I also believe it to be the product of a generous heart. The two attributes do not often go hand-in-hand, unfortunately.''

She sighed. "I could tell you stories never-ending about the kindhearted, disorganized people who waltz into my office, expecting dispensation for their benevolent thoughts, even though thoughts are all we ever get from them." The Mother Superior gave a grimace that did amazing things with her wrinkles.

James was more than a little put out by the nun's odd attitude and odder conversation, and he did not sit again immediately. He felt quite huffy, in fact. He hated talking about his father. As far as James was concerned, he and J. P. Drayton did not see eye to eye about anything on the face of the earth except that James was not the son his father wanted.

"Please sit down, Mr. Drayton," Mother Francis Mary said in a voice of boundless serenity. "I'm afraid my old neck gets a crick when I have to look up for too long a period. Too many years spent on my knees with my head bowed, I expect." Her smile was almost, but not quite, wicked in it playfulness.

With a nod to Raymond, James sat. Raymond sat, too.

James was not amused. "Are you interested in my proposal, Mother?"

The nun peered at him for some seconds; long enough for the urge to fidget to attack him. James had been taught well, though, during those long-ago lectures in his father's study, and he suppressed his urge.

Finally Mother Francis Mary said, "I am very interested in your proposal, Mr. Drayton. I am very interested in you, as well." She gave him another creaky smile. "Your father must be very proud of you."

James gaped at her for a moment before he said, "No. My father is not in the least proud of me."

"Are you absolutely certain about that, Mr. Drayton?"

Wondering if the old woman was completely out of her mind, James muttered, "Absolutely."

When Mother Francis Mary laughed, the strange rustling sound was so unexpected that James and Raymond looked at each other in surprise for a moment. Then they both stared at the nun.

At last she rose. She was no taller standing than she had been sitting. Wiping her eyes on a pristine white handkerchief, she murmured, "Ah, Mr. Drayton, it has been such an unexpected pleasure to meet you. I seldom receive unexpected pleasures, you know. I fear both my vocation and my age preclude excitement." She extended a papery hand. "I look forward to meeting your Chinese criminals tomorrow, Mr. Drayton."

"They're not criminals, Mother Francis Mary," James grumbled as he shook her hand.

"Of course not." Her smile got bigger. "And you, young man, will be bringing them to us. Is that right?" She turned so abruptly toward Raymond that he gave a start.

"Er, yes, ma'am," he said in a voice that wasn't quite steady.

"Good." She nodded sharply. "Good. I shall expect to see you then. Noon sharp."

"Noon sharp," Raymond repeated, a little dazed.

James and Raymond heard the nun's rusty laugh all the way out to the street.

"My goodness," murmured Raymond. "I don't believe I've ever met anyone quite so singular before."

"Me neither," grumbled James. He was glad of it, too. "Hop in, Raymond. I'll drive you back home."

Even after he cranked his new motorcar into submission and drove off, James was still annoyed.

Polly felt warm all over as she stared at herself in the mirror. Although it was late and she needed to rise early in order to go to her job, she hadn't been able to resist putting on the beautiful gown. Now she was glad she'd given in to her weakness.

She and her mother had found it, folded up in tissue paper, at the bottom of the trunk. The wealthy lady who had relinquished the garment had tucked lavender sachet in among its folds, and the tantalizing fragrance clung to its soft creases and kissed Polly's nostrils in powdery, elusive waves.

With a swirl, Polly watched the creamy satin skirt bell out, as though caught by the lilt of a waltz as she danced across the floor in the arms of a handsome young man. She could even picture her partner. He had dark, curly brown hair, and deep hazel eyes that warmed when they looked at her. He was tall and elegant and terribly handsome. He looked, in fact, exactly like James Drayton.

With a sigh, she wondered what James would think if he could see her in this magnificent gown. Not that he ever would.

Still, Polly had never even seen such a gorgeous gown up close before. The fact that this one was hers, and that it fit her to perfection, made her wonder if wishes might really come true. Only this evening she had wished she owned such a gown. Her ancient coin, threaded on a thin red velvet ribbon, gleamed softly from where it rested against her bosom.

Her ensemble was perfect. Absolutely perfect. Now she wished she had somewhere to wear it. With a giggle, Polly swirled once more and thought what a greedy girl she was.

The gown might have been made just for her. Sewn of cream-colored satin and overlaid with delicate ecru lace, it molded to her curves, curves she'd never appreciated until this moment. The result reminded her, although she would never say so aloud, of one of Mr. Gibson's famous drawings. The neckline was cut low—daringly low, in her estimation—and exposed an expanse of shoulders and a very little of her swelling bosom. A red satin rose was the gown's only ornament aside from its lace, and it nestled at her waist, emphasizing its smallness. There was something about the cut of the gown, or perhaps it was the color of the satin, that coaxed a glow from her skin.

Oh, how she *wished* James Drayton could see her this way instead of as he usually did, clad in her demure typist's costume. How she wished he could see her as a woman and not a mere employee.

Then she commanded herself to stop daydreaming.

Polly's stern lecture subdued her fantasies, although she still stared into the mirror with a thrill of satisfaction. Never vain, she was nonetheless elated to discover how pretty she could look, at least tonight, in the soft light of her bedroom. With

one last satisfied sigh, she stopped twirling and began to un-
hook her new delight.

I shall wear it on Christmas Eve, she decided suddenly.
*Even if I never wear it again in my life, at least this Christmas
Eve, with Mother, Aunt Grace, Cousin George, and Mrs. Plim-
sole, I will look elegant.*

Carefully, she folded up the gown in its tissue paper and
wished she had some more lavender sachet. With the thought
in mind to store her new-old coin with the dress, she took it
from around her neck. Holding it in her palm, she stared at
its ancient etchings for some time before she closed her fingers
around it.

No. She would store the ribbon with the gown. The coin
she'd carry with her. For good luck.

She giggled at her absurdity. More than most folks, Polly
MacNamara knew that luck did not abide in ancient coins.

Some time ago, Stephen had brought Polly a St. Christopher
medal from one of his many voyages. The medal now hung
on a golden chain looped over her mirror. She picked up the
chain now, unclasped it, and slipped her coin over its small
links.

There, she thought with contentment. Now she had two
charms to wear.

And, while she eschewed wearing jewelry as frivolous and
immodest for a young lady of her age and station in life, Polly
slipped the chain over her head. The two medals came to rest
between her breasts, and she placed her flat palm over them.
One of them felt cold against her flesh, the other warm. She
didn't have to look to tell which was which.

The next morning, Polly felt an unusual bounce to her step
as she walked the three-quarters of a mile to her place of
employment on Montgomery Street. Her mood was sunny,
even though the winter weather nipped at her cheeks and chin.
She still wore her charms under her chemise. The skin-warmed
St. Christopher medal made her feel as though Stephen were
nearby. And, although the old coin did not carry the senti-
mental value of the St. Christopher, she liked it, too, and en-

joyed knowing it was with her. The coin didn't need her skin to warm it; it bore its own atmosphere.

The liveried doorman at the firm of James Drayton and Associates, Attorneys at Law, smiled as soon as he saw Polly turn the corner onto Montgomery. With a wink and a little bow, he held the door for her.

"Top of the morning to you, Miss MacNamara."

Polly loved the way Marcus O'Leary's resonant voice trilled over the *r* in her name. At first she'd been a little put off by the drama-loving Irishman, but now she held him dear, a friend decorating a life thinly populated with friends.

"Good day to you, Mr. O'Leary. And how are you this fine November day?"

"Just grand, me dear. Just grand."

"Thanksgiving's right around the corner. Do you plan to dine on a turkey or a goose this year?"

"Ah, me dear. It's turkey on Thanksgiving and goose for Christmas." With another wink, Marcus said, "That's the way it should be, y'know."

The argument was an old and amicable one. Marcus embraced firm rules about everything, from holidays to the proper way of entering a building. Polly laughed, and her lighthearted mood carried her into the building.

Her smile lasted all the way through the plush entryway of the law firm, survived a wintry scowl from Mr. Gregory, James Drayton's personal secretary, and accompanied her into the typewriting room. Although she was usually the first of the four typists to arrive in the morning, Polly's three fellows were there before her today. She'd never felt comfortable with the other women. Their lives seemed so different from hers.

Nevertheless, she nodded, smiled a greeting, and sat down. Almost immediately, she shot out of her chair and looked at the seat to see what on earth she'd just sat on.

It was a box, slightly squashed now. Puzzled, Polly lifted it from her chair. The name *I. Magnin* was slanted across the box in elegant, golden letters.

A giggle from one of the other girls brought Polly's head up. Apart from a knowing look on Rose O'Brian's face, she could detect nothing amiss. Hoping for enlightenment, she asked, "Who on earth does this belong to?"

"Did you read the card, dearie?" Constance Pry was the only one of the three typists whose expression held kindness.

Polly noticed a card tucked under the box's gilt string for the first time, and saw her name scripted in bold, black strokes across it. She felt embarrassed as she untied the string and opened the box. There, on a nest of tissue paper, lay a pair of warm kid gloves.

"My goodness!" She stared at the gloves, flabbergasted.

"I'd give a good deal to know what a lady has to do to earn a gift from the boss."

Rose's nasal comment carried to Polly across the silence of the room, and she looked up. "What?"

Rose pushed herself away from her own worktable and sauntered to Polly's side. Although Polly herself had not touched the gloves, Rose picked one up and ran it through her fingers.

"Genuine kidskin. Must have done something special, all right." She gave Polly another wink and laughed. Then she dropped the glove beside its mate and strolled back to her table.

"But—but who left them here?" Polly scanned the faces of her fellows. She read on them a combination of titillation and resentment, and she didn't understand it at all.

Deciding it must be some elaborate joke, she grinned and asked, "Whose are they really?"

Juliana Kenny, the youngest and least compassionate of Polly's sister typists, sniffed, giving Polly to understand it was no joke. Her smile faded. Picking up the card, she turned it over and over in nerveless fingers, as though hoping to discern through touch the gift-giver's identity.

Snickering, Juliana said cattily, "Oh, don't play sly with us, dearie. I don't know what you did to turn the boss up sweet, but it must have been rich." Her thin, freckled face bore the marks of hard use and strain, although Juliana was no more than seventeen by Polly's reckoning.

Polly was becoming irritated by this silly mystery. "I don't understand. To whom do these belong? They're certainly not mine.''

Rose sat with a flourish and rolled a sheet of foolscap into her Underwood Visible Writing Machine. She gave Polly a smile more nearly friendly than any Polly had received since she had stepped into her work area. ''Sweetie, all I can say is more power to you. If you can get something besides a wage from the hoity-toity Mr. James Drayton, it's all the same to me.''

''Mr. James . . .'' The sentence died before Polly could even formulate the end of it. Out of developing habit, she placed her palm over the two charms hidden at her breast. ''Oh, I *wish* somebody would explain this to me.''

''I saw 'im,'' Juliana declared, resentment souring the words. ''Came in here early, he did, and looked at the nameplates on every table. When he came to yours, he smiled like, and dropped the box right there. Smack on your chair.''

''Reckon it pays to work after hours, eh, girls?'' Rose winked at Constance and Juliana.

Constance did not respond, but Juliana tittered artfully. ''What *I* want to know is, what kind of work warrants ten-dollar gloves from I. Magnin.''

''Oh, for heaven's sake!'' Polly pressed a hand to her overheated cheek.

Oh, how could he? How *dare* he! Did he consider her such a pathetic creature that he had to bestow this humiliating piece of charity on her? In full view of her fellow workers, all of whom would naturally take exception to his singling her out? And their sly insinuations! Especially given their employer's reputation with the ladies.

Well, it was simply beyond endurance. Furious, hands shaking and nerves galloping like a runaway dray horse, Polly refolded the tissue over the gloves and closed the box. Her fingers were so unsteady, it took her two attempts to retie the bow. Then she tried to smooth out the creases the box sported from having been sat on.

Taking a deep breath to calm her jitters—which didn't help in the least—Polly squared her shoulders and stepped toward the door of the typists' workroom. Theirs was a room apart from the busy center of the law firm, a carpetless, windowless, clattering cave of a room. Polly always felt as though the typewriting staff was being hidden from the world; that they were not considered grand enough to be viewed by the wealthy San Franciscans who entered Drayton's portals in search of legal advice. The thought daunted her.

Trying very hard to keep her mettle fired up, Polly lifted her chin and looked neither to the right nor to the left when her foot sank into the plush carpeting of the law clerks' room. She knew they all raised their heads to stare at her. Typists never entered the clerks' room; they were brought work by the clerks and their assistants, who picked it up again when it was finished.

It was as though typewriting were a communicable disease, Polly sometimes thought in her few dour moods.

Not today. Today Polly marched through the double row of clerks with purpose. She was proud when her hand barely trembled as she turned the knob to enter the sanctuary of the associates, Drayton, Cobb, and Bullock.

Chapter Three

As soon as the door opened to reveal this most sacred of inner sancta, Polly's fortitude almost failed her.

Oh, Lord, what had she been thinking of?

While it was true that she was proud of her self-sufficiency in a world where women were more often than not at the mercy of men, it was also true that she was not accustomed to running blithely into the jaws of danger. James Drayton's office bore all the earmarks of such a jaw.

Maybe she should have taken the gloves to Marcus O'Leary and asked him to give them to Mr. Drayton. Or sent them back to him in the parcel post. Now that she was here, this visit seemed most imprudent. After all, she thought with a gulp of dismay, who was she to visit him in his lair as though she were not a mere typist, but a woman of merit in the world?

Too late. The heavy carved-oak door shut behind her with an expensive click and Mr. Gregory looked up. It didn't take a woman as acute as Polly MacNamara to realize that Mr. Gregory resented this intrusion.

Pinning her with a malicious glare, he barked, "What on earth are *you* doing here?"

Polly had the vivid impression that his intention was to cow her. It worked. She fought the urge to shrink back against the door.

Then, with a mental kick for her trepidation, Polly took a deep, sustaining breath and stood up straight. Whatever her circumstances, she was Miss Pauline Lillian MacNamara, daughter of her mother and father and, as such, a valuable member of the human race. In spite of anything Mr. Gregory or his overbearing employer, Mr. James Drayton, might think.

"I need to speak to Mr. Drayton," she said in a voice that, miracle of miracles, wobbled not at all.

Mr. Gregory snatched his half-glasses from his ferret-like face and sneered at her. "My dear Miss MacNamara, typists employed by the firm of Drayton and Associates do not speak to the Senior Partner."

Gregory's nasty attitude ate away at Polly's nervousness and exposed the grit beneath. Polly drew herself up as tall as she could and glared right back at Mr. Gregory.

"Nevertheless, I need to speak to Mr. Drayton. If he is not immediately available, I shall wait."

So saying, and with a pert flounce, Polly passed a hand behind her skirt and sat, ramrod-straight, on a wing chair placed in the office to hold the bottoms of people more exalted than she. She knew her cheeks were pink, this time with indignation, and she didn't care. Much.

In order to keep her anger stoked, she maintained her stony glare at Mr. Gregory. His was a countenance that did not invite scrutiny, being weak-chinned and pointy. He reminded Polly of a rat, and she held the thought close to her heart for courage.

Of its own, her hand lifted to her breast. She could barely feel her two medals, but it made her feel better knowing they were there. Pressing gently, she wished James Drayton would open his door and notice her, since Mr. Gregory did not seem inclined to announce her presence.

Just as she'd begun to wonder if she should boldly walk to her employer's door and knock, another office door burst open and Lawrence Bullock's ruddy, athletic self emerged. Polly looked up abruptly and was embarrassed all over again when

Mr. Bullock, spying her, stopped short. A too-delighted smile spread across his handsome face.

"Well, well, well, and what have we here, Gregory?"

Mr. Bullock's well-oiled voice exuded pleasantness, but Polly did not like it. Nor did she like the way his gaze slid over her body, as though he knew exactly what lay beneath her demure frock and itched to uncover it. She gave him a small frown.

"Miss MacNamara says she needs to see Mr. Drayton, Mr. Bullock."

Gregory's nasal monotone conveyed none of the unpleasantness he'd used on her, but Polly could hear it anyway. Implication and insinuation oozed from each twanging syllable, and she shot him what she hoped was a withering glare.

"Does she now?"

To Polly's consternation, Lawrence Bullock advanced upon her and held out a tanned and healthy-looking hand.

"Come along, my dear. I'll take you to James. I'm sure he'll be delighted."

Polly did not care to be called "my dear." Nor did she care for the way Bullock emphasized the word "delighted." Nevertheless, although her hands did not want to leave the safety of each other's firm though increasingly panicky grasp, Polly lifted one. It was almost immediately engulfed by the moist, meaty grip of Lawrence Bullock. She stood on unsteady legs and was grateful nobody but she could tell her knees shook.

Lawrence Bullock tucked her arm beneath his and, Polly thought, held it entirely too close to his robust side as he led her to James's office door. There he rapped sharply twice and then pressed the gilt handle.

The door opened silently on well-oiled hinges to reveal James Drayton in deep conversation with a slender Chinese gentleman. Polly had time only to register surprise at the remarkable pair before James's head snapped up and he cast an annoyed-looking glance at the door.

Polly felt her cheeks burn but was encouraged when James's glare for Bullock transformed into a smile for her. A little uncertainly, she smiled back.

James stood and walked out from behind his desk. "And

to what do I owe this great pleasure, Miss MacNamara?'' Less cordially, he demanded, ''What are you up to, Bullock?''

Before Polly could form a single word, Lawrence Bullock said, ''This charming damsel was wasting away in the waiting room, James. Said she needed to speak to you and, as Gregory didn't seem inclined to announce her, I felt it my duty to see her to your office.''

There were currents and innuendoes rampant in Bullock's tone of voice that Polly could not fathom. Nor was she reassured when he gave James a sly wink. Her cheeks felt warmer. When Bullock leaned over to whisper something in James's ear and James gave him a ferocious scowl, she fought the urge to flee.

''That's enough of your nonsense, Bullock. And I'd better not hear any hints of it outside these doors, either.''

''Of course not, old man.'' Bullock gave James a large, insouciant grin. ''Well, I'd better get back to work. I'll just leave the two of you—'' a glance at the nearly forgotten Chinese man made him amend his sentence. ''That is to say, I'll just leave the three of you alone.'' Another wink saw him out the door.

Polly couldn't recall the last time she'd been this uncomfortable, unless it was last night, in James Drayton's horseless carriage. She didn't know what to say.

Although James still appeared annoyed, he said pleasantly enough, ''May I help you, Miss MacNamara?''

With an appraising glance at the Chinese man, Polly hesitated a second, then said, ''I—I wanted to talk to you about this.''

Feeling very small and extraordinarily foolish, she held up the somewhat crumpled box of gloves. James looked at the box, and a flash of irritation passed over his patrician face. Polly suppressed a cowardly impulse to tuck in her chin and stare at the floor, and kept her gaze firmly affixed to James's face.

With a brusque gesture, James motioned to the Chinese gentleman. When he rose from his chair, Polly decided he was quite young—about her own age, which was twenty-one.

James spoke to the young man as he walked back to his

desk. "Well, Raymond, I guess our business is finished, anyway. Are there any more points you want to discuss before you gather our strays together?"

Polly noticed James's smile for the person named Raymond was much more friendly than his smile for Lawrence Bullock had been. How curious.

"Don't think so, James." Raymond gathered up the welter of papers spread out on James Drayton's desk.

Then he offered Polly a shy smile and a nod. She smiled and nodded back.

James noticed their nods and his vexation bloomed. Damn, what had possessed this idiot girl to come to his office? And what had possessed her to accept the escort of Lawrence Bullock, the loosest screw in James's entire business enterprise? The only reason he tolerated Bullock at all was because he was the son of a gentleman whom James believed to have been gravely mistreated by James's father. Not that he could rescue all such people, for they were legion. Nevertheless, if Bullock didn't begin to pull his considerable weight around the law firm soon, James would have to take action.

Dealing with the situation at hand, he said, "Miss MacNamara, let me introduce you to my friend and colleague, Raymond Sing. Raymond, Miss Polly MacNamara. Miss MacNamara is the top typist in our law firm."

He smiled but was pretty sure Polly knew he didn't mean it. She looked intolerably nervous. And annoyed, a circumstance he couldn't fathom at all.

"How do you do, Mr. Sing?"

James was pleased to see her hold out a hand for Raymond to shake. Many white ladies were not so gracious. Considered themselves superior to their Chinese brethren. Like his father. James frowned.

"Good day, Miss MacNamara."

Raymond and Polly shook hands, and then Raymond beat a quick retreat.

Standing behind his desk, James gestured Polly into a chair. "Please, Miss MacNamara, have a seat." Attempting a polite smile, he said, "I see you found the gloves."

Polly sat down and then rose abruptly, as though she'd sat

47

on a tack. "Yes. And—and—well, thank you very much, but I cannot accept this gift." She walked to his desk and held out the box.

James stared at it without taking it. Her hand shook, and it looked to him as though she were embarrassed about it because with a quick gesture, she placed the box on his blotter and then withdrew her hands and clasped them in front of her. She looked intolerably ill at ease.

Slowly, James fingered the box. "Did they not fit, Miss MacNamara?"

"I don't know, Mr. Drayton. I didn't try them on."

Cocking his head in honest bewilderment, James asked, "Why not? You need them; I saw that for myself."

Actually, he'd been extremely pleased with himself when he'd passed I. Magnin last night after dropping Raymond off and noticed the display of gloves in the window. Acting on an impulse motivated solely by kindness, he had decided his pretty, fleet-fingered typist should not have to wander about town gloveless. Besides, what was ten dollars to him?

Peering up at Polly, who stood stiff as a hockey stick before his desk, he took note of the expression in her eyes. Her eyes were the most marvelously expressive ones he'd ever seen. Right now they expressed disapproval. Well, well.

Acting on his prior experience with ladies, James asked softly, "Is it the color, Miss MacNamara? Would you prefer a different shade?"

Her own color brightened considerably at his question, and he realized with surprise that the red patches on her cheeks were banners of anger.

"Of course not! I can't accept them, Mr. Drayton. I simply can't."

"Why on earth not, for heaven's sake?"

This was ludicrous, and James's patience was wearing thin. He certainly didn't mind giving this poor maiden a ride on a rainy evening. And he garnered a certain degree of benevolent good humor about the gloves. But he'd be damned if he was going to allow this chit of a typist to make more of his kindly gesture than necessary.

As though her emotions would not allow her to stand still

Christmas Pie

a second longer, Polly turned abruptly. Pacing a circle before his desk, she said, "I just can't. It's—it's not done."

"It's not done?" Still fingering the I. Magnin box, James sat back in his chair, a sardonic smile curving his lips. "I don't believe I quite understand, Miss MacNamara."

He hadn't expected this coy gesture from Polly MacNamara. Now, if it had been one of the other girls, perhaps he might have anticipated it. But not Polly, who had always seemed aloof and oh, so proper. He felt monumentally disappointed.

"I can assure you that my motives are pure. I don't expect payment in trade for a pair of gloves." James flipped the box in a negligent gesture intended to indicate just how little they meant to him.

Polly suddenly stopped pacing. Her gasp of outrage made him think that perhaps he'd done that and more.

"Oh! What a—what a perfectly horrid thing to say!"

Cheeks afire, she whirled away from James's desk and headed toward the door. She was unused to the catch and fumbled trying to open it, and he was able to dash over to her before she could escape. His big hand covered hers for only a second before she snatched it away from him and hid it behind her back.

"I would like to leave now, Mr. Drayton," she said tightly.

"Not until you explain to me why these gloves are so damned important that you refuse to accept them. They were meant as a gesture of friendship, nothing more."

"*Friendship?* There is no friendship between us, Mr. Drayton. There cannot be. You are my employer. I accepted a ride home from you yesterday. Perhaps I should not have done so. I certainly did not intend to stir your sympathies or—or to imply that I need anything from you other than an honest wage for honest work."

Her lovely eyes were snapping fire now, and James was reminded of red-hot cinnamon candies. "Well, of course you didn't," he growled, aggravated that she'd read his suspicions correctly. His words had sounded mean-spirited and jaded.

"My mother and I do not require charity, Mr. Drayton. The wage you pay is perfectly adequate. Thank you for the thought."

49

"Oh, for heaven's sake! The wage is certainly not adequate if you can't even afford to buy yourself a pair of gloves!"

"Mr. Drayton, I may not be rich. I may have expenses that are out of the ordinary because of my mother's illness, but I can assure you that I do not require gestures of pity from you or anyone else."

Polly took an agitated turn around his office while he watched, fascinated.

"And to leave them on my chair! For pity's sake, didn't you give a single thought to what the other typists must think of such behavior on your part?"

"What on earth do you mean by that, Miss MacNamara?"

She stopped suddenly. "What do I *mean*? Why, what do you *think* I mean? They all think we're carrying on some sort of clandestine affair or something!"

She apparently had shocked herself by blurting out such an incredible supposition, because her cheeks flamed anew. Although James considered the scenario she painted absurd, he was charmed by her straightforward confession, and smiled. Obviously his smile offended her; she uttered a frustrated "Ohhhh," and stamped her foot. He thought that was sweet, too.

Then she made an odd gesture, one James did not understand. Putting her hand to her breast, she whispered angrily, "Oh, I *wish* you could understand!"

All at once, James did understand. As clear and brilliant as lightning, comprehension flashed into his brain and burned itself into his consciousness.

Why, what a pompous, callous fool he was! He, James Drayton, a man who prided himself on his humane instincts, had just made an idiotic blunder his own father would have had sense enough to avoid. How on earth could he expect this proud, hard-working girl to accept charity from him as though she were of no more value than a beggar on the streets? He was ashamed of himself.

"Miss MacNamara?"

It seemed to take her a second or two, but she finally lifted her face to look at him. Her lips were pinched together as though to prevent her mouth from leaking any more indiscreet words. Such a pretty girl, James thought, with her big, luminous eyes and her flawless porcelain skin, stained now with the flush of her anger and embarrassment.

"I'm sorry, Miss MacNamara. You're absolutely right. I wasn't thinking clearly, and had no business giving you a pair of gloves. Or anything else. Particularly not in front of the other typists. It must have been very embarrassing for you, and I'm sorry I didn't realize it sooner."

His rueful grin was so sincere and so beautiful that Polly could only gulp helplessly and nod. She sank into the plush chair she'd deserted moments before, and her anger evaporated.

"Thank you, Mr. Drayton."

James shook his head. "And from what you say, I suppose the other ladies in the typewriting room have already teased you mercilessly about my inappropriate gesture."

"I'm sure it was meant kindly, Mr. Drayton. I have no doubt of that. In spite of your reputation, I'm positive that you had no ulterior motives."

She gasped as soon as she heard herself, and her hand flew to her mouth as if to stuff the words back in. James tried to stifle his amusement. He'd had no idea how utterly engaging Miss Polly MacNamara could be.

"Be that as it may, it was clumsy. Monumentally clumsy." Returning to his desk, James picked up the box and looked at it as though for the first time. "I don't recall its being quite so—so used-looking before."

Although his grin contained nothing but lingering humor, Polly felt perfectly awful. "I didn't see it on my chair, Mr. Drayton. I'm afraid I sat on it." Once her confession was out, she wanted to crawl under the grand carpet and hide.

His soft laughter gave her chills and shivers that were much at odds with her blood, which seemed to heat up and scorch through her veins.

Suddenly an awful thought struck her. "Is the box too badly damaged for you to return, Mr. Drayton? If so, perhaps you can take the cost of the gloves out of my wages. I don't think I could pay for them all at once, but—"

She quit babbling, feeling like an absolute idiot, when he

turned around. When he walked toward her with his hand outstretched, it was all she could do to keep from grabbing a cushion from the chair and holding it in front of her face.

"Please, Miss MacNamara. Truce? I'm terribly sorry for having caused you such embarrassment and hope I'll be able to rectify my ridiculous blunder with your co-workers."

Polly stared at his hand mistrustfully for several seconds, wondering what he wanted her to do with it.

When he said, penitently, "Shake hands?" she felt about two inches tall. She shook his hand.

"Now. Let me see you back to your room," he said, as though his suggestion was the most natural in the world.

"Oh, good grief, no! Please. It's bad enough already!" Then Polly wished she'd bitten her tongue.

"I'm sorry, Miss MacNamara. I obviously wasn't thinking. Again." He peered at her oddly when her hand flew to her mouth. "What's the matter?"

"I'm sorry. I—I bit my tongue."

"May I see you home again this evening, Miss MacNamara?" James asked with what Polly was sure was studied politeness. He certainly could be a charming man when he put his mind to it.

"Oh, no. But thank you. I don't go directly home on Wednesday evenings, Mr. Drayton."

"No? And what is there about Wednesdays that's so special? Is there a young man in your life, perchance?"

"Good Lord, no!" Then Polly gulped and stammered, "I mean, no. I just do—something—on Wednesdays after work."

"Well, whatever your secret is, it's safe with me, Miss MacNamara. I only hope you have a safe way of getting home from wherever you perform this secret deed."

He was teasing her. Polly knew it, and appreciated the lightness of his manner. She gave him a smile and said, "Oh, yes. Thank you. After I perform my secret deed, I'm whisked right to my mother's front door."

Another chuckle accompanied James to the door. "Thank you for coming to see me, Miss MacNamara. I appreciate your braving the gauntlet. I know all those clerks, not to mention Mr. Gregory, can be intimidating.''

He opened the door and held it for her courteously. Polly glanced up at him as she passed through it into the exquisite reception area. "Thank you."

"Thank *you*," returned James.

He watched Polly walk with straight-shouldered defiance past Mr. Gregory's desk. He noticed that she did not glance at the secretary and suspected he knew the reason. He'd been meaning to speak to Gregory for some months now. The man took his position entirely too much to heart, lording it over everybody else in the firm. He treated Raymond Sing like dirt. James could just imagine the grief he'd given poor, respectable little Polly MacNamara.

When the door closed behind her, James breathed a soft sigh. Why was he so pleased to learn she had no gentleman friend? She was certainly not at all the sort of woman who typically caught his interest. He glanced again at his secretary and found Gregory scowling at the closed office door.

"Mr. Gregory, will you please step into my office?"

Gregory leapt from his chair. "Yes, sir, Mr. Drayton." With a nasal twitter, he said, "I trust you aren't upset with me for not having gotten rid of that uppity typist, sir. She wouldn't leave the office. Said she *would* talk to you, and that was that."

The man's sniveling made James wince. Compared to Polly MacNamara, who had obviously been concerned about the possibility of losing her job but had been willing to face him anyway, Walter Gregory was behaving like a groveling toad.

With a sweep of his arm, James ushered Gregory into his office. "Actually, Gregory, it is about that which I need to speak to you."

James saw Gregory's Adam's apple bob up and down when he swallowed. Wouldn't his snobby secretary be delighted with his next assignment?

Although the day had begun dismally, after Polly's nerve-wracking chat with James Drayton it picked up. When Mr. Gregory, clearly smarting with humiliation, distributed a brand-new pair of gloves to each of Drayton and Associates' team of typists, muttering something about Mr. Drayton's having been somehow prevented from doing so himself, she felt nearly lighthearted.

Mr. Drayton, according to Mr. Gregory, was giving the gloves to his typewriting staff as an early Christmas present. The gloves were, Mr. Gregory expounded, a suitable gift since a typist's hands were her most important asset. The packets of lavender sachet, he explained, were to keep the gloves fresh in each lady's bureau drawer.

"Well, how very kind of him," Constance Pry murmured.

Juliana Kenny shot Polly a suspicious frown, but she thanked Mr. Gregory as graciously as she was able.

Rose's face went as pink with pleasure as her name when she accepted her gloves.

Fingering her medallions, Polly watched the condescending Gregory's stiff-legged passage through the grim typewriting room and wondered if she was evil to feel such satisfaction. It did her heart good to see the nasty, rat-faced little weasel trying to be courteous. Obviously, such a manner did not come naturally.

After work, she hurried the two blocks to the Sisters of Benevolence, feeling better about life than she had for some time. Although the weather was bitter, her hands were toasty warm, encased as they were in her nice new kidskin gloves. She was also quite pleased to have more lavender sachet.

Thanks to her enlightened employer's good heart—a heart Polly was beginning to appreciate in a new light—the typists employed by James Drayton and Associates worked only until five o'clock on Wednesday afternoons. Unlike the dreary sweatshops employing other women who were forced to earn their keep, Drayton paid his typewriting staff a healthy wage, too. Each girl earned fully half what a similarly employed man might make, and they were expected to toil only forty-five hours per week, as well. Polly felt herself very fortunate in her employment.

She loved her Wednesday evenings because it was then that she read to the orphaned children nurtured behind the gates of the Sisters of Benevolence. Polly often wondered whether she would ever be blessed with children. Such a likelihood seemed to grow dimmer and dimmer with each passing year, but she couldn't help wishing.

Pushing through the orphanage's merciless wrought-iron gate, Polly's heart gave its customary lurch at the thought of the children who lived here. Originally established as a sanctuary for children of Chinese singsong girls, the orphanage had expanded over the years. Now, although most of the children it housed were still Chinese or part-Chinese, scores of other parentless waifs swelled their ranks.

Polly had been reading stories to them every Wednesday evening after work for two years now, ever since she'd been hired by Drayton and Associates. The children loved the stories and always awaited Polly's arrival eagerly. And she loved them—every one of them.

"Good evening, Miss MacNamara. It's always such a pleasure to see you of a Wednesday evening, my dear."

As ever, Mother Francis Mary's sharp eyes gave Polly the feeling that the Mother Superior was staring straight through her and into her heart. With a start, Polly realized the nun and yesterday's astute little Chinese shopkeeper had the same way about them. The realization amused her, and she gave the Mother Superior a big grin.

"Good evening, Mother Francis Mary. How are my children tonight?"

"Looking forward to a good story, if my guess is correct. What delights do you have in store for them today, my dear?"

Withdrawing the two volumes tucked under her arm, Polly showed them to the nun. "For the little ones, I'll be reading *Johnny Crow's Garden,* and then I'll read chapter ten of *Huckleberry Finn* to the older ones."

"Putting mischievous ideas into their little heads, are you?"

"Oh, good gracious, no! Certainly not that. Why, *Huckleberry Finn* is a wonderful story. It's—" Polly flushed when she realized the Mother Superior had been teasing her.

The nun gave her a wry smile. "Such a serious child you can be sometimes, my dear. But you do have a lovely new pair of gloves, I see. I'm glad. I worried about your poor workworn fingers, you know."

"Oh, yes. My employer gave each of us typists a pair of gloves today. Sort of a—an early Christmas present."

Taking Polly's arm and walking with her toward the room where the children awaited their stories, Mother Francis Mary said, "That sounds like a very generous thing for an employer to do. And just who is this paragon?"

"His name is James Drayton."

The name felt strange on Polly's tongue. She was unused to saying the *James* part. Pressing her charms in a gesture that was rapidly becoming habit, she experienced a strange lifting to her heart. She wanted to say *James* again but didn't.

"James Drayton, you say?" Mother Francis Mary smiled in a way that made the creases in her face fold up on one another.

"Yes."

Polly wished her cheeks would cool off. She'd taken to blushing at the very thought of James Drayton, and she didn't like it. She and the Mother Superior walked through an open corridor, and a blast of frigid air struck her, making her shiver.

"My, my," murmured the nun, looking about, "I wonder where that came from."

John Philip Drayton stood outside his son's place of business for some time, irresolute, before he walked up to the liveried doorman. Such equivocation was foreign to him and he didn't like it.

"I should have sent Biddle," he muttered. Biddle had been his man of business for twenty-five years.

To Marcus O'Leary, who saluted sharply, J. P. Drayton gave the scowling grimace that, for him, passed as a smile. A brusque question of Marcus produced the information he needed, and J. P. made his way down the plushly carpeted corridor leading to his son's suite of offices. He eyed the trappings along the corridor with grudging approval.

Even if the dratted boy hadn't chosen to go into the family business, J. P. was pleased to see that James had done so well for himself. Not that James's success surprised him any. He'd pegged the boy for a bright, hard-working lad from the beginning. Too damned softhearted, a characteristic he'd inherited from his mother, but shrewd for all that.

Walter Gregory was working late this evening in an attempt to weasel his way back into his employer's good graces. He jumped when the door of his precious office was pushed sharply from the outside and the formidable John Philip Drayton strode in.

J. P. Drayton's person was an imposing one. Nearly as tall as his son, he stood slightly under six feet. J. P.'s six feet were more vigorously padded than those of his son, however, and his face was hawkish and sharp. James's mother, from whom James inherited his soft heart, had also softened his features.

J. P.'s glittering, icy, sea-green eyes had been transformed and become muted and mossy under his son's chestnut brows. James's chiseled nose held none of the beakish qualities of his father's, and his chin, although firm, was not sharply squared. James's chin also sported a small dimple, a feature much admired by the ladies. His father's face bore no such mawkishly romantic indentation.

Gregory had no trouble at all in identifying the personage who'd just invaded his room. J. P. Drayton's face appeared almost daily in the newspapers, as he was one of the most powerful men in San Francisco. It was said he owned more than a couple of local politicians. Rumor had it also that at least one U.S. senator didn't dare wipe his shoes without consulting J. P. Drayton first.

Peering down his beaked nose at Gregory, J. P. skewered his son's secretary with a glare as sharp as a lance. With a sneer he no longer needed to practice, J. P. took the measure of Walter Gregory. "I wish to speak to my son," he said as though he were addressing a wart.

Bolting from his chair, Gregory ran to James Drayton's door. Rubbing his hands together in an obsequious gesture that would have done justice to Uriah Heep, he bowed to J. P.

"Right here, sir. I'm sure Mr. Drayton will be more than happy to see you, sir."

With another unflattering glare, J. P. snapped, "I sincerely doubt that," yanked open the door, and stalked into his son's office.

Chapter Four

"Mother! What on earth are you doing?"

Polly's exclamation startled her mother so much that she wobbled on her shaky legs. She only just managed to grab the arms of the chair in time to prevent herself from collapsing in a heap on the threadbare carpet.

"Oh, Mother!" Racing to her mother's side, Polly carefully supported her arm and eased her into the overstuffed chair. "What in heaven's name were you thinking of?"

Polly's heart galloped so fast she thought for a moment she might faint. As soon as she was sure her mother was safely ensconced on the cushioned seat, her knees gave out and she sank to the arm of the chair. Her hand reached for her bosom and she pressed her charms as if they had some power to quell her thundering panic. Along with the panic there raced a consuming terror. And there was anger mixed in, as well. The potent combination of sensations made emotion lump in Polly's throat.

"Polly, dear, please don't scold me."

"*Scold* you?" Polly stared at her mother, hurt gobbling up the anger and fear in her bosom.

Lillian looked contrite, and Polly's heart constricted painfully. "Oh, Mother, I don't mean to scold you. I was just so frightened to see you trying to walk. You need to preserve your strength. You know what Dr. van Pelt said."

"Dr. van Pelt said there was no harm in trying, dear. I was only trying."

Quickly, Polly slid to the floor and knelt before her mother, taking her hands in hers. Her mother was so dear to Polly. It broke her heart to see her this way: shattered in heart and body. Oh, Lillian MacNamara put on a brave front, but Polly knew how much she suffered.

Of all the married couples Polly had ever seen in her life, her parents had been the happiest. They'd done everything together. Polly still felt guilty because she used to envy them their closeness. Now she would give anything to have her father back again.

The parlor was warm from the fire crackling in the hearth, and gas lamps glowed around them. The upcoming Thanksgiving holiday had inspired Polly to decorate the room with bronze and yellow chrysanthemums from Mother Francis Mary's own garden. Splashes of rusty reflection bathed the room in a toasty golden aura that, under different circumstances, might have warmed Polly's heart. Right now, though, her heart held only the chilliness of hurt and sorrow.

"I didn't mean to yell at you, Mother." Now that her terror had subsided, Polly felt foolish for having reacted so strongly. "I merely would rather you waited until I came home from work before you tried to get out of your wheelchair. Then, if you have any trouble, I'll be here to help you."

"Oh, Polly, please don't be cross with me. I know you only mean the best."

Polly nodded, unable to speak for the moment. She squeezed her mother's hand.

Mrs. MacNamara's voice was very soft when she said, "Every now and then, though, dear, I like to try something on my own."

Swallowing the lump in her throat, Polly tried to subdue an unexpected itch of irritation. "I know that, Mother. I just don't want you to hurt yourself."

Mrs. MacNamara sighed. "You know, Polly, sometimes I think it suits you to have an invalid mother."

"What?"

"I'm not being unkind, Polly. Not intentionally. But you're a young, pretty girl. You should be out and about, not shut away in here with me."

"But Mother, I don't mind. Truly, I don't—"

"That's what troubles me, Polly." Mrs. MacNamara carefully pushed herself up from the chair. Polly immediately leapt up and began to support her.

"I'm sorry, dear. You're the best daughter a mother could ever want. I guess I feel guilty about you. I *know* I feel guilty about you, in fact."

If there was one thing Polly did not want from anyone, particularly her mother, it was sympathy. "There's certainly no need to feel sorry for me, Mother. You and Father kept me well in the fat years. In the lean years, the least I can do is take care of you." Her voice sounded more sharp than she'd intended.

Another sigh saw Polly's mother to her wheelchair, where she sat with resignation. "I'm not so sure of that, dear. I often think Franklin and I were so happy together that we neglected you and Stephen shamefully. I worry that you've withdrawn from the world because you finally have your mother to yourself and you're not about to be abandoned again."

Her mother's words were so very nearly true, and Polly was so ashamed of the truth, that denial rose hot and repentant to her tongue. "No, Mother! How can you even think such a thing, much less say it? You and Father were always wonderful to us. Stephen and I—well, we never wanted for anything."

Memories of her brother and herself in the care of Cousin George's mother Grace struck Polly as she pushed her mother's chair into the dining room. She recalled the birthdays, Easters, Thanksgivings, and Christmases she and Stephen had shared with Grace and George, reading cheerful messages from their parents sent from faraway, exotic places.

Stephen had always held Polly's hand and assured her that they were the two luckiest children in the world to have such interesting parents. And their parents loved them dearly, too, Stephen used to declare. Why, did a birthday ever pass without at least a message if Mother and Father couldn't be there in person? They even telephoned, when they could. Now, how many other children received telephone calls from their parents? How many other children had gifts of exotic toys, strange ornaments, odd-tasting condiments, and fancy silks from the Orient to show their friends?

Polly was fifteen years old before she realized other children didn't receive exotic gifts and telephone calls because they were blessed with parents who weren't always darting off and leaving them. Yet she couldn't fault her parents. They had loved their children in the only way they knew how. Polly understood such things now.

She also knew, although she didn't want to admit it, that her mother was right about her. It had taken a horrible tragedy and a wrenching loss, but Polly's mother was with her now. Never again would Polly celebrate birthdays and holidays alone. Guilt made her knuckles whiten as her fingers clenched the wheelchair.

Her heart ached. First her father and now Stephen. What a selfish, miserable girl she was to have resented her parents' closeness. Although she knew better, Polly couldn't help but wonder if her greedy childish wishes might have somehow caused these tragedies. Perhaps her hopes had been captured by a mischievous devil who'd thrown them back in her face.

Polly dragged her thoughts out of the sucking pit of remorse. She knew better than most people that remorse counted for naught in this world of prosaic, everyday duties and dull responsibility.

Oh, but she missed Stephen, though, every minute of every day. She pressed her medals unconsciously and wished Stephen could be with them now. If only word would come. If they could only know what had happened. Not knowing was so difficult.

James stared at the mottling on his father's thick neck and wondered if such choler was good for the old man's heart. Almost at once he was smitten by the cynical thought that he probably needn't worry, having been offered thus far in his life no reason to suspect his father of possessing such an organ of benevolence.

Schooling his face to betray none of his emotions—James knew from bitter experience that J. P. Drayton pounced on any hint of emotion—he tried to keep his voice level when he responded to his father's insane proposition.

Insane? No. James knew better. Shrewd, is what it was. The old man would try anything to get James back into his orbit, to shove him once more under his blasted, tyrannical thumb. But James was too smart for him this time. It had taken years to wriggle out from under old J. P.'s thumb. James would be damned and crucified before he'd willingly submit to its crushing pressure again.

"I can't imagine why you'd want my firm to represent you, Father. I should think you'd prefer a firm more intimately acquainted with the ins and outs of the shipping business."

"About which, *you* have taken great pains to learn nothing."

James said, "Absolutely nothing," in as neutral a voice as he could manage. A small—virtually invisible—smile dragged at the corners of his lips. If only the old man knew.

Not for the world and everything in it would James reveal the depth of his knowledge of shipping and J. P. Drayton's business enterprises. Not to J. P. Drayton, he wouldn't, at any rate. Such a revelation would be tantamount to admitting to a weakness, and the old man could smell weakness an ocean away. Like a truffle pig in a mossy forest.

No. More appropriately, like a vulture scenting carrion, old J. P. sniffed out weakness. And once he sniffed it, the sufferer was dead meat. J. P. was the most ruthless man in America if everything James knew and read about him was correct. Hell, the old man prided himself on the attribute.

The purple mottling on his father's thick neck deepened with James's two brief words. He seemed almost to vibrate as he stood before his son, his hamlike fists pressed against the finely polished mahogany of James's expensive desk. His breath scraped audibly through his constricted throat.

"Proud of yourself, aren't you, James?" J. P.'s diamond-hard eyes glittered.

Mercifully, James could not recall the last time he'd seen his father this angry; although, his sore heart acknowledged, those times were legion. James knew he was a bitter disappointment to the old man.

On the alert, he chose his words carefully. "I've worked very hard to make my business succeed, Father. And, yes, I am proud of its success." He couldn't quite maintain his gaze on his father's face when he added, "And every one of the dollars that went into the millions I now oversee was earned honestly. Nor did it seem necessary to crush the spines of weaker creatures as I climbed the ladder of success."

Although he was prepared for something of the sort, the ringing slap of his father's hand on his desk made James jump. "Damn it, boy, you make it sound like I'm some sort of ogre! Business is business, damn it! I can't be held accountable for every idiot whose business failed in the thirty years it's taken me to get where I am."

With an enormous sigh, James recognized the refrain of an ancient, acrid argument. It was the oldest, sourest argument in his life, which spanned the same thirty years of which his father spoke. He decided to stand, too. Not only would it give him a tactical advantage since he was, after all, slightly taller than his father, but perhaps it might speed the old man on his way. James wanted to go home and read something. Something funny. Something to get the sour taste of this confrontation out of his mouth and mind.

"Of course, Father," he said wearily. "You're not responsible for the idiots. Nor are you responsible for the widows and orphans created when your ships, pushed beyond the bounds of sanity and proper maintenance, sank in rough seas. Or the poor souls whose assets you gobbled up when you wouldn't give an inch on a mortgage or a loan. Or the thousands of Chinese girls kidnapped and sold into slavery by the soulless men you hired to captain your ships. You're not responsible for any of those things."

He gave his father a thin, tight grin. "I believe we established that fact a long time ago."

63

Emma Craig

"Damn it, boy, you don't know what it was like for me."
J. P. Drayton shoved himself away from the desk and gave
James his back. The gesture didn't surprise J. P.'s son.

What did surprise him was the sight of his father's beefy
hand lifting and raking through his still-thick salt-and-pepper
hair as though the old man were distressed. James couldn't
recall another single time when J. P. had given away so much
of himself. It was an effort to keep his kind heart from flinching, but James knew J. P. Drayton too well to dare believe the
one tiny gesture meant much of anything. He did, however,
narrow his eyes and watch his father closely.

"I had nothing. Nothing. You don't know what it's like to
have nothing, James, but I do." J. P. turned with a jerk and
pinned his son with a granite green gaze. James, who knew
his father's methods, did not so much as blink.

"I had to scrape for everything. Everything. You vilify me
for being unscrupulous, boy, but you don't know the half of
it. You don't know the obstacles I faced. You call *me* unscrupulous!"

J. P. paused, a circumstance that allowed James to murmur
a gentle, "Yes, I do."

His father harumphed. "Well, if you think I'm a scoundrel,
you ought to have seen the men I was up against."

All at once James was sick of this. It was a conversation
he and his father had engaged in over and over again through
the years. Nothing in it ever changed. The words were the
same. The emotions were the same. The results were the same.
Only now, in James's elegant Montgomery Street law offices,
with the trappings of his own success all about them, his father's words rang more hollow than James could ever remember them.

"I have no doubt, nor have I ever professed any doubt, that
you overcame monstrous obstacles, Father. God knows,
you've regaled me with them often enough. And I know my
own business philosophy has always struck you as weak and
addlepated. Nevertheless, I still maintain that two wrongs
don't make a right. And I'll tell you this, Father, and honestly,
that if I'd found it necessary to grind my fellow men under

my heels the way you did in order to achieve success, I would be a poor man today.''

"Oh, for God's sake!" J. P. sounded disgusted.

All at once, James decided to take a different tack. Although he knew the words would be useless, he gave it a try. "Why don't you make up for some of that now, Father? Why don't you direct one of your Pacific ships to search for the U.S.S. *China Seas*? It vanished somewhere near the Philippines. Just think of all the wonderful publicity you'd get. Why, people might even begin to think of you as a philanthropist." James's smile felt more like a sneer than anything else, and he was almost ashamed of himself for it.

His father only glared at him. James knew he wasn't through, though. J. P. would never, ever allow James the last word, no matter what the conversation. James suspected his father would go to his grave before he admitted he'd ever been wrong to wrest his wealth away from his competitors by the heartless methods he'd employed over the years.

Before J. P. could say a word, a sharp rap came on James's office door. Surprised, James turned toward the door in time to see it creak open.

Then, as if some cheerful godlet had decided the atmosphere in the room was too grim to be tolerated a second longer, a huge hound's long, long nose appeared. Snuffling loudly and wrinkling expressively, the nose hugged the carpet. It was followed by a pair of ridiculous ears, one standing at attention and the other flopped over, as if the dog were sending signals via semaphore to a ship lost at sea. Between the ears sat two eyes, the likes of which James had never seen. The beast boasted four enormous paws of different colors, being one each brown, white, black, and spotted.

James suspected he could count the animal's ribs if he'd been so inclined. The bony torso was held aloft on legs too long for beauty and too knobby for grace. The dog's overall coloring was, he guessed, whitish, but one of those silly eyes was black and the other brown. Twin wavy lines of black and brown followed the hound's spine to terminate in a whiplike tail held aloft, a proud period to an otherwise disreputable being.

J. P. Drayton stared at the hound, speechless.

James said, dryly, "Raymond?"

Raymond Sing peered around the doorjamb, a sheepish smile on his face.

"Do you mind, James? The poor thing was starving to death. It followed me from the orphanage and I couldn't make myself—" Raymond spied J. P. Drayton and stopped speaking, horrified. "Oh, Lord, James, I'm sorry. I had no idea—"

"It's all right, Raymond." James actually was rather grateful for the distraction.

"Another of your strays, boy?" J. P. Drayton's voice was as dry as year-old toast.

"Looks to be," said James, unaffected by his father's sarcasm.

Peering at the hound and then at Raymond with withering distaste, J. P. said, "I'll say this for you, boy—nobody would ever guess. You've done an admirable job of hiding your damned eccentricities from the business community."

For the first time since his parent's arrival, James smiled. "I have, haven't I?"

With another grimace for the dog, J. P. slapped his shiny black bowler hat on his head. "Damn it, James, I *know* you're not a fool. I didn't raise you to be a damned fool!"

"Thank you, Father."

With an enormous harumph, J. P. Drayton stormed out of his son's office, having uttered not a word to Raymond Sing. The words, "Damned strays and wastrels," drifted back into the office before the door slammed shut.

"I'm really sorry, James."

"Don't waste a moment worrying about it. I was glad for the interruption." James sat down again and stared at the dog, who was inspecting his office with noisy efficiency. "Believe me."

"Whew." Raymond sank into one of the chairs opposite James's desk. "I don't recall ever seeing the old man here before. Does he visit often?"

"I've never seen him here before, either."

And that circumstance both puzzled and worried James.

He'd never even imagined his father actually visiting, in person, his place of business. The old man didn't operate that way.

"Did he tell you why he came?"

"Yes. At least, he gave me a reason. I guess it was the truth. Although with my father, truth is a variable commodity."

"Well? What was it?"

"He said he wants my law firm to represent his shipping concerns. Says he wants to switch from Forrest, Godfrey, Welles, and Boston and give the business to me."

Raymond's eyes opened wide. "Good heavens. That would mean a windfall for Drayton and Associates. Are you going to do it?"

With a bark of mirthless laughter, James said, "Are you out of your mind, Raymond? It took every ounce of my determination to get out of the old man's grasp in the first place. In fact, I had to borrow some fortitude from others and have yet to pay it back. I'm not going to sell my soul to him on purpose. Not for any amount of money."

Neither man said a word for a moment. Then James muttered, "That's why he came here. He wants to control me again."

"Are you sure about that?" Raymond's voice, always gentle, sounded especially so when he asked the question.

"Why else would he come here?" James was annoyed to hear the hurt as well as the anger in his question.

Raymond shrugged. "To make peace?"

"Peace! My father doesn't know the meaning of the word."

Another moment of silence fell between them, broken only by the interested hound. The animal had found James's heavy mahogany wastepaper basket by this time, and had started to disembowel it with evident delight. Grabbing one particularly tasty piece of crumpled paper in his teeth, the dog flopped down on the expensive carpet, held the wad between his front paws, and began to shred it.

James sighed and smiled. "What possessed you to bring that creature here?"

"Well, you've been saying you'd like a dog."

Inspecting his friend's face for signs of irony and finding none, James laughed softly. "I was thinking more in terms of a purebred, Raymond. I have an image to maintain, you know."

Raymond eyed James critically. "A poodle would never do for you, James."

"A *poodle?* Good grief. I could live this creature down before I could live down a poodle."

A lopsided grin split Raymond's face. "Well, there, you see? I've just done you a favor."

James only sighed and wondered what Mrs. Pruitt, his housekeeper, would have to say about cleaning up after an ill-kempt, ill-favored, ill-mannered hound. Nothing good, he was certain.

"I saw your typist at the Sisters of Benevolence this afternoon."

Raymond's innocent comment lifted James's brooding gaze away from the disgraceful hound. "Polly MacNamara?"

"Is that her name? I'd forgotten. The one who came to your office this morning."

"Yes. That's Miss MacNamara."

James's interest in Polly had been deepening as the day progressed. One reason he'd stayed so long at the office was to see if he couldn't work her out of his system. So far, he'd been singularly unsuccessful at doing so. "What was she doing there?"

"Seems she reads to the orphans every Wednesday evening. According to Mother Francis Mary, she's been doing it every Wednesday for two years now."

"Really?"

James's broody frown found the dog again. Hell. Why did he have the feeling he should have expected something of the sort from his pretty typist? "So that's what she does with her Wednesday evenings."

Gratitude that Polly was not seeing a gentleman on her free evenings butted head-on with James's irritation that her Wednesday-night occupation should correspond so closely with his own charitable inclinations. James had spent most of his adult life ridding himself of complications, and he'd done a remarkably good job of it. Wealthy beyond avarice, free of his father's overbearing dominance, he had established a reputation that held all but his closest friends at a comfortable distance.

He had women when he wanted them, and for none of them did he feel more than a brief hot flicker of carnal desire. He wanted nothing more. Why did he suddenly have the gut-sinking feeling that Polly MacNamara was a complication sent by the fates to test his fortitude and character?

Although he hated himself for asking, he said, "How long does she stay? It must be very late when she leaves. Does she have a safe way home?"

"Oh, yes. Mother Francis Mary sends her home in Billy Peabody's wagon, straight to her door. I asked because it worried me, thinking she had to walk home alone after dark."

"Good man, Raymond."

Raymond cleared his throat, embarrassed. "Yes. Well, anyway, Billy takes her home in the wagon."

"Well, well, well." James stared at the dog doing mischief on his office carpet.

Then he recalled that he and Raymond had begun an experiment that very day, and his attention left the hound and reverted to his friend. He chose to ignore the perceptive grin Raymond was giving him. "How did it go today? Did the boys work as well as they said they would?"

Raymond's grin transformed from one of conspiracy to one of satisfaction. He breathed a deep, contented sigh. "They did better than even I expected, James. I guess they really meant it when they said they wanted to earn an honest wage."

Pleasure overtook James's worries. "Good. That's good. If they continue to work out so well, perhaps we'll be able to expand the program; find some other institution that can use help. Hell, even businesses. Why, I'll warrant there's more than one softhearted businessman in San Francisco who'd be willing to employ the services of a young man who's made a mistake and is willing to make up for it."

"Don't judge all people by yourself, James," advised Raymond, sounding much more caustic than he usually did.

"There are more hardheaded people out there than softhearted ones."

With a grin and a shrug, James said, "Well, I don't know why a body can't be both."

Raymond only laughed.

At ten o'clock that evening, as James held the seductively swaying Cynthia Ingram in his arms and waltzed her around the Crockers' impressive ballroom, his mind was not on his partner. Several times he had occasion to be grateful to his boyhood dancing lessons when something in the room captured his attention and he realized he'd been keeping to the beat of the music without thinking.

"James, darling," Cynthia purred in his ear, "I believe your mind is elsewhere this evening."

"Mmmm?" James peered down at her and smiled.

A beautiful woman, older than he, practiced in all the arts and artifices of seduction, Cynthia was a widow and a merry one. She graced James's arms and bed more often than any other lady of his acquaintance. He even harbored faint affection for her, although he seriously doubted hers for him. He had no doubt at all, however, that Cynthia cared a great deal for his wealth.

"Sorry, my dear," he said in the artificial voice he used during these tedious social occasions.

With an accomplished pout, Cynthia cooed, "It's not very flattering when one's partner prefers staring at the walls more than into one's eyes."

James gave her an extra whirl and forced a laugh. "Ah, my sweet, you know better than that."

"Do I?"

Cynthia peered at him through artfully lowered lids. James figured she knew her lush lashes made her sapphire eyes look especially alluring from that angle, and he generally appreciated her flirtation. Tonight, though, he was hard-pressed to keep from yawning.

Almost by rote, he whispered, "Of course you know it."

"Are you bored with the party, dearest?"

"A little," he lied. He was bored to death, is what he was.

Christmas Pie

"I believe I can offer an alternative you might find more alluring." Her warm breath caressed his cheek.

James found his first genuine grin of the evening. "I'm absolutely sure of it, my love."

Cynthia had taught him more about the mysteries of love-making than any of his other amours. He often thought he owed her a good deal for that alone although, since he was a generous man, he felt in no debt to her now.

He also found himself peculiarly indifferent this evening. Although he knew Cynthia didn't expect him to speak words of love or, thank God, spend the night with her after their liaisons, he couldn't seem to drum up much enthusiasm for such an interlude tonight.

His thoughts seemed to spin exclusively around the prim, virginal Miss Polly MacNamara. Had done ever since he picked her up on that sloppy Chinatown street yesterday. He'd never been much interested in virgins. Still wasn't, if it came to that.

This attraction of his had nothing to do with Polly's innocence, however. Rather, it had to do with her character. He'd never before met a woman who fascinated him so much.

Damn.

Chapter Five

Polly decided Thursday afternoon after work would be a perfect time for her to drop into the curio shop in Chinatown. She wanted to thank her elderly benefactress properly for giving her the pretty coin that she had come to like so much.

The air was as thick and milky as barley water when Polly approached Grant Avenue. She didn't mind the weather, though. A San Francisco native, she was used to the city's famous fogs, although such a dense atmosphere was unusual during the late autumn. She felt her coin warm against her skin, and was glad to have it.

Peeking over her shoulder, she discerned Lawrence Bullock striding manfully along Montgomery Street. She frowned as she turned the corner onto Grant. There was something not entirely pleasing about Mr. Bullock, although Polly couldn't put her finger on any one quality that disturbed her.

He'd held the door for her as she left work this evening and smiled winningly as she passed by. There certainly was nothing in his manner to give her this uneasy feeling, but it nibbled at her, nevertheless.

Now if it had been James Drayton who had smiled at her

in that way—but, no. Polly wouldn't allow herself such fabulous thoughts; they led only to unhappiness.

"I'm just imagining things," she muttered as she walked swiftly up the street. "Oh, there it is."

She felt very cheery when she neared the shop. There was such an inviting air about the place. Pushing the door open, she heard the familiar tinkle of the bell, and as soon as she entered the faint fragrance of sandalwood teased her nostrils.

An elderly gentleman sitting behind the counter on a tall stool nodded to Polly. His embroidered cap caught the lamplight, and when the cap's shiny threads flung the light back into the room, Polly entertained the whimsical impression of muted fireworks. The effect was charming, and she gave the old man a big smile.

"Good evening."

With a small formal bow, the old gentleman said, "Good evening, lady." He wore his white hair in the Chinese manner and his long, tidy braid bounced against his dark blue shirt when his head bobbed.

Polly walked up to the counter and saw that his parchment-colored hands held several cards, the backs of which were ornamented with intricate Chinese patterns. He laid them on the counter and spread them out face up, as though he wished Polly to inspect them. Then he poked at one of the cards with a long, thin finger and peered at Polly with the twinkliest black eyes she'd ever beheld.

"Sad news. Happy news. Love. Contented life. Good fortune, missy. Good fortune." His voice sounded as creaky as a rusty hinge, but he smiled and gave her a cheerful chuckle after his announcement.

Polly blinked at him. Was he talking to her? About her own future? Unsure what to say, she managed a sociable, "Is that what you see in the cards?"

The old man nodded with a good deal of vigor and gave her another blithe chuckle. "Good fortune. Happy life."

Hoping he was merely eccentric and not a dangerous lunatic, and also wishing to be polite, Polly asked, "And whose good fortune and happy life do the cards foretell?"

He pointed his skinny finger straight at Polly's heart. "You."

"*Me?*"

Another creaky chuckle accompanied his, "You." Then he seemed to find the whole matter tremendously amusing. He slapped his knee and chortled so hard that he had to wipe a tear from his withered cheek.

"Oh, my." Polly wondered if one were supposed to thank a seer for predicting a rosy future and decided it couldn't do any harm, so she tacked on, "Thank you very much."

As soon as the old man's attack of levity abated, he said, "Old lady not here tonight."

"Oh, bother." Then Polly realized what he'd just said and gaped at him. "How did you know I wanted to talk to her?"

Her question provoked another spate of rusty chuckles. "She be back when you need."

Polly was beginning to feel as though she'd stepped into some melodramatic production and didn't know her lines. "When—when I need?"

He nodded again, enthusiastically. "When you need."

"When I need." Good heavens.

"Yes. Yes. When you need."

The old man collected his cards from the countertop with a swish and hopped down from his stool, smiling at Polly all the while. Then he gave her a delighted nod and hobbled through the beaded curtain into the back of the shop.

Polly watched him go and wondered if she should stop him and attempt to wrest some sense out of him. There were apparently no lights on back there and the old gentleman seemed to vanish as soon as the beads clacked together behind him. It was an odd visual illusion, and Polly shook her head and blinked to try to clear away the image.

It wouldn't be cleared, though, and she found herself alone. She wasn't surprised when silence settled on the shop again and nobody else appeared. She heard the front doorknob rattle, as if someone planned to enter. She glanced at the door, but it remained shut.

Peering around the shop and wondering what to do, she noticed one or two items she'd missed the day before yesterday. In the hope that somebody else would come out from behind the beaded curtain, Polly decided she'd peruse the shop's wares. Maybe if she waited a moment or two the old lady would show up and she could thank her in person. Of course, the elderly man said she wasn't there, but since he couldn't know who Polly wanted to see, how could he be sure?

She shut her eyes and shook her head once more, trying to rid it of cobwebs. Why on earth was she even trying to make sense of the old man's ramblings?

Still, it was pleasant to be told one's future was bright, she guessed. Even if the soothsayer did seem to be a little crazy.

After waiting as long as she dared, Polly sighed and decided she'd just have to come back and thank the old lady yet another day. Her mother worried so when she was late. She opened the front door and started up Grant Street.

"A very good evening to you, Miss MacNamara!"

Lawrence Bullock's booming voice startled her and she turned abruptly. Frowning, she saw him push himself away from the wall of the shop. Had he been waiting for her? The thought made her nervous and not a little huffy.

"Good evening, Mr. Bullock," she said with more stiffness of manner than was her wont.

Watching him closely as he approached, she read only friendliness in his expression.

Well, of course, you silly girl. What else would there be? Annoyed by her unwarranted edginess, Polly gave Lawrence Bullock a bigger smile than she had meant to.

"What are you doing out on the streets of Chinatown alone in the evening, my dear?"

I'm not your dear, Polly thought sourly. Maintaining her smile, however, she said, "I'm just on my way home, Mr. Bullock."

"I saw you go into that shop and tried to follow you, but the door was locked."

"Oh, no, Mr. Bullock. The door wasn't locked. Why, I just opened it."

"I know, my dear. I saw you."

Bullock winked at her as he spoke, and Polly's smile

dimmed. She did not approve of gentlemen winking at her. Not one little bit.

"And I also know the door was locked," Bullock continued, as though he considered it a good joke.

"You are mistaken, Mr. Bullock." Irritated, Polly turned to continue on her way.

His hand on her arm stopped her. Shocked by the overly familiar gesture, Polly turned and pointedly shook off his fingers. "Is there something you want from me, Mr. Bullock?"

Faint stirrings of alarm began to scamper up Polly's spine. She eyed her surroundings and was reassured to see the usual hustling and bustling she'd grown to expect in Chinatown, where life seemed to be lived on the streets.

Vegetable stands and meat markets did business here in a much louder and more boisterous manner than such activity was carried out in other neighborhoods. Vendors called out the merits of their wares in Chinese and English. Runners darted here and there, carrying messages and parcels. A regular Babel of voices filled the air.

"Why, yes, Miss MacNamara, there certainly is something I want from you."

Bullock's eyes, Polly noticed, were a light blue and not particularly attractive, although he was generally considered to be a handsome man. She decided it was the weakness about his eyes and chin that did not appeal to her. As if trained to do so, her brain began immediately to compare him unfavorably to James Drayton, and she had to forcefully command it to stop. Why on earth did everything and everyone remind her of James Drayton?

"Well, then, what is it, Mr. Bullock?" she asked curtly.

"I want to see you home, my dear. You shouldn't be out alone in the evenings this way."

"I assure you, I walk home every evening, and I am perfectly fine. I don't need an escort."

"Nonsense, my dear. A lovely young girl shouldn't have to walk alone."

He smiled at her in entirely too warm a manner, and Polly decided she'd taken all she intended to take from Lawrence

Bullock this evening. The thought of being walked home by him made her flesh crawl.

"Thank you very much," she said coldly, "but I do not need your assistance. I much prefer to walk alone."

"Don't be silly, Miss MacNamara. I shall most assuredly see you to your home."

Polly felt certain she heard a new edge in his voice. Oh, Lord, now what? If she were to tell one of the chief attorneys in the employ of Drayton and Associates to go away and leave her alone, she was liable to lose her position with the firm.

Some good fortune this is, she thought bitterly, and wished the sidewalk would open up and swallow Lawrence Bullock.

In a last desperate attempt to shake him off, she said, "Mr. Bullock, I walk this same route every night. I see the same people and go the same way. I live not far off and my mother is waiting for me. Please just let me go."

She turned and began to walk briskly away, hoping against hope that Lawrence Bullock would take the hint. Her heart sank when she heard him say, "Now wait just a minute, Miss MacNamara. You may be a special pet of James Drayton, but I'll be damned if I'll—"

Horrified by his ugly words, Polly whirled around to deny his assertions when all of a sudden his speech was interrupted by a tremendous grunt and he came flying through the air. She had to leap out of the way to avoid being hit by his husky body as it crashed to the sidewalk in front of her.

Caught in a moment of panic, the idea of helping Lawrence Bullock did battle in her brain with the urge to flee. Before either idea could establish precedence, another voice sailed out to her in the busy night, lifting her heart and her gaze.

With real joy, she beheld James Drayton walking toward her. So happy was she to see him, so sure was she of rescue at his hand, that at first she didn't notice the odd-looking animal loping along at his side.

"Oh, Mr. Drayton! I don't know what happened. Suddenly Mr. Bullock fell down."

"So I see." James wore a ferocious scowl when he stopped beside his fallen employee.

What he'd seen and heard when he'd turned the corner onto

Grant Street had made his blood boil. Damn Lawrence Bullock to blazes. How dare he accost this innocent girl? As much as James himself did not deserve the reputation as a ladies' man he'd tried so hard to cultivate, Lawrence Bullock did.

James knew full well Bullock would not hesitate to use his position as associate to gain Polly's compliance in a shady liaison. The knowledge made James want to kick Bullock in his most sensitive bodily area. And that area was, James thought grimly, most assuredly not his head.

As Bullock began to groan, Polly's hushed voice caressed James's ear. He liked her voice. It was at once sweet and sultry, although he was sure she'd blush up a storm if anyone ever told her so. The thought brought, hard on its heels, an almost overwhelming urge to do it and watch her color heighten.

"I don't understand it, Mr. Drayton. I had just turned to walk home. Mr. Bullock had been—talking to me—" Polly stopped speaking for a moment, flustered. "All at once I heard a terrible grunt, turned again, and it was as if he were flying through the air at me. I believe he landed rather hard." And on a new cement walkway, a fact that afforded Polly a moment of unladylike glee. She couldn't quite suppress her grin.

Another powerful groan brought Polly's gaze to Lawrence Bullock's prone form.

"Ohhhh, Lord," he groaned. "Oh, damn."

James also watched Bullock, his expression hard. "Miss MacNamara, may I presume upon your good nature for a moment to hold my dog's leash while I help Mr. Bullock to rise?"

"Of course, Mr. Drayton." Polly took the lead from James's splendidly gloved hand and, for the first time, paid attention to the animal.

"Mercy." She was perfectly astonished that James Drayton, a gentleman whom she'd always believed to be the absolute epitome of manners and fashion, should be walking a dog such as the one appended to the leash.

Perhaps it was a new breed, she mused, before her attention was once again claimed by the two gentlemen struggling on the walkway. What she heard made her stare.

"What in God's name were you doing chasing Miss MacNamara down the street, Bullock?" James growled furiously, grabbing Bullock under his armpits and trying to lift him. "And don't try to deny it, either."

Far from trying to deny James's accusations, Lawrence Bullock merely stared at his mentor blankly for several seconds. Then he shook his head, bringing to Polly's mind a bear rising from his winter stupor.

Having succeeded at last in lifting Bullock from the ground, James now found himself supporting him. He wasn't happy about it. The mere thought of Polly MacNamara being caught in the big, burly clutches of an ape like Lawrence Bullock made James want to throttle something. Preferably Lawrence Bullock.

He said savagely, "I watched you, Bullock. I saw exactly what you did. And let me tell you here and now, I will *not* have female employees of my law firm harassed by male employees. Most particularly not an associate, who should be setting an example of appropriate behavior, for heaven's sake. I trust I make myself perfectly clear."

"Wh—what happened?" issued from Bullock's lips, and James knew his trust was for naught.

"You tried to grab hold of Miss MacNamara and fell down for your efforts, is what happened. It's certainly no more than you deserved."

Blinking rapidly, Bullock seemed to see James for the first time. He lifted a hand to rub his wounded chin and muttered, "James. What're you doing here?"

"Picking you up off the street."

"But—but—" Bullock peered around fuzzily. When his gaze lit on Polly, it wobbled for a moment, then fastened and held fast. "Walking Miss MacNamara home from work, James. S'all I was doing. Walking her home."

James, who knew better, uttered a biting, "Balderdash."

Lawrence Bullock was not a pretty sight. His chin sported a scrape, and his nose and lip were scratched. There was a red welt on his forehead and a cut above one eye. Polly suspected, having had experience with such things when her brother Stephen was a boy, that the eye would be swollen and black come morning.

His clothes were crumpled and covered with dust and worse. His hair, generally pomaded and brushed impeccably, now tumbled everywhere. His hat, a once-proud member of the bowler species, had been crushed between his chest and the pavement. It now lay abandoned on the sidewalk like a fallen soldier.

Feeling desperate about the situation and the lateness of the hour, Polly said nervously, "I tried to tell him I didn't need his assistance, Mr. Drayton, but he insisted on accompanying me. I—I didn't care to have his company."

The dog seemed to sense Polly's distress. He gave her a conciliatory whine and leaned against her leg, nearly toppling her with his sympathy.

"Sidewalk opened up," Lawrence Bullock mumbled.

Polly, who had been knocked a little cockeyed by the hound, righted herself and gaped at Bullock. Before she could utter a shocked exclamation, James spoke.

"What on earth are you talking about, Lawrence?" He glanced at the sidewalk. "Oh, yes. I see. There's a big crack running straight across it." He began to pat Bullock's clothes to remove the street dust. His efforts were not gentle. "You ought to learn to be careful, man."

Polly looked at the ground, too, and sure enough, she saw the crack. It was big, all right, and ran the width of the pavement from building to street. She hadn't noticed it before. A fantastic idea shot through her brain, but it was so ridiculous she immediately rejected it.

"No." Bullock listed to port in James's arms and James straightened him roughly. "Opened up in front of me. Swear it."

"Don't be absurd, Bullock."

Steadier now, Bullock shot a queer look at Polly. "I swear to God, James, I'd just begun to hurry after Miss MacNamara when a big crack opened up. Right there in front of me." He pointed with a trembling finger.

Polly's gasp brought both men's gazes to her face and she was embarrassed. She quickly shut her mouth, but her free hand reached up to feel her two medals. Through the fabric of her worn overcoat, she felt her heart thunder beneath St. Christopher and her ancient, shopworn coin.

I must be losing my mind.

"An earthquake especially for you, was it?" James asked sarcastically. "Well, I suppose Miss MacNamara can feel grateful that the gods of geology favored you with a personal display this evening. If you hadn't tripped and I hadn't been around to see your dastardly attempt to chase her, who knows what might have happened?"

Bullock apparently felt too shaken to take exception to James's belief in him as a cad. Giving himself another overall shake, he put a hand to his aching brow. "I shall go home now." His voice sounded much more feeble than it normally did.

"Good idea." With a swoop of his hand, James plucked Bullock's crushed bowler from the pavement and slapped it against his chest. "Here, Bullock. Take your hat. If you bother Miss MacNamara again, your face will look like this. I can guarantee it."

Since James was much too sophisticated a man of the world to issue idle threats, Bullock cast him a leery glance. Then he made a hat-tipping gesture at Polly with his flattened headpiece, tried to settle it on his hair, failed, and fled down the street, reeling like a drunken man.

James and Polly stared after him until he turned onto Montgomery Street. Then James heaved a self-satisfied sigh and turned toward Polly.

"There. I don't expect you'll be bothered by Lawrence Bullock again, Miss MacNamara."

Polly felt nervous all of a sudden now that she was alone on the busy street with her elegant boss. She offered James a small smile. "Thank you very much, Mr. Drayton. I—I guess he meant well. At least—well, I *think* he did." She'd been taught to believe the best of people and, while it was difficult in Lawrence Bullock's case, she endeavored to adhere to the principle.

James's handsome smile curved downward. "I wouldn't

wager a great deal of money on that chance, Miss Mac-
Namara.''

He noticed his hound, still leaning heavily against Polly's
skirts. ''Here, Miss MacNamara, let me take that beast from
you. Thank you for holding him for me.''

Handing the leash back to James, Polly wished she could
think of something clever to say. Unfortunately, she possessed
no practice in social repartee and did not feel at all clever. So
as not to appear a complete booby, she strove for nonchalance
when she remarked, ''I don't believe I've ever seen a dog
exactly like this one before, Mr. Drayton.''

When James laughed delightedly, she was sure she'd made
a total ass of herself.

''Oh, my goodness, no, Miss MacNamara, and I don't expect you'll ever see another one, either.''

His obvious good humor cheered her somewhat.

James ordered the hound to ''heel'' in a firm voice. The
dog ignored him and seemed inclined to stick to Polly's side.
James put his fists on his lean hips and gave the animal a
mock glare.

Her employer looked terribly youthful, amused, and appealing to Polly. She'd never expected him to exhibit such
attributes, and her embarrassment faded. Catching his mood,
she eyed the dog, too, and murmured, ''One of a kind, is he?''

Another gratifying laugh greeted her small sally. Her heart
sped up and began to perform acrobatic maneuvers in her
breast.

''Indeed he is one of a kind, Miss MacNamara. At least I
certainly hope he is.''

Looking at the dog for all she was worth, since she was too
nervous to look at James Drayton, Polly asked, ''What is his
name, Mr. Drayton?''

She was probably the most enchanting female James had
ever encountered. For the life of him, he didn't understand it.
Oh, she was a good-looking girl, and pleasant. But there was
something else about her that just about held him spellbound.
He gave her a smile he hoped was charming.

''Well, now, Miss MacNamara, I haven't actually named
him yet. Perhaps, since the hour is late and you've just had

an uncomfortable experience, you would do me the honor of allowing me to see you home and we can discuss possible cognomens.''

He could tell she was leery of his offer when she stammered, ''Oh—oh, Mr. Drayton, please. You needn't bother with me. I'll be fine now that you've sent Mr. Bullock packing.''

Then, to James's utter delight, Polly pressed a palm to her lovely, reckless lips, and turned bright red. ''Oh! I mean—''

''My dear Miss MacNamara, please say no more. I'm afraid Mr. Bullock is not the most discreet of gentlemen. I am terribly sorry he bothered you, and I shall take care that it does not happen again.''

In a formally polite gesture, he crooked his elbow. Then, cocking his head in a manner he knew from experience ladies found appealing, and giving her one of his most endearing smiles, he said, ''Please? It would be my pleasure. Besides, my dog has taken quite a fancy to you. You really should help me name him.''

She paused much too long for coyness and James realized she felt genuinely uneasy about accepting his escort. ''I'm not as bad as I'm painted, Miss MacNamara. Truly, I'm not.''

''Oh, no, I'm sure you can't be.'' Then, realizing she had phrased her statement indelicately, Polly stammered, ''I—I mean—''

But James only laughed again and shook his head. This demure typist was obviously not an accomplished flirt. Why, she blurted out whatever thoughts came into her head.

''You needn't apologize, Miss MacNamara. I'm all too well aware of my unfortunate reputation. But I promise you will be safe with me.''

The dog, who had reluctantly come to James's side, took that opportunity to sit down right in front of Polly. He looked up at her with the most pleading expression James had ever beheld on a canine's face, and lifted one disreputable paw, the spotted one, as though begging Polly to give in.

Never one to miss an opportunity, James said, ''There. You see? You can't possibly resist such an invitation.''

Being, after all, only human, Polly couldn't contain her giggle. "Well, if you're sure it isn't a bother, I should be happy for your company. I'm afraid it's late. Mother worries when I'm late."

"I can certainly understand that," said James, who didn't. To the best of his recollection, nobody had ever worried about him in his entire life.

So Polly put her hand on James's arm, rather tentatively, and the three of them began to walk down Grant. The fog had lifted during the excitement of the evening, and stars now glimmered in the heavens above. Since they were in the metropolis of San Francisco, gas lamps lighted their path all the way to Pacific Avenue. Once they turned the corner, though, traffic thinned and only the moon and stars lit their way.

The picket fence beside them glittered as if gilded by the full moon's glow. Patches of staked chrysanthemums gathered starlight on their dewy petals and seemed to wink at them as they strolled past. To James, whose nature had never been whimsical, the evening seemed nearly magical, and it fairly stunned him.

"Well, now, Miss MacNamara," he said, in an effort to ward off his fanciful impression, "can you think of an appropriate appellation for this beast?"

Her walk, James decided, was as regal as that of a princess. He guessed her height to be about five feet five inches, somewhat tall. He appreciated her height since he was a tall man. Her hat had obviously seen several seasons' duty, but she wore it with flair. The two of them fell into step with each other, even with the ridiculous hound tagging along beside him, with ease and grace.

"A name," Polly mused.

James watched her take another quick peek at the hound and saw a tiny frown crease her forehead.

"Is he *really* yours, Mr. Drayton?"

Her beautiful eyes reflected starlight, her soft smile an enchanting accompaniment. A faint flush stained her cheeks, and James felt a catch somewhere in his chest. My God. Polly MacNamara, his staid, prim typist, at this moment looked to James like an elfin being, an enchantress sent to earth to tempt him.

84

"He certainly is, Miss MacNamara." He knew his smile had gone lopsided.

Polly gave a brisk, businesslike nod and the spell was almost—but not quite—broken.

"Well, then, in order to preserve your dignity, I believe the first thing we should do is establish a breed for him." She peeked at him, as if to ascertain his reaction to her imaginative suggestion.

His reaction was so strong he had to restrain himself from pulling her into his arms and kissing her right here on the street, the dog and the public be hanged.

Good Lord.

After clearing his throat with some difficulty, he grinned. "So you think my already tarnished reputation won't survive this creature?"

Polly, unused to bantering conversations with adult males, had to still her racing heart. She couldn't believe she'd just said so pert a thing to James Drayton. Yet some compulsion with which she was totally unfamiliar seemed to be guiding her tongue this evening, and she said, "Well, I'm not altogether sure how tarnished your reputation is, but, well—" she peeked at the dog once more "—a breed wouldn't hurt."

James couldn't recall another time when he'd been so delighted by a female companion. "Well, then, what breed do you recommend, Miss MacNamara?"

"It will have to be a rare one," she said with feigned gravity.

He nearly choked. "Of course."

"He looks rather like a hound."

"Yes, I believe he does exhibit a certain houndish quality."

"Perhaps he could be—" Another look at the dog prompted Polly to finish with, "—a rarely seen Portuguese Tapir Hound." Upon her pronouncement, she honored James with a large, mischievous grin.

Laughing so hard he could scarcely speak, James managed to stammer at last, "Are there tapirs in Portugal?"

After a considering pause, a small frown wrinkled Polly's brow. "You know, I'm not altogether sure. Perhaps we should select another animal."

"Or another country."

"Of course! Why didn't I think of it before? He can be a rarely seen Philippine Tapir Hound. I believe there are tapirs in the Philippines, and very few people have been there, so nobody will ever suspect."

The urge to kiss her was so strong, James had to grab the lapel of his overcoat to keep his hand from reaching out to her. "And just what will nobody ever suspect, Miss Mac-Namara?"

The warmth and delight he detected in his voice surprised him. He'd never heard it there before; never felt it before. Delight was an emotion entirely foreign to James Drayton. Warmth was something one got from a stove.

"Why, that his origins are dubious, of course. That he's an American, Mr. Drayton. A blue-blooded, dyed-in-the-wool, low-bred American mutt."

James couldn't help it. The street was dark and his companion enchanting, and he simply couldn't help it. Holding Polly's kid-encased hand in his, he turned her toward him and gave her lovely cheek the kiss he longed to bestow on her succulent lips.

Chapter Six

James, who had flirted with innumerable society maidens and done infinitely more than that with several of those damsels' more experienced sisters, aunts, and mothers, heard Polly's gasp of astonishment and knew he'd made a grave tactical error. This was one female whose sensibilities were too fine even for such a chaste kiss as this.

Immediately, he lowered Polly's hand to his arm again and hoped she wouldn't remove it and bolt from his side. When she stiffened up like a retriever on point, he guessed she was too shocked to run.

Polly put her free hand to her breast in a gesture he was coming to recognize. His burgeoning irritation at her dramatic recoil from his prim kiss melted. Poor Polly. First Lawrence Bullock and now James Drayton, a man who should have known better.

He murmured uncomfortably, "I'm sorry, Miss Mac-Namara. I meant no disrespect. It was wrong of me to presume such a liberty."

"Oh! I—I—I mean—it's—it's all right, Mr. Drayton."

"No, it's not all right. I had no business to kiss you." With a rueful grin, he asked, "Will you forgive me?"

"Of—of course," came out in a voice so small, James barely heard it.

When she peered up at him, her glorious eyes a testament both to her amazement and her longing, he very nearly lost control of himself again. Good Lord, what was the matter with him?

With an effort, he suppressed his baser instincts and cleared his throat. "Well, now that we have this animal's breed taken care of, what do you suggest I name the beast?"

At that very moment, "the beast" took exception to a cat James hadn't noticed. With a sudden lunge and an impressive bay, it jerked James's arm nearly out of its socket in a frenzy to reach and slay the feline.

James stumbled forward, leaving Polly to grab at his hand in an effort to keep him upright. She missed, and James ultimately brought his exuberant pet to a halt by yanking on the leash. The dog, unhappy at having its attempt at assassination thwarted, strained at the lead so hard it began to choke. Still, it wouldn't give up.

"Stupid dog," James muttered.

Then he heard Polly's tinkling laughter and looked over to find her giggling. He grinned and guessed the dog wasn't so stupid after all. James hadn't expected that so simple a thing as being made to look a fool would smooth over an awkward social situation with such ease.

"Miss MacNamara," he said severely, "I believe you're laughing at me."

"Oh, no, Mr. Drayton," Polly gasped through her giggles. "Certainly not."

"Humph."

The dog didn't seem inclined to give up its pursuit, even though the cat had shown the good sense to flee the second it heard the hound's bay. James, through vigorous tugging and firm commands, tried to convince the animal of the futility of its endeavor. His attention was divided, though, because he kept looking at his beautiful typist.

After watching in amusement for a moment or two, Polly said, "Lurch."

James cocked a brow. "Lurch?"

"I believe you should name that particular rarely seen Philippine Tapir Hound Lurch."

Utterly charmed, James could only grin. After another moment or two, during which man and hound fought for dominance, he brought the dog under control. It seemed to sulk when James made it behave, a circumstance James found did not surprise him. He walked the animal back to Polly.

"Miss MacNamara, I don't believe even *my* besmirched reputation could withstand the snickers sure to greet a rarely seen Philippine Tapir Hound named Lurch."

"You really think not?"

James found it telling that Polly did not seem at all shy about taking his arm this time. Nor did she exhibit any of the restraint his indiscreet, though pure, kiss had earlier precipitated. If she only knew the manner in which he truly wanted to kiss her, she'd run like that spooked cat.

"I'm absolutely sure of it."

The rest of the walk to Polly's home was accomplished without incident. The dog, nameless and with a soul unblemished by homicide, moped along at James's side while James and Polly tested appellations. None quite seemed to fit, and they arrived at the MacNamara porch without having decided on a suitable title.

"Perhaps a name will occur to you after you've lived with him a little longer," Polly offered without much hope.

James peered at his pet doubtfully. "Perhaps."

They climbed the porch steps and James was about to take a reluctant leave when the door flew open. They both jumped.

Polly whirled around and James was sorry to see a flash of guilt cross her face. Lillian MacNamara's worry was clear to see, thanks to the gaslight spilling onto the porch from inside the house.

"Oh, Mother! I'm so sorry to be late!" Polly darted to her mother and quickly bent to kiss the older woman's cheek.

"Good evening, Mrs. MacNamara. It's a pleasure to see you again." James swept his hat from his head and bowed formally before giving Polly's mother his patented, ice-melting smile. "I'm very sorry to be bringing your daughter home so late.

Emma Craig

I'm afraid she ran into some trouble on Grant Street, and I was seeing her home. Then this creature who has recently adopted me caused us another slight delay.''

"Good evening, Mr. Drayton." Lillian's voice sounded strained. "I confess I was a little worried about her. What sort of trouble did you run into, Polly dear?''

"It was nothing really, Mother. Mr. Bullock—from the law firm?—Well, I'm afraid he suffered a small accident. Fortunately, Mr. Drayton was walking his dog in the area and came to the rescue.''

She smiled gloriously at James, and he smiled back. "Yes, and Miss MacNamara has been helping me think of a name for the animal on the way here.''

"I see." Lillian offered him a gracious smile. "Well, won't you and your dog come into the house and have a cup of tea, Mr. Drayton? I'm sure you can use a cup of tea to warm you before you walk home again. You don't have your fine motorcar with you today, and the weather is chilly.''

James, who had been warmed by Polly's company, hadn't given a thought to the weather. Mrs. MacNamara was correct, though. The autumn night air held a distinct snap. There would undoubtedly be frost on the ground tomorrow morning.

"Thank you, Mrs. MacNamara, I should like that, if you're certain I won't be a bother." Looking down at his hound, however, he had second thoughts. "Er, although, I'm not entirely sure what to do about this—''

"Rarely seen Philippine Tapir Hound," Polly supplied in all apparent innocence.

Her expressive eyes twinkled merrily and provoked another smile from him. "Exactly. I'm not sure what to do with my rarely seen Philippine Tapir Hound.''

"Why, that's no problem at all, Mr. Drayton. Your dog can take a nap in the hallway. Stephen's dog Bruno used to sleep on the braided rug there all the time.''

At the mention of Polly's missing brother, a fine mist of sadness seemed to settle on them for a moment. Polly dispelled it with a shake of her shoulders. "Oh, my, it really is chilly out, isn't it? Let's go inside where it's warm.''

Her feelings ran riot as she guided her mother's wheelchair

around and pushed her into the house. Ecstasy at being in James Drayton's company for a few moments longer warred violently with the certain knowledge that she shouldn't be taking such pleasure in it.

In spite of her turbulent emotions, Polly enjoyed the tea the three of them shared in front of the fireplace. The MacNamara parlor owed little to wealth, but it was a pleasant place for all that. Its air of coziness seemed especially potent this evening.

Oriental pieces from earlier, more prosperous times, nestled artistically on the mantel and inside a glass-fronted hutch. Polly had been able to refresh her arrangement of chrysanthemums, thanks to Mother Francis Mary's generosity. A wicker cornucopia preserved from her childhood and filled with wax apples, pumpkins, and squash added an autumn flair.

The fire warmed Polly's chilled bones. Her mother's alarm at the lateness of her arrival soon faded and a jolly mood prevailed, thanks in large part to James Drayton's polite manners and easy good humor, a circumstance Polly thought strange. None of the things she'd heard about him ever gave mention of his personable social graces. In fact, most of the whispers she'd heard spoke of a cold man, one who did not care for the company of his fellows. Constance and Juliana hinted he was, moreover, one who treated females in much too cavalier a manner.

As Polly watched James tease her mother out of her worries, she could detect nothing of the roué in his deportment. Rather, he appeared to strive to please. He pleased Mrs. MacNamara's daughter, for a fact.

Polly fingered her charms absently, wishing they could spend more time like this, just the three of them, getting to know each other in an easy, friendly atmosphere. His offices were so formal. So cold. So—so—

So much his life and not yours, Polly MacNamara, you foolish, foolish girl.

The grim reality of their lives stole Polly's smile for a good five minutes until James noticed its absence and teased it back again.

He remained with the MacNamara ladies through supper.

Polly's mother offered the invitation, much to Polly's initial dismay.

"Oh, surely Mr. Drayton doesn't care to dine with us, Mother. I'm certain he has much more important engagements this evening."

With a grin designed to beguile, James demurred. "Why, what could possibly be more important than dining with two lovely ladies, Miss MacNamara?"

Since Polly, in her innocence, could think of no light, bantering rejoinder, she blushed instead.

Her rosy flush stole James's breath. It would, he thought cynically, take a good deal more than one of his usual insipid evening engagements to wrench him away from her charming company tonight. He hoped Cynthia Ingram would forgive him. Then he decided he didn't much care one way or the other. Besides, Cynthia had dozens of gentlemen friends with whom to occupy herself.

"Well, do come into the dining room then, Mr. Drayton. Polly will set a place for you, and we can enjoy an informal supper together. I'm sure you're a hungry man. You must be just about my Stephen's age, and he's forever hungry."

"And how old is your son, Mrs. MacNamara?"

With a sigh, Lillian said, "He will be thirty the end of January, Mr. Drayton."

"Ah, then I have him beat by two months. I'll be thirty on the twenty-eighth of this very month."

He appropriated the handles of Lillian's wheelchair before Polly could do so. He did it so deftly and with such an engaging smile that Polly felt momentarily bereft, although the impression was so fleeting it did not leave so much as an aftertaste. She did, however, finger her charms for a split-second before she dashed to the pantry to fetch more silverware and china.

Supper was a much more lighthearted affair than Polly thought it might be. James Drayton proved to be a charming, articulate dining companion. He was so adept at dealing with Lillian MacNamara that Polly had to stifle a stare of amazement when she realized he'd managed to get her mother to talk about the accident that had claimed her father's life.

"It was six years ago, Mr. Drayton. We'd been to China, where Frank had contracted for a large quantity of beautiful silks. There were porcelains and jade-ware in the order, too, and we were bringing everything back home to San Francisco. He was quite successful in his importing business."

"Did you travel with him often, Mrs. MacNamara?"

"Too often, I'm afraid," Lillian said, glancing ruefully at Polly. "We often left the children with my sister Grace for months at a time. I'm afraid they felt like orphans sometimes."

"Of course we didn't, Mother."

Polly squeezed her mother's hand and hoped the lie wouldn't count against her in the Book of Records kept by God's agents. She felt James's gaze on her. When she lifted her eyes and met his, she knew he knew she'd been fibbing. Her face felt hot when she returned her attention to her meal.

"At any rate, we were on our way home, and the ship had just arrived at the mouth of the harbor when the boiler blew up. Frank was felled by the blast."

When Lillian paused in her narrative James said gently, "I didn't mean to cause you any distress, Mrs. MacNamara. I guess we attorneys are just naturally nosy people."

"Oh, I don't mind really, Mr. Drayton. Maybe it's good to talk about it."

"I've often heard it said a burden shared is a burden halved, Mrs. MacNamara."

Polly, who had tried for years to get her mother to unburden herself, wished with all her might that Lillian would do so now. Even though she didn't understand why James Drayton seemed able to draw the information forth when she couldn't, she hoped, for her mother's sake, that he would continue to do so.

"I've heard that, too, Mr. Drayton." Lillian drew in an audible breath and continued.

"I could see Frank lying a few feet away from me, and I tried to reach him. My legs were pinned under a pile of shattered wood, though, and I was unable to move. It was awful. I don't know if I could have helped him if I'd been able to reach him—but I couldn't."

With a trembling hand, Lillian lifted her napkin to her eye. "Oh, I'm sorry. I'm being silly."

"No you're not, Mother."

James had never heard anything like Polly's voice. It fairly trembled with love. He watched her put a comforting arm around her mother's shoulders. Never having experienced comfort from another human being, James discovered himself envious. How very strange.

When Polly's gaze lifted to capture his, her eyes were luminous, glowing with candlelight and love. He felt a catch in his chest.

"My parents were very close, Mr. Drayton. I've never seen a couple who—who belonged with each other as my parents did."

She returned her care to her mother, and James was left to contemplate the two ladies. They were both lovely. It was easy for him to see from whom Polly had inherited her grace and elegance. He wondered if his own parents had ever been as close as Frank and Lillian MacNamara. Somehow he couldn't imagine it.

"Oh, Polly," Lillian murmured, "I'm sure that one day you too will find a man to love as deeply as I loved your father."

"Perhaps you're right, Mother."

James could tell Polly didn't believe her mother. And she also seemed uneasy with the topic of love and marriage, so he decided to turn it.

He waited until Polly felt comfortable returning to her knife and fork. Deeming Lillian able to handle a little more gentle probing, he asked, "What was the name of the vessel, Mrs. MacNamara?"

The smile she gave him almost broke his heart, it was so brave. He'd never considered courage among the lives of ordinary folks, yet it lived here, in this room. His father would never understand the fortitude these two women exercised every day of their lives.

"It was a ship called *Golden Liberty*, Mr. Drayton. I liked the name. I recall telling Frank that our voyage was sure to be lucky." *Lucky* broke on a small sob she obviously tried to control.

"Oh, Mother, if it's too hard for you to talk about it, please don't."

Although he regretted its necessity, James was grateful for Polly's consoling admonition. He hoped he'd been able to disguise the sudden surge of horror Lillian's words evoked in him.

Golden Liberty. Damnation. No wonder Polly's brief recitation of her father's unlucky demise had stirred a memory. The *Golden Liberty* disaster was among several last straws that eventually culminated in the final, acrimonious breach between James and his father. The ship had been one of the Pacific-Orient's China Express line. Until the *Golden Liberty* catastrophe, James had tried to preserve a semblance of familial affinity. Afterwards, he'd felt no such compunction.

An investigation after the calamity—which claimed ten lives beside that of Frank MacNamara, if James's memory served—was hushed up, thanks to liberal doses of J. P. Drayton's golden panacea. His father had spread money around like butter, James remembered bitterly, and very few people ever learned the investigation's results.

But James had learned them. He knew that the inquiry had revealed a drunken ship's captain and a bet between him and the captain of another vessel, *Pacific Winds.* The details escaped James's recollection at the moment, but he knew they were sordid. James considered them only one more manifestation of his father's guiding principle: succeed at any cost.

It was a principle etched on a gilt plaque in J. P.'s office, but J. P. had been singularly unsuccessful in teaching his son to live by it. James told his father it was because he, James, possessed a conscience. His father told James it was because he, James, was a fool.

The argument was one neither of them would ever win or lose, because ultimately James had given up the fight and moved on. Now, as he watched Polly try to give her mother solace, his brain whirled with ugly thoughts and memories.

When he believed he could speak without spitting in anger, he cleared his throat and asked softly, "Was your husband's shipment not insured, Mrs. MacNamara?"

Lillian took a deep breath and seemed to draw her inner

resources together. "I tried to determine that very thing, Mr. Drayton, but I'm afraid my health was not good for some time after the accident. Polly was only fifteen years old and had to spend all her time caring for me. Stephen was out of the country, so there was no one to see to things. Frank's man of business was, I'm afraid, not of much help."

"I'm sorry to hear that."

"Believe me, I was sorry to hear it, too," Lillian said with an admirable attempt at wry humor.

"I still think that man didn't tell you everything, Mother," Polly said. It was the first time James had heard her sound bitter.

Lillian sighed heavily. "I know you do, dear. Perhaps you're right. But I'm afraid I wasn't up to fighting with him any longer, and now it seems too late."

"What's his name?"

"William Boedecker, Mr. Drayton."

"Boedecker? Why, he's—"

James stopped before he could reveal that Boedecker's was one of the names bandied about during the investigation into *Golden Liberty*'s tragic fate. According to some sources, Boedecker had been backing the *Liberty*'s captain in his race with the captain of *Pacific Winds*. James knew for a fact that Boedecker had profited handily from J. P. Drayton's largesse.

"He's what, Mr. Drayton?"

Polly's lovely, inquisitive gaze almost made James blurt out his suspicions, but his knowledge was too sketchy. He resolutely determined to say nothing on the matter until—unless— whatever he said could be helpful. The MacNamara ladies didn't need any more loose ends in their lives.

"His is a name well-known in the shipping business, I believe."

The unsuspecting Polly nodded, seeming to be satisfied with his half-answer.

After a little more subtle, gentle probing, James decided that he'd learned enough and allowed the conversation to veer into cheerier channels. His heart ached, though.

When he left the MacNamara residence and set out for home, his as-yet-unnamed hound lumbering along at his side, he could think of little other than the distressing facts of Polly MacNamara's life.

First her father, and now her brother. James knew good and well that life wasn't fair, but this seemed too much for one person to be obliged to bear. His firm stride ate up the distance between Pacific Avenue and Russian Hill, where he lived on a grand estate much at variance with the modest home Polly MacNamara shared with her mother.

She deserved better, James thought angrily. Polly Mac-Namara wasn't a woman who should waste her life away typing for a law firm. She should marry a man who would love her and provide her with a gracious home. Heaven knew she possessed the flair for it; James could tell. And children. She deserved children.

All women loved children. It was something in their nature, or so James had been told. He was sure his own mother had wanted him and would have loved him. His Chinese nanny had told him so.

There was something about Polly MacNamara, though, that made James certain she'd make a better mother than most. Maybe it was her sweetness. Or maybe it was the sense of humor she allowed out every now and then.

She'd make a good wife, too. How James decided that, he didn't inform the indifferent air or his dog, but he was sure of it.

By the time he'd marched home, he had determined on a course of action. He'd never even dream of taking such action for any cause of his own. But Polly MacNamara's was an entirely different matter. Her cause called for desperate measures, and James was not about to shrink from them, however distasteful they were certain to be.

Yesterday he'd been shocked when his father showed up in his office. He wondered how his father was going to feel when James visited him on the morrow.

Polly sat on her bed fingering her medals for a long time before she crawled under her quilt. Her attention was not on St. Christopher, however, but upon the strange indentations on the ancient coin she smoothed between her fingers.

It did feel warm, she decided, glad to have cleared up any confusion about the matter. She stared at the coin for several more minutes before she shook her head hard. No. It was too fantastic. It couldn't be. Such things simply didn't happen. Why, they were approaching the twentieth century, for heaven's sake. They were entering an age governed by machines and motors, industry and science.

Polly knew it was her imagination which made her feel as though the old, worn coin pulsed a response.

"No," she whispered aloud. If ever there had been magic on this earth, it was long gone now.

Lying back on her bed, Polly pressed her coin and stared at the ceiling. A soft smile crept over her as her thoughts tiptoed backwards through the evening.

"He seemed so kind," she whispered to the ceiling, which was used to such musings from her. He'd been awfully polite. And he was so very, very handsome.

Although the ceiling remained mute, Polly could feel her heart hammer against the coin beneath her fingers. She could understand how he'd earned his reputation. She guessed women in his social circle probably threw themselves at him all the time.

A momentary pang that she was not of his circle smote Polly, but she resolutely thrust it aside. She didn't want dismal reality to slay her fanciful reverie so soon. She had to deal with reality every day. One evening of wistfulness surely couldn't hurt.

Everybody deserved to dream.

Her smile broadened and she said aloud, "All right, coin. If you're magic, send Stephen home to us. For Thanksgiving." In spite of her whimsy, a tear slipped from her eye.

Polly wiped it away and said, still smiling, "And send Mother a goosedown quilt. She's always wanted a real goosedown quilt. They're so soft and warm. A goosedown quilt would keep her legs toasty this winter. She suffers so badly with the cold."

Of course, if the coin were really magic, Polly might as

well ask for her father back. Or for James Drayton to fall in love with her. Her smile went awry.

The truth was that Polly MacNamara, who might every now and again take a turn at the fanciful, knew better than to believe in magic.

Chapter Seven

Friday morning found James in a pose consciously borrowed from his parent, with his hands splayed flat on the glossy black finish of J. P. Drayton's gigantic ebony desk. He leaned over the desk and stared into his father's eyes. J. P. glowered back at him ferociously. Used to such displays from the man who sired him, James remained undaunted by J. P.'s tempestuous expression.

"Well? What do you intend to do about it?"

J. P.'s jowls quivered with fury and his bristly brows almost met over his tyrannical nose. His green eyes glittered dangerously. "Damn it, James. When Biddle let you in this morning, I thought it was because you'd come to your senses. I thought you'd come because you planned to accept my offer."

James, his own expression an almost-perfect imitation of his father's—he'd practiced long and hard in his youth—snapped, "I came to my senses years ago, Father. I'd work for the devil himself before I'd work for you. What I'm here for is to see justice done."

"Damn it, boy, there is no justice in this world. There are only people. There are people who succeed and people who fail. I succeed, and I don't care if you approve or not.''

James stood up straight and lifted the engraved gilt plaque gracing J. P.'s desk. He deliberately marred its shiny surface with his fingerprints.

''Yes, I know how you pride yourself on succeeding.'' He put the now-soiled plaque back on the desk in a manner designed to leave no doubt in his parent's mind what he thought of J. P.'s guiding principle.

J. P.'s scowl deepened. ''And I'm not accountable for every improvident female whose husband manages to get himself killed, either.'' He grabbed the plaque and polished it vigorously with a monogrammed linen handkerchief snatched from his breast pocket.

James, who seldom harbored savage thoughts about his fellow human beings, had to consciously control the urge to belt his father in the jaw. In a voice straining with repressed violence, he said, ''You're responsible for these two, Father. Franklin MacNamara didn't 'get himself killed,' as you phrase it; he was killed at somebody else's hand, a hand that ultimately points directly to you. And, by the way, there's not an improvident bone in either of those ladies' bodies.''

To keep from doing J. P. physical harm, James flung himself away from the desk and tramped across the expensive Oriental carpet to stand, glowering, in front of the gleaming black door. He'd always thought it interesting that his father favored bold black and gold in his office decor. There was something so cold and uncompromising about the combination of colors.

''For God's sake, now that her brother's disappeared, Polly MacNamara supports the two of them typing—*typing*—for a living.'' He whirled toward J. P. again.

''By all that's holy, you *are* responsible! They were used to living in comfort until your captain, Horace Witherspoon, a man well known for his excesses, got drunk and decided to make himself a little extra money at their expense.''

''Horace Witherspoon was suitably disciplined.'' J. P. did not look at James when he spoke, but stared out his office window at the bustling wharf just beyond the sparkling glass.

Emma Craig

"Disciplined? You call sending him to work the West Indies route *discipline?*"

"It was a tremendous step down, James, and you know it." J. P. fiddled with his elaborate inkstand. "We made him sign the pledge."

Apparently even J. P. Drayton was unable to recite the disciplinary measures meted out to the man responsible for eleven deaths and maintain his aplomb. He cleared his throat and, for the first time in James's immediate memory, looked slightly abashed.

"He took the pledge." James repeated his father's words, giving them the emphasis he believed they deserved. The way he said them made Witherspoon's discipline sound as pathetically absurd as, in fact, it was.

J. P. seemed to regain his equanimity. "What about the ship's insurance? Why didn't your precious females take advantage of the insurance?"

"You tell me, Father. I wondered the same thing." James crossed his arms across his chest and glared back at J. P.

"Anyone who applied was given a fair portion. You know that, boy."

"What about people who didn't apply, Father? What about Mrs. Franklin MacNamara, whose husband was dead, who was herself in the hospital, whose son was out of the country, whose daughter was fifteen years old, and whose man of business was one of Witherspoon's chief backers? What about her? I'm sure she never even heard about any insurance. Boedecker made a bundle, thanks to you, but Lillian MacNamara sure as the devil didn't."

In two strides, he covered the office carpet and slammed his hands back down on his father's desk. *"What about her, damn it?"*

"You can't mean it, James." Lawrence Bullock sat in one of James Drayton's overstuffed office chairs and stared at James, an expression of utter disbelief on his broad, bruised face.

James, whose mood was still barbarous as a result of his earlier encounter with his father, frowned. There was not a hint of pity in his heart, and he suspected his mood showed on his face, because Bullock looked worried for the first time in James's memory. Generally, Bullock's demeanor was one of hearty good fellowship.

"Yesterday was the last straw, Lawrence. God knows you've been given plenty of chances. I won't have employees of my law firm assaulted on public streets by other employees."

With an air that strove for perfect innocence and achieved only artfully manufactured righteousness, Bullock cried, "Assaulting? Why, I had no such intention, James. I only meant to see her home."

James eyed his junior associate with distaste. Bullock's right eye was blue and nearly swollen shut this morning. His scraped chin and brow each bore a piece of white sticking plaster, and bruises decorated both cheeks. He looked more like he'd been in a barroom brawl than tumbled over a crack in the sidewalk.

"I watched you, Lawrence. I saw exactly what you did. I saw Miss MacNamara beg you to leave her alone and, when that didn't work, I saw her try to shake you off."

He leaned forward in his chair, the injustice of Polly's situation vivid in his mind. "Damn it, I could practically hear her struggling with herself. 'Should I tell him to go to hell? If I do, I may lose my situation, and then my mother and I will starve.' I could almost hear that, Lawrence."

For the second time in as many hours, James wanted to punch another human being. "Damn it, you callous bastard, you'd have done it, too, wouldn't you? You'd have made that poor girl a victim of your bestial appetites because you know she needs her job."

"Oh, come now, James—"

Bullock got no further because James slammed down his open palm, hard, on his desk, and made him jump.

"Be quiet, Lawrence. I've put up with a good deal from you, but this is it. No more. You're done with this firm. I'll give you a reference, although it goes against the grain."

James could read the impotent fury on Bullock's once-handsome face. He wasn't surprised when Bullock protested.

"I'm a good attorney, damn it, James. What do you mean, 'it goes against the grain'?"

"Just what I said, you pompous jackass. You may have the ability to be a good attorney, but you're a shirker and an idler and fancy yourself a damned ladies' man. You haven't ever pulled your weight at the firm, and I'm not giving you any more warnings. This is it."

Apparently deciding further discussion would be fruitless, Bullock adopted a beseeching expression. "You'd turn me out before the holidays, James? Before Christmas?"

With a grimace prompted by his associate's sniveling, James snapped, "I'm turning you out today, Lawrence. Pack your things and be out of here by noon."

"But—"

James's upheld hand stopped Bullock's whine.

"I'll pay you through the end of the year and give you a reference, but I want you gone today."

"But—"

"No!" James rose and leaned over his desk. He wanted to leap across it and beat Lawrence Bullock to a quivering jelly.

"Damn it, Lawrence, don't say another word. I've had it up to my eyebrows with your sniveling and whining. You're a disgrace to the legal profession. And to me. I thought to help you once, but you don't deserve it. Get out."

Although Bullock opened his mouth, a good look at James made him shut it again. He rose stiffly.

"Very well. I hope you don't regret this, James."

James pushed himself back from his desk and gave Bullock a black frown. "My only regret is for Miss MacNamara."

With a petulant look, Bullock said, "I knew you were sweet on her. That's what this is all about, really, isn't it? You're sweet on her, and she was flirting with me."

James's hands fisted involuntarily. Through gritted teeth, he said, "You'd better get out now, Lawrence. Before I have second thoughts."

A pouty harumph preceded Lawrence's exit. "She's nothing but a sassy little tart," he said as he yanked open the door. The door slammed behind his arrogant rear end a scant second before James's heavy glass paperweight smashed into it at the level where his head had been.

Both Bullock and Mr. Gregory jumped at the sound. Gregory, who had obviously been listening at the keyhole, had not quite made it back to his desk when Bullock emerged from James's office. Bullock eyed James's secretary malevolently.

"Fetch some cartons and the carriers, Gregory."

"Yes, sir."

Polly was pecking away industriously on her Underwood Visible Writing Machine when Mr. Gregory's imperious form graced the typewriting room of Drayton and Associates. She didn't notice him until his body cast a looming shadow over the paper in her machine. Its sudden presence startled her into a rare typographical error and she frowned, irked.

She was glad for her temper when, lifting her head, she discovered the interloper to be James Drayton's stuffy secretary. Her posture stiffened and she offered Gregory her coldest glare.

"Miss MacNamara," Gregory intoned.

"Yes, Mr. Gregory. What do *you* want?" Polly said right back, her regal timbre a perfect imitation of his own.

"Mr. Drayton wishes to see you."

All at once Polly's haughtiness deserted her. Her hand lifted to her medals as she sought courage. "He wants to see *me?*"

Impatiently, Gregory snapped, "Yes. Now come along." He turned and headed toward the door.

Polly peered at the error glaring back at her from the legal brief she'd been typing, then glanced at Gregory's back. A quick peek at her co-workers revealed them all staring at her, eyes wide.

Juliana was the first to recover. "Getting a little above ourselves, don't you think, girls?" She shot a spiteful smile at her fellows.

"Mr. Drayton," Constance murmured. "My, my."

Desperately trying to make her world regain its lost balance, Polly said, "I can't imagine what this is about."

"No?" Rose gave her a wink. "Well, I guess my imagination is just better than yours, then, Polly.'' She shared a giggle with Juliana. Even Constance smiled.

Mortified and angry, Polly decided she'd correct her type-writing error later. ''Oh, for heaven's sake, stop it! I have absolutely no idea what you're talking about, Rose.''

With as much poise as she could summon, she strode out of the typewriting room and followed Walter Gregory, who did not bother to look to see whether she'd obeyed his summons.

Polly felt her indignation bubble and steam as she followed the self-important secretary, although her anger only made it as far as Gregory. It never quite reached James Drayton. Still, this was the second time her employer had singled her out from among her fellow typists. She knew Constance, Rose, and Juliana must think the worst.

Yet try as she might—and she tried heartily—she couldn't quite find it in her heart to be angry with James. He'd been so sweet yesterday about Lawrence Bullock. And then, when he'd kissed her cheek . . . She decided she'd better stop thinking.

Gregory opened the door to James's office for her and gave her an almost imperceptible bow. Polly suspected his courtesy was no courtesy at all, but rather stemmed from his not wishing his employer to know what an unpleasant man he truly was.

''Miss MacNamara, sir,'' Gregory announced in his most lordly voice.

With a hot glare she hoped roasted Gregory's ridiculously sparse mustache, Polly walked into James Drayton's lush office. The door shut behind her with a louder click than it should have, and Polly felt a swell of satisfaction, knowing she'd managed to annoy Gregory. Then she looked at James Drayton.

He had stood at her entrance and now he smiled at her. His smile ate away at any of Polly's remaining irritation over his summons. It lit his face, softening his sometimes arrogant countenance, and warming his gaze until it heated Polly through and through.

Merciful heavens.

In an effort to hide her reaction, Polly tried on a cool, polite smile. "Good morning, Mr. Drayton."

"Good morning, Miss MacNamara." James's voice, infinitely warmer than Polly's, held only pleasure at seeing her again. "Please, take a seat." He gestured to one of the chairs.

"Thank you."

Polly, clad as usual in a dark gored skirt and pleated white shirtwaist, smoothed her skirt and sat. She settled her folded hands on her lap and consciously made herself not knead them together with anxiety.

Now that she was here, basking in the warm glow of James's smile, all the things she'd ever heard about him reared up in her mind to unsettle her. Was that smile false? Had he assumed it to put her off her guard? His expression hinted of benevolence, but she'd never once heard James Drayton spoken of as benevolent.

Surely he hadn't called her in here to dismiss her, had he? Had he reconsidered the incident on the sidewalk? Had Lawrence Bullock been vilifying her behind her back? Oh, Lord. Who would James believe? A mere typist or a fellow attorney? She jumped when James spoke.

"Miss MacNamara, I felt it imperative to see you this morning to apologize for the behavior of Lawrence Bullock."

Polly's gaze had been firmly affixed on the elegant paperweight on James's desk. She'd just started wondering how it had become chipped when James's statement brought her gaze abruptly to his face.

"Apologize? Oh, my goodness. There's no need for that, sir, really. Why, you sent him on his way and saw me home and . . ." She stuttered to a halt, unable to continue, and felt very self-conscious.

"Nonsense. The conduct of my employees is my responsibility, Miss MacNamara. I am fully aware of all of Lawrence Bullock's shortcomings, and I should have dealt with him before now."

He paused for breath and Polly felt at sea. "D-dealt with him, sir?"

"Yes. I should have done something about him before this

time. He's never been an asset to the firm, and you may be sure he will not bother you again.''

Completely unnerved, Polly stared at James for several moments. Shock and burgeoning understanding jumbled in her breast. She didn't dare believe what she thought James's words meant. At last, feeling she should say something, she stammered, "I don't think I understand, Mr. Drayton."

James gave her the warmest smile she could recall ever having received from a gentleman. The heat from his smile made her blood bubble and her heart march a quickstep against her ribs.

"I'm sorry I'm not making myself clear, Miss MacNamara. What I'm trying to say is that, as of today, Lawrence Bullock is no longer an associate of James Drayton and Associates, Attorneys at Law. He should pose no further menace to you or to any other young lady employed at this firm."

Polly's eyes opened wide. "You mean you *fired* him?" She pressed her coin, elation and disbelief nearly lifting her out of her chair.

"Don't worry about Bullock, Miss MacNamara," James advised dryly. "I expect he'll land on his feet. His kind always do."

Polly frowned. "I'm sorry to hear that," she said before she thought about it. Then she felt her face flame.

James burst out laughing. After a moment, during which she wished the floor would open to swallow her up, Polly smiled a little bit, too.

"I didn't really mean that." An honest girl, she added, "At least, I did mean it, but I shouldn't have said so." Then she wished she'd had sense enough to keep her mouth shut and dropped her gaze to the floor. A fairly large hole gaped from James's beautiful carpet right at her feet. How odd. She hadn't noticed it before. She felt the color drain from her cheeks as an incredible thought struck her.

With a sigh, James said, "Well, I gave him a tolerable reference, Miss MacNamara. Which, I might add, is more than I wanted to do. Unfortunately, one must play ball according to the rules if one wishes to survive in the business world. And, while I deplore the despicable way in which Bullock acted toward you, I recognize the necessity of preserving a show of unity with a brother attorney. I expect he will pass it about that he wanted to make a change, that Drayton and Associates turned out not to be his cup of tea.''

"Oh." Fingering her medals, Polly kept staring at that hole, wondering.

James had been leaning back negligently in his chair, but he sat forward now, drawing Polly's attention away from his carpet. His expression was intense.

"Miss MacNamara, I realize that my reputation is not the most savory to be found in San Francisco but, believe me, what Bullock tried to do to you passes the bounds of tolerable behavior. It was insupportable. I won't have it, and I want you to know that.''

James frowned at his desk and fingered his chipped paperweight. "And when I think of what he might have been able to force you to do. And all because of his status with the firm. Well, it's intolerable.''

The thought of what Lawrence might have been able to force her to do brought the color back to Polly's cheeks. Nevertheless she managed to say, "Thank you, Mr. Drayton.'' Until two days before, she'd never guessed she'd find kindness in her employer.

James looked up from his paperweight and smiled at her. "Believe me, Miss MacNamara, you're entirely welcome. Besides,'' he added, his grin broadening, "I owe you a great debt for endowing my disreputable hound with a pedigree. Getting rid of Bullock was the least I could do.''

Mentioning the episode with the dog introduced an element of lightness to the conversation, and Polly forgot all about the hole in the carpet. She returned James's grin with a broad smile. "How is your dog doing, Mr. Drayton?''

"My rarely seen Philippine Tapir Hound is doing quite well, thank you, Miss MacNamara.''

"I'm glad.''

"Yes.''

"Have you decided on a name yet, sir?''

"Not yet.''

Polly nodded sagely. "You'll think of something. My

brother Stephen always said that when you're around an animal long enough, his name will come to you.''

James cocked his head and grinned at her brother's wise words. "Did he?"

"Oh, yes. And Stephen was—is very good with animals."

Still fiddling with the paperweight, James studied Polly's face for a moment, his smile fading. His perusal lasted just long enough for Polly to become nervous again.

She began to rise. "Well, Mr. Drayton, thank you very much for your consideration." She wanted to get back to the typewriting room before the girls' speculation got out of hand.

"Wait."

His voice startled her, and Polly stopped halfway to her feet and looked at him. When she noted his unwavering expression, she slowly seated herself again.

Sensing her alarm, James said, "I mean, please, Miss MacNamara, don't run away yet. There's something else I need to discuss with you."

Mystified, Polly sat back in the chair and refolded her hands in her lap. "Certainly, Mr. Drayton. What is it?"

"It's about your father."

"My father?"

"Yes. I have been—making inquiries into the accident with *Golden Liberty*."

Polly's heart suddenly took to thudding painfully. "Thank you," she murmured, afraid to look at him for fear her emotions would get the better of her and she'd start to cry. Never in a million years had she expected this man to take an interest in her family's tragedy.

"Don't thank me yet, please, because so far I've not managed to do much. I'm still making inquiries."

Looking up, Polly found James rubbing his finger across the nick in his paperweight. He looked almost angry, and Polly didn't know how to account for it.

Before she could disgrace herself by bawling, she said, "Mr. Drayton, my mother and I will be forever grateful to you for anything you've done. Please don't think you need do more. I'm not sure what happened after the accident because I was quite young and not at all conversant with the ways of the business world, but—but I certainly do thank you for look-ing into the matter.''

When he lifted his head and eyed her again, his gaze seemed harder than she'd seen it in several days. He looked like the James Drayton she'd observed from afar before he'd offered her a ride home in his lovely new motorcar. Unconsciously she lifted her fingers to her charms again and wished his eyes would soften once more. He looked very nearly approachable when he wasn't sporting that hard look.

His grin came out of nowhere, so sudden and beautiful that Polly's lips parted in wonder. ''Nonsense. I'm going to do more than merely look into the matter, Miss MacNamara. I plan to get to the bottom of it, and make sure you and your mother get everything due you.''

His smile could have melted a polar ice cap. ''I know justice has not been done, and I plan to see that it is.''

Where she found the wit to thank him, Polly didn't know. Oh, my, he was *so* handsome. More than that. Polly suddenly had the absurd notion that if a man were to be crafted specif-ically for her by one of God's minions, that man would be James Drayton.

James continued to smile at her for a moment or two, and she continued to bask in the glory of his stunning maleness. She'd never been so conscious of a man's presence before. James Drayton's quite took her breath away.

At last James said, ''Well, I suppose we both need to get back to work.''

''Oh, of course!'' Polly rose out of the chair as if she'd been goosed, mortified to have been staring at her handsome employer. ''Why, I left an error glaring from the page and must get back and erase it before the ink sets too deeply.''

Feeling like an absolute imbecile for having uttered such an inane thing, Polly almost ran to the office door. All that stopped her from flinging the door open and bolting through it was James's amused voice.

''Miss MacNamara, please wait a moment.''

She whirled around and faced him. To keep her hands from wringing each other to death in front of her, she consciously dropped them to her sides and strove for dignity. ''Yes?'' She was pleased when her voice betrayed none of her disquiet.

She was sure his easy grin was proof that he considered her a lunatic. But then he asked, "Aren't you interested in who will be taking Lawrence Bullock's place with the law firm, Miss MacNamara?" and she wasn't so sure.

After a moment and a gulp she was sure James could hear from his desk, Polly said, "Why, certainly."

"I'd like your opinion on the matter, actually. Will your error last for another minute or two?"

He spoke softly and with no irony, but Polly wasn't sure of anything anymore. With a coolness she did not feel, she said, "Of course," and went back to sit again. Although she assumed an air of polite concern, she did not relax.

"What do you think of Drayton and Associates hiring a Chinese attorney, Miss MacNamara?"

"A—a Chinese lawyer?" Polly, who'd never had occasion to think one thing or another about Chinese lawyers before, was at a loss.

"Yes. You seem to be such a sensible person, I'd like your opinion. Do you think San Francisco would spurn Drayton and Associates if we were to take a Chinese associate into the firm?"

James's question was a serious one. Polly recognized the fact, and was gratified that he'd asked for her judgment. Because he seemed to expect a thoughtful, honest opinion, she did not respond immediately but considered the impact of such a move by his law firm before answering. When she did answer, she chose her words carefully.

"Well, I expect there might be some people in town who will look askance at the addition of a Chinese attorney to the firm of Drayton and Associates. I believe, however, that there will be even more people who will applaud such an addition as a shrewd business move on your part."

James's mossy green eyes opened wider. "Do you really?"

Polly'd never before been asked to give an opinion on such a weighty matter, and trepidation skittered up her spine on prickly feet. But she had given him her considered recommendation. She was committed now and would not back down from her reasoned conclusion. Besides, whatever the world thought, her opinions were as valid as anybody else's. She sat up straighter and nodded firmly.

"Yes. I do, because there is such a large community of Chinese living in San Francisco. And, although they are not allowed to own property, they manage a good deal of it. We also do a vast amount of trade with China, and one needs Chinese translators and agents in order to conduct business properly."

"I presume your father did business in such a manner."

"Oh, yes. Yes, he did. Why, Mr. Chang even dined at our home several times."

Deciding her statement had been intolerably priggish, Polly hurried to say, "I mean, he was almost like a member of the family. I looked on him as an uncle. When one gets to know and like another person, one forgets the color of his skin." She looked James straight in the eye, wondering if she'd shocked him by voicing her candid view. "At least, that's what I think," she added, almost defiantly.

He smiled at her for so long, Polly almost lost her nerve and dropped her glance. Only the strength of will she'd acquired over the last several brutally hard years kept her gaze steady.

At last James said, "I am very happy to hear you say so, Miss MacNamara."

Astonished, she said, "You are?"

"I am. And I hope you're right. The gentleman who will be joining our firm is the same one you met the other night. Raymond Sing."

"Oh! Why, I had no idea he is an attorney, Mr. Drayton. He looked to be no older than I am!"

A crooked grin accompanied James's. "And just how old might that be, Miss MacNamara, if I may be so bold as to inquire."

Polly said, "Twenty-one," before she could think about it and felt like a fool again.

"So young," James murmured.

Polly clamped her lips together and decided she'd humiliated herself enough for one day.

"Actually, Raymond is older than you are, Miss Mac-

Emma Craig

Namara. He is a graduate of a prestigious law school, who granted him a scholarship on the weight of his brilliant academic achievements in school. He is a member of the California Bar Association and a dear friend of mine.''

''Oh.'' Polly began to relax again. ''You know, I thought you were friends. You seemed so comfortable with each other the other day when I barged in on you.''

James gave her another brilliant smile. ''And I'm very happy to hear your sentiments on the matter, because they correspond absolutely with my own.''

With another ''oh,'' Polly felt a wash of relief.

''And now, I suppose you have an error waiting.''

James rose from his chair and stepped over to Polly. He extended a hand to help her rise and she took it without hesitation. Neither one of them wore gloves, and his hand felt very big and warm and masculine gripping hers. There was something truly thrilling about feeling his flesh press against hers. Polly wished her cheeks would lose the intense color she knew they sported.

''I certainly hope we will have an opportunity to chat again soon, Miss MacNamara. I find your company refreshing.'' James opened his office door.

''Thank you, Mr. Drayton.''

It took every ounce of Polly's composure to walk in a stately manner past Mr. Gregory. She wanted to pick up her skirts and run like a jackrabbit away from James Drayton and the tremendous pull she felt toward him. But walk in a stately manner she did. She even gave Gregory a frosty glare as she passed his desk. He glared back, and Polly smiled, feeling superior. She'd bet James Drayton never asked Gregory *his* opinions about hiring Chinese attorneys.

When she got back to the typewriting room, her error awaited her. So did Constance, Rose, and Juliana, and they were in a catty mood. Polly put them in their place with a few well-chosen words and went back to work.

The other girls didn't like her. Polly knew it, but she didn't know what to do about it. Her life was just so *different* from theirs. She didn't have time for all the frivolities they shared. That was all.

114

As for James, he shut his office door and meandered back to his desk, all the fury of his day's earlier encounters forgotten. He sat down and fingered his broken paperweight once more. Then he stared at his office door, a moony smile on his face, for a good ten minutes before he made himself get up, don his overcoat and gloves, and go out to pay a call on Raymond Sing.

The Wednesday before Thanksgiving, Polly read the eleventh chapter of *The Adventures of Huckleberry Finn* to the older children at the Sisters of Benevolence and *Doll Rosie's Days* to the younger ones. Just as she prepared to leave, she was caught up short by a friendly voice.

"Miss MacNamara!"

She turned and was surprised to see Raymond Sing, brand-new associate at Drayton and Associates.

"Why, Mr. Sing, what a pleasure to find you here. Don't tell me you support the Sisters of Benevolence, too?"

"Well, all right, if you insist, Miss MacNamara. But it will be a lie, because I do."

Raymond gave her a conspiratorial smile and Polly laughed. "That is a pretty silly expression, isn't it, Mr. Sing? I understand there are no such ambiguities in the Chinese language."

"Oh, there are ambiguities aplenty in Chinese, ma'am, but we manage."

"I'm quite fond of this organization myself," Polly told him, looking around at the walls of the orphanage.

Old and built from California stone, those walls might have been grim except that Mother Francis Mary had allowed the children to paint murals on them. Now they wore gay pictures of flowers and animals. There were even some scenes inspired, Polly knew, by the fairy tales and nursery rhymes she read.

"I've been reading to the children once a week for a couple of years now. I love doing it. I wish I could come more often."

"Is that so?"

"Yes. I'm quite fond of children, and these children, in particular, need love and attention. Don't you think so?"

"I certainly do."

For just a moment, it looked to Polly as though Raymond

wanted to say something more, but Mother Francis Mary joined them and he didn't.

"Good evening again, Polly. Are you acquainted with Mr. Sing?" The Mother Superior's eyes were more twinkly than usual this evening, Polly thought, and she wondered why.

"Indeed, we have been introduced, Mother. Mr. Sing has just joined the law firm where I'm employed."

"Is that so? My, my, it's a small world."

Mother Francis Mary hooked an arm through Polly's and Raymond's elbows and walked between them toward the gates of the orphanage. They both had to look down at her when she spoke to them.

"We're having our annual charity ball on Christmas Eve, Polly, and you're invited again, you know."

Polly smiled. "Thank you very much, Mother Francis Mary. I can't imagine attending such a grand function, though."

"Why not, Miss MacNamara?" Raymond asked, over the nun's black wimple. "I'm nobody, and I'm going. I think it might be fun to mingle with the few kind hearts in our fair city."

With a little laugh, Polly said, "Oh, no. I've never been to a function of that nature. I wouldn't know what to do."

"Well, I wish you'd go," Raymond said seriously. "Then at least I'd know two people there."

"Two people?"

Polly peered at him and was curious to notice he seemed uncomfortable, as though he'd said too much.

"Er, yes. Another gentleman of my acquaintance plans to attend the ball."

Mother Francis Mary's creaky laugh drew Polly's attention. To the best of her recollection, she'd never heard the nun laugh before.

"Oh, my," the Mother Superior said, catching her breath. "I think you should both attend. Why, you even have a proper gown to wear, my dear, don't you?" She winked at Polly. "You told me all about it. Remember?"

Dumbfounded to be winked at by a nun, Polly murmured, "I—I—why, I guess I did."

116

Mother Francis Mary left Polly and Raymond at the gate. She chuckled all the way down the corridor, and the two of them stared after her until she was out of sight.

Finally Polly shook herself. "Well, I'd best be getting along, Mr. Sing. Billy Peabody drives me home on Wednesday evenings, and he doesn't like to be kept waiting."

Raymond laughed. "Ah, yes. Good old Billy. I suppose you're right. I understand he gets quite cranky when things don't happen right on schedule."

It was Polly's turn to laugh. "Your understanding is absolutely correct, Mr. Sing." She ran to Billy's wagon. He sat hunched over his reins, his cap pulled down on his forehead, an impatient frown on his face.

"Well, hell, Raymond," James said grumpily. "Why didn't you ask her if we could give her a ride home?"

Raymond shrugged and smiled. "You always say you don't want anybody to know about your charitable leanings, James. I figured you'd hate it if word got out in the typewriting pool that you're a closet philanthropist."

Raymond's words brought a shudder to James's expensively garbed shoulders. "I suppose you're right."

He didn't like it, though, and he rapped on Mother Francis Mary's door a little harder than was necessary.

"Come in, come in, Mr. Drayton," the tiny old nun said, swinging the door open in James's face. "It's a pleasure to see you. We have much to talk about."

"Er, yes. Thank you, Mother."

Mother Francis Mary waved James and Raymond onto the two chairs across from her desk. "Oh, my, yes, we do indeed have lots to discuss. I just realized you've not only sent us criminals, but your firm's loveliest typist as well. The children all adore her."

James stared at the nun. Her sparkling eyes held a degree of humor for which he couldn't account. "Do they?"

With a large sigh, Mother Francis Mary sat down and folded her leathery hands on the stack of papers she seemed to keep on her desk for the purpose. "Oh, my goodness, yes, Mr.

Drayton. They do indeed love her. She's wonderful with children. She'll make a splendid mother one day. When the right man comes along.''

James could have sworn the old nun winked at him.

Chapter Eight

On Thursday morning Polly did not have to rise early since the employees of Drayton and Associates, Attorneys at Law, were given the Thanksgiving holiday off. With pay. It was a consideration Polly deemed one more indication that James Drayton was nothing akin to the scoundrel he liked to make people believe he was.

She was luxuriating in bed, her thoughts tangling wistfully around memories of her chat with him the day before. All at once her blissful daydreams were shattered by a tremendous ruckus coming from the street below.

Good Lord, it sounded as though somebody were being murdered.

Scrambling out of bed, Polly threw on her morning wrapper and stuffed her feet into her slippers. She tore down the stairs and raced to the front door. When she threw open the door and darted outside, the sight that greeted her eyes drew forth an exclamation of dismay.

Then she burst out laughing.

Flapping furiously through the neighborhood were at least fifty indignant geese, each one squawking up a storm. A terrified dray horse had apparently bolted and now stood, sides heaving and eyes rolling, several yards away, having managed to get its traces tangled around a picket fence. The cart itself listed at a drunken angle against the same fence.

Ignoring both horse and fowls in favor of the poor drayman, who looked petrified and clung desperately to the almost-naked lower branches of a maple tree, lurched James Drayton's rarely seen Philippine Tapir Hound, baying fit to kill. Its disreputable tail whipped back and forth in a whirlwind of happiness over having discovered such good sport in Polly's neighborhood.

"Oh, my goodness."

Polly dashed down the six steps and out into the street. She still wore her nightgown and robe but was willing to sacrifice modesty for the sake of rescuing a fellow human being in distress. After all, it *was* Thanksgiving Day.

"Help!" cried the drayman.

"Come, doggie. Come here." She added, "Good doggie," and nearly laughed again.

The dog turned to look at her, but all she got for her efforts was an especially big wag.

"Get him off me!" the poor drayman hollered. "Get him off me! He's scattered my geese all over creation, and I've got to get 'em to market for Thanksgiving!"

"I'm trying," Polly told him, all inclination to laugh now squelched.

For several tense minutes, she tried to persuade the dog to draw off, but the tenacious beast wouldn't be swayed from its purpose. Every time she got the animal by the collar and tried to drag him away, he resisted. Since the dog was nearly as heavy as Polly and had twice as many feet, he won each skirmish.

Finally, Polly put her fists to her hips and told the drayman, "I guess I'll have to go into the house and fetch a rope. Try not to worry. I don't think he's really vicious." She eyed the fellow skeptically and shook her head, knowing her recommendation was for naught. He was obviously quite worried already.

Just as she turned to hurry back to the house, she heard a loud and enormously angry voice.

"Dewey! Dewey! What do you think you're doing?"

Her spirits soared, and Polly turned on the second step to peer in the direction of the voice. Her anxiety vanished instantly when she spied James Drayton, a leash held aloft, tearing down the street. Amusement returned and, with it, her laughter.

"Mr. Drayton, we're so happy to see you!"

James saw Polly on her porch steps, screeched to a halt, and nearly collapsed from shock at the foot of the stairs. He could only stare at her for a moment, speechless.

Good Lord in heaven. He'd always been under the impression that women looked their worst in the morning. Polly MacNamara belied that commonly held belief. There she stood, in her night wear and tousled from sleep, looking as serene and lovely as a Grecian goddess. Her hair, still braided for bed, captured the morning sun's rays, perfected them, and sent them back into the world in glimmering auburn flashes. Her utterly fascinating cinnamon-colored eyes shone with humor.

James realized he was gaping and shut his mouth. "I—I lost my dog."

A giggle erupted from her rosebud mouth and he gulped.

"So I see. But I think you'd better fetch him now. He's managed to chase that poor man up a tree and scare away all his geese."

Tearing his gaze away from Polly, James eyed the devastation his hound had wrought. "Oh, my God," he muttered. "Here, Dewey!"

As he ran over to rescue the poor drayman, he heard Polly's laughter ripple through the air. His whole insides smiled.

"I can't believe you actually named that animal Dewey, Mr. Drayton!"

James could tell she was trying to contain her giggles and was having a hard time of it. He was glad. She was so lovely when she laughed. As he grabbed his hound by its collar he said, "It was the least I could do, Miss MacNamara. After all,

Commodore Dewey was the hero of Manila Bay.''

Another silvery laugh kissed his ears as he began to haul the hound from its prey. Dewey dug in his paws and proved recalcitrant, but James was stronger than Polly and made the hound obey.

"I'm very sorry, mister," he told the drayman. "Please let me deal with this beast and then I'll take care of the rest of this mess."

The drayman still clung to his branch, apparently unwilling to trust James's strength and the paltry leash. James smiled sheepishly when he walked Dewey up to Polly.

"Miss MacNamara, may I call upon your kind heart one more time? If you will take this animal inside, perhaps I can deal with the havoc he's wrought on your formerly peaceful street."

"I'd be delighted to do so, Mr. Drayton," she said just as the front door opened.

"What on earth is going on out here?"

Lillian MacNamara wheeled herself onto the porch and stared incredulously at the street. When she saw James and Dewey, her eyes bugged out momentarily, but she regained her composure almost immediately.

"Good morning, Mr. Drayton." Lillian's voice sounded weak.

Geese still flapped here and there. The drayman, on his feet now, wasn't happy about the state of affairs. His glower raked James's back, skidded over the geese, and pounced on his horse. The equine had relaxed by this time and was now occupied in devouring the unpainted pickets around which his traces were wrapped.

Wandering geese nipped at each other and neighborhood flowers. Some, apparently of a more nervous disposition than their sisters, continued to cackle with agitation. MacNamara neighbors, alerted by the noise, peeked out from doors and windows.

"Good morning, Mrs. MacNamara," James said, striving for a formality he did not feel. In spite of everything, he felt just fine.

Polly, leading the now-docile Dewey, said, "Come inside,

Mother. I'll explain everything to you while I dress."

"Well . . ."

"Your daughter has come to my rescue yet again, Mrs. MacNamara," James said gallantly. "I have some business to clean up out here, and I'll join you soon to express my appreciation."

"Well, all right." Lillian looked perfectly bewildered.

The drayman finally found his voice. As Polly waited for her mother to precede her into the house, he cried, "*Some* business! *Some* business! You've got geese to round up, mister, and no mistake!"

"And so I shall, sir." When the front door clicked behind Polly and his hound, James realized his voice had gone dreamy and he snapped to attention. "And so I shall," he repeated, with much more appropriate firmness. "But let's tend to your horse first. Then we'll see to your geese."

"A fine thing it is when a gent can't even make an honest dollar on Thanksgiving."

Polly, peeking out the window at the mess, giggled yet again. "Oh, my, what a stir."

Then she turned, deposited Dewey in the hall with firm instructions to behave, and wheeled her mother to her bedroom. There she explained things while she washed up, dressed, and brushed her hair. By the time she had put the last pin to her upswept hair, she heard a knock at the door, followed immediately by an intense baying as Dewey, ever alert, announced that a visitor had appeared on the porch.

Both MacNamara ladies were laughing when Polly reached the front hallway. Holding on to Dewey's collar for insurance, Polly opened the door to an extremely contrite James Drayton. In his gloved fist he held a creature that had, in life, been a superior example of the goose family. James presented the bird in a gesture of conciliation.

"May I offer you a Thanksgiving goose?"

Dewey lunged for the fowl and nearly broke Polly's arm. She was laughing too hard to take exception.

"Oh, good Lord." Very carefully, James handed Polly the deceased fowl and took over the care of his dog.

After a few awkward moments, during which the fate of the

MacNamaras' hall carpet and James's peace offering remained in doubt, tranquility descended on the house once more. As they walked toward the pantry to deposit the goose, Mrs. MacNamara said, "We were going to have a roasted chicken from our coop out back, but this will be much more festive, Mr. Drayton. Thank you very much."

"There's no need to thank me, Mrs. MacNamara. Your daughter saved the day."

"Actually, I wasn't able to save much of anything. I'm afraid old Dewey is bigger than I am."

"And much less disciplined," murmured James.

He was having a hard time keeping his gaze directed at where he was going. It kept sliding over to Polly.

"However did you solve matters with that poor man, Mr. Drayton?"

"We managed to work out a solution satisfactory to everyone. I'm afraid his cart was badly damaged, but I'll take care of the repairs. He managed to find a boy to fetch his brother with another cart. Fortunately the horse wasn't injured, although the poor thing was scared to death." He frowned. "I'm not sure about that fence, though. I suppose I should replace the pickets he ate."

Polly's laughter bubbled out as though she couldn't keep it contained, and James grinned. Lord, she was lovely. He'd had no idea the staid typist who looked so stiff and somber in the office could transform into this relaxed, delightful woman in her own home.

"How did you ever make that man come to terms, Mr. Drayton?"

"First we had to catch the geese. Then I offered him a reasonable price for the lot, and a good deal extra for his trouble. At least, he seemed happy to accept it."

"You bought the whole lot?" Polly turned to stare at him. "Good heavens, that must have been fifty geese! What on earth are you going to do with fifty geese?"

Bother. James had difficulty stifling his scowl of annoyance. He'd never let information of this nature slip out before. He must be going soft. Or daft, in the company of the enchanting Polly MacNamara.

"There are one or two charitable organizations I know of that can use the geese, Miss MacNamara. I paid the drayman to deliver them."

Polly's smile could have melted a heart of ice, and however much he chose to pretend, James's heart was definitely not made of ice.

"Oh, Mr. Drayton, how kind of you. I wish I'd known. There's an organization run by the Sisters of Benevolence with which I am associated in a minor way. They operate an orphanage and two soup kitchens, and I'm sure they could use an extra goose or two."

"I am aware of the Sisters of Benevolence, Miss MacNamara. I sent thirty of the geese to Mother Francis Mary."

It would be easy, James decided, to become obnoxiously bigheaded if he were to be the recipient of very many glowing looks from Polly MacNamara. At the moment, in fact, he felt almost heroic, when he knew he wasn't any such thing. His only interest in the charities he supported was motivated, as Mother Francis Mary had so appropriately pegged it, by guilt. He returned Polly's smile, though; he couldn't help it.

Lillian interrupted James's contemplation of her daughter's charms. "However it came about, I'm sure this goose will be delicious, Mr. Drayton. And since you're the provider of the feast, it seems only fair that you partake of it. Can you join us for Thanksgiving dinner, or will you be dining with your own family?"

Dining with my own family. The words twisted bitterly through James's middle. "Indeed, Mrs. MacNamara, I have no family with whom to dine, and I should be delighted to join the two of you."

He noticed that Polly's cheeks went pink, and hoped they did so with pleasure and not mere embarrassment. When she seemed about to lodge a protest, he forestalled her with, "But what's this about you dining on chicken? It's Thanksgiving, ladies. Thanksgiving is a time for turkeys and geese, not chickens."

Polly seemed to accept James's conversational detour. She smiled when she said, "Mother's sister Grace, my cousin George, and our friend Mrs. Plimsole were all going to join us for dinner today, but every single one of them seems to have taken to bed with a cold." She looked delightfully self-conscious when she confessed, "Mother and I decided not to waste the price of a turkey on just the two of us."

"Well, Miss MacNamara, now you will have the pleasure of wasting a goose on the three of us." James bowed the ladies into the parlor.

Polly, to whose lot it fell to cook their Thanksgiving goose, felt as though she were treading on clouds for the rest of the day. Mrs. Ragsdale had made a mince pie the day before, and Polly barely noticed peeling potatoes, preparing the stuffing, putting the goose in the oven to roast, and snapping the green beans.

Her fingers kept straying to her medals, hidden beneath her shirtwaist and apron. Each time they did, she smiled. Of course, there was no such thing as magic. She knew that.

She hummed "Three Little Maids from School" for a moment or two as she sliced carrots, then giggled.

It was fun to pretend, anyway. And she *had* wished they could spend more time together, just the three of them.

She tried to recall whether they'd received messages about their invited guests' various illnesses before or after she'd made her wish. Then she giggled again.

Not, of course, that she'd ever wish Aunt Grace or Cousin George or Mrs. Plimsole to become ill. But the fact that they had all done so was certainly interesting.

The brazen thought that James Drayton might ask her to walk out with him after dinner flitted into her mind and was thrust aside. She told herself not to be ridiculous. He was only dining with them because he had no family.

Poor thing.

Polly had never thought she'd be the type of wicked person to take pleasure in the misfortunes of another, but she found herself grateful to James Drayton's family for being dead.

When James appeared at the MacNamara ladies' door for the second time on Thanksgiving Day 1899, he was dogless. He also carried a bottle of champagne under one arm and a box of chocolates under another, and he clutched a pretty bouquet of fall flowers in the hand not holding his hat. His Benz Landaulet-Coupé rested at the edge of the sidewalk. Harboring a slim hope that the very proper Polly MacNamara might agree to drive out with him after dinner, James had decided to bring his horseless carriage this evening.

A flushed and glowing Polly opened the door almost before he'd finished knocking. It was refreshing to meet a young woman who was not conversant with the arts and airs of flirtation. The other ladies of his acquaintance would have made him wait at least five minutes, if only to promote the flimsy illusion that they did not crave his wealth and status.

"Please come in, Mr. Drayton." A dimple peeked at the corner of Polly's mouth. "I see you decided to leave the good admiral at home this evening."

"Indeed, Miss MacNamara. I thought even so formidable a personage as yourself might find two encounters in one day with my rarely seen Philippine Tapir Hound daunting."

Taking his hat and coat, Polly hung them in the entry closet. Then she seemed adorably confused when she spied the bounty James had brought with him.

"Oh, Mr. Drayton, you shouldn't have bothered. Such beautiful flowers." She took the bottle, then murmured, "Oh, my goodness. Champagne," and blushed rosily.

The woman simply couldn't be coy. James, used to the company of people who posed and simpered with every word they uttered, felt as though he'd been bewitched. He wanted to kiss her. He wished he'd brought two bottles.

"It was the least I could do, Miss MacNamara. After all, it was my idiotic dog who roused you out of bed so early on a holiday morning." The thought that he envied his dog, that he would like to rouse Polly in the morning, flashed through his mind. He told his mind to behave.

"But if he hadn't done it, Mother and I would be eating chicken," Polly reminded him, tilting him a look that ate away at his resolve to behave. "Alone," she added.

James fingers tightened so solidly around the box of chocolates, they made five little indentations in the stiff, gilt cardboard. He noticed the dents when he lifted the box and presented it to Polly.

"After we've supped on the goose, perhaps you would do me the honor of partaking of a chocolate."

"Oh, Mr. Drayton, you're entirely too generous."

"Nonsense."

The idea of ripping open the box and asking Polly to take a chocolate from his fingers popped into his head. He could almost feel her velvety lips close over his fingertips as she nibbled the sweet. His reaction to the thought was indelicate and predictable. He gave himself a little shake to cool his ardor.

"Do you have a chill, Mr. Drayton?" Polly asked innocently. "It's quite brisk outside."

With a grin, the wickedness of which he knew she'd never comprehend, James said, "Not at all, Miss MacNamara. I drove here in my motorcar and hardly felt a nip of cold air."

"How nice."

James chuckled. "Yes. I well recall how fascinating you find motorcars, Miss MacNamara."

There went that dimple again. James controlled himself and only smiled at her.

"I guess I like horses because one can pet them, Mr. Drayton."

"Miss MacNamara, you may pet my motorcar any time you desire." And me, too, a baser part of his anatomy cried. James told it to be still.

Polly laughed. "Please come into the parlor. Mother is there. Perhaps you and she would like to chat in front of the fireplace while I set out dinner."

"Do you need any help?" asked James, who had never helped set out a dinner in his life.

"Of course not." Polly was obviously shocked that he'd even asked.

A ribbon of disappointment fluttered through James when her artless comment reminded him of their relationship. Polly MacNamara remembered their disparate stations in life, even if he didn't. She couldn't possibly know that he didn't give a fig about a person's social standing. He'd gone to such pains to present himself as a snob, how could she?

Although James and Lillian praised her meal, Polly was

ever afterwards unable to remember how anything tasted. She felt as though she were living a happy dream.

After dinner, they took coffee and chocolates in the parlor, and Polly felt more relaxed and comfortable than she could remember feeling for years, if ever. Of course, the fact that she'd tasted her very first glass of champagne with dinner might account for some of her fuzzy good humor. Polly suspected, however, that the company had more to do with her attitude than the wine.

James proved to be an amusing and solicitous guest. He treated her mother with a lighthearted respect that made Polly's heart sing. People often didn't understand how trying it could be for an invalid to be constantly pitied and fussed over. James didn't fuss, and he exhibited no pity. If it seemed appropriate, he offered his assistance, but he didn't hover.

With each passing second, Polly discovered more to like about him. And, even though she knew herself to be in peril of foolishly throwing away her heart, she couldn't seem to help it.

"These chocolates are delicious, Mr. Drayton," Lillian said as she reached for a second piece. "I don't usually make such a pig of myself, but these are truly special."

"A fellow in town makes them, Mrs. MacNamara. I believe in supporting local businessmen, and I guess others feel the same way because his business is booming."

"They really are wonderful," Polly murmured.

She peeked at James just before she bit into a dark, glossy, delightfully lumpy chocolate mystery and found him staring avidly at her lips. His gaze seemed awfully warm. At least it heated Polly. By the time she finally tasted her chocolate, she was sure her cheeks were pink.

James cleared his throat and looked away. "The chocolates are a mere trifle, Miss MacNamara. Your dinner was superb. I had no idea your skills included a flair in the kitchen."

Unsettled both by his expression and his words of praise, Polly couldn't look at him when she said, "Well, we have a cook, Mrs. Ragsdale. But, of course, she isn't with us on holidays. She did make the pie."

The information about the pie was added hastily, as a disclaimer, because Polly didn't want to take credit for anything she hadn't done.

Suddenly James looked at Polly's mother. "Mrs. Mac-Namara, may I have your permission to walk out-of-doors with your daughter for a moment or two? If you don't mind?"

He looked quickly at Polly. "If, of course, you care to take the air with me, Miss MacNamara."

To Polly's utter amazement, he appeared to be nervous. She'd never considered even the possibility that the suave, sophisticated James Drayton might ever be nervous. Especially around her, of all people.

"Why, certainly, Mr. Drayton. I believe a little walk would be nice."

Lillian smiled at them. "I think that would be fine, Mr. Drayton. The exercise undoubtedly will do the both of you good after such a large meal."

"Would you like to go with us, Mother?"

Polly asked the question out of form and realized she hoped her mother would decline the invitation. Although her nerves had begun to jangle at the thought of being alone with James, she wanted to be. Oh, mercy, how she wanted to be.

"Good heavens, no, Polly. Why, I'm sure two bright young people don't want anybody's old mother tagging along. It's a crisp, beautiful autumn evening, perfect for a nice walk."

James rose and extended his hand to Polly. "In that case, let's take a stroll. Perhaps you can advise me about your neighbor's picket fence, Miss MacNamara. I looked at it again before I left this morning and decided it might be more appropriate to replace the whole thing."

"I'd be happy to." Joy and trepidation sent Polly's emotions flapping around as wildly as this morning's frightened geese.

James helped her on with her coat, something no gentleman had ever done for her before. Then she donned her one good hat, pulled her nice new gloves over her fingers, and said, "All ready, Mr. Drayton."

When he opened the door for her and stood aside as she walked through it, Polly felt like a princess. Then he took her hand and placed it, just so, on his arm, and she wished the day would never end.

They walked for a moment in silence. Polly breathed deeply of the crisp autumn air and felt happiness bubble up in her. It had been a long time since she'd been happy. Long before Stephen's disappearance, a stifling sense of disappointment had begun to claim her waking hours. She didn't know why, but she had a feeling the emotion stemmed from her self-imposed isolation. She didn't feel isolated today, though. Today she felt as though she belonged to life; that life belonged to her.

"It's a perfect day, isn't it?" James's question seeped into Polly's thoughts smoothly, as though his voice belonged there.

"Oh, my, yes."

Another moment or two of silence followed, broken by the pleasant crunching sound of autumn leaves under their feet.

Then James said, "It must be difficult for your mother to get around, Miss MacNamara. How do you manage the steep steps to your front door?"

"There's a ramp at the back door. Mother didn't want one in front." She grinned. "There's a ramp next door, too, for old man Fleischer's beer kegs."

"Beer kegs!"

"Oh, yes. Mr. Fleischer is from Germany, you see, and he's most particular about his beer. He has a keg delivered every two weeks. The delivery man rolls a new one in and rolls the old one out."

"Good heavens."

Polly laughed. "He's really a very nice man. And I don't believe I've ever seen him so much as tipsy."

"I'm glad you have nice neighbors, Miss MacNamara." James considered her thoughtfully. "Your mother is a lovely lady."

"Yes, she certainly is."

"I can see where you come by your beauty and manners."

Never having been complimented by a gentleman before, Polly didn't know what to do or say. She stammered, "Oh, but—well—thank you."

James smiled, charmed by her discomposure. "It's nothing

but the truth, Miss MacNamara. But it must be difficult for you, keeping house for the two of you. Do you get out much?''

"Get out?'' Polly peered up at him, wondering what he meant, her heart still bumping crazily from his compliment.

"Get out,'' he repeated. "You know, with friends. Go to the theater or to musical offerings in the park. Attend lectures. Visit museums.''

"Oh.'' All at once Polly's joy took a tumble and she felt very small and naive. A bumpkin, disconnected and alone.

Of course. Regular people did all of the things James mentioned. Regular people had friends and laughed, ate taffy on the wharf, listened to the band in the park on Sunday afternoons, went to see the amazing new coin-operated juke box in the Hotel Royale, picnicked in Golden Gate Park, and took the steamer to Marin County to visit Mount Tamalpais. Polly knew about those things from listening to the happy chatter of Constance, Juliana, and Rose in the office.

Polly herself had never once seen or done any of them. Instead, she hid in her mother's house, caring for a woman who would prefer it, Polly realized in a flash of dismal clarity, if she'd behave more like a lively young woman than a caretaker.

"Well?''

James continued to smile at her, and Polly couldn't hold his gaze. She dropped her head and said softly, "No. I—I don't get out much, Mr. Drayton.''

"Does your mother require so much of your attention, Miss MacNamara?'' James inquired in a very gentle voice.

Polly heard his solicitude and was shamed by it. Motives that had once seemed noble now felt empty, warped by intentions gone awry, twisted by a young girl's longings into a young woman's loneliness. It was true what everyone said: the truth hurt.

Taking a deep breath, she answered him honestly. "Actually, no, Mr. Drayton, she does not. I suspect I have fallen into the way of caring for my mother to the exclusion of other activities. My mother believes me to be too anxious about her, and I'm afraid she may be right.'' She paused for a sustaining breath and admitted, "Why, just the other day she tried to walk by herself and I scolded her for it.''

"I see.''

"I believe Mother is right about my clinging to her now that she needs me. Stephen and I—well, Stephen and I were alone together a good deal when our parents were away. I think I've gotten into the habit of staying with Mother because I longed to have her with us when we were little.''

She peeked up at him, hoping her candid confession wouldn't produce a display of maudlin sympathy. She wanted him to understand her, not feel sorry for her, although she wasn't sure why.

To her unutterable relief, James was not looking at her. He stared into the distance, seeming not to notice the neighborhood, lost in his own thoughts. Polly glanced around, too.

Still pleasant, the homes here were well tended, with flower gardens and neat, albeit tiny, yards. Polly was sure, because she'd seen illustrations in newspapers, that James's own neighborhood was opulent by comparison. Still, hers was tidy, and she was not ashamed of it.

They walked on in silence, the holiday afternoon fading into dusk. The street was deserted, everyone having taken to the warmth of their homes where they were, Polly was sure, sharing festivities with family and friends. Like her. The thought brought the lost smile back to her lips.

"Perhaps we should do something to rectify that situation, Miss MacNamara.''

Polly had been so involved in scrutinizing her neighborhood and thinking that James's voice surprised her. Before she could ask what he was talking about, though, he spoke again.

"Are those men approaching your door, Miss Mac-Namara?''

There was a shade of worry in his words. Polly looked up quickly.

"Oh, my goodness.'' Fear slammed into her with such force it robbed her of breath. "Oh, my goodness.''

As though he understood, James quickened his pace and hurried her toward her home where three gentlemen, clad in the uniform of the United States Navy, were climbing the front steps.

Chapter Nine

James felt anguish shiver in the MacNamara parlor when Lillian MacNamara read the telegraph she held in a trembling hand. He wanted to throttle the three men standing grim-faced and rigid in front of her. He wanted to wrap Polly in his arms and hold her, let her weep hot tears on his breast, comfort her.

Since he had no earthly right to do any of those things, he stood still and watched, aching with the certainty that the telegraph message boded tragedy. Damn. Helplessness was not a new sensation for James, but he couldn't recall ever having felt it for another human being until now. He'd made a career of fixing things, but he couldn't fix this.

"You understand, Mrs. MacNamara," the navy chaplain said in a high-pitched twang, drawing James's swift gaze, "that this information is preliminary. Nothing can be certified and there may still be hope."

"Although," the vice-admiral intoned, his deep voice sounding much more like that of a preacher than the chaplain's, "the facts are such that we felt it best to prepare you."

"What does it say, Mother?"

Polly's eyes were as round as dinner plates and her whisper

quivered in the heavy atmosphere. James realized with a powerless ache that all of her considerable vitality seemed to be channeled into dread.

He could almost feel Polly's mother fight for composure as she cleared her throat. "It says that wreckage from the U.S.S. *China Seas* has been located near one of those nameless Philippine Islands, Polly. Several islands have been searched, but no survivors have been discovered."

Lillian lifted her head and looked at her daughter. "They fear Stephen is dead, dear."

Lillian's voice broke and Polly abandoned her stoic pose next to the door and flung herself onto her knees in front of her mother. She shook her head violently.

"No, Mother. No, don't believe it. Please don't believe it. They don't know. He might still be found. I'm sure I would feel it if Stephen were dead, Mother. You know how close we are."

"Oh, Polly."

Polly put her head in her mother's lap, gave up her fight for poise, and wept. Lillian finally stopped trying to be brave, too. James saw her shoulders shake for a moment. Then she laid a hand on her daughter's head and succumbed to tears of her own.

Unable to stand idly by while these usurpers shattered the lives of two women for whom he'd begun to care a great deal, James pushed himself away from the wall and spoke softly to the vice-admiral. "Will you please give me the particulars, gentlemen? My name is James Drayton."

He pulled out his engraved gold card case and handed the gentleman an embossed business card. "I'm a friend of the family, and perhaps I can be of some help."

The vice-admiral looked at James with interest. "Drayton? Are you perhaps related to J. P. Drayton, the shipping man?"

James felt his jaw tighten. "J. P. Drayton is my father, gentlemen. This matter does not concern him, however."

Shaking his head sadly, the vice-admiral said, "Never hurts to have others watching, Mr. Drayton. It's a sad case."

James lowered his voice when he said, "Did you have to bring this news today? On Thanksgiving?"

The chaplain answered him. "There is no good time for a message of this nature, Mr. Drayton. Our purpose is to tell people what we know as soon as possible. In this case, there are many families to visit. *China Seas* was a heroic vessel with a heroic crew, and we felt it imperative that relatives be notified immediately."

"It's still possible some of the men may be found," offered the third man.

"Well, I would appreciate being informed of any progress you make."

"Are you the family's attorney, Mr. Drayton?"

Making a swift decision, James said, "Yes."

"Mr. Drayton?"

Lillian's gentle voice jerked James around as surely as if she'd shouted at him. He took a step toward her and then stopped, unsure of himself. In all his years of giving alms and sprinkling his wealth judiciously on the heads of his impecunious fellows, he'd never encountered such an immediate problem. All of his good works were done behind the scenes. He'd never seen the victims of tragedy face-to-face before; he didn't know what to do.

Wiping her eyes with a lacy handkerchief, Lillian said brokenly, "Can you please help Polly, Mr. Drayton? I feel the need to ask these gentlemen a few more questions."

Her hand stroked her daughter's head. Polly's usual austere reserve seemed to have crumbled under the weight of her shattered hopes. Her despair ripped at James's heart with razorlike talons.

"She and Stephen were—are—were—Oh, dear." Lillian took a shaky breath. "She and her brother have always been very close. I'm afraid—I'm afraid Stephen was more a parent to her than a brother. Than Frank and I were."

Another of Lillian's ragged breaths nudged James to action. "Of course."

Without another word, glad to have been offered the task, he knelt next to Polly. Wrapping one arm around her back and supporting her shoulder with his other hand, he urged her to rise. She didn't resist. Nor did she demur when he guided her to the sofa and sat with her, holding her against him, pressing her face to his shoulder. He shut his eyes, wishing he could do something to ease her grief.

Time seemed such a variable commodity sometimes. The day until now had sped by, full of happiness and discovery. The few minutes since the naval contingent had arrived at the MacNamara home seemed much longer than the rest of the day. Minutes slogged past, and Polly still cried.

Defying censure, at last James quit being formal. He hugged her close, willing her burdens to shift to his own, much broader shoulders.

"Polly? Polly, I'm so sorry. I'll do everything I can to help."

His voice seemed to penetrate her misery and also to remind her in whose arms she was weeping. James was sorry when she stiffened and tried to draw back. He didn't want to let her go and loosened his arms only after a momentary struggle with his better nature. Pulling his monogrammed handkerchief out of his pocket, he eased her back against the sofa cushions. Then he tried to dry her poor cheeks, but she forestalled him.

"Oh, I'm so sorry, Mr. Drayton."

Her eyes had the look of wet copper pennies. Her nose was pink and her hair, neatly arranged for the festive day, now sported escaped, bedraggled wisps at odds with her usual cool demeanor. For all that, she was the most attractive woman James had ever seen, and her less-than-perfect appearance struck him as appealing.

Lord, he wanted to help her, to help them both. To make everything all right again. She looked uncertain and a little afraid, and James heaved a big sigh.

"At least take my handkerchief. Please."

"Thank you." She accepted his offering and dried her cheeks. Since her eyes still leaked, the hankie was soon soggy. Her hand gripped the fragile cloth as though it were a lifeline, and James was glad. A handkerchief seemed of pitiably small support, but at least she could use it.

"I'm so sorry, Mr. Drayton. I don't usually fall apart this way."

Her contrite expression, her obviously bruised pride, nearly broke his heart. In spite of convention and propriety he squeezed her shoulder.

"I know that, Miss MacNamara. You have every reason to be sad, but please don't give up all hope. I have connections with people in the shipping business. Perhaps I can help."

"Oh!" For the first time in what seemed like hours, she brightened a fraction. "Do you think you can—can get information? Anything? Any information at all would be welcome."

With a smile he hoped didn't convey the turmoil in his breast, James said, "Of course. I'll do everything I can."

Even ask my father.

Since the significance of the act would be lost on Polly, and since he couldn't believe he meant it, James didn't tell her about it.

Leave-taking was awkward. Lillian was as gracious as circumstances allowed. Polly saw him to the door, leaving her mother to deal with the navy.

"I'm terribly sorry you had to be here during this—this revelation, Mr. Drayton."

"Not at all, Miss MacNamara. Until this evening, the day was glorious, and I'm glad I was here when the unhappy news arrived. There may be nothing I can do to help, but I'm certain that through my connections I can at least discover everything there is to learn about the matter."

"Thank you."

Polly couldn't seem to meet his gaze, and James felt a painful tightness in his chest. Nudging her under the chin, he made her look him in the eye.

"Please promise me you'll let me help you," he whispered. "Please let me help."

For several moments Polly only looked at him. Then she gave him a tiny nod and said, "Thank you."

The last of James's determination to be a proper gentleman dissolved under the weight of Polly's unhappiness. He murmured, "Oh, Polly," and drew her into his arms. When his lips captured hers, he felt as though he'd found the one thing he'd been searching for all his life. She melted into his em-

Emma Craig

brace, unresisting. He tasted her salty tears and ached to ease her sorrow.

She was sweet as honey, hot as fire, and a balm to his soul. She fit his arms perfectly. Her untried ardor blossomed under his touch. He longed to hold and pet her, to soothe her worries with his kisses and caresses.

His kiss was neither chaste nor carnal, but was, rather, a promise. James had never before kissed a woman for whom a kiss was a promise, had never wanted to. But he meant this pledge. No matter what it took, he would keep it.

Although he wanted to keep kissing her, to kiss her again and again, to assuage her misery with passion, he knew better than to try it. Very gently, he broke off the kiss and looked down at her face. She seemed dazed. He smiled and put his hand to her cheek, cupping it tenderly.

"I'll come by tomorrow, to let you know if I'm able to learn any more information about the discovery of the *China Seas*' wreckage. There may be information these men don't have or aren't telling you."

"Thank you, Mr. Drayton," Polly whispered, obviously bewildered by everything that had happened during the last hour or so. Most particularly during the last few minutes.

She watched until James cranked up his horseless carriage and drove off into the star-spattered night, fingering her medals the whole time. Closing her eyes, she made a conscious decision not to think about the many times she'd wished to receive information about Stephen's whereabouts. Then she heaved a deep sigh and turned to brave the heavy, disconsolate atmosphere of her home.

She and her mother sat and talked after the chaplain, vice-admiral and the third man—whose name and rank they never did learn—left them.

"Please try not to give up hope, Mother." Polly offered Lillian the advice she was herself trying desperately and without much success to follow. It was hard, hanging on to hope when every circumstance seemed determined to grind it to dust.

"I am trying not to, dear."

"Mr. Drayton said he would attempt to discover any infor-

140

mation about the ship those men might not have known or might have kept from us. I guess he has connections.''

"How very kind of him. He seems to be a very nice man, Polly.''

Polly couldn't quite withstand her mother's steady gaze. She said, "Yes. Yes, he does seem to be,'' into her lap. The feel of James's lips still lingered on hers, and she could feel the warmth of his arms yet. She wished she could still be within the sweet cocoon of them.

"He seems to be taking a great interest in our affairs, too.''

"Yes.''

"Polly—'' Lillian stopped, unsure how to phrase her next comment, her expression troubled.

"What is it, Mother?'' Polly asked softly, almost afraid to know.

"Oh, Polly, I don't know. I just—I just don't want you to be hurt, dear. Mr. Drayton is an important man of business. Although I can certainly understand why he seems to be interested in you, because you are a girl of rare character and beauty, still—still, Polly, please be careful.''

On top of the dreadful news regarding *China Seas,* and especially after the beautiful kiss James had shared with her, Lillian's warning was almost too much for Polly to bear. Her heart felt like lead, and she could only stare at her mother for a moment, unable to speak for the sorrow that lumped in her throat.

At last she said, "If there is one thing I never lose sight of, Mother, it is that James Drayton and I occupy vastly different stations in life. He has been kind to me.''

She dropped her gaze. "I am absolutely certain that Mr. Drayton harbors nothing but benevolent interest in a common typist employed by his law firm.'' The bleak truth emerged taut and strained, quivering with suppressed emotion. It took a great deal of Polly's fortitude to say the words aloud, because they hurt so much.

Tension jangled in the room. To Polly it felt as though invisible waves of pathos jolted through her like painful electrical charges.

Neither woman spoke for a moment.

141

Then Lillian reached for her daughter's hand. "Oh, Polly, I wanted so many things for you and Stephen. When you were little I didn't realize how fragile life could be, or I never would have left the two of you so often and for so long. I'm sorry, dear. I'm so awfully sorry."

"Oh, Mother." Polly squeezed Lillian's hand and couldn't say more.

The MacNamara ladies remained together in their warm, once-cozy parlor until very late. Polly needed to be near her mother that night, and apparently Lillian felt a similar need. They didn't talk much. Polly tried to concentrate on the book she held in front of her, and Lillian pretended to embroider.

When they finally did go to their separate bedrooms, Polly lay on her bed with her hand clutching her St. Christopher medal and her old coin for a long time. Just feeling the medal Stephen had given her made her feel not quite so alone, although there were moments, too, when the loss of her brother was so acute, it seemed to tear at her very soul.

James Drayton's face haunted her as well, and the way she'd melted when he held her. She felt almost worse now for having received such comfort from him. She wondered if she was beyond hope for ever being other than a complete fool. When she slept her dreams were filled with loss and abandonment.

She awoke in the morning red-eyed and groggy, her heart heavy, her head aching. Nevertheless, she dressed and prepared to go to work.

"But, Polly, I'm sure Mr. Drayton doesn't expect to see you at work today."

Polly had anticipated her mother's shock, and felt guilty about leaving her alone. But she couldn't bear to be trapped in the house today, mourning. "I can't not go, Mother. If I stayed home from work today, it would be—it would be as if I believed Stephen to be dead. I won't do that. I won't believe he's dead until I see his body!"

Lillian stared in dismay as Polly virtually ran out of the house.

* * *

J. P. Drayton glowered when James walked through his office door. "I don't intend to sit still for another lecture about integrity from you, boy, so don't even think about it."

James sighed with weariness as he removed his hat. "I don't intend to give you one, Father." He stood before his father's desk, silent for a moment before he asked, "May I sit down?"

"Go ahead." J. P. spoke grudgingly.

So James sat, put his hat on his lap, and stared at the floor. He didn't know how to begin. How did one ask a favor of a man to whom one had barely spoken for ten years? How did one approach a man whom one hated and loved and—James felt idiotic admitting it—feared with all one's heart?

"Well, did you come here to stare at my Turkish carpet, James? It's quite a nice piece and I got it at a bargain, although I'm sure *you'd* tell me I cheated the rugmaker out of a fair profit."

I'm sure I would, James thought cheerlessly.

His head felt heavy when he lifted it to gaze at his father's face. For the first time in years, James really studied the old man's features and realized he looked tired. Tired and careworn.

Strange. James had been so busy resenting J. P. Drayton all these years that he hadn't given a thought to his father.

He'd lain awake for hours last night, thinking about Polly MacNamara, her brother, her mother, and her father. All that thinking about Polly's problems stirred up the mud of his own long-buried memories. He was sorry for having dirtied the waters with all that sloppy emotion. Disinterring the ancient, bitter memories had made him think—about his father and about himself.

What he discovered was that it was easy for him to despise an unscrupulous businessman. It was infinitely more difficult for him to hate his father. Now, as he peered at the man who had sired him, James's heart hurt. He didn't want to hate J. P., but he didn't know how to love him.

With a deliberate shake of his head, he plunged into his subject. "I've come to ask your help, Father."

James saw surprise flash across his father's face. Almost at once, the old man's "J. P." mask descended, and James was

Emma Craig

left sitting face-to-face with the shipping magnate.

"What for? I thought you needed nothing from me. You've told me so often enough."

Although he might have imagined it, James had the fleeting impression of hurt in his father's words. Certainly there was nothing in J. P.'s expression to give him that perception. And J. P.'s voice was as hard as steel.

Oddly enough, James did not bristle immediately. "This particular favor isn't for me."

J. P. scowled. "No?"

"No."

James said no more for a full minute. He'd been thinking all night and all this morning, trying to come up with the words he needed to say, but they'd never come. Now he sat in his father's office with nothing planned, and inspiration, if it was striking anywhere, seemed to be avoiding James like the plague.

He'd heard somebody say once, "When all else fails, tell the truth." He'd thought it a funny, slightly sardonic epigram at the time, but now he decided to let the maxim guide him.

"Do you recall several days ago when I asked you about finding the U.S.S. *China Seas,* Father?"

J. P.'s eyes narrowed. "I remember."

"Well, Mrs. and Miss MacNamara received word yesterday that wreckage from *China Seas* has been found on one of the Philippine Islands."

"So? What has that to do with me?"

"Stephen MacNamara, Polly's brother, was chief petty officer on that ship. He is presumed dead."

J. P. only stared at James, his frown deepening by the minute, so James forged onward.

"The MacNamaras don't have any resources, Father. They barely scrape by from day to day. You have an entire fleet of ships at your command, and some of them are undoubtedly in the area right now. I wondered—" James stopped and sucked in a breath, doubting his sanity. "I wondered if you could direct one of your ships to search for survivors."

Silence settled over the two men. It broke when J. P. began thrumming his fingers on his desk. James's nerves jumped,

144

and images of war drums thumped in his brain with each roll of his father's fingers. Time, that ever-changeable element, seemed to stretch until it pulled so taut, James thought either it or he would snap.

At last his father said, "Just what is your interest in this MacNamara chit, James? I thought she was a typist in your law firm. I know your heart is soft as pap, but it seems to me you're taking a good deal of interest in a mere employee."

James felt his jaw tighten. An old familiar rage snaked up his spine, overriding all the philosophical musings in which he'd been indulging. Anger gouged away at his control like acid. "Polly MacNamara is not a chit, Father. Nor is she a mere employee."

"No?"

His father's bushy brow arched ironically and James felt his hands fist around the brim of his hat. With an effort, he relaxed them. "No. She is not."

An unpleasant grin twisted J. P.'s lips. "I'd always heard you had a yen for ladies in a different echelon, my boy. Ladies with experience, who had a few years behind them. Never expected you to get caught in the maws of a designing innocent. A sinless typing maiden might expect more from you than a quick tumble, you know. I understand such affairs can become quite nasty. Thought you had more brains than that, boy. Always heard you did."

His father's words made James think about the kiss he had given Polly last night. It had been a beautiful kiss, and James had endowed it with all of his finest motives. Now, in the withering light of J. P. Drayton's scorn, both kiss and motives seemed silly, callow, somehow spoiled. James's anger churned and his clenched jaw ached.

"There has been no 'quick tumble,' Father, nor will there be," he said with barely suppressed violence. "Polly MacNamara is a young lady of firm moral principles. Even if I weren't cognizant of her virtue and didn't respect her for it, she would never sink to such depths."

The hearty, beefy face of Lawrence Bullock rose before his mind's eye, and James's fists tightened again. Damn these men. Damn them all. Damn every one of them who treated

innocent women as playthings. The thought of Polly Mac-
Namara in the clutches of such a man made James's temples
throb.

J. P.'s eyes opened wide. James couldn't tell whether the
gesture was one of genuine surprise or if it was meant sarcastically. He didn't suppose it much mattered.

"A regular paragon, is she?"

"As a matter of fact, she is."

J. P. stopped drumming and sat back in his chair. He stee-
pled his hands and held them to his lower lip as he contemplated his son.

"You know, James," he said dryly, "you speak of the
wench as if you were in love with her."

It was all James could do to remain seated. He wanted to
lunge out of his chair, stomp out of his father's office, and
never set eyes on the heartless old scoundrel again in his life.
For Polly's sake, he remained seated. For Polly's sake, he
would endure this monster's sarcasm and innuendo.

"Do I?"

"You do."

"And do you disapprove, Father?"

For a moment J. P. appeared almost surprised. Then he
shrugged. "It's not my business, boy. You made sure of that
years ago."

His father's shrug hurt James almost more than his words.
Pain speared him and his anger bubbled over. That damned
careless shrug typified J. P.'s attitude for a certainty. That's all
James had ever been: a nuisance to the old man. What did a
hard-hearted, hardheaded businessman like J. P. Drayton care
about a boy, even his own?

Oh, James might have been able to curry J. P.'s favor once
upon a time if he'd been willing to sacrifice his principles,
character, mind, and soul. But he hadn't, and his father had
never forgiven him. Well, J. P. Drayton could go straight to
hell. James wasn't about to start bowing and scraping now.

James wanted to help Polly MacNamara more than he'd
ever wanted anything in his life save, possibly, his father's
love and approval. Now he could see clearly that any help
Polly got would happen without J. P. Drayton's support. No

matter how much he *could* help or how little it would cost in effort and his precious money to do so.

As casually as he was able, James rose and put his hat back on. "Well, I see I've wasted my time."

With what he hoped was a contemptuous smile, he said, "Good day then, Father," turned on his heel, and reached for the doorknob.

"James—"

But James was in no mood for further discourse with J. P. Drayton today. Or any day. He'd abased himself this morning for the first time in ten years. It would be the last time he'd ever do so.

Never again, chanted through his brain. *Never again.* He managed to control his rage until he walked clear of J. P. Drayton's elaborate office building. Then he ducked into a narrow alleyway between two abandoned buildings and pounded the wall of one building until his hand bled.

He emerged from the alleyway not much relieved, and walked the long way to his office, churning with bitterness.

God, what a fool he'd been to think that man had ever possessed a heart.

People stared at him because he was muttering to himself, but James didn't care. Things he'd liked to have said to his father pounded like artillery fire through his head. Oh, how he'd love to give the old man a piece of his mind!

He'd never do it, though. Old J. P. would never sit still for James's opinions. Even if he listened, a doubtful prospect, he wouldn't hear.

Or, perhaps more disheartening, he wouldn't care.

"Damn. Damn, damn, damn, damn, damn."

James was still angry when he reached his office.

"Well, curse it all, if the Lord High Drayton won't help, there are still plenty of things I can do," James growled savagely as he shot past Marcus O'Leary, leaving the doorman staring in dismay at James's flapping coattails. "I have almost as many resources as my father, except for his ships, damn it."

It wasn't until he had ignored Walter Gregory, flung his office door open, slammed it again, thrown his coat and hat into a chair, and sat down behind his desk that he realized the tightness in his throat and the burning in his eyes were the same sensations he'd experienced as a boy. When he'd wanted to cry.

But James hadn't cried as a boy. And he didn't cry now.

Constance, Rose, and Juliana chattered happily about their Thanksgiving holiday while Polly tried not to listen. Occasionally one of the three women directed a comment at her, and she tried to answer appropriately.

Desperately, she concentrated on the legal transcript she was typing and wished it documented a thrilling criminal court case instead of a boring civil lawsuit. Distraction. She needed distraction. Not the chattering distraction of her three co-workers discussing families and holiday parties, which only seemed to emphasize her own loneliness and loss. No. Polly needed something absorbing, something to take her attention away from everyday life for awhile; something to redirect her thoughts, draw them away from dwelling on Stephen's possible fate.

Suddenly all four typists were taken up short by a commanding voice.

"Miss MacNamara!"

Surprised into stiffness, Polly's fingers paused over the keys of her Underwood. She lifted her head to seek the source of the voice. Her breath froze when she beheld the form of James Drayton, standing rigid with anger at the door of the typewriting room, his gaze directed squarely at her.

Chapter Ten

All at once Polly's numb misery evaporated in a blinding flash of rage.

How dare he?

She wanted to scream the question at him, but prudence—only a dim but nonetheless helpful presence today—held her tongue.

As soon as the shout left his lips, James regretted it. He hadn't meant to yell. It was only that he was disconcerted to see Polly here today. He'd expected her to be home, giving comfort to her mother; taking comfort from her mother. Leaving everything to him.

What on earth did she think of him? Did she honestly believe he'd begrudge her a day or two to compose herself? What kind of heartless, soulless, callous brute did she think he was, anyway?

She said, "Mr.—" and the word came out so hoarse, she was obliged to clear her throat. Then she said, more firmly and with a very sharp edge, "Mr. Drayton?" The two words sounded as cold and hard as ice.

With a quick glance around the typewriting room, James

took note of the curious stares of the other three typists and didn't blame Polly for her annoyance. He decided he'd best not question her here. Irritation blossomed like a spring bud in his breast when he comprehended the field day the three women would have speculating about the boss's interest in Polly MacNamara.

He wanted to kick something but knew that would only make things worse. If they could be worse.

He said curtly, "Will you please step into my office for a moment, Miss MacNamara?"

She hesitated for just long enough to let James know how much he had provoked her. Her lips flattened into a thin line. He wished he could just start the day over, knowing what he knew now.

Polly swallowed before she said, with a fair show of courtesy, "Certainly, Mr. Drayton."

She rose with the dignity he'd come to expect of her and walked toward him. She didn't peer at him as she passed by him into the clerks' room. Except for the red patches burning on her cheeks, nobody would guess her composure had just been rattled. All the clerks stared at her, of course.

James couldn't recall another time in his life—at least not since he'd broken with his father—when he'd made such a hash of things.

They walked in silence to his office. James couldn't help scrutinizing her. She looked almost ill, and the fact made him feel even worse. It didn't appear as though she'd slept at all. There were purple rings under her eyes, and her normally peaches-and-porcelain complexion was sallow except for the two telltale marks of fury blazing on her cheeks.

Signs of strain were evident, too, in her pinched lips and the rigid set of her jaw. He noticed that her eyes were red and swollen and wished he could put his arms around her, hold her tight, absorb her pain.

For the second time that morning, James ignored Mr. Gregory as he and Polly entered the reception area. His attention was focused firmly on Polly when he opened his office door and stepped aside to allow her to enter.

As soon as he shut the door, he murmured, "Please take a seat, Miss MacNamara."

She did. She wouldn't look at him, though, but rather directed her gaze at her lap. James got the feeling she was holding herself on a tight string, that she might snap at any second, and prepared himself.

He cleared his throat. The sound drew her gaze to his face. Lord, she looked furious.

"I'm very sorry to have startled you, Miss MacNamara," he said, feeling incredibly inadequate.

She didn't respond. James picked up an engraved gold fountain pen and began twisting it in his fingers.

"I was surprised to find you at work today. You shouldn't be here. There was no need. The news you received yesterday was—was such that you shouldn't have felt obliged to come to work for—for a few days. Of course, you will be compensated for the time."

She stood so suddenly, she startled James into a jump of surprise.

"How could you?" Her voice throbbed with fury. "*How could you*, Mr. Drayton? How could you yell at me that way?"

She whirled around to face the wall. James saw her hand lift as though she were wiping away an angry tear, and felt about two inches tall. Her shoulders shook for a moment, and he was seized by the impulse to leap up, put his arms around her, and draw her to his chest. Of course, he did no such idiotic thing.

When she turned around again, she had regained a modicum of composure. She held herself rigid and knotted her hands into fists at her sides. James suddenly wished he could just put his head down on his desk and shut his eyes.

"I don't know what I've done to anger you, Mr. Drayton. Whatever it was, I apologize. I certainly didn't—" Her voice shook and she stopped abruptly to clear her throat. "I certainly didn't mean to do anything to aggravate you, to make you shout at me in that awful way."

James opened his mouth, but Polly cut him off before he could say a thing.

"I know it's not my place to reprimand my employer.

151

You hold my livelihood and that of my mother in your hands. But—but, for heaven's sake! Why, those girls in there already think we're having an illicit affair!" She lifted one arm while she spoke and pointed in a direction James guessed she thought was toward the typists' room. It wasn't, but he didn't suppose he'd better mention it.

"How could you yell at me like that?" The color in her cheeks deepened. "They're probably babbling right this minute, speculating, wondering what sort of business we could possibly have together. For heaven's sake, how *could* you?"

"Miss MacNamara—" James stopped, wondering where to start.

Polly barked out, "Yes," then passed a hand over her eyes, as though she'd reached the end of her endurance.

"Miss MacNamara, I'm very sorry. Please sit down and let me try to explain." He was surprised at how soothing he could make his voice sound when he wanted to.

Polly sat abruptly, folded her hands, and arranged them on her lap. Her back was as straight as a spike, and her face held a poignant combination of defiance, grief, and misgiving.

"I'm very sorry," James repeated. "It's only that I was surprised to see you here today. I didn't mean to startle you or to give the other typists food for gossip."

She made no response, although her lips pinched even more tightly together. James had a feeling she'd love to splash invective all over him. He sighed and decided to start at the beginning.

"Miss MacNamara, I visited my—an associate this morning, hoping to enlist his support in searching for survivors from the U.S.S. *China Seas*."

Defiance faded and a lick of hope flickered in Polly's expression. Encouraged, James hurried on.

"I'm afraid I did not meet with much success there." The hope died instantly and, had James been fiddling with something less sturdy than his fountain pen, it would have snapped in half when his fingers tightened abruptly.

"I came at once to the office and began using the telephone." He gestured to the elegant candlestick phone on his desk. Her gaze strayed to the instrument, a modern invention

James was sure she'd never used before, her circumstances being what they were.

"Raymond Sing is on his way now to the naval office. His assignment is to determine exactly where the wreckage of *China Seas* was found, and to glean any information the men who came to your home yesterday might not have told you. I believe it is often the case that family members are not given elaborate details because such details are not deemed to be of use to them. With the resources at my command, however, any such details may prove invaluable."

"Thank you, Mr. Drayton." Polly ducked her head and added in a very small voice, "I—I'm sorry for my tantrum."

"There's no need to apologize, Miss MacNamara. I fear I deserved it."

"No." Polly shook her head, still staring into her lap. "I have an unfortunate tendency to speak before I think. I had no business taking you to task. After all, you are my employer." As if she couldn't help herself, she added grimly, "Even though you did startle me terribly."

He gave her a small grin. "It is I who should be apologizing, Miss MacNamara."

She almost managed to return his grin. "May I return to work now, please?"

James rose from his chair precipitately, his gold pen falling with a click to his blotter. Anger, directed at no one particular person or thing, propelled him. Damn it, her brother might well be dead, and her circumstances were truly uncertain, but that didn't mean she had to give up on life entirely.

"Miss MacNamara, will you please come with me?" Less a question than a command, James nevertheless held out a chivalrous arm for her to take.

Her anger seemed to have evaporated completely by now, leaving in its wake numb despair. He could detect bewilderment in her expression when she placed her hand on his coat sleeve and rose from her chair. Her demeanor nibbled painfully at the edges of his heart. He'd seen her stiff, polite, terrified, happy, relaxed, and angry. But he'd never seen her defeated, and the attitude did not suit her.

He strode through his office door with Polly on his arm and

stopped so quickly she bumped into him. Without thinking about it, he steadied her with an arm about her waist.

"Gregory, run to the typewriting room and fetch Miss MacNamara's things. An—incident has occurred, and she is needed at home."

He didn't bother to look at Polly; he could see her well enough out of the corner of his eye, gaping at him.

"Yes, sir."

Mr. Gregory rose stiffly, gave Polly an imperious once-over which, James decided, ended Gregory's services with the law firm. Damn it, having a soft heart was one thing. Putting up with insolence and rude behavior in paid subordinates was something else entirely, and James was through with it. Never again would he tolerate a Lawrence Bullock or a Walter Gregory in his employ.

"*Now*, Gregory," he barked.

"Yes, sir."

Gregory scuttled out of the room on quick, fawning feet, James's hot glare burning his back. James stared after him and contemplated the many changes he planned to make in his life.

"Mr. Drayton?"

So busy had he been with his own thoughts that Polly's soft voice startled him. He frowned when he looked down at her, but the moment his gaze caught her expression—solemn, worried, and puzzled—his anger melted. He patted her hand.

"What is it, Miss MacNamara?"

"If you don't mind, I'd just as soon stay at work today."

"Why do you want to stay here? You have enough on your mind today without having to worry about your job, too."

"But that's just it. I need the distraction. Without something to divert my mind, I keep thinking about—about Stephen. About where he might be and—and—"

"Well, for goodness' sake, then seek diversion, Miss MacNamara. But not diversion of such a burdensome, uninteresting, depressing nature as typing legal briefs for litigants squabbling over money in a court of law. You need distraction of an amusing nature."

"But—"

Mr. Gregory gave a quick rap on the door before he entered. His face spoke eloquently of the imposition he considered he had suffered having to fetch a menial's coat and handbag.

Perhaps, when James sacked him, Walter Gregory could go work for Lawrence Bullock. They deserved each other.

"Thank you, Mr. Gregory." With a smile full of promise, James said, "I shall be speaking to you after I conclude some other business."

"Yes, sir," Gregory squeaked.

James helped Polly into her coat and ushered her to the door. "Take care, Miss MacNamara. Please let me know if I can be of help to you or your mother."

"But—" Polly's mouth snapped shut. "All right, Mr. Drayton. Thank you."

James wondered why she looked so angry when she left the office.

A smile that would have astonished his son wreathed J. P. Drayton's face. He positively beamed as he spoke into the fancy, gilt-inlaid receiver of his telephone.

"When?" he asked in a voice so mellow it might have rivaled honey. He was gratified by the answer he got and chuckled with satisfaction.

"Good. Good. Where are they now?"

The answer given to that question pleased him, too. His laugh became quite hearty when he heard it.

"Wonderful! Then do you suppose this miracle can be accomplished by Christmas Eve?" A longer pause ensued, but J. P.'s smile never wavered. "Wonderful."

J. P.'s second "Wonderful" completed the conversation. He replaced the receiver on its cradle, then sat back in his enormous leather chair. For the first time in his life, he rubbed his hands together in glee.

His eyes positively sparkled when he chortled, "Damned arrogant pup. I can't wait to watch his face at that snobby charity ball of his when I give him the news."

Polly's brain and heart both roiled with conflicting emotions as she hurried along Montgomery Street, away from Drayton and Associates, Attorneys at Law.

155

Emma Craig

How could he? She huffed angrily, her breath coming out in a puff and trailing in the air beside her as she hurried past. Why, he'd as much as kicked her out of his office.

Tears stung her eyes, but she wouldn't let them fall. She wouldn't cry. She *wouldn't*. She'd cried enough yesterday. Tears were for weaklings, and Polly MacNamara was no weakling.

It wasn't until she'd turned up Grant Avenue that her pace slowed and she allowed her mask of anger to fall and reveal the hurt underneath. Oh, Lord. It wasn't bad enough that Stephen might well be dead, but James Drayton didn't want her.

Well, why should he? Just because he'd taken Thanksgiving dinner with her didn't mean anything. Just because he'd been kind yesterday didn't mean he'd ever be kind again. Just because he'd kissed her . . .

She didn't dare even finish the thought. After all, Polly knew what his reputation was. She'd heard all about him. Why did it hurt so much to discover his reputation, however much *he* denied it, was true?

She harbored a suspicion that she was being irrational, but she didn't care. Irrationality fit her mood right now. She needed to wallow.

She was wallowing with fervor when a familiar voice startled her.

"Well, well, well. If it isn't Miss High-and-Mighty-MacNamara, typewriting mistress to the lordly Mr. James Drayton."

Shocked, Polly whirled around to face her mocker. Her lips tightened when she beheld Lawrence Bullock.

He didn't appear so hearty and fit today. In fact, he looked drunk. He leaned against the door of a disgraceful-looking saloon and leered at her, a toothpick dangling from his loose lips.

Well, Polly didn't need to worry about offending him today. He held no further power over her life and livelihood. She gave him a raking glare to let him know without words how disgusting she considered him. Then she turned deliberately and, back straight, continued on her way.

His yank on her arm nearly sent her sprawling. Without

156

thinking, she whirled around, and the flat of her palm connected with stinging accuracy on his cheek. She felt a moment of astonishment when she encountered the flab on that cheek. At once she realized his demeanor of athletic good health was nothing but a charade.

She didn't have time to think about it. Although Bullock staggered back under the force of her blow and his own surprise, he righted himself quickly. His grip on her arm tightened, his fingers digging into her painfully.

"Bitch!"

"Let me go!"

Bullock hauled her up close to him until his whisky breath nearly made her pass out. "You little tart! You sassy little bitch. Who do you think you are?"

"Let go of me!" she yelled again. This time she added emphasis to her words by slamming the heel of her shoe down on his instep.

Yelping in pain, Bullock nevertheless did not release her arm. Rather, his free hand was raised as if to slap her.

"You bitch!" he screamed, drawing stares from everybody on the street.

Dimly aware that they were attracting a crowd, Polly reached for her hat. She'd never had to defend herself in earnest before, but instincts borne of childhood scuffles with Stephen came to her aid in this moment of need.

She didn't give Bullock time to hit her, but stabbed savagely at his upraised arm with her long hat pin. She wasn't sure about the accuracy of her aim but felt a surge of gratification when he bellowed in pain. His grip loosened, and right before she felt herself spin away from him, spurred on her way by his push for spite, she kicked at him with her pointy-toed shoe. Since he had hunched over, her shoe connected with his soft stomach. Her heart swelled with satisfaction.

Hopping on one foot, doubled up in pain, gripping his wounded arm, Bullock looked ridiculous loping about on the pavement. Her emotions rioting, Polly put a hand to her heaving bosom and spat, "I wish to God somebody would teach you a lesson, Mr. Bullock. You're a disgrace to the whole human race!"

All at once, Polly became aware of two surprising circumstances. The first was that the spectators on the sidewalk, who had been watching avidly, began to applaud.

The second was that James Drayton, coattails flapping, was racing up the walkway toward the commotion. Fright and worry radiated vividly from his features, and Polly felt a rush of pleasure when she realized both emotions were for her.

"What's going on here?" James seized Polly by the shoulders, his expression intense. "I was worried about you and followed you. When I saw Bullock grab you, I—I—"

James apparently couldn't finish his sentence. With a movement so abrupt it left Polly staring, his hands dropped from her shoulders, and he whirled around to confront his former law associate.

"Damn your eyes, Lawrence Bullock!" With those words, James drew back his fist and propelled a punch at Bullock's still-bruised face so furious, Polly was sure the crack when it met its mark could be heard by her mother on Pacific Avenue.

The blow was apparently hard enough to hurt James. He grimaced almost as soon as his fist connected with Bullock's cheek. Cradling it in his other hand, he turned around in another swirl of coattails, without even waiting to watch Bullock crumple up on the ground with a loud groan.

"Polly—"

Wide-eyed, Polly opened her mouth to speak just as James did. They were both silenced by the approving roar of the crowd.

Flinching from the noise, Polly cast her startled gaze around and found what seemed like hundreds of people clapping, stomping, and yelling.

"Hear, hear!" cried one large, whiskery gentleman. "Hear, hear! Show the bully that's no way to treat a lady!"

"That's the way to go!" hollered another.

"She was doin' pretty good on her own, young feller," a third pointed out.

"All right, what's going on here?" another voice bellowed. Even before Polly could take in the supportive comments of the horde surrounding them, the sea of people parted and a uniformed policeman dashed up. He held his nightstick in a threatening manner and glared around, as if to thwart any would-be evildoers. "What's going on here?" he repeated, skidding to a halt in front of Polly and James.

A moment of silence descended on the scene. Lawrence Bullock took that very moment to utter another painful moan. The policeman eyed him suspiciously. Then he looked at Polly.

"Did that feller try to bother you, ma'am?" The way he said it made it sound as though bothering Polly was one of the worst crimes he could imagine.

With a quick glance at her tormentor, Polly's heart hardened against him. She said firmly, "He certainly did, Officer. He assaulted me on the street, in fact."

Immediately, she felt guilty. "Well, perhaps he didn't *assault*, exactly. Actually, he—"

James interrupted her. "He did, too, assault her, Officer. I saw it."

Polly stuttered, "Well, yes, but—"

"The cad doesn't deserve your sympathy, Miss Mac-Namara," James interrupted again. Still pampering his hand, he added, "Miss MacNamara will be filing a complaint against him, Officer." With a glance obviously meant to quell any misplaced compassion on Polly's part, he added, "I'm James Drayton, Miss MacNamara's attorney, and I'll see to it."

Polly took another, longer look at Lawrence Bullock, and her compassion dwindled. She felt somewhat penitent about kicking him in his soft, disgusting stomach, but not very.

"Yes, I shall be lodging a formal complaint. I guess." The perfidy of Lawrence Bullock struck her, and she lifted her chin, defiant. "It's a crime when a respectable female can't walk on a public street in San Francisco without being accosted by a drunkard."

Her speech drew another roar of approval from the crowd. Several rugged-looking men began to advance upon the wretched form of Lawrence Bullock, and Polly wondered if she'd gone too far. Bullock had managed to sit up by this time and was massaging his jaw with shaky fingers. Blood seeped onto his coat sleeve, leaking from the wounds inflicted by

Emma Craig

Polly's hat pin. She saw it and felt guilty again.

Her compassion faded when Bullock, eyeing the crowd with fear, whimpered, "Don't let them hurt me."

With a revolted grunt, the policeman stalked over to Bullock and took charge. "Don't worry, you piece of scum. I won't let the big, bad men hurt you." His conspiratorial wink at the crowd drew smiles. "Hell, if a lady can do this to you, heaven alone knows how you'd survive if you had to deal with a couple of *men*."

The crowd loved it. The policeman hauled Bullock to his feet amid a chorus of threats and jeers.

Grinning, James said, "I'll come down to the station later to file the complaint, Officer."

"That's fine, Mr. Drayton. That's just fine." The policeman jerked Bullock's arm, making him wince. "I'll just take this fine specimen down to the precinct jail." Another contemptuous look at his prisoner prompted, "Disgusting daylight drunk," out of him as he began to lead Bullock away.

Amid congratulatory comments from their audience, James drew Polly away from the scene. She went willingly, all thought of anger toward him having dissipated long since.

"Let's get out of here, Miss MacNamara."

"All right."

He'd meant to rescue her! The thought made her heart, which had alternated between the heaviness of loss and the anger of frustration, sing. What did it matter that she'd already rescued herself by the time he showed up? He'd meant to rescue her!

All at once her burdens didn't feel so heavy. Hope, which had sunk to her toes and lain dormant for many hours, revived. Somehow, just knowing James Drayton wanted to be her champion cheered her.

"Thank you for coming to my rescue, Mr. Drayton."

"I'm not sure how much rescuing you needed, Miss MacNamara. You were doing quite well by yourself."

She nibbled on her lower lip. "You don't suppose he'll be imprisoned for long, do you?" she asked, beginning to feel guilty again.

He looked at her, surprised. Then a rueful grin lifted his

160

lips. "Miss MacNamara, you're the only lady I know who'd feel any compunction about Lawrence Bullock. The man," he said succinctly, "is a rat. When I saw him grab you, I—I—"

Polly guessed she was never to learn what emotions James felt when he'd seen Lawrence Bullock grab her, because he quit speaking abruptly, as he had at the scene. Suddenly he stopped short, startling her yet again.

"Miss MacNamara, you said you needed distraction."

A sudden flood of sorrow filled Polly's heart. "Yes."

"If you will allow me, it would give me great pleasure to distract you. The way you need to be distracted. Not by typing dull legal briefs, but the right way—the real way."

Surprised, Polly said, "But—" and was cut off by James's hand held up in a gesture commanding her silence.

"No. I won't hear any protests. Just once, just today, I want you to know what it's like to be young and alive and healthy and a citizen of our remarkable city."

With that, he took her by the arm and began to lead her away.

And Polly let him.

Chapter Eleven

The first place James took Polly was to Market Street where, in spite of her protests, he bought her an enormous ice-cream soda. Since he did not believe one should drown one's sorrows alone, he indulged, too.

As the unsettled expression on her face softened, his heart grew lighter. Polly's eyes nearly sparkled when she said, "Oh, my, Mr. Drayton. I haven't had an ice-cream soda since I was a little girl."

"Well then, it's long past time you had another one."

Polly's lips kissed the straw as she sucked, and James had to look away. Good heavens. He'd never been unable to control his reactions in this unseemly way before; he had to get a grip.

Polly sighed and said, "It tastes so good. Sometimes when we were children Stephen took me out after church on Sundays to buy me an ice-cream soda."

She looked sad again, and far away. Although he longed to take her hand and squeeze it, James settled for gripping his frosty glass more tightly. His father's words stinging his brain, he reminded himself that he was much too sophisticated to fall into the trap of maudlin romanticism. He admired Polly, sympathized with her, and, yes, desired her. That was all. That must be all. He couldn't imagine anything else.

After they drank their sodas, James marched her to the Hotel Royale, where he pumped pennies into the juke box and watched her dimple reappear. Hers was a mouth designed for laughter. And kisses. Its former grimness was totally inappropriate.

"I've never seen such a contraption, Mr. Drayton," Polly admitted as the rousing "Stars and Stripes Forever" filled the air around them.

"Nobody has, Miss MacNamara. This is brand new."

"It's quite wonderful, isn't it?"

"It's more than wonderful. It's the beginning of a new era. Why, it won't be long before every home in America will be equipped with an automatic music box. I anticipate even motorcars will sport them one day."

"My goodness! But how on earth will you ever be able to hear it over the roar of the motor?"

"Don't you worry about that. People like my partner, Ransom Olds, will solve the problem. Motorcars and telephones and music boxes are just the beginning. Have you ever heard of motion pictures?"

Polly seemed amazed by this catalog of coming wonders. She shook her head.

"Well, you will. The day is right around the corner when you'll be able to go to a theater and watch a play on a screen in front of you, projected from film, just like the negative for a photograph. You just wait and see."

He knew his plan to distract and amuse her was succeeding when her air of wonder gave way to amusement. She gave him a grin and said, "Well, I guess I'll just have to wait, won't I?"

It was all he could do to keep from picking her up off the Royale's crimson carpet, swinging her around, and kissing her, right on her sweet lips. He laughed, though. He couldn't help it.

"Well, there's something you won't need to wait for, and that's another ride in my motorcar. I plan to drive you to Cliff

House, and there to partake of a light luncheon in the restaurant overlooking the sea.''

''Oh, no—''

James put two fingers against her lips and Polly said no more. She seemed almost as shocked by the feel of his warm flesh against her lips as he was by her lips against his fingers.

''I won't hear a word against my plan, Miss MacNamara, so don't even offer one.''

He'd seen her eyes widen at his touch and wondered if she felt the same incredible attraction for him that he felt for her. Just touching her made him loath to stop. He wanted to continue to touch her, in every way imaginable.

''But—but, my mother . . .''

Her plea jerked his mind away from pleasant fantasies about what he'd like to do with her. Poor Polly. Worried about her mother. Worried about her brother. James wondered if she ever spared one of her worries for herself. Probably not.

''Your mother thinks you're at work, Miss MacNamara. And you are. You are in my charge today just as you are any other day. I'll have you home before the time you usually get home from work. Unless,'' he said, an amusing thought having struck him, ''there's time to visit the zoological gardens after our luncheon at Cliff House.''

''Oh, my goodness.''

It looked to James as though his silver tongue had finally stilled her protests. He wondered whether it was him or the lure of the zoological gardens that had finally sent her over the edge into acceptance and decided he'd best not ask. He wasn't sure his vanity could stand the truth.

A quick cable-car ride brought them to the foot of Russian Hill. James was pleased to note that fresh air had returned the bloom to Polly's cheeks, where it belonged. It had hurt him to see her looking so sallow-cheeked and unhappy. He supposed there was nothing to be done about the hint of bleakness still lurking in her eyes but, by God, if he could brighten her life even a little bit, he'd do it.

As she observed James Drayton's home, Polly decided she had never been this close to absolute luxury in her life. Even when she was a child and her father's business prospered, they'd never lived like this; like royalty.

She sat on a plaster bench in James's Japanese garden, patting Dewey's disgraceful head, while James fetched his horseless carriage and cranked it up. Although she tried not to stare like the peasant she knew herself to be, her gaze kept roaming the manicured lawns, green even as winter's frigid feet tiptoed over them.

"I wonder how much money it takes to keep a lawn green in the wintertime," she mused. Dewey seemed not to know, for he kept silent except for his adoring pants.

This place was amazing.

Cunningly pruned camellia bushes and yews gave the place a truly Oriental flair. Raked paths led here and there, and Polly could discern a teahouse perched in pastoral serenity atop a small hill in the distance. A stately willow dripped over a carp pond spanned by a red-lacquered footbridge. She wished she could climb the bridge and throw bread crumbs to the fish, but she didn't have any crumbs. Anyway, she didn't quite dare take such a liberty.

Although Polly generally took great pride in her independence, at this moment, surrounded by the glory of James Drayton's millions, she felt timid. It was an unusual emotion for her, and one she did not like.

James's house rose in glorious splendor beyond the pond, its white walls gleaming in the late fall sunlight. Lacy Queen Anne edging gave the house the charm of a wedding cake, but it was saved from cloying sweetness by its size and tasteful design. Polly could not recall ever having seen such a beautiful home.

And yet . . .

She would never say so to James Drayton, but it seemed almost indecent for one human being to live so elaborately. Her mind's eye strayed to the Sisters of Benevolence's orphanage, and she wondered how many destitute children might be fed and clothed for the price of the bench on which she sat.

Still, it was not for her to dictate how James Drayton spent the money he earned by the sweat of his brow.

As she stroked Dewey's silky ears with one hand and fingered her medals with the other, though, she couldn't help but wish some of his wealth might make its way to her poor orphaned children. They had so little and he had so much. And, while she guessed James had probably worked hard for his fortune, those poor children had done nothing to earn their grief but be born.

The growl of a motor startled Polly out of her contemplation of these splendid surroundings. Looking up, she beheld James Drayton decked out in motoring goggles and waving at her. His smile was as wonderful as the day, and she couldn't help but smile back.

It was becoming more and more difficult for Polly to remember he was her employer. She must make herself do it, though. She simply must.

James guessed his grin probably gave him the dazzled look of an addlepated adolescent, but he couldn't help it. When he'd driven up and seen Polly seated on his garden bench, staring about somberly, idly petting his ridiculous dog's ridiculous ears, his heart gave a giant leap and his insides lit up.

She belongs here, shot through his brain like an arrow. She fit into the scene as if she and it had been crafted for each other.

For the space of a breath or two he tried to imagine Cynthia Ingram on Polly's bench, only to recoil at the idea.

No. Absolutely, positively not. Decadence followed in Cynthia Ingram's footsteps as surely as Christmas follows Thanksgiving. Of course, James thought with a sprinkling of regret, he'd enjoyed Cynthia's decadence once, and he was certainly not about to despise her for behaving in the same manner as he did himself.

Giving himself a mental shake, he acknowledged that he might even enjoy Cynthia's practiced charms again. Right now, though—in fact, since the evening he discovered Polly MacNamara hurrying along that muddy Chinatown street—he seemed to have no use for Cynthia Ingram.

There was a poise, an innocence, a rightness about Polly MacNamara that was as refreshing as a new dawn. And he craved her rightness in his life as surely as a flower craves water. He felt thirsty for her goodness; he felt as if he'd been missing something all his life and she was it. She filled places he hadn't realized were empty. She endowed his home with grace and purity, as though her very presence were cleansing.

As if he were observing one of the moving pictures he'd told Polly about, James envisioned her here, surrounded by a flock of laughing children. Her children. His children. Their children.

Good God. What on earth was he thinking of?

With another, harder, shake of his head, James leapt out of his motorcar and strode toward her.

"Miss MacNamara, I have another pair of goggles and a motoring scarf in the carriage. Let us be off, my dear. Wonders yet await."

Still, James couldn't shake off the idea that the greatest wonder of all was right here, right now.

Polly couldn't recall another single time in her life when she'd had so much fun. She wondered if this was the sort of adventure Constance, Juliana, and Rose chattered about in the office. Did other people really do these things, see these sights? All the time? Any time they wanted to?

To Polly, who had lived a life of rigid circumspection for six years now, it seemed impossible that such joy was available for the taking by just anyone. Yet, when she examined the day closely as she and James drove back to town, she had to admit that perhaps it was. After all, except for the motorcar and their luncheon at the Cliff House, neither of which she could ever in a million years afford, the day had hardly cost a thing.

Even she, Polly MacNamara, the modest typist, could afford an ice-cream soda every now and again. And she could certainly afford a wagon ride to the Cliff House and admission to the zoo. By rights, she needn't even come this far. A walk along the beach to look for shells, such as the one she and James had shared after luncheon, cost nothing at all.

Amazing. It was truly amazing. Her mother's words filtered through her brain like wisps of smoke. This sort of activity is

what her mother wanted for her, she guessed. Lillian didn't
want Polly devoting her life and youth to the care of an invalid. She wanted her to experience the fun of being young
and alive. She wanted her to be a participant in her genera-
tion's prime years rather than a stiff and lonely observer.

Right now, Polly felt more alive than she had since her
father died. Even with Stephen's fate uncertain, she felt vital
and more animated than she could recall feeling in ages and
ages. That so simple a thing as getting out in the fresh air
should revive one's spirit and energy astounded her.

"I believe she's right."

"What's that, my fair Polly?"

Polly hadn't realized she'd spoken aloud until she heard
James's teasing question. She also couldn't recall when he'd
begun referring to her as his "fair Polly," either, but she liked
it, even if it was shockingly familiar.

She shot him a look, and a giggle took her by surprise. The
two of them must look like a couple of alien creatures out of
a Jules Verne novel, draped in their scarves and motoring
coats, with their goggles wrapped around their faces.

"I said I believe my mother was right when she told me I
should get out of the house more often, Mr. Drayton."

James's answering grin might have lit the darkest winter
day. "I believe your mother and I are of a mind about that,
my fair Polly."

Since Polly could only take a small dose of his glorious
smile without blushing, she turned her head and peered at the
scenery once more. She was observing how the cedar trees at
the edge of the road were being whipped into a frenzy by the
wind made by their motorcar when James's voice surprised
her.

"I don't suppose I could prevail upon you to call me James,
could I, fair Polly?"

His request startled her, and she turned quickly to stare at
him, caught between joy and uncertainty for a moment. When
reality hit, it did so with an almost shattering burst of focus.
She felt the smile she'd been working on shrink.

"Thank you, Mr. Drayton, but I don't believe that would
be a good idea. I can't thank you enough for today. But as an

employee of your firm, it wouldn't be appropriate for me to address you by your first name.''

She realized the motorcar was slowing down and a flutter of alarm assailed her. When James pulled it over and parked in a gap among the trees beside the road, the flutter grew into a gale-sized tempest. He turned off the engine and the sudden silence almost deafened her. She turned to stare at the trees again, fearing another glance at James would be her undoing.

''Look at me, Polly. Please?''

His gentle voice sent rivers of warmth coursing through her. When she dared take a peek at him, his expression heated those warm sensations and set them to dancing a crazy, hot reel.

She realized he was removing his gloves and goggles and gulped. ''Wh-what are you doing, Mr. Drayton?''

He reached over to remove her goggles, and Polly stiffened. She'd been so relaxed and happy a moment ago. Now tension held her rigid in her seat, her back so straight and her jaw so set, they both hurt.

''I'm making you listen to reason.''

After the goggles, he began working on her next layer of defense: the big motoring scarf tied over her hat.

Polly felt James untie the knot at her throat and immediately lifted her hand to stop him. As soon as her fingers touched his, even though hers were still swaddled in the motoring gloves, she realized what a mistake that had been. It took every ounce of her resolve to keep from twining her fingers through his and drawing his hand to her lips. She wanted to kiss him so badly she ached.

Oh, sweet Lord, have mercy.

Quick as lightning, Polly snatched away her hand and hid it in her lap. She wasn't sure whether she was more afraid of what he planned to do to her or of what she wished she could do to him.

Then James cupped her cheeks in his two big hands and Polly realized what she really feared was the pleasure she took from his touch. She couldn't afford to feel this pleasure. The disparities in their social standing rose up in her mind, an insurmountable barrier to any kind of relationship other than that of employer to employee.

Frantically, she tried to hold that thought in her mind. Almost immediately, James's tender, stroking fingers put it to flight again.

"Please, Polly, what can I do to make you see us as a man and a woman rather than an employer and employee? There must be something I can do."

Polly opened her mouth to speak but nothing emerged. She felt her eyes widen as James's face came closer and still closer to hers. Her gaze fastened on his full lips until she could no longer see them; then she felt them, and reason fled.

She heard a little noise and knew it had come from her. She couldn't help herself. His lips grazed hers softly, their touch undemanding yet compelling. She didn't know what to do and felt foolish. She was dimly aware of James's other arm as it inched around to draw her closer until her gloved hands were trapped between his chest and her breasts.

James drew away only far enough to murmur, "You're so lovely, Polly. So sweet."

His words blended with his gentle assault to create a steaming kettle of emotions in Polly. Although her brain screamed at her to remain alert, her eyes fluttered shut and her resistance seemed to melt.

She heard him whisper, "Please, Polly. Relax for me," and wished she could. For once in her life, she wanted to forget her troubles and be a woman in this man's arms; to forget he was the boss and she a mere typist. More than that, she wished *he* would forget it; really forget it; to look upon her as a woman who was his equal in every way save one.

A groan from James shot through her like wildfire, and all at once Polly abandoned reserve. So what if she wasn't experienced? She didn't care. Never in her life had she savored the feelings James's touch evoked. His hands seared through her confining clothing, sending the sweet heat of passion burning through her veins. Liquid pressure coiled deep within her, and oh, how she liked it.

Forgetting herself entirely in the thrill of the moment, Polly slid her hands from James's chest. Then she wrapped her arms around his shoulders and pressed into him shamelessly, her breasts flattening against his chest. She could feel them, tingling like the rest of her body, and felt her nipples harden. She knew her behavior was shocking, but she didn't care. If this was lust, then hooray for lust. It felt just grand.

She wished their passion could last forever.

It was while James was in the process of discovering the sweet taste of Polly's mouth and wondering how delectably soft her naked flesh must feel that his scrupulous nature reared its ugly head and smote him. Hard. Right in the conscience.

Good Lord, what on earth was the matter with him? Here he was, alone with Polly MacNamara in his horseless carriage—an improper circumstance to begin with—and he was taking shameless advantage of her. Him. A person who, as a gentleman and her employer, was charged with her protection. Polly MacNamara was no Cynthia Ingram to trifle with and be trifled with in turn. She was an innocent, demure young lady who deserved better at his hands than this.

No matter how right it felt. No matter how much he wanted her.

No matter what.

Unless he was prepared to declare his honorable intentions, a notion so new and startling he could barely contemplate it, he was behaving in a manner that declared him to be no better than a cad. A roué. A bounder whose reputation, no matter how ill-founded until this minute, he had just proved he deserved.

With a groan of thwarted desire—and of regret that his character should be so weak—James gently eased the embrace he and Polly shared. Good Lord, what was wrong with him? Lawrence Bullock, that great profligate ox, held nothing over James Drayton when it came to tawdry seduction.

Polly looked stunned when he peered into her eyes. Her innocence could not disguise her passion, and a beastly part of James reveled in the fact that he'd stirred her. He knew it was the first time she'd been so moved, and was glad it was he who had done it.

As soon as the thought entered his head, a blinding awareness nearly leveled him, and he knew he wanted to be the only one ever to stir Polly's passions. And, by God, he wanted to be the only one ever to satisfy them, as well.

He sucked in a breath and could only hold on to her shoulders and stare at her in amazement for several seconds. Her lovely eyes were round as holly berries, her cheeks pink as Christmas punch. He wanted to kiss her again and knew he'd be demeaning her if he did. He would die before he dishonored her.

He loved her. God help him, he loved her.

No. Good Lord, no. That was absurd thinking. Ridiculous. James Drayton knew better than to believe in romantic love. Physical love, the love of a man for a woman, was a transitory thing; a mirage. The only real love in the universe was a transcendent spirit of helpfulness. James knew he was fortunate to be endowed with enough wealth to act upon his love of mankind. Why, he took in stray dogs, helped orphans and downtrodden Chinese boys, and—and even heartsick typists.

There was no such thing as love on a personal level. The concept of romantic love was one fostered by poets and idiots to beguile people into stupid acts. It was promulgated by people who probably believed in fairies and elves and little green folk. The notion of love was akin to a belief in magic, Father Christmas, and perfect happiness.

Still, as he continued to stare into Polly's eyes, James couldn't help but feel regret. His gaze strayed to her hand. She had lifted it, as she often did, to her breast. For the first time, he noticed she seemed to be clutching something beneath the fabric of her shirtwaist.

Because he had no idea what he could say to explain his wretched behavior, he put his own hand over hers. Even through her motoring gloves, he could feel the smallness of her hand. A world of wishes jumbled up in his head; wishes for her; wishes for him; wishes for both of them together. On top of the other wishes—and in spite of all he knew about life, the world, reality, and everything else—was the wish that he and Polly could share the kind of love the poets wrote about.

He couldn't say that. It was too stupid. Instead, he said,

"What are you clutching so tightly, my fair Polly? Why does your hand so often stray to your bosom?"

She blinked once or twice, as though he'd spoken to her in Urdu or Swahili or some other exotic foreign language. Then her gaze fell to their hands, too. His was so large it had hidden hers.

"I—" She had to clear her throat. "I wear a St. Christopher medal Stephen sent me from one of his journeys. And a coin given to me by—by an old Chinese lady."

He squeezed her hand and said, "I wish I could see them someday."

"What?" Polly lifted her head suddenly When James's gaze met hers, she was staring at him in open-eyed amazement. "What did you say?" she asked unsteadily.

James could feel his lips lift in a grin. She was so adorable. With his hand still covering hers, he wished he could take her home and keep her forever.

"I said I'd like to see them someday, fair Polly. They seem to be dear to you. You touch them often."

"No."

James lifted his brow wryly at the one curt word. There she went again, blurting out her first thoughts. When she gave herself time to think, she was generally the most diplomatic of females. The stain of embarrassment immediately painted her cheeks pink. James was delighted.

"I—I mean—I mean, no, that's not what you said." Polly looked down at their hands again and whispered, "You said you wished you could see them. I heard you."

Tilting his head, puzzled by the odd note of vehemence he detected in her voice, James said, "Well, I suppose I might have, at that."

"You did."

"Is it important? I would like to see the medal and coin that seem to mean so much to you. May I? Someday?"

Obviously trying to pull together her composure, Polly said more firmly, "Of course you may, Mr. Drayton. Someday. Certainly."

Although he was almost vibrating with the need to kiss her again, James drew away and opened his arms. He dropped his hand, and Polly inched away from him. He saw her shoulders slump when his hand left hers and wanted to draw her into his arms again.

"I guess we'd better get you home now. We don't want your mother to worry about you."

"Oh! Oh, no. No, of course not."

She looked uneasy, and James could have kicked himself for being so maladroit. If he knew nothing else about his companion, he knew that any mention of her mother immediately stirred her guilt.

A long-ago conversation with Mother Francis Mary slithered into his memory and his grin wobbled a bit. "Such a useful emotion, guilt," the tiny Mother Superior had told him. He wondered how those wry words applied to Polly.

Although he tried several times, he was unable to draw her into any sort of sustained conversation the rest of the way home. Every time he looked her way, it was to find her staring at the scenery to her right. He got the impression that she wasn't seeing the trees, though, but was lost in her own thoughts. He hoped those thoughts were not unpleasant.

They drew up to the MacNamara residence a little earlier than Polly was used to getting home from work. James hurried to help Polly out of the car, afraid she was so upset with him that she wouldn't let him see her to the door.

"May I say good evening to your mother, Polly?"

He held her arm, being very careful to show her nothing but gentlemanly courtesy. She still seemed distracted, and James was certain she was recalling the kiss he'd thrust on her and hating him for it. And probably hating herself. Damn. What had possessed him to do such a cursed fool thing?

"Of course, Mr. Drayton. I'm sure Mother would be happy to see you. She enjoyed meeting you and having you join us for dinner yesterday."

"It's kind of you to say so, Miss MacNamara."

He grimaced, aware that he was becoming more formal with every step he took away from the freedom of his motorcar. Somehow calling Polly by her Christian name in the recesses of the home that had been her—what?—prison?—for so many years—seemed almost sacrilegious.

"Oh, no," she blurted. "I'm not being kind. It's the truth."

The charming flush crept into her cheeks again, just as it always did when she uttered one of her spontaneous truths. Even though he scorned the institution, he wished they were married—or at least formally promised—so he could snatch her up off the porch steps and hug her.

Alas, such a pleasant fate was not to be. Instead, Mrs. MacNamara met them at the door, and James's conscience was wrung yet again when he beheld Lillian's pallor and the dark circles beneath her eyes. Apparently neither MacNamara lady had slept much last night.

Lillian smiled when she saw James. "My goodness, Mr. Drayton, how nice of you to bring Polly home this evening."

"It was my pleasure, Mrs. MacNamara."

"Oh, Mother, he didn't just bring me home. Why, he—he showed me every kindness. Every kindness."

"Won't you come in and have a cup of tea, Mr. Drayton?"

James shook Lillian's proffered hand. "Thank you. I should enjoy that above all things."

Deftly, James took the handles of Lillian's wheelchair and turned her around. He was a little surprised to see Polly's quick look of dismay. She hid it again immediately.

As he wheeled Lillian into the parlor, he said, "I have to admit I was annoyed at finding her at work today, Mrs. MacNamara. I had no idea I'm such a hard taskmaster that my employees don't feel free to take time off under circumstances such as these."

With a heavy sigh, Lillian said, "I told her the same thing, Mr. Drayton, but she wouldn't hear of it. Said she needed distraction."

"I know. She told me the same thing."

"It's true," Polly said sharply, as though she didn't care for being talked about this way. "I couldn't bear to sit here all day and worry about Stephen. I couldn't bear it."

James said soothingly, "I understand completely, Miss MacNamara. I probably would feel the same way."

"I suppose I understand, too." Lillian sighed. "Heaven knows, I wish I'd had a little more distraction myself."

"Oh, Mother." Polly's hands flew to her cheeks. "I'm so sorry. I never should have left you. I didn't think."

Her mother forced a look of sternness. "Now don't go blaming yourself, Polly, or I promise you I shall have the vapors."

The three of them smiled at her threat.

Chapter Twelve

Polly was glad for the opportunity to leave her mother and James for a few minutes while she prepared tea. Her nerves were completely scrambled.

While the water heated, she leaned against the kitchen counter, reliving the feel of James's lips on hers. His kiss had taken her breath away. Not to mention her self-control. She pressed her medals.

He made a wish, she thought as the teakettle began to sing. *He made a wish on my coin.*

She tried to dislodge the fanciful thought, but it wouldn't be dislodged.

His spoken wish had been fairly benign. Had he wished for anything else? Had he wished, as she had, that they might meet as man and woman rather than employer and employee? Had he wished for her love as, heaven help her, she'd wished for his?

She felt perfectly distracted as she took the teakettle off the stove.

When she toted the tray into the parlor, Lillian and James were carrying on a desultory conversation. Both seemed to greet her interruption with relief. James leapt to his feet and helped her with the tray, nearly upsetting everything in his enthusiasm. His chivalry made her smile.

"Truly, Mr. Drayton, you needn't help. I'm used to doing this." She gave him a pert look. "You, I see, are not."

"You're right, Miss MacNamara. I'm about as useful in the kitchen as an elephant."

Polly felt almost gay as she served the tea.

"Oh, Polly," Lillian said, accepting her cup, "I forgot to tell you that you received something interesting in the post today."

"I did?" Polly's thoughts had begun to swirl around coins, kisses, and wishes again, and her mother's words barely registered.

"Yes. I have it here in my pocket. I believe it's an invitation."

"An invitation?" Her attention captured, Polly put down her teacup and reached for the gold-and-white envelope in her mother's hand.

Well, this was certainly intriguing. Polly had so effectively hidden herself away from the world that she seldom received invitations to anything. And a gilt-edged invitation received through the post—well, if a peacock had flown through the window, perched on the table, and fanned its regal tail, Polly wouldn't have been much more surprised.

"My goodness."

As soon as Polly read the engraving, she smiled, her puzzlement banished. "How kind. It's from Mother Francis Mary. Last week she threatened to invite me to the charity ball again, and she's carried through on her threat." Her giggle robbed the words of unkindness.

"How nice of her. When is the ball, Polly?"

"Christmas Eve."

"Oh." Lillian gave a small frown. "Well, it's a little awkward, but I'm sure we can arrange things. Perhaps Grace and George can come on Christmas Day instead of Christmas Eve, dear."

With a dismissive wave, Polly said, "Don't be silly,

Mother. Of course I won't go to the ball. But it was sweet of her to invite me.''

"Why not?"

Polly turned, startled at James's brusque question. Lillian looked at him, too.

James cleared his throat. "I beg your pardon, ladies. But, I mean, why not? Why don't you want to go to the charity ball? I understand it's a lovely affair and benefits several local charities; a good many people of goodwill attend it. You'd be among like-minded folks, as you're kind-hearted, too."

"Is this ball an annual event?" Lillian smiled at him.

"Yes. Yes, it is."

"Have you attended it before, Mr. Drayton?"

He cleared his throat again. "Well, no. I have, however, been invited for several years now."

"You have? *You?*"

Polly sounded so astounded that James took umbrage. He frowned and fiddled with his teacup.

"I don't generally care to advertise my involvement in San Francisco's charities, Miss MacNamara, but I'm truly not a complete wastrel."

But Polly waved aside his repressive manner, barely hearing his words. "Is that why I saw Mr. Sing at the orphanage, Mr. Drayton? Was he there at your behest? Are—are you a benefactor of the Sisters of Benevolence?" All at once Mother Francis Mary's amusement and Raymond Sing's nervousness began to make sense to her.

She didn't give James a chance to formulate an answer. Sitting so far forward that she nearly fell out of her chair, she cried, "So *that's* why you sent them the geese. *That's* why you already knew about them. Why, you've been supporting them all along!"

"No!"

Surprised, Polly sat up straight again. James took a gulp of tea.

"I mean, no, I have not been supporting the Sisters of Benevolence's orphanage for very long, Miss MacNamara. I have—um—been a contributor to their cause through another—um—organization. My personal involvement came

179

about out of another—project—Raymond Sing and I were working on."

Polly didn't know what to say.

"What project is that, Mr. Drayton?" Lillian asked after a moment of silence.

James cleared his throat. "I have established a program whereby young Chinese boys who have been ensnared through poverty or ignorance into working for the Tongs and have been arrested for it may be given an opportunity to avoid deportation and earn their ways honestly here in the United States."

Her heart swelling with wonder, Polly breathed, "Really?"

"Er, yes." James looked at Polly and Lillian nervously and stole another gulp of tea. "You see, I believe that given the chance, most of these young men can offer great contributions to our society. If the law has its way, they'll be shipped back to China, and who knows what will happen to them then."

"I see," Lillian murmured. "How very kind."

James made a gesture as if to brush Lillian's comment aside.

Polly's heart sang. Hah! She'd known it all along. Underneath everything—her worry, her distress, her fear, her sorrow, her pain, her uncertainty about James's motives as regarded herself—she'd just *known* he possessed a kind heart. It made her very happy to discover that her heart had known the truth all along, even when her mind had fussed.

He seemed terribly uncomfortable to have been found out, too, a circumstance that only made her love him more. Yes. She acknowledged it to herself here and now, even knowing naught would ever come of it. She loved him.

"Yes. Well, um, anyway—" James stopped speaking and took another swig of tea as though to fortify himself. "Anyway, as I was saying, er—Miss MacNamara, would you consider going to the ball with me? As my guest? It would be my honor to escort you."

Lillian, who had been watching the two younger people shrewdly, immediately said, "Why, what a perfectly splendid suggestion, Mr. Drayton." She turned to Polly. "You have that beautiful new gown to wear, Polly. It would be a shame to waste it on the family."

Polly had been on the verge of politely but firmly declining James's invitation, however much she wanted to accept it. But her mother's suggestion stopped her cold. Her mouth opened, but nothing came out. Her dress! She'd forgotten all about her dress!

James seemed relieved by Lillian's timely intervention. "There. You see? It's all settled, then."

She gulped and stammered, "Oh, but—"

"Why, yes, Mr. Drayton," Lillian cut in smoothly. "Certainly. I've been longing for Polly to get out in the world. She's hidden herself away here with me for so long. And truly, I'm not *that* much of an invalid! Why, I've even started climbing the stairs when Polly's not around to scold me."

"*What?*" All thoughts of balls and ball gowns vanished and Polly gaped at her mother, stricken.

Lillian patted Polly's knee. "There, there, dear. I knew you'd fuss if you found out. But Dr. van Pelt encouraged me to try it. I hold very tightly to the banister, so there's no danger of my falling. And I rest when I get to the top before I start down again."

"But—"

"That's wonderful news, Mrs. MacNamara," James interrupted with a too hearty joviality.

Before Polly could so much as breathe, Lillian sighed happily. "Yes. I'm quite proud of myself, really."

Again, Polly opened her mouth to speak, but James said quickly, "And well you should be, ma'am. And I'm sure your daughter is proud of you, too."

When Polly caught the warm look James cast at her, she only managed to stammer, "I—" before Lillian cut her off again.

"Yes, well, you don't know Polly as well as I do, Mr. Drayton. I'm afraid it sometimes suits her to have me bound to my chair."

Polly could do no more than utter a horrified, "*Mother!*" before Lillian continued. "You see, although we didn't consider it at the time, I'm afraid Frank and I must have created a feeling of abandonment in our children. I believe Polly, especially, felt the loss of her parents."

Before James could continue the exclusive conversation he and Lillian were carrying on around Polly, she stood up in a furious burst of energy.

"Stop it! Stop it, both of you!"

She glared at her mother and James accusingly. "How dare you speak of me as though I weren't even in the same room with you!"

With a sigh, Lillian held out her hand. "I'm sorry, dear."

A guilty flush stole across James's cheeks, astounding Polly, who never dreamed that the urbane, sophisticated James Drayton could blush.

"I apologize as well, Miss MacNamara," he said sheepishly. "I guess I was afraid you'd somehow manage to refuse my invitation and didn't want to give you the chance."

"And I guess I was afraid to tell you about trying to walk, dear."

Polly felt her anger evaporate, leaving in its wake a feeling of desolation. She sat down again but did not smile.

"I had no idea I was such a difficult attendant, Mother," she said in a tight little voice, hurt clamping round her heart like a steel band.

"Oh, Polly, you're not. Not really. Not at all."

James took another sip of tea, staring at Polly over the rim of his cup. She couldn't quite meet his gaze but slanted a peek at him from under her lashes.

He put his cup back on his saucer with a little clink and took a deep breath.

"Will you please go to the San Francisco Christmas Eve Charity Ball with me, Miss MacNamara? It would be a great honor to escort you."

His air of formality vanished and was replaced by a mischievous grin. "If you wish, I can pick you up in my horse and carriage rather than my motorcar."

Polly didn't answer for a minute. She forgot her hurt as her mind spun back to the evening when she received the beautiful new ball gown and danced in front of her mirror, wishing she had someplace to wear it. She could almost smell the elusive lavender scent now, here in the parlor. Her fingers crept to her medals and she fingered them through her shirtwaist. When she saw James's gaze drift to her hand, she dropped it into her lap once more.

"Well . . ." she said, watching her mother and the man she loved, wondering how she could punish them for treating her so—so honestly. She sighed inwardly when she admitted it to herself. Suddenly finding a shimmer of humor in the situation, she decided self-vilification could wait until later.

"Hmmmm . . ." She gave James a severe, narrow look.

"Please?" he asked sweetly, nearly robbing her of breath.

"Well . . . Do you really promise to leave that noisy, smelly motorcar at home?"

"Absolutely."

Polly sniffed and lifted her chin, striving for a majestic angle. "And is your carriage suitably grand?"

With a grin, James said, "My carriage is most grand, mademoiselle. In fact, I shall have it bedecked as suits the season. And my horses are glossy, jet black, and eminently petable."

Polly inclined her head imperiously. "Then I should be happy to accompany you, Mr. Drayton." She spoke in the most lofty tones she could manage and then spoiled the effect completely by giving him the broadest grin in her repertoire and laughing.

"But you must know that I've never been anyplace elegant before. I won't know how to go on. I hope I won't embarrass you."

"Don't be silly, Miss MacNamara. Any day of the week you take the shine out of the useless society damsels I've met."

Lillian nodded firmly. "There, Polly. You see?"

Polly remained unconvinced, however happy she felt. Now that she'd accepted James's escort, she grew nervous. At least, thanks to Stephen and Cousin George, she could dance and curtsy and possessed a small inventory of social chitchat. Both relatives used to practice their gallantries on Polly before they tried them out on their lady friends. As long as nobody spoke to her about anything besides the weather, she'd probably not stammer.

Still . . . Attending a grand Christmas Eve charity ball with James Drayton was not at all the same as waltzing around the living room with her brother or pretending to take formal afternoon tea with her cousin.

James rose from his chair, startling Polly out of her frets. "Well, ladies, I've had a delightful time, but I regret to say I must get back to business." With a speaking look for Polly, he said, "I'm afraid I've loafed a little too much today. There are legal matters to attend to and a complaint to file. Also, I need to talk to Raymond to see if he's been able to discover any information concerning *China Seas*."

"You mean you're checking into the matter, Mr. Drayton?" Suddenly Lillian looked as if she might cry.

"Yes, ma'am." James took one of Lillian's hands in both of his. "Mrs. MacNamara, I can't promise to find your son, but I can promise you that if there's anything more to be discovered about the matter, my associates and I will find it."

"Oh, Mr. Drayton, I don't know how to thank you."

With a charming, lopsided grin, James said, "Just persuade your daughter not to break our Christmas Eve engagement, if you please."

"I will, Mr. Drayton. You may depend on me." Lillian couldn't quite maintain her composure, but had to dig into her pocket for a handkerchief with which to wipe her eyes. "Thank you."

Before he left the MacNamara house, James exacted a promise from Polly not to go to work on Saturday.

"Saturdays are only half-days anyway, Miss MacNamara and, although I tell you, frankly and truthfully, that you're the best typist in our employ, I believe we can manage without you for half a Saturday."

"Thank you, Mr. Drayton," she said formally.

Her austere composure was shattered when the loud "aaooga" of James's horn smote her ears. She couldn't help laughing when he waved at her, his motoring scarf flying out behind him like a banner in the wind, his grin a mile wide.

Polly and Lillian retired to bed early that evening, as both ladies were exhausted from not having slept the night before. Polly sat cross-legged on her bed, her flannel nightgown drawn up under her knees. Her ancient coin lay nestled in her open palm and she gazed at it gravely. The old metal felt warm and, as usual, she sensed or saw—she couldn't even tell anymore— a subtle light emanating from the coin.

"Are you magic?" she asked softly. "Are you *really* magic?"

Stillness settled around her, sweet and peaceful, calming nerves that had been strung taut all day. The ache in Polly's heart for Stephen remained, but even it seemed to relax until she was left with only a vague, melancholy uncertainty. Not knowing her brother's fate was hard; but she no longer felt the piercing despair that had kept her company earlier in the day.

"I never realized how many things I wish for every day," she told the coin. It seemed to pulse a tiny response, and Polly smiled. She didn't know if her fancies were making her believe in magic or if magic was enhancing her fancies.

She didn't suppose it mattered.

The coin seemed to brighten and Polly glanced toward her candle to see if it had flared. It hadn't; at least not while she was looking.

She heaved a tired sigh. "Well, if you are magic, please send Stephen back to us." After thinking about her wish she amended, "If it's meant to be."

Another few minutes' thought produced, "I mean, does anybody really know what's meant to be? Perhaps if, God forbid, Stephen is never found, one of Mr. Drayton's genius friends will be inspired to invent some great navigational device to assure ships are never lost at sea."

The thought brought tears to Polly's eyes and she wiped them away, still feeling philosophical. "Who really knows what's best for the world? We think we know what's best for ourselves, but I'm not sure we even know that, truly. Look at Mother."

Her mother was right. If Polly had known she was practicing climbing stairs, she'd have stopped her. She liked having Lillian an invalid because she couldn't get away when she was confined to her wheelchair. What a dismal statement that was about her.

The coin caught her attention by heating her palm until she

noticed. She looked down in surprise, wondering if it had just become warmer or if her imagination was carrying her away.

Then she grinned. "Are you trying to tell me there's no value in self-pity, coin?"

As if on cue, she felt an infinitesimal pulse against her palm. Shaking her head, torn between enchantment and concern, she murmured, "Maybe I'm just going crazy."

Then she decided to try an experiment. Squinching her eyes up to help her think, she tried to come up with a suitable test. After all, how did one examine an object to determine whether it contained magic? It was not a topic discussed in textbooks, in Polly's experience.

Now, let me see . . . She didn't want to ask for anything big. Eyeing the coin thoughtfully, she mused, "It seems to me that when I wish for things they don't come to me exactly as I would expect them to. Maybe you're a devious little coin."

After several more minutes of deep contemplation, she said, "I have it!" Clearing her throat, she sat up straighter on her bed and stared hard into her palm.

"If you're really a magic coin, let me see Dewey, Mr. Drayton's dog, tomorrow. Now, this sighting doesn't have to be anything dramatic; just let me see him."

She heaved a satisfied sigh. *There. That's not difficult, and I can't see how it can occasion harm to anybody. And it will be a splendid test.*

Pleased with herself, Polly snuggled under her quilts. She went to sleep with her coin clutched in her hand and tucked up under her head. Her dreams were full of happy wishes for her future. With James.

The very first thing James did when he left the MacNamara ladies was visit the Grant Street Police Station and file a formal complaint, as Polly MacNamara's attorney, against Lawrence Bullock. He was a little disgruntled to discover that Bullock had managed to bail himself out before he got there. He'd love to have given his former associate a stern lecture.

Sighing philosophically, he decided it couldn't be helped. And he still had lots to do today.

Raymond was in the process of unpacking his law books

and setting them on the shelves in his new office when James returned to the law firm.

"Sorry, James. So far my sources have come up completely dry."

"*All* of them?" James scowled at Raymond's back. This was bad—and strange—news indeed.

"All of them." With a large tome clutched in his hand, Raymond turned around. "I know this sounds suspicious— maybe even fantastic—but I swear, it's as though somebody's clamped a lid on the *China Seas* investigation."

James's scowl faded into bemusement. "But that's crazy, Raymond."

With a shrug, Raymond stuffed the volume onto his bookshelf. "I don't know what to tell you, James. Everywhere I looked, everybody I talked to, was shut up tight as an oyster. Some of them even started to say something and then clammed up, as though they just recalled they'd been told not to speak about it. I couldn't find out a single, solitary thing. Not one." He stooped to pick up another two books and frowned when he straightened up again. "It was very frustrating."

"Yes, I can see that it would be." James squatted down and began to help Raymond with his books. "I don't understand it."

"Neither do I."

In the comfort of the parlor in his mansion on Nob Hill, J. P. Drayton spoke into his telephone. An air of satisfaction hovered over him and imbued his cheeks with a ruddy glow. If one didn't know him for the Scrooge he was, a body might mistake him for Father Christmas himself. He chuckled, a sound so foreign in his household that his Chinese butler, setting out the brandy decanter, peered at him as if to ascertain whether or not he needed medical attention.

"Wonderful, wonderful," J. P. chortled into the receiver. "No. For heaven's sake, don't tell anything to a single soul. This is going to be the surprise of that damned insolent young pup's life."

A roar of laughter greeted the response he heard on the other end of the line. His butler, with a frightened glance at J. P., finished his work quickly and hurried out of the room. At the door, he cast one last look at his employer, shook his head in amazement, and scuttled out, making sure the door was securely closed.

His butler's behavior and expression of concern didn't escape J. P.'s attention, but he didn't care. For the first time in his life, he was having fun. And, as in his business affairs, he didn't plan to let anyone or anything interfere with it.

It took James a long time to fall asleep that night. Thoughts of Polly MacNamara bounced up against the puzzling fact of Raymond's thwarted attempt to gather information about *China Seas* until James's brain was in a muddle. He finally decided to set the *China Seas* mystery aside and concentrate on Polly, a much more pleasant occupation.

"She's wonderful," he murmured to Dewey who, much to his initial annoyance, insisted on sharing his gigantic bed.

He'd almost become used to his dog's nightly presence by this time, although he still had to nudge him every so often when the hound took to snoring. James figured Cynthia Ingram would have a fit if she ever saw a dog in his bed, but by this time he had a pretty shrewd notion that Cynthia Ingram would not be visiting his bedroom again.

Ideas of an entirely different—and infinitely more permanent—nature had begun to spin in James's head. They were ideas he'd never expected to entertain, and he found it necessary to tiptoe up to them carefully and examine them only obliquely. Otherwise, they scared the tar out of him.

"She likes children, too. And dogs." He poked Dewey with his big toe, and the dog sighed in his sleep. With a chuckle, James continued, "She even bestowed upon you a dignified pedigree, God save us all."

His laughter died. "But I wish to heaven I could find out something about her brother's ship. And there's still the matter of her father's death. I'll be damned if I won't see them compensated for that disaster."

A scowl carved two deep ruts in his forehead. "I'll see justice done there, if I have to dog my father's steps from now to eternity."

At the word *dog,* Dewey sighed in his sleep, lifted a paw, and slapped James on the leg, startling him. His dour mood broken, he shook his head in amusement and lifted his knee to dislodge his affectionate hound's paw.

"Good grief. If I *do* end up proposing to her, I'd better find you another place to sleep. She's no Cynthia Ingram, but even my sweet-natured Polly might object to sharing her bed with you, Admiral."

Dewey rolled over onto his back. The exercise lifted the flaps of his muzzle and made him appear to grin. James couldn't help laughing. Then he gave up thinking, turned off his fancy Edison electrical bedside lamp, pulled up his covers, and closed his eyes. Just before sleep claimed him, he decided to shock his entire household tomorrow and have his housekeeper decorate the mansion for Christmas.

He went to sleep with a smile on his lips. All night long he dreamed of Polly.

Chapter Thirteen

The next morning found Polly and her mother feeling cheerier than they had the day before. Polly scanned the early edition of the *Chronicle* while she and Lillian ate their breakfast. This Saturday morning was much more relaxed than usual, since Polly didn't have to hurry off to work.

"Do you see anything about Stephen's ship, dear?"

"No. Not a word, I'm afraid." Polly heaved a little sigh.

"Well, I expect they haven't found out anything more yet. I wonder if they ever will."

Polly's hand paid a brief visit to her charms. "I don't know. I hope so."

"I wonder if Mr. Drayton will be able to discover anything," Lillian murmured into her teacup.

Polly found herself smiling in spite of the painful topic of their conversation. "I don't know."

A dreamy mood overtook her, and she commenced to staring out the dining-room window, the newspaper forgotten in front of her. Thoughts of James Drayton floated gently through her head. Just think: In only another couple of weeks, she'd be dancing the night away in his arms. The notion made gooseflesh rise in the most embarrassing places.

A loud knock on the front door jolted her out of her pleasant daydream.

"Good heavens!" Lillian squinted at the clock on the sideboard. "Who on earth can that be?"

"I'll see, Mother. Don't trouble yourself about it." Polly shoved her chair away from the table.

Even though she knew she was merely indulging in idle fancies, her heart lifted at the idea that it might be James, come to pay a morning call. She told herself not to be ridiculous.

Still, her hope lasted until she opened the door to discover a uniformed messenger holding an official-looking envelope in his hand. Her spirits, which seconds before had been singing merrily, suddenly plummeted like a popped balloon.

"Special delivery." The man held the envelope out to her. *Oh, my God,* her heart cried, *Stephen's dead.*

Then her sensible nature asserted itself and told her to calm down; the navy always sent a chaplain to deliver news of that depressing nature. Nevertheless, her hand trembled when she took the envelope.

"Thank you."

The courier saluted smartly and left her holding the door, staring blankly after him.

"What is it, Polly?"

Her mother's voice jarred her and, with a shake to settle her nerves, Polly called, "It was a special messenger with an envelope, Mother." Polly scanned the envelope, searching for a return address. She saw nothing. "I don't know who it's from, but it's addressed to you."

"Special delivery?"

"Yes." Polly handed her mother the envelope and noticed that Lillian, too, seemed worried about what the envelope might contain.

"It's probably nothing, Mother."

Lillian peered up at her. " 'Nothing' via special delivery?"

Polly sat with a sigh. "No, I suppose not."

"Well, I'd better get it over with."

Lillian opened the envelope and pulled out several pieces of paper. She read one while Polly watched, on pins and needles with anticipation.

Then Lillian lifted her gaze and the utter incredulity on her face made Polly exclaim, "Good heavens, what is it?"

"I—I'm not altogether sure."

To Polly's intense frustration, Lillian dipped her head and re-read the paper. When she lifted her gaze again, Polly was on the verge of an unladylike shriek.

"It's from Mr. J. P. Drayton, Polly."

Polly stared at her mother in astonishment. "J. P. Drayton? The shipping magnate?"

"Yes." Lillian looked from the paper to her daughter and back again. "He says his son, James, just informed him of Franklin's death as a result of the accident on the *Golden Liberty.* He says he's terribly sorry my health precluded our taking advantage of the insurance settlements offered after the accident."

"His son *James!*" All at once Polly's world tilted. Her thoughts whirled. Then she thought: of course. Why hadn't she made the connection before? A pain began in her heart and spread until her chest felt as though it were being squeezed by fiery metal tongs.

Lillian held up another piece of paper, this one much smaller than the last. Her hand shook and Polly heard the paper rattle. "He enclosed a bank draft."

Polly took the draft from her mother's hand and read it. When she saw the amount scripted on the paper, her mouth dropped open and she stared, unable to believe the amount inscribed thereon in stark black and white.

"My God," she whispered. "My God."

Lillian cleared her throat. "He says—" She had to stop and swallow. When she spoke again, her words were thick. "He says he's included interest and also added a stipend by way of apology." Lillian nodded and blew her nose. "He says he never knew of our situation before, or he would have done something sooner."

For several moments, Polly just watched her mother, her brain spinning.

James Drayton. J. P. Drayton. James—her James—son of the powerful, rumored-to-be-brutally-sharp-and-hard-hearted shipping millionaire.

The pain in her chest pulsed and she frowned. What on earth was she thinking of? *Her* James? Not very likely.

All of her fragile fantasies shattered like glass, leaving her feeling empty. A wry smile curved her lips. It was almost funny. She'd fought those beautiful fantasies so hard. Only reluctantly—and with what she perceived as encouragement from James—had she allowed them freedom to blossom. And now the same stroke of fortune that would be the salvation of her family had blasted those delicate blossoms until they stood withered on their stalks, pallid and bloodless. Dead.

She felt like crying.

"I had no idea your employer was related to J. P. Drayton, Polly." Lillian sounded almost numb.

It was an effort for Polly to reply calmly, "No. No, I didn't know it either."

"Of course, we might have suspected by the name, I guess."

Polly stared into her teacup. "I guess."

But she hadn't suspected. Not a thing. Yet, all unsuspecting, she'd allowed herself to dream. If she'd known about his family connections, she never would have done such a foolish thing as dream.

Frowning, she recalled her mother inviting him to Thanksgiving dinner. Hadn't he said he had no family? Yes. She was sure he had. He'd lied to them. He'd *lied*.

Why on earth would he lie about something like that? It didn't make any sense.

Unless . . . With a stab of anguish, Polly remembered James Drayton's reputation with the ladies.

Suddenly she couldn't sit in the stuffy house any longer. She needed to be out in the cool, fresh autumn air so she could ponder her suspicions, unobserved.

"I believe I shall write to Mr. Drayton right this minute, Polly." Lillian's voice had still not regained its full timbre.

Undertaking a demeanor of happiness—after all, she should be happy; her family had just been saved from the clutches of grinding poverty—Polly rose from the table and borrowed a smile. "That's a wonderful idea, Mother. Would you like me to help you? I—I'd like to take a little walk first, if you don't mind. I need to think about—everything."

Lillian gave Polly a tender smile. "My dear, you just take your walk. I'm sure we both need to think." She stared at the draft in her fingers and her voice broke when she whispered, "Now, if only Stephen would come home, this would be the happiest Christmas ever."

Swallowing back her tears, Polly said, "Yes. Yes, indeed." Then she fled out the front door before she could burst out crying.

Still pulling on her coat, she began striding along the street, blindly kicking fallen leaves out of her path. Her eyes were so blurry she hardly saw the bare maples or the Christmas wreaths and boughs of holly people had begun to hang on their doors. Polly had always loved Christmas. Until today. Right now she felt hollow, the Christmas spirit and holiday joy as far away from her as her brother.

How could James lie to them that way? She'd believed—she'd honestly begun to believe—that he cared for her. If only a little bit.

Bitterness filled her heart. Perhaps he'd found her amusing. Maybe he'd tired of sophisticated ladies and decided to toy with a poor little typist for a change. An angry tear slid down her cheek and she wiped it away viciously. Her bare hands were cold. Her gloves resided in the pocket of her coat, but she wouldn't put them on, vowing to freeze to death first—although the likelihood of such a wretched fate seemed dim, given the weather. They'd come from *him*.

She didn't see the bulky, hulking form of Lawrence Bullock step out from behind a tree and begin to follow her. It wasn't until her steps began to flag and sorrow overtook her anger that she noticed him. She couldn't help it, since he grabbed her by her coat sleeve and yanked her around. Polly was so startled, she screamed.

"Shut up, you bitch! You got me arrested, damn you!" His step was unsteady, his expression malevolent.

Since she wore no gloves, Polly's slap sounded a loud, satisfying smack when it connected with his beefy cheek.

"How dare you! Let me go at once!"

"Be damned to you," yelled Bullock. "You damned little tart. Well, you might be James Drayton's little whore, but you're nothing to me but trouble."

"How dare you?" Polly shrilled once more, aiming another blow to Bullock's head and kicking at him for good measure.

He was big, though, and much stronger than she. With a vile curse, he restrained her by pinning her arms at her sides. Then he lifted her right up off the pavement, slung her lopsidedly over his shoulder, and began to stagger away.

"Put me down! Put me down this instant!"

"Be damned if I will! Damn you! I'll teach you to get *me* arrested."

Polly's head hung at an odd angle and she couldn't see much except the leafy sidewalk jolting along beneath her. Lifting her head as much as she could, she tried to scan her surroundings. She screamed again, a piercing, wordless noise that shattered the daylight.

Why didn't anybody come to her aid? Where was everyone? Dismally, she recalled the peculiarities of her neighborhood and realized her neighbors were probably at work or doing the weekly marketing on this crisp December Saturday morning. Oh, Lord.

All at once an unearthly roar ripped the air, and Polly's terror surged. She screamed again, this time with fright. An appalling growl followed the roar, bringing to her mind tales of grizzly bears and packs of bloodthirsty timber wolves. The awful noise came closer and closer until suddenly Bullock yelled. His bellow was filled with such horror, Polly could only squeeze her eyes shut and pray.

Then she didn't have time to be afraid, for she found herself slipping off Lawrence Bullock's shoulder and tumbling to the ground. With a good deal of arm-flapping and dancing, she managed to remain upright and not fall on her face. She was still teetering when she found herself grabbed and yanked around yet again this morning by two big strong hands.

"Polly!" she heard through the terrified screams of Lawrence Bullock and the increasingly furious growling noise. "Polly! What did that animal do to you?"

James Drayton steadied her and pulled her toward him,

195

away from the racket. But Polly's senses had been jerked about too much already in the last several seconds. Every nerve vibrated with alarm.

With a wild, *"No!"* she wrenched herself out of James's grasp and whirled around to see what was making that blood-curdling noise. "Oh, my God!"

Lawrence Bullock's sobs were a combination of pain and panic as he wrestled on the ground with Dewey. The hound, his formerly untried gallant nature having been stirred by Polly's distress, was doing his valiant best to slay Bullock. In the effort, he was attempting to locate Bullock's throat. Bullock had thrown his arm across that particularly vulnerable body part, and Dewey was chewing the fabric of his coat energetically. It looked to Polly as though he intended to chew through Bullock's wrist as well, and she turned to James and grabbed him by the lapels of his expensive overcoat with both hands, her heart slamming a crazy rhythm and her senses reeling.

"Oh, please, Mr. Drayton! Call him off! He's liable to kill Mr. Bullock."

James, whose heart was hammering, too, tore his gaze from Polly's face with difficulty and aimed it at Lawrence Bullock. Hate filled his being when he realized that Polly was right. An unchivalrous swell of triumph seized him.

"No," he snarled, feeling something like a knight of old might have felt as he watched a dragon eat his fair maiden's captor. "Let the dog have him. It's all he's fit for."

Horrified, Polly cried, "Oh, but James! Dewey will be destroyed if he kills Mr. Bullock. I'm sure the authorities will destroy him. We can't let that happen. Oh, the poor dog!"

Although he didn't like it, James recognized the reason in Polly's plea. Besides, she'd called him "James."

"Well, all right, then."

He grabbed the leash dangling from Dewey's collar and tugged hard. Without releasing his grip on Bullock's coat sleeve, Dewey found himself being dragged away from his prey. He didn't like it and turned to scowl at James. But in order to do so, he was obliged to let go of Bullock's sleeve.

"Come on, Dewey, we'll let the police take care of this bit

of trash.'' James glowered at Bullock as he said it.

Her rescue assured, Polly's terror gave way to rage. She stormed over to stand above Lawrence Bullock. He whimpered, hunched on the sidewalk, and peeked up at her with dread.

"You miserable coward!'' she cried. "You fiend! Why, you're no better than a toad. Worse! A toad would never try to kidnap a woman who's never done anything to it. You wretched excuse for a human being!''

Bullock groaned pitiably, his little round blue eyes a testament to his fright.

"Ooooh! I hope you *are* in pain, you fiend. I wish I could kick you!'' Bullock flinched away and she cried scornfully, "Oh, I won't do it. They say you're not supposed to kick an opponent while he's down.''

Her words tickled a thought, though, and she frowned when she added, "Although I don't know why not. You're too big and fat to kick when you're not down. Why, you're *twice* as big as I am, you horrible bully!''

Bullock tried to roll himself up into a ball. Then Polly said, "Oh, why not? That old saw was undoubtedly made by men for men, just like everything else in this stupid world!'' And she hauled her leather-clad foot back and kicked Bullock hard, on the shin.

Bullock yelped and struggled to his hands and knees, spurred on his way by James's, "Get up, you miserable coward. Get up and face *me*. I'll teach you to kidnap ladies off the street!''

It was unclear how James was going to deliver his lesson, since it was all he could do to keep Dewey in check. He longed to fight the miserable villain, though, right here, right now. He ached to avenge Polly.

Staggering to his feet, Bullock blubbered, "No! No! I'll go 'way. I won't do it anymore! Please.''

Polly looked at him with utter contempt. "Why, you sniveling brute. I do believe you're inebriated again, too. You're a *fine* excuse for a man, aren't you?''

Her gazed scorched Bullock up and down and he backed away from her. Unfortunately for him, that put him within

Emma Craig

Dewey's orbit again. The hound, with a mighty growl, lunged at his heel, grabbing his trouser cuff in powerful jaws.

"No, Dewey!" James commanded.

As usual, Dewey paid no heed to his master. He whipped his head back and forth in a frenzy of joy, Bullock's shod foot going along for the ride since he couldn't draw his trousers out of the dog's mouth while still wearing them.

With an inarticulate screech, Bullock tugged with all his might. The fabric of his trousers gave way with a loud rip. Suddenly Dewey found himself flapping a piece of empty cloth in his teeth. Lawrence Bullock's foot, at the end of his white, hairy leg, naked from the knee down, hit the sidewalk. Apparently taking it for a sign, the scoundrel sobbed once and began to run away.

James glared after him, then looked at Polly. Her breasts heaved with exertion and anger. Two brilliant patches of red shone on her cheeks, and her eyes snapped fire. She was absolutely glorious.

With difficulty, James kept his mind on business and asked, "Do you have a telephone, Polly? We can call the police."

She seemed to find such a prosaic question inappropriate and glowered when she barked, "No. We could never afford such a luxury."

Staring down the street, she watched the erratic escape of Lawrence Bullock. A smile curled her lips and then faded. Lawrence Bullock was a brute and a bully, but he had just lost his job. Although Polly could think of no real justification for his having assaulted her—twice—on public streets, she did begin to feel a thread of compassion twine itself around her anger and justifiable indignation. Bullock was a bumbler and a weakling, but she didn't suppose he was evil. Exactly. More misguided, perhaps. She frowned, wondering if there was a difference. The result was the same, and always seemed to end with her. She didn't understand it.

Then she remembered something. All thoughts of Lawrence Bullock faded, and Polly whirled around to face James and Dewey. By this time the dog had settled down on the sidewalk and was contenting himself with eating Bullock's trouser cuff.

James felt an unsettling premonition as he watched Polly.

198

She looked furious, and this time her mood seemed directed at him.

"At least we couldn't afford it until this morning," she amended, anger swelling her voice. Then she took James completely by surprise. "You *lied* to us!"

James, who had expected her to throw herself into his arms in gratitude, could only stammer, "Wh-what?"

"You lied to us!"

She whirled away and began to dash back toward her home. For a dumbfounded second or two, James could only stare after her, his sense of order in the universe having been knocked cockeyed by her anger.

"What the hell . . . ? Come on, Dewey. We've got to get to her before she makes it to her house."

It took a tug or two, but James ultimately managed to get his hound to give up chewing his victory prize and run alongside him as he pursued Polly. Dewey didn't relinquish his trophy entirely. It fluttered out behind him, a streamer proclaiming his mastery over a fallen foe.

"Polly! Polly, wait! What are you talking about?"

By this time, the few MacNamara neighbors who were home on this crisp Saturday morning had begun to peek out their windows and open doors to determine what was going on in their normally quiet neighborhood. James saw them, cursed under his breath, and speeded up his pursuit.

He caught Polly about a house or two away from her own. Since he wanted to talk to her alone and she didn't seem inclined to stand still and listen to him, he reached out and, very much as Lawrence Bullock had done earlier, grabbed her by the coat sleeve and jerked her around.

"Polly—" was all he managed to get out before Polly, just as she'd done with Lawrence Bullock, slapped him on the cheek. Hard.

"Ow!" James wanted to coddle his burning cheek with his hand but didn't dare let go of her to do so. He contented himself with saying in a lamentably bemused voice, "What did you do that for, Polly?"

She'd begun to cry, a circumstance James guessed he might have understood if she were still under the influence of Bullock's villainy. But these tears seemed somehow connected with him, and they bewildered him.

"You lied to us," she cried again. "You lied to us."

Although he didn't dare let go of Dewey's leash, James tried to put an arm around Polly to ease her distress, whatever it was. She resisted so fiercely that he gave up. He did not, however, relinquish his hold on her coat sleeve.

"Polly, please tell me what's wrong. Why do you think I lied to you? I've never lied to you. Honestly, I'd never do such a thing."

She shook her head hard, and James began to entertain the unhappy suspicion that she was hysterical. Oh, Lord.

"You did!"

With a huge sigh, he said, "Please, Polly. Please. Let's sit down on the porch steps and talk for a minute. I can't recollect ever having lied to you. Please tell me what you mean, so I can understand."

"Oh, you wretch. And here I thought you liked us. I thought you liked *me!* But no. You were merely playing a devil's game with me, the poor little typewriting wench."

Perplexity began to give way to irritation. With a glance up the street, James noticed a scattering of interested spectators peeking out of their houses at them. A little roughly, he dragged Polly to her porch steps.

"Sit down, Polly."

"I don't want to sit with you!"

"Damn it, Polly, quit screeching. Everybody's watching us. They'll have the police drag *me* away pretty soon, and it was Bullock who kidnapped you!"

"Good!"

But she, too, glanced at her neighbors. James saw her cheeks heat up again, he presumed with embarrassment. Thank God. If *he* couldn't get her to shut up and explain things to him, maybe the fear of public humiliation would.

He managed to get her to sit down. Dewey immediately flopped at her feet and laid his big hairy head in her lap. She took a hicuppy breath and begin to pet the hound. Relieved, James sat down next to her. Still, he held on to her coat sleeve for insurance.

"Now, will you please tell me why you keep saying I lied to you, Polly?"

Polly shot him a wicked look. "My name is *Miss Mac-Namara,* Mr. Drayton."

James let out a disgruntled sigh. "Miss MacNamara."

For several moments Polly stroked Dewey's head and said nothing. Her shoulders heaved every now and then when a sob shook her. James began to wonder if he was supposed to discern through second sight why she was so mad at him. He'd heard women did things like this—made you figure out, without offering clues, what you'd done to upset them—but he'd never expected Polly MacNamara to be so contrary.

Just when he decided he was going to have to drag it out of her syllable by syllable, Polly said stiffly, "You told us you have no family."

Puzzled, James said, "That's not a lie. I have no family. My mother died shortly after I was born."

Polly turned on him as if she'd just discovered him to be Jack the Ripper, moved from Whitechapel to San Francisco for the express purpose of plaguing her. "Hah! And what about your *father,* Mr. James Drayton? What about *him?*"

James's compressed his lips and narrowed his gaze. His father? Was all this hysteria about his father?

"My father is still living." Coldness congealed the words into hard icy lumps.

"Hah!"

She began to dig into her pocket, James suspected for a handkerchief. She withdrew a glove—one of the brand-new, ten-dollar kidskin gloves he'd bought especially for her from I. Magnin—glared at it, and stuffed it back in. Absently, he whipped out his pocket handkerchief and handed it to her.

"Thank you," she said rigidly and snatched the handkerchief and blew her nose.

Frowning, James said, "Polly, I broke connections with my father almost ten years ago. Until a couple of weeks or so ago, I hadn't spoken to him in six years."

With the handkerchief pressed to her cheek, Polly eyed him suspiciously. Her eyes still swam with tears, her nose was a bright cherry pink, and her normally porcelain skin looked blotchy. James longed to draw her sweet body to him and give her a measure of comfort, but he didn't dare. Yet.

He drew in a deep breath. "My father is a hard, unscrupulous businessman. He hated it when I objected to his business practices. He hated it even more when I chose the legal profession over his shipping concern, but I had to get away from him and his ways. He's—he's a monster, Polly."

Slowly, the handkerchief dropped. Polly looked as though she wasn't going to bolt, so James dared let go of her coat sleeve. His hand was beginning to cramp. He took her expression of interest for a signal that he should continue.

"My father's philosophy has always been to succeed at any cost. As I grew up, I realized the cost was always to others. He ruined people with no more compunction than you or I would feel for an ant we happened to step on. I couldn't live like that, Polly."

"Really?" Her voice was small, scratchy.

"Really." Another deep breath fortified James to continue. "After I went to law school, I tried to maintain a relationship with him, but he wouldn't let me be. He kept trying to draw me into his business, to make me work for him. Well, I couldn't work the way he demanded, with no regard for the welfare of others, so six years ago I finally broke away completely. I couldn't take any more of his pressure.

"I worked hard and made my own way, without my father's help or support. I won't say that his name didn't help, because I'm sure it did, but my own code of ethics would never allow me to treat others the way my father does. I made my way honestly, and without destroying other people in the process."

Another peek convinced him that Polly wasn't going anywhere. She seemed fascinated by his depressing narrative.

"I don't advertise the fact, Polly, and I would be pleased if you wouldn't, either, but I have tried over the years to make up in some small way for the damage my father has done to innocent people during his rise to riches. My experiment with the Sisters of Benevolence is an example."

A brief period of silence followed James's confession. After a moment or two, Polly asked in a near whisper, "Do you honestly believe him to be all bad, James?"

After a moment required to think, he said, "Yes. Yes, I do." He looked at her steadily and strove to put the sincerity he felt into the words he uttered. "I didn't mean to lie to you, Polly. It's just that I consider myself to be without a family. As I said, until a couple of weeks ago, I hadn't talked to J. P. Drayton in years."

"What—what happened a couple of weeks ago?"

"He came to my office and asked if my law firm would represent his shipping business."

"What did you say?"

Surprised, James exclaimed, "What did I *say*? Why, I said no. For heaven's sake, I don't want anything to do with that miserable, cruel old man!"

"You don't think he came to you to make peace?"

"Not on a bet."

"Are you sure?"

"Absolutely."

"Oh, James, don't you think you should give him another chance? I'm sure he came to you to make amends."

"You don't know him," he said sharply. With difficulty, he suppressed the jolt of anger her words had provoked. "You don't know him, Polly. He just wanted to get me under his thumb again."

"Are you sure? Absolutely sure?"

For some reason, he didn't want to look at her when he answered, "Yes." His heart gave an enormous plunge on the word.

"Oh, James," Polly whispered. "I'm so sorry. How sad for you both."

Chapter Fourteen

As much as James wanted Polly's understanding, he disliked hearing the pity in her voice even more. He almost flinched when she put her hand on his arm and said, "Oh, James, I had no idea."

"Well, it's not a worldwide catastrophe, Polly. It's only a schism between a father and a son. Worse things happen every day." He sounded terribly cynical.

"Oh, but James, think of it. It's a catastrophe in *your* world. You're all the family the both of you have, and you don't even speak to each other." Polly shook her head sadly. "When you might be each other's solace, give one another love and comfort, you each have nobody."

Enough of this maudlin nonsense, James thought irritably. "It's not like that."

She lifted her head and her gaze met his. He couldn't maintain her honest scrutiny and turned to scan the street. Thank God they no longer had an audience. Why was it that all of his encounters with Polly seemed to take place on public streets? James, who disliked public displays, found the fact extremely aggravating.

"And at Christmas, too. Oh, James, I'm so sorry." Polly's voice made him hunch up as he tried to ward off the emotions that threatened to escape the prison into which he'd stuffed them so many years before.

"Christmas is just one more day in the year." James chose to ignore the memories of a little boy who longed to sit on his father's lap and sing Christmas songs. Of course, he'd never dared. Long ago, those childish needs had hardened into a demeanor of world-weariness fostered to keep the world at bay so that it couldn't disappoint him, too. "People make a big thing of it, but it's just another day."

"It's not!"

James winced again.

"Oh, no, James. Christmas is a wonderful time. It's a time of love and joy and forgiveness. And families and friends and closeness. One shouldn't be estranged from one's family at Christmas time, of all times."

He cleared his throat, an angry sound that tore through the feelings lumping up around them. "Nonsense," he said, his voice hard and crisp. "Not all of us are blessed with close families. It's nothing to do with the season."

Polly didn't say anything, but he knew she didn't believe him; that she believed him to be deprived somehow. Him! Of all people. And her! To feel sorry for him, a man who had wealth she couldn't even dream of. Polly MacNamara—what had she called herself? A poor little typewriting wench? Feeling sorry for him, James Drayton. It was ludicrous. Laughable.

James didn't feel like laughing, though, and the fact disturbed him.

"And here I thought you were deliberately withholding information from us." She sounded even sadder now, and James turned toward her, annoyed.

"Now, why would I do that?"

She shrugged. "To lure me into your snare, I thought." Her confession came out almost casually, as though it didn't matter anymore.

It mattered to James. "To *what?*" His roar startled both Polly and Dewey, who lifted his head from Polly's lap to direct a soft growl at him.

205

Polly at least had the grace to look embarrassed. "Well, you know. You have such a reputation. I—I thought you wanted to dally with me for your amusement. Because I'd be such a departure from the rich, sophisticated ladies you usually see."

James knew it was irrational, but fury rose in him, hot and painful. He wanted to yell at her for believing the pretense he'd gone to such great pains to encourage.

"I see. Well, it's nice to know what you think of me, at any rate." The hurt he heard in his voice bothered him.

"I don't think it anymore," she said softly. "Truly, I don't."

"Good." Relief washed over him and he couldn't be scathing, although he wanted to be.

"But, James, don't you think you're being a little hard on your father?"

Oh, good heavens, now they were back to his father. First she demolished his character and now she was harping on his rotten old man. James wasn't sure he could stand it.

"No," he said shortly. "I don't."

"I'm sorry to hear it. You know, people can change. Maybe he's changed. He's getting older. Maybe he wants another chance."

"Good grief."

"But you're his only son, James. His only relative. And he's your only relative. You only get one father in this life, you know."

Aggravated beyond endurance, James surged from the cold porch step and took an agitated turn in front of Polly, his hands jammed into his overcoat pocket. "You don't know him. You have absolutely no idea what a ruthless son of a bi—buzzard he is."

He stopped still and glared down at her. "It was his ship that killed your father, Polly. Your *only* father. Did you know that about *my* sainted father?"

Her sad little nod completely flabbergasted him. His mouth dropped open. "You did?"

She nodded again. "Just this morning."

"This morning?"

"Yes."

Recovering his composure with an effort, James rasped, "Well, do you know how it happened? How he hired a drunkard who staged a race between *Golden Liberty* and another ship, who taxed his vessel so far that a boiler blew up and killed your father? Left your mother an invalid? And all for the sake of saving a few paltry dollars. Eleven people died because my father wouldn't pay the salary to hire a competent captain or keep his ship in repair!"

"Perhaps you're being too hard on him, James," Polly said gently. "I've never seen you be unkind before."

"Unkind? *Me* unkind?"

His voice had risen and he stopped talking, unwilling to shout on a public street. They'd already given Pacific Avenue quite a show this morning; he wasn't about to make a fool of himself for the amusement of Polly's neighbors.

She reached out to him, as though she wanted to offer him a dose of solace, but he jerked back from her touch. He didn't want her damned sympathy; he wanted her to see reason. For heaven's sake, his father was a monster! He watched her hand drop to Dewey's head and felt, irrationally, as though his last hope had just deserted him.

Livid, he said, "I can't believe what I'm hearing. You're telling me I'm being unkind to the man who killed your father, who has never felt a drop of compassion for another human being in his life? I come over here to see how you're faring, to tell you how my investigation into your brother's ship is coming along. I find you being accosted by a villain and sic my dog on him. Then you vilify my character and yell at me for lying to you. And now you try to tell me I—*I*—am being unkind to my father. My father, the vilest man on the face of the earth."

He turned away and ran a hand through his hair. "I can't believe it. I simply can't believe it!"

"Oh, James, I'm so sorry."

He jumped when he felt her hands settle on his shoulders.

"I'm so sorry. I don't know anything about your father. Or you. It just hurts me to hear the unhappiness in your voice when you speak of him."

Her hands felt warm even through the thickness of his overcoat. He wanted to turn around and take her in his arms; to kiss her as she'd never been kissed before; to feel her body against his; to lose himself in her.

But he was a civilized man in a civilized city, and he wouldn't do it. Damn the constraints of society.

He felt Dewey bump his leg and absently reached down to pat his head. His throat felt tight and he had to force himself to speak. "How did you discover that J. P. Drayton was my father?"

"Mother and I got a special delivery letter this morning. It contained a letter from him and a—a bank draft." Her voice almost gave out when she said, "It was a bank draft for a—for an enormous sum of money."

"What?" Incredulous, James turned and took Polly's hands in his.

He knew there was some mistake. There must be. J. P. Drayton was not the sort of man to make amends. How could he be, when he never acknowledged culpability for any of the evils he perpetrated? It must be a joke or—no. Somebody else must have found out about Polly's plight and sent the draft. Some secret benefactor. Some—no.

The whole thing was impossible.

"Are you sure the letter came from my father, Polly?"

"Yes."

"Was the letter signed? Maybe it's a mistake. Maybe it's some sort of vile joke. Maybe—" James ran out of possible alternatives just when Polly shook her head.

"It was a letter signed by him, James. Anyway, who else would do such a thing?"

"But that's just the point, Polly. *Anybody* would do such a thing before he would. Hell, he practically scoffed at me when I told him about you and your mother."

Her smile, when it happened, was so soft and beautiful that James could barely look at it. It was a smile that spoke almost painfully of love and gratitude.

"I guess he stopped scoffing after you left, James."

He turned around, unable to withstand the purity of Polly's

expression. He still didn't believe it. He *couldn't* believe it. If J. P. Drayton had actually—really and truly—made amends for a wrong he had done, there must be a trick involved. There had to be a catch.

With his back to her, James asked, "Did he make any demands? Request your silence? Anything of that nature?"

"No."

He turned around again and demanded curtly, "Are you certain of that, Polly?"

"Well, you're welcome to read the letter yourself, James. I'm sure my mother will be happy to see you."

As if to make up for her prior expression of doubt about his morals, Polly added, "It was very sweet of you to come by this morning to see how we're doing. And I truly appreciate being rescued from that awful man."

James waved away both her apology and her thanks. He wanted to see that damned letter. There had to be a mistake.

"Thank you. I should be happy to read the letter, if you don't mind."

"Of course."

Neither of them spoke again until they were seated in the MacNamara parlor. Then Polly excused herself to make tea. James gritted his teeth and managed to endure Lillian's effusive thanks. When she offered him the letter from his father, it was all he could do to keep from snatching it out of her hands.

First he scrutinized the signature, searching for hints of forgery. There were none. Then he read the letter carefully twice, and yet a third time, dissecting its every phrase, searching for hidden catches in the text. Again, he found none.

When he lifted his gaze at last, Polly had returned to the parlor with tea, and James was filled with an almost overwhelming sense of confusion.

"I don't understand it."

Lillian looked at him oddly. "You mean there are legal ramifications I didn't discern, Mr. Drayton? The letter seemed quite straightforward to me; but then I'm not versed in legal phraseology."

Surprised, James turned toward her. "I beg your pardon?"

"Mr. Drayton believes his father to be an unscrupulous man, Mother. He is surprised that J. P. Drayton has made this compensatory gesture. I believe that's what he doesn't understand."

"Oh." Lillian looked profoundly shocked.

Polly gave James a kind smile, and James found himself wanting to yell at her, to shake her, to make her understand. The sudden thought struck him that maybe this was his father's latest plot: since he'd failed to get James's submission, J. P. now planned to turn the only woman he'd ever loved against him.

"I'm so sorry to hear that, Mr. Drayton," Lillian murmured.

"It's nothing," James said curtly. Then he sighed and said apologetically, "I'm sorry, Mrs. MacNamara. This whole situation is beyond my comprehension. If it's true—and it seems to be—I am certainly glad for you both."

Good Lord. It seemed to him that all his life he'd longed for his father to behave in just such a manner as this. And now that he had, James not only couldn't make himself believe it, he felt somehow betrayed by his father's gesture. He didn't understand it. Surely he wasn't so mean-spirited as to resent his father's helping these two women. Was he?

Turning toward Polly, he tried to smile when he asked, "And will the draft he enclosed be enough to negate your having to work so hard for a living, Miss MacNamara? If it will, I confess it will go hard on my law firm if you leave us, although I will, of course, be happy for you."

An ungentlemanly flood of bitter satisfaction assailed him at Polly's shocked expression. So she hadn't begun to consider all the consequences of his father's saintly gesture, had she? James wasn't surprised.

"I don't know, Mr. Drayton. I—well, I haven't had a chance to think about it yet. I guess." She gave him a bewildered look, then turned toward her mother, as if hoping to find an answer from that quarter.

Lillian smiled from her seat at the little writing desk in the parlor. She hadn't moved from her seat since James had entered the room, and for the first time he realized her wheelchair was nowhere in sight. Good heavens.

"Mrs. MacNamara, did you walk into this room?"

"What?"

Taken aback by the shock in Polly's voice, James turned his attention from Lillian to Polly. He noted that Polly's cheeks had gone pale and wondered, not for the first time, how much of her own worth Polly gained from serving her mother. As much as he gained from righting his villainous father's wrongs? It bore thinking about.

Lillian gave her daughter a sheepish grin. "Please don't scold me, Polly. It's not far from the dining room to this little desk, and I've been trying to practice my walking as much as possible. This morning practicing seemed especially appropriate in light of the good fortune already visited on us."

James saw Polly swallow before she said, "How—how wonderful. That's wonderful, Mother."

James decided he didn't care to sit here and puzzle out Polly's reaction to her mother's news. However much he enjoyed a mystery, this morning had already been too full of them for his taste. He rose from his chair.

"Thank you for your hospitality, ladies, but I believe Dewey and I should be off now. I have a business to run, after all. I'm very happy for your good fortune, although I find it—" He struggled for an appropriate word and finally settled on, "—incredible."

Polly stood, too, and looked contrite. "Thank you for coming, Mr. Drayton. And—well, I didn't mean to say anything to upset you."

"No. No, that's quite all right, Miss MacNamara." In truth, James had never been so ruffled, and his usual urbane manner was straining at the seams. "But I truly do have lots of work to do."

"Please thank your father for us, Mr. Drayton. I was just writing him a letter when you paid your call, but please thank him for us." Lillian smiled up at him.

James couldn't think of a single thing to say.

Polly murmured, "I don't believe the Draytons have much to do with each other, Mother."

James wanted to hit something when Lillian looked surprised and said, "Oh! Oh, I'm so sorry, Mr. Drayton. I had no idea things were so bad between you. I . . ." Her words drifted off and she looked disconcerted.

Groping almost desperately for his society manners, James pasted on his patented smile and said, "It's quite all right, Mrs. MacNamara. Please don't be embarrassed. The truth is, I did speak with my father about you lovely ladies. And, although I find myself enormously surprised because he didn't seem receptive at the time, I'm glad he did the right thing."

"Well," said Lillian, "we do thank you both, very much."

James offered her a glittering parting smile and a little bow.

"I'll see you to the door, Mr. Drayton."

Although he did not want Polly's company at the moment, James said, "Thank you."

At the door, she took him by the arm. "James, please don't be angry. I guess it's difficult for my mother and me to understand the feelings you have for your father." She bowed her head. "My own family is so precious to me, it's hard for me to imagine someone choosing to sever such relationships."

"Yes, well, not all of us are as lucky in our families as you are, Polly."

He knew she watched him long after he and Dewey had descended her porch steps and begun to walk away. It wasn't until he turned the corner onto Grant that he realized how ludicrous his last statement had been.

Cynthia Ingram had never visited James in his law office before. As the door opened to admit her, he almost groaned when he saw who had invaded his misery.

Damn. He wanted to sulk some more; to puzzle out his odd reaction to his father's generosity; to consider why it—yes, he admitted it to himself in the privacy of his office—frightened him so damned much. He didn't need this sultry creature interrupting his gloom. He summoned a smile from somewhere and lent it to her.

"My, my, Cynthia. What brings you here?" He almost achieved the lighthearted, irreverent tone that had once come so naturally to him. Before he met Polly and began to care about things other than Chinese criminals and vague, impersonal societal wrongs.

"Hello, James, darling." Cynthia even made door-closing provocative. "I'm surprised there's no secretary out there to block my entry. Do you allow just anybody to enter these sacred portals?"

Her smile glittered. It annoyed James and he snapped, "I sacked him, Cynthia. Darling." His voice curdled on the last word.

"Oh, my, how brutal you are, my love."

Cynthia seemed to slither to his desk. James eyed her with distaste. Why had he never noticed before the way Cynthia's every movement, every gesture, was aimed at seduction. He told himself he was being silly. Of course he'd noticed before. That's why she and he were lovers, for heaven's sake. Had been lovers. Once.

"Well, James, since you seem to have deserted me, I decided I'd just have to visit you in your lair."

The way she mouthed *lair* made it sound as though she considered his business office a den of iniquity. James felt his grin slipping. "Don't be absurd, sweetheart."

"Am I?" Cynthia picked up the paperweight James had thrown at Lawrence Bullock's head and ran a gloved finger over the nick in its polished surface.

"Of course." His annoyance came out in the words, and James was peeved with himself.

Cynthia sat on one of James's specially upholstered chairs as though the mundane act of sitting were a prelude to the act of love. "But darling, you haven't called me on the telephone or dropped by to see me for simply ages." Her pout was perfection itself.

"Don't be silly," he spat. Then he reined in his irritation and sighed. "I've been very busy, Cynthia."

"I see." Cynthia's sapphire eyes appraised him candidly. "Well, James, my love, I do value our—association. But if you've found another playmate—"

"Don't be absurd, Cynthia." He rapped out his disclaimer too quickly and with too much force, and he knew she knew he was lying. He sighed again and wondered where his famous detachment had hidden itself.

Her smile mocked him. "Well, my dear, since you haven't

seen fit to telephone me or return my calls, I decided to visit you and ask whether you plan to attend the grand charity ball on Christmas Eve.''

Suddenly on the alert, James eyed her sharply. "I do plan to attend the function, Cynthia, but I don't believe you and I ever discussed it before.''

With a sly, slanting look from under her lush lashes, Cynthia murmured, "No, I don't believe we ever did, James. But I wanted to determine exactly how the wind blew with us before I accepted another gentleman's kind offer of escort.''

Still wary, James murmured, "That was nice of you, Cynthia. I believe you may accept the other gentleman's offer with a clear conscience, however, as I have made other plans.''

"I see.''

Her eyes seemed to harden as James watched. They were sharp as diamond facets when she said, "You seem to have made other plans quite often lately, my sweet.''

Suddenly sick of Cynthia and everything she stood for— including his former way of life—James stood abruptly. "Yes, I have, Cynthia. And I expect I shall continue to make other plans in the future, as well.''

Cynthia's lips tightened. "I see. Well, James, I can't say I'm glad to hear it. We had a good time together, you and I.'' She held out a gloved hand and smiled.

Her smile looked grim. James could see tight little lines radiating from her pinched lips. He took her hand.

"I hope we can still be friends, James.''

"Thank you, Cynthia. I appreciate your understanding.''

"Oh, I don't understand at all, darling, but you've been most generous and I do care for you.''

"Thank you, Cynthia,'' he said dryly.

He saw her to the door, silently cursing himself for ever having become entangled with her. Then he walked slowly back to his desk, sat, and resumed brooding.

Polly's thoughts were in such a jumble, she found it impossible to hold on to one of them long enough to reach a sensible conclusion about it before another one bumped it out of the way.

What an incredible morning.

Their financial problems were over.

Lawrence Bullock had actually tried to kidnap her!

And she'd been rescued by James and Dewey.

She needed to file a police report. Had James already done so? Should she ask him? Did she dare?

James Drayton was the son of J. P. Drayton. And they apparently hated each other.

She needed to thank J. P. Drayton. Oh, she knew her mother had written to him, but she felt the need to thank him personally.

Why? Why did she want to do such a thing?

Her motives were murky to her, and she shook her head. Immediately thoughts of thanks were nudged aside by another incredible fact.

Her mother was walking. Walking! She was actually walking.

Pretty soon she wouldn't need Polly at all. A shudder made Polly's feet speed up until she was almost running down the sidewalk.

Would she keep her job?

And the ball. The charity ball. Good heavens, what should she do about that? Nothing? Something? Had anything changed between James and herself? Was there anything between them to change?

She'd barely been able to help her mother back into her wheelchair before she felt compelled to flee the stuffy house for the second time that morning. And she'd made a botch of helping her into the chair, too, fumbling, stuttering, wondering if she should offer, wondering if it would upset her mother if she didn't.

Ultimately, Lillian had asked for her assistance, and Polly had given it silently, unable to think of a thing to say.

And then there was the coin. Her coin. Her *magic* coin?

The facts remained, though, and spoke louder than words. After wishing on her coin last night, she'd seen Dewey today. She hadn't asked for anything dramatic, but—

And Stephen was still missing.

Emma Craig

Oh, Lord.

Polly raced down Pacific Avenue, heading like a bee to its hive, toward the Sisters of Benevolence's orphanage on Grant and Rampart.

Chapter Fifteen

"Why, Polly! Whatever are you doing here on a Saturday morning?"

Mother Francis Mary looked up in astonishment from what she'd been writing. Polly could barely see her dear black-and-white head over the huge pile of papers on her desk. She had time to register surprise that it was still morning before she burst into tears and sank onto the hard chair across from the Mother Superior's desk.

She realized she was dabbing at her eyes with a kidskin glove just as Mother Francis Mary handed her a white linen handkerchief. "Th-thank you."

Polly appreciated the nun's hand on her shoulder as much as her affectionate smile. Making a monumental effort to get her ragged emotions under control, she sucked in a shuddering breath.

"Are you all right, my dear?"

"Yes. Yes, I think so. Thank you."

"Do you want to talk about it, Polly? I presume that's why you came to visit."

The Mother Superior waited by her side until Polly said,

"Yes. If you have a moment or two, I need to talk to somebody and—and I have no friends."

She made the confession in a bleak little voice and felt ashamed of its truth. But it was the truth. She'd managed to hide herself so effectively behind the facade of wage-earner and mother's-helper these last six years that she counted Marcus O'Leary and Mother Francis Mary as her only true friends. Of the two, she could talk of personal things only with the Mother Superior.

Even as she felt a rush of tenderness for the nun, she realized her friendless condition was a telling statement about herself. And she didn't like what it told. Martyrdom made a cold companion indeed.

"Well, my dear, you just sit still and compose yourself for a minute while I get us a nice cup of tea." Mother Francis Mary patted Polly's shoulder and left the room.

Polly looked around the office. It was a cheerful, cluttered room, with papers and religious icons nestled next to one another on the desk. Pictures of Jesus and the Blessed Virgin Mary shared wall space with photographs and letters from orphans who had lived here over the years.

One missive, sent ten years earlier, expressed gratitude for the Sisters of Benevolence's kind offices during the letter writer's formative years, and credited the Sisters with his success. Polly stared in amazement at the signature, for it was that of Sien Luke Chang, her father's old business associate Uncle Chang. Imagine that!

She didn't hear the door open and started when she heard the nun's creaky voice ask, "Are you feeling better now, dear?" Polly jumped up from her chair to help with the tea things.

"Yes. Thank you." Embarrassed, she added, "I'm sorry for my outburst, Mother. It's just been such a—such an amazing morning. My nerves are skipping."

"Well, you just sit down and tell me all about it," Mother Francis Mary said, pouring out a cup of tea and handing it to Polly. "That's what I'm here for."

"It is? But I'm not even Catholic." Polly felt stupid when she heard herself.

Her companion didn't seem to mind. In fact, her rusty laugh gave Polly the impression that the question had been expected.

"Indeed it is, my dear. I'm here for all of God's creatures. Even non-Catholic typists need a sympathetic shoulder to cry on every now and then." With a queer little sideways look, she added, "Or so I've been led to understand."

"Thank you very much."

After a sustaining sip of tea, Polly plunged into her morning's tale. She began at the beginning, since to do otherwise would lead a short path to chaos, given her unsettled nerves.

The old nun breathed a pleased, "My goodness!" when Polly told her about J. P. Drayton's letter and bank draft.

"Yes. It's a lot of money, Mother."

"Indeed, it is. I expect you won't have to work your fingers to the bone typing for a living any longer, my dear."

Although she had been staring into her teacup, wondering how one went about reading tea leaves, Polly jerked up her head. "I—I don't know. That's what Mr. Drayton said, too."

"Did he now?"

"Yes."

"Ah."

Polly didn't know what to make of that "Ah," any more than she knew what to make of her feelings about her job. For four years now, she had taken great pride in her ability to earn her mother's keep and her own. Earning her living in a world notorious for its unkindness to women and being her mother's nursemaid were all she knew how to do. It was how she defined herself. Now, at the stroke of J. P. Drayton's pen, both occupations seemed to be slipping away from her.

With a little shake of her head, Polly decided she would think about all that later.

Mother Francis Mary's eyes opened suitably wide as Polly told her about Lawrence Bullock's perfidy. The nun's disapprobation melted into pleasure at James Drayton's timely arrival, and she laughed when apprised of his noble hound's derring-do. "Might have known that lad would own an heroic canine," she said with a chuckle.

"Oh," Polly cried—too quickly, she later thought—"do you know him?"

219

"James Drayton's dog?" Mother Francis Mary peered at Polly over her stack of papers. "No. Can't say that I do, dear."

"No." Polly cleared her throat and took another sip of tea. "No, I meant Mr. Drayton. Do you know him?"

The nun's thousand wrinkles crinkled into a smile that seemed to take up her whole face. "Oh, my goodness, yes, dear. I know James Drayton."

"I—I believe he and Mr. Sing, his new associate, are conducting an experiment here?"

As a spy, Polly guessed she'd be a miserable failure if Mother Francis Mary's sly twinkle was anything by which to judge.

"Ah, yes, Mr. Drayton and his Chinese criminals. Indeed, I do know him, Polly." The old nun's wrinkles bent again, this time into a mock frown. "Such a serious young man he is, too, as he sets about to right the world's wrongs."

"Or his father's," murmured Polly. Her heart gave an odd twist.

The Mother Superior gave her another sparkling look. "Of course."

Polly looked at the nun hard. "You—do you know about James and his father's estrangement?"

"I know what he's told me, my dear." The old nun sighed. "He truly understands his father to be some kind of evil being, I believe. And I'm sure he has his reasons."

Her amused smile didn't seem to go with her words, and Polly felt confused, as though she wasn't in on a secret everybody else knew. "I'm sure he does."

"And what else has happened to upset your composure, my dear?"

"Well, when we got the letter from J. P. Drayton this morning, it was the first indication we'd ever been given that James is his son. I—" She licked her lips. "I guess I felt betrayed."

It sounded silly when said aloud in Mother Francis Mary's messy office. Polly felt her cheeks burn and, since the Mother Superior did not make an immediate comment, she rushed to explain.

"I mean, I don't suppose he owed us any explanations, but

when he brought us the goose for Thanksgiving and Mother invited him to dine, he said he had no family." She was staring intently into her teacup and feeling like a fool when she said in a small voice, "I thought he'd lied to us."

Polly peeked at the nun to find her taking a delicate sip of tea. When she put the cup back in its saucer and looked at Polly, her eyes glittered like polished obsidian. Her smile turned the wrinkles in her old cheeks into a map of mysteries Polly couldn't even begin to fathom.

"I see you refer to him as James," Mother Francis Mary observed mildly.

Striving to maintain the nun's steady gaze, Polly said, "He—he asked me to, yes."

"Ah." The old woman seemed to be finding her amusement difficult to contain. "And did he make this odd request at work, dear?"

"Oh, no! Heavens, no. It was right before he kissed me."

Realizing what she'd said, Polly's mouth dropped open in horror. She pressed a hand to her burning cheek, removing it from her teacup so suddenly she almost upset the cup in her lap.

With a pleased chuckle, Mother Francis Mary said, "I see. Then, perhaps you had reason to feel a bit upset that he didn't confide his parentage to you, my dear."

"Oh, dear. It's not the way it sounds, Mother. Truly, it isn't."

"No?"

"No. At least—well—I don't know." Polly looked up and cried, "I don't know! I don't know, Mother. That's the problem."

"Ah, I see. I figured it was something of this nature. So now you're unsure of your young man's affections and are worried that he may be trifling with you. He is, after all, a man of substance in the community and you, while perfectly respectable, are quite poor."

The glance the nun gave Polly from under her eyelashes made her look like a wise little gnome. "At least you *were* quite poor. Unless James Drayton is right about his father, and old J. P. is a certifiable scoundrel, you are no longer poor at all.''

"I guess not,'' Polly said, for the first time almost believing it.

"Tut, tut; a quandary, to be sure. Has he given you any other indications of his regard, my dear?''

Hundreds, Polly thought. And none. "Well, when we got news that the wreckage of Stephen's ship had been discovered, Mr. Drayton was—quite kind to me.''

The nun sat up straighter in her chair. "I'm sorry to hear that, my dear. I didn't know.''

"No. No. I haven't been here since then. But he was kind to me. And—and he is looking into that situation, too.''

"My, my. A virtual paragon,'' Mother Francis Mary murmured.

"And when he heard you'd sent me an invitation to the Charity Ball, he asked me to accompany him.''

Another smile rearranged the wrinkles on the old woman's face. "What a splendid idea, to be sure.''

"Yes, but now I don't know if I should go with him or not, Mother. I don't know.'' Polly lifted her cup to drink more tea, realized it was empty, and replaced it on its saucer with a clink. "Oh, I don't know what to do,'' she said unhappily.

"Did you accept his offer?''

"Yes.''

"Well, I believe it would be impolite to withdraw your acceptance now, dear,'' Mother Francis Mary said in her schoolteacher's voice.

"You do?''

"Indeed. Most impolite.''

She shook her wimpled head, and Polly wondered if she was making fun of her. Too rattled to voice her suspicion, she went on to her next problem. "And then there's Mother.''

"Oh, my goodness. Is something wrong with your mother, my dear?''

"No. That is, not really. I mean—she's walking.''

"Why, how wonderful!''

"Yes. Yes, I guess it is.''

Mother Francis Mary shot her a keen look, and Polly said

hurriedly, "I mean, yes. Yes, it is wonderful. It's just—" But she didn't know how to say it. When she gave her thoughts voice, they sounded mean and petty.

"It's just that your whole life has revolved around your job and your invalid mother for the last several years, and you aren't sure what you'll do with yourself without either one of them," the Mother Superior finished for her.

Grateful, Polly could only nod.

"Add to that a young man who seems one day to be paying you court and the next to be keeping dark secrets, and you're about as confused as a pretty young girl can get." Mother Francis Mary smiled warmly. "Oh, Polly, child, don't feel so bad about feeling bad. Your emotions are perfectly understandable."

"They are?"

"Of course they are. Why, your whole life has just been turned cock-a-loop." The nun shook her head. "You young people, though. You're all so terribly serious about everything. James Drayton and his father; Polly MacNamara and her mother. Goodness gracious."

"Do you really think we're too serious, Mother?"

"Oh, Polly, I suspect I'm just too old to take the vagaries of life so seriously, my dear. When you get to be my age, you're thankful for life's absurdities as welcome relief from the trudging monotony of the endless days. But if it makes you feel better to be serious about things, you certainly have my permission."

She laughed her creaky laugh. "You will, anyway, with or without it."

Polly actually felt her mouth lifting of its own accord. Her heart felt lighter, too.

"And you know, Polly, whether you work or not and whether your mother can walk or not, there are still things that need doing in this world. You need never feel useless." Mother Francis Mary made a sweeping gesture with her arm. "Why, right here we have a hundred children longing for attention. They already love you, dear. You're certainly welcome to spend more time with them."

The nun's simple words caught Polly off guard. All at once

a whole new world opened up before her. Why, how narrow-minded she was being! Her heart lifting like magic, she exclaimed, "Thank you, Mother. Thank you for listening to me for being my friend."

"Oh, my dear, it is my great pleasure. I'm so old now and the problems of youth are so far behind me that it's a delight for me to hear about them every now and again, just to keep in touch with how other people live."

They walked arm-in-arm to the severe wrought-iron gate separating the denizens of the Sisters of Benevolence's charitable institution from the world. Polly's step felt much springier and her mind much less muddled than it had before she came here. She sighed when the big gate closed behind her.

Then, just as she was about to walk back home, she made a quick turn and headed into Chinatown. As long as she was here, she might as well pay another visit to her shop and see what, if any, fey creatures resided within it today. Polly felt her medals through the thick fabric of her coat and knew she'd always be grateful to that old woman, whether this coin was magic or not.

And after she visited the shop . . . Well, she'd think about that later.

She pushed open the door to the familiar jingle of the little bell and stepped inside. With a sigh, she saw neither the tiny old woman nor the jolly old man behind the counter. The beaded curtain hung unmoving between the shop and the secrets housed in back.

Although the day outside was bright, inside the shop a twilight aura reigned. Polly smiled and decided it must be the delicate scent of sandalwood and the dimness of the lighting that were responsible for her fanciful impression. The subtle aura was certainly not unpleasant; rather, the soft atmosphere gave her a feeling of peace.

I'll just look around for awhile, and maybe somebody will show up.

With that thought and a grin for the infinite possibilities the shop afforded, she commenced to prowl the small, cluttered room. Oh, my. There was such an abundance of beauty to please the eye in the confined space. Her smile widened when she saw Christmas decorations—a holly wreath above a small crèche—settled next to carved Chinese figurines of the Nine Wise Ancients, as though the disparate cultural artifacts all belonged together.

Fingering the baby Jesus in the crèche and thinking about it, Polly murmured, "I guess they do."

"May I help you?"

Polly's heart nearly leapt out of her throat and she must have jumped a foot when she heard the soft voice at her elbow. Turning with a start, she beheld a beautiful young woman, about her age, standing very near her. She hadn't heard the beads click. She put a hand to her thundering heart and felt her coin, glowing warm through her coat.

"Oh, I'm sorry. You startled me."

The woman gave her an enigmatic smile. Polly thought she was perhaps the loveliest female she'd ever beheld and harbored a sudden, unworthy thought; she was glad James wasn't with her today.

Not, of course, that there was any reason he *should* be. Or that, if he were, it would matter whether or not he admired this woman. Or that Polly should care one way or the other.

She cleared her throat. "I was sold some ivory hair combs in this shop a while ago by an elderly lady shopkeeper."

Her statement was greeted by another mysterious smile. "Yes?"

"Well, I wondered if she might be in today."

"You wish to speak to her about the combs?"

The young lady's voice was low and musical. Although she stood no more than three feet away, Polly felt as though an enormous distance separated them. The impression was a strange one, and she couldn't account for it. Like the old woman who had given Polly the coin, this lady stood with her arms folded across her stomach, her hands nestled in the long embroidered sleeves of her Chinese pajama jacket. Unlike the old woman, this one was very still. If she hadn't spoken, Polly might have taken her for a statue.

"No," Polly said, "The combs are lovely. But while I was here, the shopkeeper gave me a coin."

"Ah."

The woman smiled again, and Polly got the distinct impression that she knew all about the coin—and her own connection with it—already. Well, for heaven's sake.

"Is she here today?"

"No."

The news didn't surprise Polly.

"She will be here when you need her," the woman added in a very soft voice, as though speaking to a child who needed a gentle reminder. Her smile did not waver.

"When I need her?"

A nod was Polly's answer. Hmm, she thought, this should be most irritating. Strangely enough, it wasn't. In fact, amusement bubbled inside her; amusement and a strange lilting sensation, as of anticipation.

She almost giggled when she asked, "And do you have any idea when that will be? I keep coming back here to thank her, and she's never here."

With a slight inclination of her head, the lady said, "It's fine to thank. You may come here as often as you need."

Mercy. So much for that. Polly guessed this trip, too, had been wasted. At least she hadn't been given any predictions this time. Not that she minded. She felt a little bit the way she expected Mother Francis Mary felt when given reports about life outside the Order. It was as if Polly had stepped straight from her everyday, humdrum life into an enigma. The feeling was not unpleasant; rather, Polly felt a glow of excitement.

"Well, thank you." On an impulse, she asked, "And the old man who predicted a happy life for me? Is he here?"

For a moment, the woman's expression broadened fractionally, then it smoothed out into the Mona Lisa–like smile she'd maintained since Polly first set eyes on her. She shook her head, and Polly sighed.

"No. I expected he wouldn't be."

She was surprised when the woman withdrew one of her hands and put it on Polly's arm. Her hand looked like that of a China doll: tiny, perfect, white, with beautifully manicured nails.

"He, too, will be here when you need. And he is correct."

She withdrew her hand and put it back into her sleeve. Her

movements were so graceful, the garment barely moved.

"He's right? You mean about the fortune he predicted for me?"

A nod.

"My goodness. I'm glad of that, anyway." With another little sigh, Polly said, "Thank you for your time."

"Certainly."

Just before she shut the door behind herself on the way out, Polly peeked back into the shop. It didn't surprise her to see the shop empty and the beaded curtain hanging as still as a painting. Of course, she'd not heard it click.

"My goodness," she murmured again.

Then she took a peek around outside and smiled as she viewed the busy, bustling streets. Stepping out into the bright sunlight was like walking into another world. She loved Chinatown. It was so alive, so unlike her own cloistered life, which today seemed as closed and compressed as a jail cell.

With a firm nod for courage and a bracing gulp of fresh air, Polly decided she might as well finish what she'd started. Her cheerful mood lasted until she had walked almost all the way to J. P. Drayton's imposing office building on Commercial Street.

Once she neared the docks, her step slowed and she began to feel uneasy. The Pacific-Orient Freight Shipping building was the only one on the block that didn't look as though it had seen better days. The location of J. P. Drayton's business was, by its very nature, somewhat unsavory. Polly understood docks were always unsavory, being, as they were, the meeting ground of many worlds.

Not only that; the idea of encountering J. P. Drayton himself, face-to-face, was a daunting one.

She decided she was glad it was Saturday. With so many people scurrying around doing their weekly marketing at the fish stands, it was easy to dismiss the lurid accounts of kidnap and murder she read in the newspapers. Still, as she peered at the crowds, there were enough rough-looking individuals among the Saturday shoppers to make her shiver and pull her coat closer to her breast. When she did, she became aware of her coin, warm against her skin, and felt better.

She climbed the stairs inside J. P. Drayton's building with mounting trepidation. Oh, Lord. What if he turned out to be as mean as James believed? What if he told her it was all a horrible mistake, and to give the bank draft back? What if—

No.

Polly breathed in a deep, fortifying breath redolent of fish, tar, creosote, and salt air, and told herself to stop borrowing trouble. The man to whose office she headed had just done her mother and herself a tremendous kindness. Indeed, he'd rescued them from the jaws of poverty. As soon as James had told him about her father's accident and its outcome, he had done his best to rectify the situation. If some measure of blame for Franklin MacNamara's death lay at J. P. Drayton's door, at least he was trying to make up for it. That's all Polly needed to know.

Bravely holding that thought close to her heart, she turned the knob on a door proclaiming itself to be the office of J. P. Drayton and stepped inside. At first she saw nobody, and a cowardly rush of thankfulness washed over her. Then she noticed the open door of an office leading from this room, apparently the reception area, and realized that a man sat behind a desk in that room. What's more, he was glaring at her.

Breathing a silent prayer for courage, Polly shut the door behind her and walked to the office door. There she stood her ground and said, "Mr. Drayton?" Her voice, amazingly enough, sounded clear and resolute.

"I am J. P. Drayton," the man growled. "And who the devil are you?"

Swallowing her recoil at his brusque manner and improper language, Polly squared her shoulders and walked quickly toward J. P. Drayton, her hand held out.

"I am Polly MacNamara, Mr. Drayton. And I came here today to thank you for your kindness to my mother and me."

Her heart had taken to pumping like a piston in her chest but her hand didn't shake as it was enfolded in the huge, burly hand of J. P. Drayton. From somewhere within, she found the mettle to smile at him.

"You can't imagine what it means to us, sir. These pas

few years have been difficult. You have given us the means to a better life. Thank you.''

J. P. Drayton had never been so astonished in his entire sixty-four years. When he'd had Biddle prepare the letter and bank draft for Lillian MacNamara and her daughter, he'd done it out of spite, because James had acted as though he were some sort of vile monster. He'd never expected to actually see either MacNamara lady, to meet one of them in person. Oh, certainly he'd expected to receive letters gushing thanks. Maybe even a fruitcake or two come Christmases in the future. But meet them? Never.

In short, he'd thought of them as objects, as a means to an end; as a joke. Yet here was one of them, in the flesh, shaking his hand.

It went against the grain to acknowledge it, but he guessed they weren't merely objects. They were flesh-and-blood people. Polly MacNamara's hand was as warm with life as his own. As soon as it flickered into his brain, J. P. snuffed out the thought that maybe his dratted uppity boy had a point when he called him indifferent and hard.

He barked out a gruff, "You're welcome." Then he eyed her with interest, liberally laced with disapproval.

So this was the chit his son was so enthralled with that he'd visited the father he professed to despise for the purpose of pleading her cause. Well, well. She didn't look like much to J. P. Looked like a simple working girl, in fact.

He acknowledged grumpily that he guessed she was.

She didn't seem to know what to do with herself now that she'd said her thanks. J. P. frowned. Silly girl had used up all her pluck marching in here to thank him and didn't know how to carry through. She'd never get anywhere that way.

Still . . . If the things James had yelled at him were true, this absurd baggage had been supporting herself and her mother for quite a few years. She must have some grit behind all that fluff. Narrowing his eyes critically, J. P. guessed she wasn't *too* fluffy. Looked almost prim, in fact. And nervous as a cat, too. He wondered just what slanders James had told her about him, and his scowl deepened.

"Well, sit down, for heaven's sake." He gestured peremptorily at one of the chairs across from his desk.

"Thank you."

Polly sat with a plop and remained stiff-backed and edgy. J. P. could tell she didn't have a clue what to say or do now. She hadn't planned this out very well, he decided critically. Obviously the girl had no common sense. She was impetuous. J. P. Drayton greatly disapproved of impetuosity.

"You work for my boy?"

"Yes, sir."

"How long?"

"Two years."

"A typist, are you?"

"Yes, sir."

"You like it?"

"Yes, sir."

"He tell you about me?"

"Yes, sir."

J. P. curled his lip. "Can't you say anything besides 'Yes, sir,' girl?"

He saw her lips flatten in annoyance and felt a tickle of amusement. Maybe the chit had some spunk in her after all.

"I didn't come here to chat with you, Mr. Drayton," she said tightly. "I came to thank you. I'm sorry if I seem clumsy, but I am quite nervous."

J. P. sat back in his chair and studied Polly some more. "Yes," he growled, "I see. And I also see that James has told you about me. The boy thinks I'm a monster." With a sudden move, he leaned across his desk "What do you think?"

At his precipitate movement, Polly gave a start of alarm. J. P. grinned. He didn't fault her for her jump. His tactics had been known to make strong men quail. He admired her for not leaping up and screeching, although it always annoyed him when a person didn't do as he expected.

"As to that, I'm not sure what to think, sir. I don't know you."

"Humph." Settling back once more, J. P. frowned. "Well, I'm not a monster, and you can tell that frippery son of mine so." He watched in surprise as Polly's eyes narrowed in irritation.

Christmas Pie

"Well, sir, I believe I must withhold my judgment on that issue for a while yet. My mother and I will be forever grateful to you for your generosity, although I believe the settlement is not outrageous, considering the circumstances contributing to my father's death."

"Not outrageous?" J. P. laughed unpleasantly. "Why, you impudent little baggage."

She looked really angry now, J. P. noted with displeasure.

"I don't believe telling the truth should be called impudence, sir."

"The truth? And just who are you to be talking to me about the truth, young lady?"

Admiration for Polly's courage in standing up to him began to give way to annoyance that she should speak to him so plainly. He gave her his hottest scowl and felt a tingle of satisfaction when she had to tighten her grip on the chair's arms. His satisfaction evaporated with her next words.

"I am the daughter of a man who died aboard one of your ships, Mr. Drayton, apparently as a result of your captain's incompetence."

"Nonsense!"

"Is it?"

"Of course."

"I believe there is some doubt about that, sir."

J. P. glared at Polly. Polly glared back.

"And as far as your son goes, Mr. Drayton," she said, after taking two or three deep breaths, "I believe both you and he should reassess your familial relationship."

Furious by this time, J. P. gave her one of his best glowers. She ignored it. He could hardly believe she'd done such an astounding thing.

"Oh, you can give me all the black looks in the world, sir, but they won't stop me from speaking my mind. For heaven's sake, you and James are the only family you each have. To be at odds like this is a terrible shame, especially at Christmastime, when men of good will forgive one another and—and try to get along."

"*Christmas,*" J. P. roared. "Christmas? Bah!"

With a triumphant look, Polly cried, "Aha! You sound *just*

231

Emma Craig

like Ebenezer Scrooge before the spirits visited him! You and
your son are cut of the same cloth!''

"Well, of course we are, you silly fool!''

Polly bristled. "I may be a fool, Mr. Drayton, but at leas
my mother doesn't have a child who considers her no bette
than a fiend! And should my mother ever, God willing, be
blessed with grandchildren, her child doesn't detest her so
much that she'll never be allowed to meet them!''

Silence slapped between them like a beached whale, huge
obtrusive, and quivering with emotions.

Finally, J. P. growled, "Well, you've said your thanks and
a good deal more, young lady. Now, I have a business to run.'

Polly popped up from her chair as if she'd been pinched
He could read the relief on her vivid features.

"Of course, sir. Well—well, I just—well, thank you, sir.
hope you won't let my run-away tongue invalidate the genuine
thanks in my heart, Mr. Drayton. It was very good of you to
compensate us. Your kindness means the world to my mothe
and me.''

J. P. was on the verge of telling her kindness had nothing
to do with it. Nor did goodness. J. P. didn't believe in good
ness any more than he believed in kindness. Goodness could
be bought and kindness led to foolishness and ruin.

Deciding a lecture would be wasted on this ridiculous little
idealist, he grumped, "You're welcome,'' and turned his at
tention back to the papers on his desk.

"Good day, sir.''

"Good day.''

J. P. heard Polly's feet clatter down the steps after she left
his carpeted reception area, sounding as though she couldn'
escape fast enough. Damned silly girl. She deserved James
the prig.

He gave up pretending to write as soon as her footstep
faded. Then he sat back in his chair, stared out the window o
his third-floor office, and thought for a long time. Damned
annoying, foolish little chit. Still . . .

J. P. couldn't recall ever having been thanked for anythin,
before. Yet when he tried to remember ever having done any
thing requiring thanks, he couldn't think of a single instance

232

His brow deeply rutted, J. P. grunted, "Bah!"

The word made him think of Polly's comparing him to Scrooge and he wished she were still here so he could holler at her. Then, of its own accord, his mind veered down another thorny path.

"Grandchildren. Hah! Damned girl. That's why I tried to get my boy to represent my firm, damn it. I *tried* to mend our fences. Blasted boy wouldn't even give me the time of day."

He sat in fulminating silence for another several minutes until a reluctant grin crept up on his frown, eventually obliterating it.

"She has nerve, though. Damned if she doesn't have nerve enough for the both of them."

His smile broadened when he thought about the surprise yet to be sprung on the annoying Polly MacNamara and his own irritating son James.

"I'll teach 'em. I'll teach the both of 'em." He went back to his business much more cheery than he'd been before Polly invaded his office.

Chapter Sixteen

Polly was still frowning about her visit to J. P. Drayton the next morning as she wheeled her mother's chair to church. Lillian and Mrs. Plimsole, who walked with them, were deep into a discussion about the MacNamaras' increased fortunes, so Polly's thoughts were undisturbed.

James's father really was a beastly man, she decided. She got the distinct impression that he was deliberately abrasive with her yesterday, as though to put her off. *Her,* of all people. As if anything she said or did could cause him any distress. Why, she was no more than a mere fly whom a flick of J. P. Drayton's autocratic finger could send hurtling into infinity.

He'd actually seemed to enjoy discomfiting her. Polly did not approve. She wished James were here so she could tell him so.

With a sigh, she realized what a silly wish that was. Then, recollecting the charm she wore, she grinned and decided, oh, why not? Lifting one hand from the wheelchair grips and pressing her coin, she wished she'd have an opportunity to speak with James that day.

Then, recalling how her wish to see Dewey had been fulfilled yesterday, she wondered if she should have wished at all.

It was too late to worry about it now, though. The wish had been made and she didn't know how to call it back. Anyway, they were at church, so she had no time to experiment.

Organ music filled the air as the three of them entered the sanctuary. Polly, Lillian, and Mrs. Plimsole always sat in the back pew so that Lillian's wheelchair wouldn't inconvenience other parishioners. Polly actually enjoyed it back there because she was given an unrestricted view of the entire congregation. She liked watching people and making up stories about them when Mr. Carter's sermons became boring, as they so often did.

She frowned when she noticed one particular worshiper.

"Now what on earth is *he* doing here? I've never seen him here before."

"Who's that, dear?" Lillian craned her neck so she wouldn't have to speak loudly. The hard-of-hearing Mrs. Plimsole didn't realize Polly had spoken.

Polly leaned over to whisper in her mother's ear. "Mr. Gregory, Mr. Drayton's secretary. I've never seen him here before."

"Which one is he, dear?"

"The sour-looking man next to the wall. The one with the pinched face and the bilious green suit."

Polly felt a little contrite that her voice should reek of such unchristian malice. After all, while it was true that Mr. Gregory was a deplorable human being and a bully, he had just lost his job—partly because of her. She tried to feel guilty, failed, and sighed, wondering what her lack of compassion told about herself.

"My goodness, he looks rather unpleasant, Polly."

"He is." Again, she felt a stab of guilt, and took a breath to soften her pronouncement.

They were obliged to quit talking when Mr. Carter held up his arms for silence. By the time the service concluded, Polly had forgotten all about Walter Gregory.

Walter Gregory, however, had not forgotten about her. He followed the three ladies at a discreet distance, distaste for this task making his ratlike nose wrinkle. When he saw them turn down the narrow pathway separating two of the tall framework houses on the block, he scowled.

How was he supposed to give Lawrence Bullock her precise address if he couldn't tell which house she was going to? He might have known the girl would give him trouble in this, too. His life had been quite pleasant until *she* waltzed into it. It had been a black day for Walter Gregory when Miss High-and-Mighty MacNamara decided to speak to his boss. His former boss. Gregory's thin lips pursed in animosity.

Idiot girl. Thought she could parade right into Mr. Drayton's office as if she had the right. She was probably one of those infernal suffragists. What did people call them nowadays? Suffragettes? Bah! As if women had brains enough to be trusted with the vote!

And then, to crown her impudence, Mr. Uppity James Drayton had the nerve to call *him* on the carpet. *Him!* Walter Gregory, his loyal personal secretary. Gregory sniffed imperiously. And what was going on in *that* quarter? he'd like to know. It didn't take as shrewd a customer as Walter Gregory to figure out what a nobody of a typist and a rich businessman were doing behind closed doors.

Gregory's mood did not improve as he hid himself behind a prickly camellia bush and waited. After tarrying for what he decided must be time enough for three ladies to sort themselves out and get indoors, he dashed down the alleyway, wondering if he'd waited too long. What if he'd lost them entirely? If they were already inside one of the houses, he'd never be able to guess which was the MacNamara abode.

Slithering to a halt at the back of the two houses, Gregory stuck his head out just far enough to get a glimpse of their respective back doors. Peering to his right he saw not a soul. There was, however, a wheelchair ramp leading to the door. He smirked.

Then he turned his head and peered to his left, just to be on the safe side. He scowled when he observed the third lady, the one who had been chatting with the MacNamara female's mother. With a start, Gregory recognized her as his Aunt Martha, and jerked his head out of sight at once.

"Good God," he muttered, momentarily unnerved.

He'd noticed a ramp leading to that door, too, though, and he recovered his composure and smiled nastily.

That was it, then. That was the one. He scuttled off down the leaf-strewn street, Aunt Martha forgotten, bearing glad tidings to his new employer.

James wished he'd taken his motorcar. Walking took so much time. Time that could be used more pleasantly—or, rather, he meant, more efficiently—in talking with Polly. He hurried up Pacific Avenue and barely heard the leaves crunch under his feet. Autumn had slowly fallen into winter, and there was barely a leaf left on the maple trees lining the street. The air was brisk and a salt tang from the bay hung in the air.

James wasn't thinking about the weather, though. His thoughts clung, with the persistence of Dewey after a scent, to Polly MacNamara. He guessed it wasn't absolutely necessary to bring these legal papers for Polly to sign tonight, but—but—he wanted to get them filed. Yes, that's exactly why he was racing down the street toward her house.

Besides, his honest, albeit less noble heart told him, he hadn't seen her since yesterday afternoon. He'd been in a snit at the time, too, annoyed that she seemed determined to feel sorry for him. What if she still thought he was angry with her? What if she'd decided she was angry with him? She'd sure been aggravated for a while there yesterday. James grinned when he remembered the scene.

His grin vanished with the intrusion of another, awful thought. What if she'd decided to quit his employ? Could he convince her to keep seeing him? As absurd as it seemed to him—because he truly didn't believe in such things—he couldn't get over the sinking sensation that he loved her. Or at least—James's brain rebelled at the word *love*—he cared deeply for her. At the very, very least, he'd certainly enjoy keeping company with her for a while.

She was—she was—she was refreshing. Yes. That's what she was. Love might be too strong a word today; although, he admitted ruefully, it hadn't seemed too strong on that other day, when he'd been alone in his motorcar with her. That day in his horseless carriage, it had seemed like the truth.

At any rate, Polly MacNamara was definitely soft and feminine and lovely. He particularly liked the hint of womanly charms that showed in spite of those starchy, prim shirtwaists she insisted on wearing. She was passionate, too. James knew that for a fact.

His eagerness increased as he mentally cataloged Polly's virtues, and his footsteps sped up until he was almost running. Suddenly an unpleasant possibility rampaged into his brain. Good Lord. What if his father had thought better of his generosity and stopped payment on that enormous bank draft?

The bastard.

James scowled. It would be just like the old man to do something of the nature. After all, this was the first time in his entire thirty years that James had known J. P. Drayton to compensate a victim of his unscrupulousness.

"Maybe he's turned over a new leaf," James ventured aloud to see how it felt. It felt nonsensical, and he shook his head. No, there was something else going on in that shrewd old head of his. It wasn't like J. P. Drayton to make amends.

It had just gone dark as James approached the MacNamara residence. A delightful day had turned into a perfect December evening. The cloudless sky had darkened and begun to sport a sprinkle of stars. By the light of a solitary candle lamp on a porch newel, James noticed that some Christmas elf had bedecked the picket fence he'd recently replaced with red ribbons. The big bows looked festive against the sparkling white of the freshly painted pickets.

Suddenly he wished Polly could see his house. Even he, who eschewed Christmas celebrations as a foolish waste of time, had to admit the place looked pretty. He knew she'd love it. She seemed to take a good deal of pleasure in all this holiday nonsense.

Yet when James himself had observed the handiwork of his housekeeper—who'd tackled the formidable task of decorating his huge mansion with glee—he'd felt only emptiness. His reaction made him uncomfortable, and he didn't care to examine it.

Years ago he'd adopted an air of sophisticated nonchalance about Christmas and the syrupy emotional craziness about family, hearth, and home that always accompanied seasonal celebrations. This year his disdain seemed to have been replaced by a hollow feeling of loss. For the life of him, he couldn't figure out what it was he'd lost.

When Polly answered his knock at the door, a smile lit her countenance. His chancy mood lifted like magic.

"James! What a delightful surprise!" Her cheeks grew pink, and James knew she was embarrassed by her spontaneous, honest greeting.

"I came over to have you sign the complaint against Lawrence Bullock, Polly." So that she wouldn't think he'd gone to any particular trouble, or misinterpret the businesslike nature of his visit, he added, "It's best not to leave these things too long."

His explanation sounded lame. When he saw the sparkle of happiness fade from her eyes, he wished he hadn't said anything. She still smiled, though, when she held the door and bade him enter.

"How kind of you. I'm so glad you've come. I have so much to tell you."

"You do?"

"Indeed I do." Polly stepped back to allow him entry. "But first, come into the parlor. Mother and Mrs. Plimsole are there. We're just taking tea while I decorate the Christmas tree."

Although James's primary reason for this Sunday-evening visit was to chat with Polly—about the Bullock case, of course—he said, "Thank you," with suitable docility. He followed her into the parlor, his briefcase tucked up under his arm.

Polly was clad in a plain dress that shouldn't have made James lick lips that suddenly went dry as he watched the subtle sway of her hips, but it did. The fabric was well-washed and had probably been a bright azure in its youth. It was now a soft blue-gray, and it hugged Polly's graceful curves with seductive delicacy. Before he entered the parlor, James managed to pry his gaze away from her body and adopt a friendly, family-attorney's smile for Lillian MacNamara and her friend.

"Please come in," Polly said with a smile when she led him into the front room.

Immediately, he noticed that Polly had already been busy in the parlor. Gone were the browns and golds of Thanksgiving. They'd been replaced with the greens and reds of Christmas. Swags of evergreen boughs graced the fireplace and holly berries winked from the greenery. A ceramic figure of Father Christmas, an overfilled pack slung over his shoulder and a pipe clamped between his ruby lips, stood on the mantel between two cranberry glass candlesticks. Cotton-fluff snow nestled at his black-booted feet.

"Why, good evening, Mr. Drayton. Please join us." Lillian stood up from her wheelchair. She didn't try to go to him, but she smiled proudly when James walked over to shake her hand.

"You seem very well this evening, Mrs. MacNamara. You've been practicing."

"Indeed, I have. I am well, thank you. And this is my very good friend Mrs. Plimsole. Martha, this is Mr. James Drayton."

James realized Mrs. Plimsole seemed to have to strain to hear, so he spoke distinctly when he said, "It's a pleasure to meet you, Mrs. Plimsole."

She responded with suitable civility and shook his hand.

"Polly's told me about what that terrible Mr. Bullock did to her yesterday, Mr. Drayton, and I can't thank you and your dog enough for coming to her assistance. It's a shame people find it necessary to do such awful things, especially at this time of the year." Lillian sat down again and shook her head.

"Yes, it is. I confess I feel somewhat responsible, too, ma'am. I'd known Bullock was not an asset to my law firm for some months, but I failed to take action until recently. I'm afraid he has taken it into his head to hold your daughter accountable for his downfall. His thinking is absurd, of course, and another indication of his refusal to accept his proper duties."

"Yes. But please don't hold yourself to blame. Mr. Bullock is the master of his own actions, not you. If his character is so weak that he fails to be responsible for himself, there's not a thing anyone else can do about it."

"I'm afraid you may be right, Mrs. MacNamara."

"But have a cup of tea, Mr. Drayton. Polly has just brought it in, and we have gingersnaps, too. Mrs. Plimsole bakes every Christmas and we have some wonderful treats. She took some over to our very nice neighbor, Mr. Fleischer, earlier today."

"Mr. Fleischer claims Mrs. Plimsole's gingersnaps go quite well with beer." Polly grinned as she held out the plate.

With an appropriate shudder, James said, "I think I'll enjoy them more with tea, ladies. This is a treat. Thank you."

He took a cup of tea and a cookie and sat back feeling more content than he had for a day or longer. The parlor smelled of cinnamon, gingersnaps, and Christmas, a scent he'd never paid much attention to before. Tonight he liked it.

The MacNamara tree was a small one, he noted. It sat on a table in the corner with a white flannel sheet at its base. It looked as though Polly had just begun the task of decorating it. A tinsel star sparkled on its uppermost point, but no other ornaments had been applied.

"Would you like to help me decorate the tree, James?" Polly asked. "We can go over those depressing papers later."

James, who had never decorated a Christmas tree in his life, was about to decline her pleasant invitation. As if sensing his reluctance to participate in such a jolly, childlike activity, Polly grabbed him by the hand and dragged him out of his chair.

"Come along now. If you won't help me, I won't tell you my news."

"Well, if you put it like that . . ." James knew he'd not be able to deny her anything if she kept smiling at him in just that way. Of course, as ever, she had no idea the effect she had on him. It was one of her charms.

She began with enthusiasm, "Now, you see, we have all these ornaments. There are cherubs and bells and tiny wicker baskets. Here are some satin roses. And I have yards of red satin ribbon for bows. And, oh, yes! I almost forgot. Look at

241

these.'' With a quick, graceful movement, Polly knelt. When she stood again, she bore an enameled wooden box, obviously Chinese.

"Just look, James. They're absolutely beautiful. My father brought them back one year from a trip to China.'' She opened the box to reveal a set of lacquered cut-out figures, all in elaborate Chinese garb, as though dressed for a ceremonial occasion.

"Chinese Christmas ornaments?''

She shrugged. "Why not? Christmas is for everyone.''

When he looked down into her eyes, he felt a catch in his chest. Her lovely eyes glowed with excitement. And something else. His breath caught when he realized the something else was love. And it was aimed directly at him.

The catch in his chest ached for a moment. Then, as if an angel reached inside his body and unlocked a steel barricade, it broke open. Suddenly his heart flooded with joy.

Lifting his hand, he touched Polly's face. She gently brushed her cheek against it, a reaction he considered most telling. Then he dropped his hand and said, a queer, unfamiliar sensation making his throat feel tight, "I'd be happy to help you decorate the tree, Polly.''

So they decorated the tree and drank tea and ate gingersnaps for an hour or more. The longer James participated in the exotic activity, the more he relaxed. It wasn't long before he was laughing along with Polly about whether it was proper to hang a Chinese lacquered figure next to a distinctively Western, albeit tiny, sombrero, or if a wicker basket—which Polly deemed to be more Western than the figure—should be tied next to the hat.

Finally Polly declared, "Oh, why not?'' She added the Chinese figure to the tree.

She laughed as she stood back, hands on hips, and tilted her head to peer at the odd grouping. James had a tremendous impulse to grab her and kiss her.

He restrained himself and hung a minuscule English bulldog next to the sombrero. "Might as well make it a truly international grouping.''

Polly's delighted laugh was interrupted by a tremendous

blast, followed by a blood-curdling scream. Chatter in the MacNamara parlor stopped with a shock.

James was the first to recover. "My God, that sounded like a shotgun being fired."

"Did it? I've never heard one." Polly pressed a hand to her hammering heart.

"Dear gracious." Lillian stared at Polly and James in alarm.

Even the nearly deaf Mrs. Plimsole had heard the noise. She lifted a hand to cup her ear and said, "My word, what was that?"

"I don't know, but I'm going to check on it. Better stay here, ladies." James hurried to the front door and flung it open.

Polly, unwilling to miss out on the excitement, ran after him. They burst out onto the porch together and stared up the street, from whence the noise had come.

"Oh, my goodness, I believe something's going on at Mr. Fleischer's house."

"You'd better stay here, Polly. I'll investigate," said the gallant James.

"Oh, no you don't." Polly barreled down the porch steps in front of him. "I'm not going to miss out on this."

"Wait!" Laughing because he couldn't help it, James dashed after her and caught her around the waist. "At least stay with me. If it's a madman with a shotgun, we should be careful."

"I don't think it's a madman, James," Polly told him in a truly bemused voice. "I think it's Mr. Fleischer. And, oh, my goodness, who's that with him? Look."

Sure enough, James followed Polly's pointed finger with his gaze and saw her rotund neighbor step out of his house. Mr. Fleischer wore the tops to his long underwear, trousers, suspenders, and no shoes. His bushy gray side whiskers bristled and his heavy lips were working their way around a mouthful of blistering German.

He held a shotgun in a menacing manner at the backs of a couple of black, huddled figures. There was only one light burning on the MacNamara porch and another at the Fleischers', so it was difficult to see, but James thought at least one of the people held at bay by the intrepid Mr. Fleischer wore a mask. Both cowered and covered their heads with their hands.

"Good God," he muttered as he and Polly ran over to offer assistance.

"Mr. Fleischer," Polly cried, "what on earth is going on? Are you all right?"

After they had run up the Fleischer steps, James could clearly tell that Mr. Fleischer was monumentally irate, and that his anger was directed at the men at the end of his shotgun. The old German's cheeks were bright red, and his bristly brows met over the bridge of his nose.

"Yah, yah, I'm all right. But these two rascals! Come sneaking into a fellow's house at night and try to scare him. These two rascals I believe I should shoot."

One of the rascals shrieked, "No! No! For God's sake, James, don't let him shoot us!"

Fleischer poked the man in the back with his gun and snorted angrily.

James stared at the masked figure in astonishment. He turned to look at Polly, who was looking at him. Then they both turned their attention to the masked men.

"Bullock?" James reached out and twitched the mask away. Sure enough, the face revealed was that of Lawrence Bullock, and he was trembling with fright.

James heard Polly gasp and put a comforting arm around her shoulders. She leaned against him, and he directed his attention to the other masked villain; the shorter, more slender of the two.

Grimly, James said, "And I wonder who this idiot can be."

To the accompaniment of Mr. Fleischer's offended muttering, he ripped the mask away to reveal Walter Gregory's weasel's face. Only tonight, the supercilious sneer he had adopted during his tenure as James Drayton's secretary was gone. Right now he looked merely terrified, and tears dribbled from his small, beady eyes and dripped from his pointy chin.

"Good heavens!"

James tightened his hold around Polly's shoulders. "What

in the name of all that's holy do the two of you think you're doing?"

"We only meant to frighten her, James," Bullock blubbered. "Honestly, we didn't mean any harm."

"Frighten *her?*" Polly gasped. "You meant to frighten *me?*"

Gregory nodded.

"Buy why did you try to frighten me by going into Mr. Fleischer's house?"

James saw her eyes widen as understanding hit her between the eyes. "Why, you horrid little man! You were spying on us in church today! You used the Lord's house to *spy* on us!"

"I'm sorry!" Gregory whimpered. "I'm sorry!"

"He got the wrong house, James," Bullock whimpered. "We didn't mean to break into this man's house. We didn't mean anything. We didn't take anything. There's no harm done. Honest!"

"Bah!" Mr. Fleischer hit the barrel of his shotgun against Bullock's fat buttocks once more, eliciting a small yelp from him.

"No harm? No *harm?*" Polly stiffened in outrage.

James believed her to be suffering from justifiable female spasms of fright. When he tried to give her another comforting squeeze, however, he suddenly found himself empty-armed as she burst from his embrace in an explosion of wrath.

"No *harm!* Why you imbeciles! How dare you sneak into this good man's house in the middle of the night? How *dare* you!"

"We didn't mean anything," sniveled Gregory. She turned on him with the power of a Fury, and he shrank back until he felt the shotgun. Then he burst forward, nearly colliding with Polly, who reached up a hand and shoved him, hard.

"Don't you *dare* touch me, you miserable creature." Whirling on Bullock, who cringed, she said, "And *you!* First you accost me on the street, then you try to kidnap me!" With a nod of contempt, she told Mr. Fleischer, "And he was inebriated both times, too." Returning to Bullock, she said scathingly, "And now this—this monstrous criminal act! And here I had been feeling sorry for you! Well, I guess my sympathies were misspent, weren't they?''

Neighbors had begun to gather at the foot of the Fleischer porch. James eyed them with resignation and thought, *Of course.* Whenever he and Polly were together, they seemed to draw crowds. He wondered if it was some sort of omen.

Since the captives seemed in no danger of escape, what with Fleischer holding his shotgun at their flank and Polly covering their front, James conferred with one of the throng. The man nodded, and sent his son running to the police station on the corner. Then James returned to the scene of crime.

Grinning, he leaned back against a porch pillar and crossed his arms over his chest. He wondered how long Polly planned to harangue the pair of scoundrels and decided to let her do her best. Or worst. She deserved it, after what Bullock and Gregory had put her through. He also decided it would be to his advantage not to irritate her in the future.

''And *you*,'' she cried, rounding on Walter Gregory again. ''You spiteful, nasty creature! I felt sorry for you in church today, knowing you'd lost your job for being such a nasty man. Why, I actually thought that perhaps you'd turned to God in an effort to straighten out your life. But I was wrong! You're a bully and a wretch, just like this awful pig!'' In case Gregory didn't know who the ''awful pig'' was, she slapped Bullock on his belly. This evening, Bullock was not dressed in a suit and vest, and his rounded belly protruded slightly, making an easy target.

Bullock whimpered, ''Ow!'' and Polly scowled at him.

''What on earth is going on?''

James, amused when Polly seemed vexed at the interruption, turned to tell Martha Plimsole, ''These two men tried to break into Mr. Fleischer's house. He objected.''

''Men!'' Polly scoffed. ''They aren't *men.* They're cowardly *beasts!*''

Mrs. Plimsole, panting when she reached the top of the Fleischer steps, stared in astonishment at the two men quaking before Polly's lashing tongue. A tiny beaded handbag dangled from her wrist, and she fumbled in it for a moment and then drew out a pair of eyeglasses. She put them on and squinted at Walter Gregory.

When she said, "Walter? Walter, is that you?" Polly stopped in mid-screech.

She stared at Mrs. Plimsole in surprise. "You mean you know this creature, ma'am?"

Mrs. Plimsole's mouth pursed in distaste. She snatched her spectacles from her nose and announced, "*Know* him? He's my sister Mary's child. My nephew." She spat out the word *nephew* as though it tasted bad.

"My goodness," Polly said. "How astounding."

"Astounding, my foot!" Mrs. Plimsole walked up to Walter Gregory as if she and Polly had been assigned the task of vilifying him and it was now her turn.

"You always were a sniveling, spiteful child, Walter Gregory, but this goes completely beyond the pale. I can't believe even *you* would stoop to breaking and entering."

"But, we weren't—"

"Oh, be quiet, you fool." Mrs. Plimsole whacked Gregory sharply with her beaded handbag, making him screech and cower.

"Aha!" Mrs. Plimsole cried. "Cringe away from me, you coward! Just wait until your mother hears about *this!*"

"Oh, no!" Gregory fell to his knees, wringing his hands. "No! Please, Aunt Martha. Don't tell Mother! Please!"

"Don't snivel, you wretched boy," Mrs. Plimsole told him with unutterable distaste. "I most certainly *shall* tell your mother."

She turned abruptly and marched toward the porch steps. She stopped long enough to tell the gathered crowd, triumph ringing in her voice, "I always told Mary she coddled the boy too much. I guess she'll believe me now!"

Head held high, she strode back to the MacNamara residence where she would, James guessed, regale Lillian MacNamara with the juicy details of the evening's adventure.

Apparently Mrs. Plimsole's interruption had taken the wind out of Polly's sails. She still looked like a storm cloud about to burst and rain on Bullock and Gregory, but she no longer hollered at them.

247

Turning with a whirl, she asked James, "You know those papers you brought for me to sign this evening?" With a glance over her shoulder at Lawrence Bullock, she added, "The ones pressing charges against that fiend?"

"Yes, Polly," James said mildly.

"Well, I won't sign them until they've been amended to include this night's work. And you can include that wretched Mr. Gregory, too!"

"Yah!" bellowed Mr. Fleischer, who had been severely out-shouted by Polly up till now, "and me, too! I'm going to press them too!"

Gregory whimpered. Bullock sniffled.

James shook his head and chuckled. "Actually, I think we'll have to draw up another complaint about this incident." He eyed his two former employees with distaste. "But I shall certainly see to it first thing in the morning."

With an imperious nod, Polly said, "Good."

A policeman hurried up at that moment, and the crowd parted like the Red Sea for Moses.

A brief flurry of confusion ensued. Mr. Fleischer offered to shoot the two men, believing such action would effectively thwart attempted escape, besides having the additional advantage of saving taxpayers' money. The policeman declined, much to the general disapproval of the crowd.

"He's got the right," one neighbor cried.

"Aye! Them two rascals broke into his house."

"Shoulda shot 'em when you had the chance, Fleischer," another gentleman proclaimed, causing Bullock and Gregory to sob and lean toward the protection of the policeman.

James held Polly firmly around the waist during the altercation. At last, when the policeman finally managed to get the crowd under control and clapped cuffs on Bullock and Gregory, he squeezed her gently. She was the most perfect of feminine bundles. He was sure she had no idea how delightful she felt in his arms.

He was wrong. Polly knew very well how delightful she felt. She'd never, in fact, felt anything quite as wonderful as

248

James's arms around her. She felt safe, cared for and protected in his strong embrace. They were conditions that had been in short supply in her life, and she longed to snuggle against his broad chest and bask in the warmth of him forever.

Chapter Seventeen

The entertainment value of Lawrence Bullock and Walter Gregory's perfidious deed lasted until almost midnight, much later than the MacNamara ladies generally stayed up on a Sunday night. Mrs. Plimsole, shocked and more than a little pleased that her dire warnings about her sister's only child should have been so spectacularly validated, seemed too excited to go home. Mrs. MacNamara, also titillated by the evening's events, demanded to know what had happened in thrilling detail.

Polly, repentant now that she'd cooled down, wondered if jail terms might not be too harsh a punishment for the misguided bumblers. James rolled his eyes, and Mrs. Plimsole expressed his sentiments.

"Nonsense," she said roundly. "They're housebreakers, Polly. They meant to do you a mischief, and it was only chance that made them enter the wrong house. Who knows *what* they'd have done if they'd entered the right house."

"Well, but they'd have found us inside and wouldn't have done anything," Polly said reasonably.

Mrs. Plimsole snorted. "Ha! They'd have waited until the

lights went out. You don't know men, my dear.''

Mrs. Plimsole, thought James, had a way of emphasizing certain words that changed their meaning entirely. For example, she made the word *men* mean *snakes*. He was impressed, although he rather resented being thrown into the same pit as Gregory and Bullock.

Polly looked unconvinced. ''Well, I'm not so sure. They both just lost their jobs, after all.''

''For good reason,'' James interposed. All three ladies turned to look at him as if they'd forgotten he was present.

Mrs. Plimsole nodded. ''Yes, indeed, Polly. There was good reason for them to be discharged. Remember that when your soft heart gets to aching for them. They're not worth it.''

''I believe Mrs. Plimsole is right, Polly dear,'' said Lillian thoughtfully. James smiled at her, pleased at her common sense. His little Polly was too blasted kind-hearted.

''Hmm,'' Polly said. ''Perhaps you're right. I still feel bad for yelling at them, though. I don't suppose my behavior was very ladylike.''

''At least you didn't kick Mr. Bullock this time, dear,'' said Lillian.

''No,'' Polly said. ''At least I didn't do that.''

The three ladies looked at each other and then burst out laughing.

James watched them with amusement. Maybe this was what a family was all about. He'd never experienced it before. He understood Polly's feelings a little better now. If he'd grown up with all this warmth and sharing, he might feel sorry for someone who was estranged from his family, too.

As it was . . . Well, the funny sense of loss he'd been feeling lately seemed to have gone away in the last couple of hours. What James couldn't figure out was how he could feel loss for something he'd never had to lose in the first place. It was too confusing to think about now, so he concentrated on the conversation.

He sat next to Polly on the sofa, everybody apparently too excited about criminal activities in the neighborhood to wonder at the liberty he was taking. He even, from time to time, dared take her hand in his. Polly, leaning forward on her seat

251

to swap suppositions and possible ramifications with her mother and Mrs. Plimsole, would send him a smile over her shoulder each time he did it. He knew she thought he was only agreeing with her opinion when he took her hand. But he wasn't.

He loved the satiny feel of her skin against his. When, at long last, Mrs. Plimsole departed for her home up the street and Lillian wheeled herself off to bed, James begged a moment or two alone with Polly.

"We should discuss these papers, Polly," he said, knowing he dissembled.

"All right, James."

"And you haven't told me the news you were going to share, either."

"Oh, that's right. Well, just sit down and I'll tell you all about it."

So James sat and took her hands in his as she related her visit to J. P. Drayton's office the prior day.

With a frown, James said, "I don't like the idea of you wandering into that neighborhood by yourself, Polly."

"Wandering? I wasn't wandering, James. I knew exactly where I was going. And while I know the docks are rather unsavory for an unescorted lady, still, it was Saturday and a market day. There were dozens of respectable people there at the fish stands."

On the point of arguing with her, James suddenly gave it up and grinned. "You're quite an independent little thing, aren't you, my fair Polly?"

He watched with approval as her darling little chin lifted with pride. "Indeed, I am, James. I've had to be."

Right before James could wrap her in his arms and kiss her, she pulled back and announced eagerly, "And you were absolutely right about your father, James. He's perfectly awful!"

All thought of improper behavior fled James's brain in an instant. "Really? You really think so?" He guessed he shouldn't be happy to hear somebody call his father awful, but Polly's approbation had come to mean a good deal to him, and he couldn't help it.

"Indeed, he is. But you know, James, I think he's honestly

trying to change his ways. He simply doesn't quite know how to go about it.''

Rolling his eyes, James muttered, "Good Lord." Then he tipped up Polly's chin and gazed into her eyes. "Don't believe it for a minute, Polly. It wouldn't be a wise thing to do.''

"Why not? What can he do to me? Or me to him, if it comes to that. He did us a kindness, James. Don't forget that.''

When he opened his mouth to protest, Polly put a finger against his lips, sending a shock of awareness through him.

"Oh, I know you don't think he was being kind. And I agree that he did owe us some measure of compensation for my father's death, especially if it happened because he'd hired an incompetent captain. But, James, according to you, he's never done anything of this nature before.''

Reluctantly drawing his mind away from what he wanted to do with Polly, James muttered, "That's true.''

"Well, then, you see? I think this change in his behavior is most telling, because people don't generally do things that are out of character unless they're trying to better themselves. It may be a small gesture on his part—although it seems quite generous to me—but it's a step in the right direction. I think he's begun to contemplate growing old and missing out on the joys a family can bring.''

"The joys of a family?'' James realized he sounded sarcastic and regretted not tempering his irritation. But the joys of a family? What did his father know about the joys of a family? With a jolt, he recalled his feelings earlier in the evening.

As if she hadn't heard him, Polly continued, "I told him so, in fact. I told him he'd better mend his ways or nobody would ever want to have anything to do with him.''

"You did?'' It must have curled old J. P.'s hair to have little Polly MacNamara read him the riot act. James couldn't stifle his chuckle.

"Yes, I did. I believe he was quite taken aback when I reminded him that if he continued to be estranged from you, he might never know his own grandchildren.''

253

"You told him that?" To his knowledge, nobody ever, ever ever said things like that to J. P. Drayton.

"I certainly did. I believe I caught his attention, too."

"I'm sure you did." James nearly choked on his laughter Polly MacNamara, holding her own with J. P. Drayton. Oh my.

"Don't you dare laugh at me, James Drayton."

"Of course not." Oh, how he wanted to hold her and kiss her and teach her all the wonders of passion. She'd be an ap pupil; James was sure of it.

Unfortunately, Polly's attention seemed to have a depress ing tendency to hone in on the business at hand.

"Well," she said with a sigh, "I suppose we should go over those papers."

"I suppose we should. It's getting late."

"Yes." She stood up and smoothed her skirt. "It's very late. And I have to get up early and go to work. The boss doesn't like it when his typists are late coming in to work you know."

James leaned back on the sofa and grinned at her. "He doesn't, eh? So you've decided not to quit?"

She stopped smiling. "As to that, I'm not sure yet, James I—well, I enjoy the independence of earning my keep. On the other hand, if I don't need to earn our living any longer, may choose to devote more of my time to charitable cause and leave the paying jobs to those women who need them."

"A noble decision, my fair Polly."

"Don't be silly, James. Besides, Mother Francis Mary ha asked me to direct the children's chorus. They're going to sing Christmas carols at the Charity Ball on Christmas Eve."

"Really? I didn't know you were musical as well as beau tiful, my fair Polly."

"Well, I am," she told him with a saucy grin.

"My, my. A virtual font of womanly virtues. Typewriting and music; your skills are never ending. I'm not sure my firm can survive without you."

"No," she said pertly. "I'm not, either."

Throwing his head back on the sofa cushions, Jame

aughed with unfeigned good humor. He hadn't felt so good
n years, if ever.

Polly settled her fists on her hips and honored him with a
stern frown when he stopped laughing and wiped the tears
rom his eyes. "You know, Mr. Drayton, you are in many
ways an enlightened employer."

"Thank you."

"But it's still not *that* much fun working for James Drayton
and Associates."

"No?"

"No. Especially if you plan to hire another rude secretary
ike Walter Gregory."

James rose from the sofa and took her by the shoulders. He
stared down into her lovely eyes and said, "I wouldn't dream
of doing such an addlepated thing again, Polly."

"No?"

"No."

"Well, it's a good thing."

Pulling away from him as though she were nervous, Polly
turned around and eyed the parlor, still adorned with boxes
rom decorating. "Yes. Well, I suppose I can pack up these
boxes while we chat about those papers."

"Come here, Polly."

"I beg your pardon?"

"I don't want you to be scurrying around the parlor while
we talk, my fair Polly. I want you by my side."

James's soft, seductive voice, his gentle, suggestive words,
iltered through Polly's senses like a fine mist. She turned under the pressure of his hands and found herself caught in the
warmest gaze she'd ever seen. Suddenly she felt monumen-
ally nervous. And terribly warm.

"You—you do?"

"I do."

As gently as a kitten's paw, his lips brushed hers. Her eyes
uttered shut at his touch. She leaned toward him and felt a
well of disappointment when he didn't follow up on his dis-
reet kiss with another, deeper one; another like the one they'd
hared in his motorcar.

Feeling drugged, she opened her eyes and peered at him.

255

Her lips tingled where he'd touched them, and she felt them with her tongue, longing to taste him on her. She didn't understand why James groaned softly when she did it.

"Oh, Polly," he murmured.

Then he folded her in his arms, and Polly was lost. Heat rushed through her until her body felt too small to contain it. Sensations she'd never experienced drove her to encircle James's neck with her arms and cling to his shoulders, pressing herself against him. She could feel her breasts flatten against his chest, knew her nipples were hard and that he could undoubtedly feel them, and instead of withdrawing as a gentle maiden should, she pressed harder.

Lord, he made her feel good. He made her feel things she'd never known a woman could feel.

"Oh, James." She knew her words were swallowed by his mouth, and the knowledge made her burn even hotter.

His hands, which had been gripping her waist, began to move. They stroked a hot path up her body until they rested on her rib cage beside her breasts. She felt a wanton need for him to touch her there, too.

When he did, she whimpered, and didn't care. She felt glorious. Wonderful. She felt like a woman, and the feeling almost overwhelmed her.

"Oh, Polly, Polly, Polly. Whatever am I to do with you?"

James's ragged voice penetrated the mush he'd made of Polly's brain only slowly. She wondered if he expected her to answer and decided he probably didn't. If anybody knew what to do with her, that person seemed to be James. Her hand crept up the back of his neck to sink into his luxurious hair, and she heard him groan again.

A shock of triumph that she could make this sophisticated older man of the world moan in passion jolted through her. And she knew it was passion, too. She might be innocent, but Polly MacNamara knew what was what. She recognized his hard, heavy arousal against her thigh for what it was and moved her leg against it, eliciting another ragged moan. Elation stabbed her, sharp and hot.

"Oh, Lord, Polly."

Polly was monumentally disappointed when James pulled

away from her. She opened her eyes to see whether he seemed as affected as she by what they were doing together. She felt a small ripple of joy to note that he looked ruffled. His eyes glowed like hot, dark-green pools. His chest heaved with exertion. His hair was mussed. His face was flushed. He looked, in short, the way she felt: aroused and ready.

Ready for what? Polly wasn't sure, but she knew she was ready. Heat steamed inside her, and a delicious pressure had begun to spiral until it formed a pulsing pool of need between her thighs. Instinctively, she knew James was the only man she would allow to satisfy it.

James stared at her for quite some moments without speaking. Polly was grateful for his silence. She needed time to gather her wits, which had been sent scrambling in a thousand directions by his kiss. With a shimmer of understanding, she realized he needed the time, too, for the same reason.

Good. She didn't want to be alone in this, for heaven's sake.

She'd just begun to feel uncomfortable, to wonder whether he was merely trifling with her, when he spoke again, shattering the unworthy thought.

"I'm sorry, Polly." He still sounded rattled, as if his wits, too, had gone begging.

"S-sorry?" Her voice was tiny, a mere thread of the voice that had recently ripped Lawrence Bullock and Walter Gregory to ribbons.

She gave a tiny start of alarm when he said, forcefully, "No. Damn it all, I'm *not* sorry. I've been wanting to kiss you again ever since I kissed you in my horseless carriage."

"You have?"

Giving her a look hot enough to toast bread, James said, "God, yes."

"Oh, James, I'm so glad."

So he did it again.

Never had Polly expected to feel as she felt now, vital with life and passion. James's lips devoured hers. Then, to her amazement, they left her mouth and began to move against her skin, scorching a path to her cheek, her throat. He nibbled her earlobe and she almost cried out in surprise and pleasure. His hand ventured up into her hair, loosening pins, cradling

Emma Craig

her scalp, holding her still for his tender assault. His hand
sculpted her body. For the first time in her life, Polly wishe
she was not wearing a corset. She wanted to feel his hands o
her flesh, unhampered by those ridiculous, confining stays.

As his hands and mouth toured her body, James murmured
"Oh, Polly, you're so lovely, so perfect. I've dreamed of this
I've dreamed of you."

"You have dreams too?"

"Oh, yes. Oh, yes."

Polly felt his tongue press against the frantic pulse on he
throat and almost fainted.

Her quick gasp apparently touched a gentlemanly nerve i
James, because he lifted his head. "My God, Polly."

Breathing hard, he drew away from her. As soon as hi
hands dropped, she almost did, too. When he withdrew hi
support, she staggered and, with a soft thud, sat in an armchai
Unable to speak, she looked up at him, her heartbeat ragged
her hand pressing her medals. Oh, my Lord. She wished the
could do that again. And again and again. She wanted to b
able to do it forever.

Running a hand through his tumbled locks, James rasped
"I guess we'd better get those papers signed now." H
grinned ruefully, obviously striving for control. "Mind yo
I'd rather kiss you again, but I'm afraid your mother migh
object."

Polly tried to agree with him, but her throat wouldn't work
She cleared it with difficulty and said, "Yes." Because sh
didn't want him to think she'd minded, she said, "Althoug
you do it so well, it's a shame to stop."

She'd shocked him. She knew it because he stopped fum
bling in his briefcase and shot her a look over his shoulde.
His dark brows lifted. "Well, we'll have to practice agai
soon."

Oh, Lord, she hoped so. He brought her the papers, whic
she pretended to read, although she couldn't concentrate on
single sentence. Then she signed her name on the appropriat
line and James folded the papers back up, stuffed them int
his briefcase, closed it and tucked it under his arm.

258

Realizing he was preparing to leave, Polly popped up from her chair. "I'll see you to the door, James."

"Thank you."

She felt awkward as she walked him to the door and reached out to open it.

"So I will see you at work tomorrow, Polly?"

His question made her hesitate, her hand resting on the knob. "Well, yes. I haven't decided to give notice yet. And I'll give you notice, James, if I decide to leave the firm. I know you need the four of us typists. I won't leave you in the lurch."

"Nobody could ever replace you, Polly."

She could only whisper, "Oh."

Then she was in his arms again. She felt bolder this time, and it took her no time at all to wrap her arms around him and return his embrace. When she felt his tongue against her lips, she opened her mouth, and almost fainted when his tongue invaded her mouth to spar with hers. It felt like heaven. Pure heaven.

Unfortunately, James Drayton was a consummate gentleman. The kiss was entirely too brief in Polly's estimation. Her heart thundered like an electrical storm when he drew his head back. Her hand instinctively sought her charms and clutched them tightly as she peered into James's eyes. He had the most beautiful eyes. They were dark and mysterious and the most wonderful, rich shade of hazel.

His hand covered hers. "I still want to see your medal one of these days, Polly."

"Yes."

"I wish I could—"

His eyes went round when she quickly pressed her hand over his mouth. "Be careful what you wish for. I think it's magic."

"Magic?" He looked at her quizzically.

"Oh, I know it sounds crazy. Maybe it is. But—but—" She looked down at their twined hands. "But, I swear, James, when I touch my medal and wish for things, they happen."

He was silent for a moment. At last he said, "You're serious, aren't you, Polly?"

He sounded as though he wasn't sure he approved, and Polly sighed. She'd been afraid of this. "Oh, James, I know it sounds impossible. It probably is. It's just that so many strange things have happened when I wish for them, I can't help but—well, I've begun to believe that maybe there's something about the coin that—well—*makes* things happen. Only strangely."

"Like what?"

Taking a deep breath, figuring herself for a blazing fool, Polly plunged into her explanation. "It started the very day that strange lady gave me the coin, James. I wished I was home already, and you showed up right then, at that exact moment."

"I see."

"And then I wished I had a gown to wear with the coin, and I got one. And when I wished the sidewalk would open up and swallow Lawrence Bullock, he tripped over that crack. And when I wished for a goosedown comforter for Mother, your silly dog upset that goose cart."

"You didn't get a comforter," James reminded her with grin. "You got a goose."

"I know. I told you things don't happen exactly as I wish for them. And—and then I wished Mother's life could be easier, and she began to walk, and your father sent that bank draft. And yesterday, as an experiment, I wished I'd see Dewey, and he showed up and nearly chewed Mr. Bullock's leg off."

She looked up at him, hoping he wouldn't think she was raving lunatic, and said, "And today, I wished I'd see you."

"You did?"

"Yes."

He stroked her cheek with the back of his hand, sending shower of sparks rioting through her. "And what else have you wished for, my fair Polly?"

"Oh—oh, lots of things, James. I can't even remember them all." She dropped her gaze and a spasm of sorrow made her heart ache. "I wished Stephen would come home for the holidays, and we heard about his ship the very next day."

James gave her a quick, sympathetic hug. "I see. You were

ight when you said your wishes don't come true exactly as you wish them."

"No, they don't. That's the strange part. I think——" She stopped speaking suddenly, embarrassed. Then she took a quick breath and plunged on. "I've thought about it a lot because it seems so crazy. But I think the coin is so old that some of the magic has rubbed off. I know it sounds silly, even idiotic, but there it is." She smiled up at him bravely. "I guess I'm just an idiot."

"You're not an idiot, Polly. You're almost making me believe in your magic coin."

"I wish you did."

James sighed and said, "I do, too."

They both seemed to realize what they'd said at the same time. Polly felt her eyes open wide and watched James's eyes do the same.

Then he laughed. "Well, I reckon we'll find out now if that thing is magic, won't we?"

"I guess we will."

"May I see this amazing magical coin, Polly? I'm too curious to wait any longer."

"Of course."

Reaching under her demure high collar, Polly caught the gold chain with her fingers and withdrew it from her bodice. Slipping the chain over her head, she held the St. Christopher medal and her ancient coin in her palm. St. Christopher's golden outline looked, as always, stoic and calm, ready to help the weary traveler along the road of life. A dull glow radiated from the coin. It shone like no other metal object Polly had ever seen.

She said softly, "It always looks as though it bears its own atmosphere. It's as though it's from another world, and this one can't quite touch it."

"It is a queer little thing, isn't it?" James reached out and touched the coin with his finger. "It's quite pretty. May I pick it up?"

"Of course."

"It's warm, too." All at once he closed his fingers around it, shut his eyes, and stood stock still.

"What are you doing, James?"

He opened his eyes and smiled down at her. "Wishing." Then he put the coin back in her hand. "Take care of that thing. If it's magic, you don't want to lose it." Putting his hat on his tousled head, he added with a grin, "Or wear it out."

She laughed softly. "No. I don't want to do that."

Slipping the chain around her neck again, Polly watched him stride away from her. She pressed the charms in her hand and wished he'd never leave her again.

The next three weeks passed in a blur for Polly. She continued to work, although she no longer needed to. For some reason, during those weeks she felt strange, as though she were a different person; or the person she used to be had undergone some magical transformation.

Often she found herself pondering the phenomenon and wondering if the bizarre feeling came from knowing she and her mother were no longer poor. Or maybe, she thought with a rush of warmth suffusing her body, James Drayton's kisses had done something to her brain and beguiled her. Or then again, maybe it was her coin. Her magic coin? Some nights she'd sit on her bed for an hour or more pondering the ancient charm; turning it over and over in her hand and wondering, wondering, wondering.

Whatever the reason for the change in her mood, this was the first time since she'd gone to work for James Drayton and Associates that she'd felt expansive. She found herself actually laughing and chatting with her co-workers, as though she were one of them instead of a breed apart. It surprised her to realize they all seemed to like her once she let down her reserve and opened up.

Could it have been she who'd set herself apart from them and not they who'd created the chasm yawning between them? She'd always just assumed they didn't like her.

Good heavens. Maybe they thought *she* didn't like *them*. It was a daunting notion.

"Why, Polly MacNamara, a body would think you'd fallen in love, the way you're acting," Constance teased.

When Polly blushed, Rose giggled and said, "I declare, you

must have hit the nail right on the head, Constance.''

Juliana, looking for once almost kind, said, ''Well, whatever it is, it's improved your attitude, Polly.''

Polly decided they were hitting too close to the truth for her to take exception. She laughed, thereby further thawing the invisible wall of ice she'd built between herself and the three women who'd only known her as aloof and stiff.

When Constance ventured a tentative question about her charitable activities, Polly waxed eloquent about her orphans, and another foot or two of the wall melted. She'd never had anybody to talk to before except her mother. She hadn't realized how satisfying it could be to chat with girlfriends and swap tales about individual interests and activities.

She was able to give her three co-workers daily updates on her choir's progress. Now that she had acknowledged that her mother was capable of fending for herself, she didn't feel she had to rush home after work. Every day she visited the Sisters of Benevolence. Taking her job as choir director seriously, she taught the children a small symphony of Christmas carols. She couldn't recall ever having a more satisfying job than dealing with the delightful orphans.

''I suspect it's a sure bet you'll have to have some children of your own someday then,'' said Constance.

''Oh, how I'd love to.'' Polly sighed.

Rose grinned. ''I guess you'll just have to get that fellow of yours to marry you, then.''

For the first time in days Polly's bright mood dimmed.

Her fellow. Did she have a fellow? James hadn't so much as spoken to her since the night they'd shared those glorious kisses. Prior to that evening, she'd honestly come to believe he wasn't the insensitive ladies' man people thought him to be. She wasn't sure any longer.

''Oh, Polly, Rose didn't mean anything.''

Polly looked up in surprise to discover that it was Juliana who'd caught her mood and accurately guessed its cause. For heaven's sake.

She made a concerted effort to cast her doubts aside. After all, even if James Drayton proved to be a cad, even if she never married and had children, she could still live a happy, fulfilling life.

"I know it, Juliana. I—I was just—thinking about something."

Juliana gave her a smile of sympathetic understanding. The smile effectively told Polly that Juliana didn't believe her for a minute.

James deliberately kept away from Polly during the weeks before Christmas. When he'd closed his hand around her silly charm that night, he'd wished for guidance. Then he couldn't believe it of himself. Was he going completely daft?

As if a hardheaded businessman needed guidance in personal matters from an ancient Chinese coin! He frowned in exasperation as he prepared to interview a secretarial candidate.

He didn't need guidance. What he needed was to keep away from Polly MacNamara. Any more kisses like the ones they'd shared in her parlor and he'd end up having to marry the girl. And James Drayton definitely did not need a wife. In spite of what he'd thought the other day.

For the Lord's sake, a wife—especially one who believed in magic coins—would expect him to be forever declaring his love for her. And, while James was willing, tentatively, to acknowledge that he cared deeply for Polly, he knew better than to believe, honestly and truly, that romantic love existed on this mortal coil. Not the kind the poets wrote about; the kind that lasted forever and ever, through space and time and thick and thin, it didn't. Certainly he'd forget about her if he just stayed away from her. He was sure of it. Or, at least, he was relatively sure. A little bit sure, at any rate. He thought he might, anyway.

He did have Raymond Sing visit the jail and ensure that appropriate charges had been filed against Lawrence Bullock and Walter Gregory. They had. Mr. Fleischer had scurried down to press charges the very evening the bumbling pair had broken into his house. Under ordinary circumstances, James would have seen to the matter himself. Right now, however,

he didn't want to be anywhere near the MacNamara home and
the temptation of Polly.

The whole time Raymond was away from the office, James
was unable to concentrate. Then he nearly bit Raymond's head
off when he returned.

"Good heavens, James, everything's all right," said Raymond, surprised and more than a little annoyed by his friend's
touchiness.

James raked a hand through his hair, a gesture he'd adopted
lately, much as Polly pressed her coin. "I'm sorry, Raymond.
I—I don't feel well."

That was the truth. He was cranky as a boiled owl, and he
felt like hell.

He was also more frustrated than he could recall being in
years. Neither he nor Raymond had been able to dig up the
tiniest shred of information about the U.S.S. *China Seas*. It
was as if a hole in the world had opened up and swallowed
not merely the ship and Polly's brother, but every single par-
ticle of information about either one of them. Or anybody else
who'd been on the damned ship. The whole mysterious situation set James's teeth on edge.

And those ridiculous Christmas decorations he'd had his
housekeeper put up were driving him crazy. Every morning
he got up and had to wade through a sea of greenery to find
his way to the dining room. Even his stairway was hung with
garlands. He couldn't put his hand on the banister, for God's
sake, without stabbing himself with a damned pine needle.
And the woman had put red candles and a green bough in the
middle of the dining-room table. The dining-room table, of all
places!

The fact that she'd done so at his request galled him almost
beyond endurance. He couldn't recall another single time in
his life when he'd so completely lost his head. Christmas decorations? Bah!

He thought about his father, too. According to Polly, J. P.
was trying to mend fences between them. As if *she* knew anything about the matter! Still, the fact remained that J. P. had
approached him about representing his shipping firm. And
he'd more than made up for any financial losses incurred by

Emma Craig

the MacNamara ladies as a result of Franklin MacNamara's death, even if he couldn't bring him back to life. In fact, when James had learned the amount of money J. P. had sent the MacNamaras, he'd been struck speechless. Such largesse was unlike the J. P. Drayton James knew.

Yet, if J. P. were changing his ways, would it be churlish of James to reject his peace overtures? Did he dare believe the signs?

The truly depressing part of the whole confusing matter was that James had discovered a gaping hole in his life when he experimented with mentally removing the cloak of villainy from his father's shoulders. Without J. P. Drayton's bad example to rebel against, James found himself at a loss; floundering for a foothold on the slippery slope of life.

His reaction made him take a critical look at himself. He didn't like what he saw, and was intolerably irritated by that fact.

And, as if all that wasn't enough, he couldn't get Polly MacNamara out of his mind. She was with him day and night. He couldn't even get away from her in sleep, because she haunted his dreams. And every time she popped into his head, his body stiffened with desire. Good God.

His mood was really rotten as Christmas approached.

Chapter Eighteen

Polly stared at herself in the mirror and wondered if the vision she beheld could really be Polly MacNamara, until recently a mere typist in the firm of James Drayton and Associates, Attorneys at Law.

With a somewhat dazed smile, she decided it must be.

Then she twirled in front of the mirror, watched her cream-colored ball gown bell out, threw back her head, and laughed. The transformation was positively incredible.

She was nervous as a tabby in a room full of tigers about this evening, though. James had sent a message that he would pick her up at seven o'clock. For three weeks he'd been avoiding her. His deliberate neglect had hurt her feelings. She felt a little as though she'd been used, although she knew she shouldn't feel that way. After all, she could have rejected his advances. Instead, she'd responded to his kisses with heavenly abandon.

It might have been humiliating, but Polly's pride was such that she refused to brood. Tilting her chin at a defiant angle, she muttered, "If that's the way he is, then who needs him?"

Almost immediately the thought that *she* needed him thrust

itself into her head and nagged at her until she sighed with frustration.

She commanded herself to stop thinking about possibilities. Then she took the unprecedented step of complimenting her reflection. "At any rate, you look lovely this evening. This gown might have been made for you." She fingered her coin, hanging tonight on its carefully preserved red velvet ribbon. "And my coin has never looked more beautiful."

She stopped fidgeting for a minute and stared at herself. Her bright cinnamon eyes stared back. They looked big, and she couldn't recall her lashes appearing so dark and lush before this evening. Perhaps she'd just never noticed. Why, her eyes looked almost mysterious.

The creamy satin and lace of her gown made her skin seem to glow. The red rose at her waist sat at a place and an angle that accentuated her trim figure and added a hint of naughtiness that Polly decided she liked. A lot.

Polly'd never done so novel a thing as appreciate her looks before. As she acknowledged her own attractiveness, the color rushed to her cheeks, enhancing her image.

Then a smile lit her countenance and she swept herself an elegant curtsy. Oh, she was going to shine tonight. If only she didn't get too nervous and spoil the effect of all this beauty by stumbling or spilling punch on her skirt or something equally awful.

She remembered the night she'd tried on this gown and wished James Drayton could see her wearing it. And now he would! She was sure he'd appreciate the way she looked. She certainly would not disgrace him, at any rate.

With a haughty sniff, she decided that even if he ignored her all evening long, she would not pine. She'd just amuse herself with the children. And with Mother Francis Mary.

She was ever so thankful that the Mother Superior planned to accompany the children's choir to the ballroom. Polly didn't know what she'd do with herself if she had to stay in a ballroom full of people without knowing a single soul there except the man who'd been avoiding her like the plague for three weeks. Her heart ached painfully, and she told it to stop.

She'd been fine before she met him; she'd be fine again. A

little sadly, she acknowledged that it might take time. But she'd be fine; just fine.

Although she did not allow herself to dwell on the thought, she feared she'd never truly be fine again. In fact, she had a sinking feeling there would forever be an empty spot in her heart; a spot reserved for James.

Wrenching her mind away from the maudlin contemplation of unrequited love, Polly squared her shoulders. She heard the doorbell ring, and an arrow of anxiety pierced her. She shook it off impatiently.

With one final glance at her reflection, she muttered, "Well, he may not love me, but he can't fault my dress or looks tonight."

Polly grabbed her tiny beaded handbag—bought especially for the evening with some of her newly acquired wealth—wrapped her mother's elegant Chinese silk shawl carelessly over her arms—as Rose had demonstrated she should do—angled her chin just so and marched to the staircase.

James stood in the front hall, chatting with her mother. Polly took a deep breath, said a little prayer for courage and descended the stairs.

"I'm very well, thank you, Mrs. MacNamara," James said in response to Lillian's polite question. "And how are you? You seem to be faring remarkably well. I don't believe I've seen you walk before."

"Oh, I've been walking for about two weeks now. I can't go far yet, but I try to practice as much as possible."

James, his nerves raw, got the impression that Lillian was barely repressing her disappointment that he'd not been to call on her daughter during those weeks. Then he decided he was being unreasonable and wished he'd get over this strange, aggravating mood of his.

He wished this damned night were over.

He wanted to rub his jaw, to pass his hand through his hair, to straighten his tie. Since none of those things needed to be done, he curtailed the impulse. This urge to fidget was only a manifestation of his irritable nerves. That's all. As soon as this last onerous task was completed, he could relax. He was a fool for having invited Polly to go with him to this idiotic ball.

"Is that a corsage, Mr. Drayton? How nice of you."

James's wandering attention snapped back to Lillian MacNamara. "Yes. Yes, it is."

James looked at the flowers he'd had his new secretary buy for Polly and frowned. He hoped she'd be wearing something that went with red. His secretary, Collis Philpott, said the florist recommended them as being appropriate for Christmas. Well, James guessed they were, but he certainly couldn't imagine what could possibly go with white orchids and red roses.

"I expect Polly will be down in a minute, Mr. Drayton. Oh, yes, here she is."

James turned toward the staircase, his scowl firmly in place. When he saw the glory that was Polly walking serenely down the stairs, he lost his train of thought.

"My God."

Lillian smiled with motherly affection. "Doesn't that gown suit her, though? I think she looks perfectly lovely."

James had to swallow. "Er, yes. Yes, she does."

"And that corsage will look beautiful at her shoulder, too."

"Yes."

He shook himself out of his trance when Polly negotiated the last stair and stepped onto the carpeted hallway. With a lunge, he reached her side.

"Here. Here, let me help you, Polly." His voice, he noted, sounded foreign. Hoarse.

"Thank you, James."

"I—I brought you some flowers. A corsage."

Her face lit with pleasure. "How sweet of you. Thank you." She looked at the corsage he held and exclaimed, "Why, they're perfect! Did you ask Mother what color my gown was?"

"Er, no. No, I guessed."

Or, rather, Collis Philpott had guessed. All of a sudden James felt a wash of shame.

"Here, Polly, let me pin it on your dress."

"Thank you, James. I've never been given a corsage before." Then she looked a little peeved, as though she wished she'd kept her artless confession to herself.

James didn't mind. Oh, he guessed he felt as though he'd

just been kicked by an army mule, but he didn't mind. Or maybe he'd just had the sense knocked back into him. Peering at Polly's perfectly blameless face, he wondered why he'd been in such a godawful snit for the last few weeks.

Why on earth had he been in such a dither, refusing to acknowledge the almost overwhelming attraction he felt for her? Why, for heaven's sake, had he stayed away from this delightful woman, who seemed to take such pleasure in his company? Why had he punished himself by refusing to see her? Why in God's name did he want this glorious feeling to go away? In the name of all that's holy, he should embrace it with both hands, grateful to have the bland nothingness that had been his life revitalized by Polly.

Why had he been in such a confounded lather to refuse to love this perfectly lovable woman?

He had no earthly idea. His foul humor seemed silly to him now: a sulky child's reaction to something he didn't understand and didn't want to recognize.

But, for God's sake, he loved her! The truth seemed so reasonable now, tonight, in her spectacularly feminine presence.

By God, she was perfect. In every detail. Cynthia Ingram, with all her seductive beauty, couldn't hold a candle to Polly MacNamara. She was perfect. She was what he'd been missing all his life. She filled up the empty places in his heart. She'd given him laughter. She'd shown him joy. She'd taught him that he didn't have to try so damned hard not to be his father.

He loved her. He, James Drayton, was as much a fool as the poets; as much a fool as anybody else on earth. He loved her.

James felt like shouting it from the rooftops. By damn, he loved her!

His delicious trance lasted during their good-byes with Lillian, through the door and down the front porch steps. It was Polly's delighted exclamation that ultimately brought him back down to earth.

"James! You actually did it! You brought your horses and carriage."

Polly skipped the last several paces to the carriage, her efforts to appear elegant clearly forgotten. James grinned like a kid in a candy store when she stood in front of one of the glossy black steeds and stroked his head.

"Oh, they're just beautiful, James! And you had them decorated for Christmas, too."

It was true. Earlier in the day, glowering and grumpy, he'd told his stable manager to put the damned Christmas bells and ribbons on the damned horses. He had to go to the damned charity ball this evening, and he'd made a stupid damned promise.

At this moment, James wished he'd done even more. More bells! More ribbons! Bring them all on! He was ready. He resolved to give his stable manager an extra bonus this Christmas for putting up with his sour mood.

James contemplated the stir they'd cause if they could arrive at the ball late and make a grand entrance. Oh, how he'd love to do that. All the people he knew as business associates, the ones who were used to seeing him with the likes of Cynthia Ingram or any number of the other well-traveled ladies with whom he used to keep company, would gape when James walked in with Polly MacNamara on his arm. He'd never been seen at a society function—or anywhere else, for that matter—with such an obvious innocent. He could imagine the gossip that would surely ensue.

Such satisfaction would be denied him, though, because Polly needed to arrive early to arrange her orphans. He didn't mind. In fact, as he stood in the back of the ballroom near a cluster of chairs and watched Polly with the children, his insides lit up like the candles on a Christmas tree.

She was perfect, he decided with delight. She was absolutely perfect.

"You going to marry that baggage, James?"

James stiffened and turned quickly. Good God, it was him. J. P. Drayton. His father. Here. He frowned. "What on earth are *you* doing here?"

As a greeting it lacked finesse, but James could hardly believe the evidence of his own eyes. His father at a charitable event! What was the world coming to?

J. P. took his son's greeting amiss. He matched James's frown with one of his own. "I was invited, you damned impertinent whelp. What do you think I'm doing here?''

Annoyed with himself for succumbing to impulse, James reined in his temper and said more mildly, ''I'm unused to seeing you at such affairs, Father. I beg your pardon for being abrupt.''

''Abrupt? Bah! You were damned rude to me, James, and I don't like it.''

Deliberately refusing to be baited by this man who was an expert at the game, James turned his back on J. P. and murmured, ''What a shame.''

''Hah!''

James could feel his father seething behind him. It wasn't a new sensation, but he didn't like it. He stifled his sigh.

''You still didn't answer my question, boy. Are you or not?''

James peered over his shoulder and asked, ''Am I what?'' His voice, he noted irritably, sounded brittle. Damn. He hated showing emotion before his father.

For once J. P. seemed not to notice his son's emotional condition. ''Are you going to marry her? That girl there.'' J. P. pointed at Polly. He sounded cross. He looked cross, too.

''That's right. You've met each other, haven't you?''

J. P. glowered. ''Don't smirk at me, boy. She's a sassy little piece of goods, is what she is.''

Bristling, James opened his mouth to refute his father's outrageous assessment of Polly. J. P. stopped him short when he said, ''She'll do you some good, boy. Damned if she won't.''

''What?''

James left off watching Polly and trying to be immune to his father, and turned around to gape at the old man. He wanted to clean out his ears. He couldn't believe what they'd just heard.

His scowl perfectly ferocious, J. P. repeated, ''I said she'll do you some good. You got mud in your ears?''

Ignoring his father's question, James sucked in a deep breath and said, ''Would you care to sit and talk, Father?''

J. P.'s bushy brows arched ironically. ''You want to chat with me, boy? Whatever is the world coming to?''

Trying to hide his exasperation, James said, "Please, Father. Can't we just sit down and talk to each other without hurling barbs for once?"

Eyeing his son doubtfully, J. P. said, "Seems to me you're the one who hurls the barbs, boy. I tried to patch it up, if you'll recall."

Rather huffily, he sat in the chair James held out for him.

"Is that what you were trying to do when you asked me to represent your business?"

"What in God's name did you *think* I was trying to do?" J. P. crossed his arms over his chest and gave James his very best glower.

James, looking for the first time past his father's gruff demeanor, thought he detected the hint of a plea in the sharp old eyes. On the other hand, it was probably his imagination. James wasn't about to take any chances; he felt almost as though his soul were at stake in this battle.

"To tell you the truth, I wasn't sure what you were trying to do, Father." James peered at this stranger's face for a long time without speaking. J. P. continued to scowl, but the longer James stared at him, the less rigid his expression became. Finally, for the first time in James's memory, the old man dropped his gaze first.

J. P. cleared his throat.

Then he straightened his tie.

He crossed his left foot over his right. Then he crossed his right foot over his left.

At last he said, almost querulously, "Well, what are you staring at, damn it?"

With a start, James realized he had been staring, and rather rudely, too. "I'm sorry, sir."

J. P. gave a huffy harumph and took to watching Polly and her orphans.

"It was good of you to send that letter and bank draft to the MacNamaras, sir."

J. P.'s grizzled bulldog head snapped around, and he pinned James with a glare holding more than a hint of astonishment. "Well, you're the one who told me to do it, you cheeky puppy!" The words came out in a roar, the tone J. P. usually adopted with his son, and he had the grace to look embarrassed.

More mildly, he said, "How the hell was I to know there were people who hadn't taken advantage of the offered settlements? I didn't know until you told me."

James's first impulse was to demand to know why J. P. hadn't looked, but some angel of mercy held his tongue and he didn't disparage his father's good deed. The first good deed James could remember him ever having done.

"Well, they can certainly use the money. What with Polly's brother being lost with the *China Seas,* the money he used to send home hasn't been coming. If they determine the crew is dead, I suppose they'll get some sort of settlement, but until then—well, their lives haven't been easy."

An odd look crossed his father's face, one James had not encountered before. It looked almost as though the man were contemplating a private joke, although James knew that couldn't be the case. If there was one individual on the face of the earth devoid of a sense of humor, it was J. P. Drayton.

J. P. waved a hand, as though he didn't care to discuss the situation further. "Here comes your young woman, James," he said gruffly. "Appears fit this evening, doesn't she? Hasn't wasted any time spending her new money, it looks like."

James bit back the retort teetering on the tip of his tongue. He wouldn't give the old bastard the satisfaction of showing him a reaction. Besides, he'd be damned if he'd let Polly witness him fighting with his father.

When he turned toward her, all thought of chastising J. P. Drayton fled. Struck again by how perfect Polly was, he could only stand and grin like a lovesick fool as she neared. He saw a flicker of trepidation cross her face when she beheld J. P., but she didn't break her stride. Good for her. James knew it wasn't his place to be proud of her, but he was anyway.

"Good evening, Mr. Drayton." Polly smiled and offered James's father her hand. J. P. had risen, too, and now he frowned at her.

"Going to reproach me some more this evening, miss?"

"Of course not, Mr. Drayton. I'm glad to see you here and chatting with James."

Her glorious smile traveled from J. P. to James, and James wasn't sure he could survive many more of them without sweeping her away and ravishing her.

"I didn't know you'd be joining us this evening, Mr. Drayton," Polly said.

"Had to. That dratted Mother Superior needled me until I had to come or have her praying over my immortal soul and telling me about it every time she had to kneel." He sounded dreadfully vexed.

Polly laughed. "Indeed, Mother Francis Mary is a formidable personage. I expect anybody she prayed over would go straight to heaven."

J. P. gave another harumph.

"Why did Mother Francis Mary invite you?"

Polly turned to gape at him, and James knew she was startled by his blunt question. She just didn't know his father or she wouldn't look so surprised. J. P. never had any truck with charity. And as far as his immortal soul went, James was pretty sure J. P. didn't have one.

"I'm practically supporting those damned orphans, young man, if you want to know."

"You are?"

The voices of James and Polly blended in a duet of shock. J. P. smirked at them.

"Surprised, are you, you silly whippersnappers? You're not the only one in the family who does a good deed from time to time, boy."

James ignored the ignominious *boy* his father insisted on calling him. "I used to be."

J. P. offered another harumph.

People had begun to fill up the ballroom by this time. James decided he wasn't about to waste a perfectly good evening of Polly's company in that of J. P. Drayton. "I suppose it's time to begin mingling, Father. I'm sure we'll see each other again during the evening."

J. P. snorted, and Polly said, "Oh, you. You like people to think you're a grouchy old bear, don't you? You're just a softie underneath all that grump. You must be, or you'd never have sent Mother and me that check or support the wonderful work the good Sisters of Benevolence do.''

Although he looked astonished, J. P. didn't have time to disabuse Polly of her absurd notion because James swept her off on his arm. J. P. noticed the ironic gleam in his son's eye and resented it.

"Couple of impudent babies. That's what they are.'' Annoyed, he turned away to seek the punchbowl.

"I had no idea your father was a philanthropist, James,'' Polly said. "I got the impression he eschewed things of this nature.''

The orchestra struck up the first notes of a Strauss waltz, and James took Polly's hand. As they began to dance, James acknowledged, "As far as I know, he's never done anything like this before in his entire life. Maybe you're right. Maybe he's changing his ways.'' He knew he sounded doubtful. He *was* doubtful.

"I'm sure that's the case,'' Polly said serenely, as though J. P. Drayton giving money to charitable institutions and poor widows and orphans were not as astonishing an event as a snowstorm in August.

James decided not to argue. Holding Polly was too delicious a pastime to spoil with an argument. She danced very well. It took them no time at all to fall into perfect rhythm. He was not surprised.

Polly decided this was bliss: to be dancing the waltz in the arms of the man she loved on Christmas Eve. James didn't seem at all standoffish tonight; she couldn't understand why he'd been so aloof during the past three weeks.

Whatever the reason, she didn't intend to dwell on his strange behavior. He was attentive tonight, and tonight was all that mattered.

The ballroom had been decorated in swags of green foliage and holly berries. Red ribbons graced the candelabra, a huge Christmas tree stood against the front wall, there was gold and glitter everywhere, and a generally festive air prevailed. A hundred or more charitable San Franciscans were expected to attend this annual extravaganza. Light refreshments were provided in a room apart from the ballroom. Polly had never attended such a grand affair.

Her choir was scheduled to sing at eight, after speeches by prominent politicians and businessmen who supported the Sisters of Benevolence. Polly, who had worried about having someone to talk to, found herself all but hovered over by James. He introduced her to everybody who fell within their orbit, and she discovered that chatting with rich people was not very different from chatting with poor ones. It was as Rose had instructed her: If she acted as though she belonged, people would treat her as though she did.

She found the whole experience amazing. There was one woman, however, who puzzled her. Was it her imagination, or was James trying to avoid her? The woman was a golden-haired beauty who hung on the arm of a gentleman to whom James had introduced her earlier. She certainly didn't seem to want to avoid James. In fact, she seemed to be staring at them, an expression of wry amusement on her face.

Oh, my, she was lovely. Polly felt a twist of jealousy and then told herself to stop being silly.

It might very well be true that the woman and James were friends. Why, the woman obviously had scads of money. Just look at the way she glittered. Perhaps she glittered a bit *too* much for refinement, Polly decided uncharitably. There was no denying, however, that she certainly caught one's eye.

The awful notion that perhaps the gilt beauty and James more than merely knew each other struck Polly and dimmed her enjoyment for a moment or two. Then she told herself severely that it was no concern of hers one way or the other. After all, she supposed James had every right to see whomever he wished.

Since the thought of James with that brilliant female made her want to cry, Polly stopped thinking about it at once. James had just introduced her to another couple of gentlemen, one a banker, the other an attorney, and she gave them her own version of a dazzling smile. The banker, a gentleman named Brundage, was dazzled enough to ask her to dance.

"We can't allow James to monopolize you all evening, Miss MacNamara," he told her with a very warm smile.

"Such a treat as you are must be shared. Right, James?"

Although James laughed at his friend's jest, Polly took satisfaction in noticing a quiver of what might be aggravation cross his handsome features. She smiled back at Mr. Brundage as she took his proffered hand.

"Just bring her back in one piece, Brundage. Be careful, Polly. Brundage has feet the size of watermelons, and everybody knows he can't dance."

"Don't be silly, James," Mr. Brundage advised with a mock scowl. "Don't pay any attention to him, Miss MacNamara. He's merely jealous."

An unworthy, *Oh, I do hope so,* charged through Polly's head.

At first she managed to pay attention to the dance and even engage in pleasant conversation with her partner. Mr. Brundage danced nowhere near as well as James.

"So, Miss MacNamara, how on earth did you manage to meet our devil-may-care James? Do you have an interest in these charities? Is that why he's here? Those of us who support these nuns' soup kitchens were quite surprised to find him at this shindig."

Polly could feel her cheeks get warm and was glad Mr. Brundage had given her an excuse not to tell him she was a lowly typist for James's firm. She also decided James's secret was safe with her, even if her heart wasn't.

"Oh, my, yes," she said, striving for an air of nonchalance. "Why, I've been devoting time to the orphanage for two years now. I'm in charge of the choir tonight." She was *so* proud of her choir, but she thought she might appear unsophisticated if she were to demonstrate her pride.

"My goodness, what a talented young lady. And what other skills do you possess?"

Typewriting, Polly thought grimly. As they executed another turn, she glanced toward James and saw that the spectacular blonde had approached him. Or appropriated him. Brundage's polite question fled from her mind.

James and the painted lady chatted easily, the woman laughing and touching him as though they were acquaintances—at the very least—of very long standing. Polly caught herself frowning when she saw the female rub James's arm and James laugh as though she'd said something witty.

Although she stopped frowning as soon as she realized she'd succumbed to the unladylike expression, Polly still wondered what the woman had said to amuse James so. She tried to decide whether she herself was witty and came to the glum conclusion that she wasn't. Not at all. The most witty thing she'd done in years was to give James's stupid mongrel dog a pedigree.

"A Philippine Tapir Hound, indeed," she muttered.

"I beg your pardon, Miss MacNamara? Who's a hound?"

Annoyed with herself for succumbing to her unpleasant thoughts, Polly adopted a bright smile and said, "Oh, I beg your pardon, Mr. Brundage. I was just thinking about a dog I'm acquainted with."

"I'm not altogether certain I deem that a compliment, Miss MacNamara."

Polly blushed, embarrassed. "I'm sorry, Mr. Brundage. Indeed, I didn't mean anything."

With a laugh, Brundage said, "That's all right, Miss MacNamara. I've brought worse things to ladies' minds, I'm sure."

Determined not to make a fool of herself, Polly paid attention to the music for the rest of the dance. When it ended, they found themselves at the other end of the ballroom, and Mr. Brundage escorted Polly back to James's side. As they approached, Polly was perturbed to see James still tête-à-tête with the dazzling blonde.

Her escort murmured, "I see Lady Midnight's found him."

Polly shot him a swift look. "Lady Midnight?"

Brundage immediately looked contrite, as though he'd been indiscreet and regretted it. "I mean, I see Mrs. Ingram has begun to monopolize James." He peered down at Polly. "Don't understand that man's taste."

Since Brundage seemed to be a friendly sort, Polly longed to query him about the ravishing creature clinging like a leech to James's arm. Unfortunately, they were nearing their destination and she was unable to do so.

Chapter Nineteen

Polly had just reached James's side when Mother Francis Mary bustled up to her. The old nun looked as out of place as a penguin in the grand ballroom. The Mother Superior, however, seemed not at all troubled by the discrepancy between her austere garb and that of the rest of the resplendent company.

Before James could begin an introduction between his two female friends, Mother Francis Mary grabbed Polly by the hand. "It's time, dear. Come along with me."

A little disconcerted, Polly murmured, "Of course. Please excuse me," she added to Brundage, James, and the lady.

Lady? Hah!

"You look absolutely glorious tonight, my dear. I believe all this folderol agrees with you."

Polly couldn't help but laugh. "Thank you, Mother. I must admit I've been enjoying myself." *Until the last few minutes.*

The more Polly thought about James Drayton consorting with that artfully painted creature, the less she liked it. Almost before she'd reached the raised staging area where the children were to perform, she'd decided the two of them were carrying on a torrid affair behind her back.

As if we were close enough for him to do anything at all behind my back, she thought, hurt giving way to anger. Why the beast had kissed her just a couple of weeks ago. And now look at him! Why, that woman was *plastered* to him. It didn' bear thinking of.

If that was the sort of female James Drayton favored, Polly guessed she should be happy she had discovered it now. A the moment, her chief regret was that she'd succumbed to the charms of such a blackguard in the first place. She though about wishing on her charm, then decided not to be stupid.

Determined to put James Drayton and his doxy out of he mind, Polly turned her attention to her orphans. They wer dressed in white robes with big red floppy bows at their throat and looked adorable. Polly was bursting with pride for then when they marched out in one long, well-behaved line an took their places in three tiers on the stage.

The chairman of the board of the Sisters of Benevolenc Charitable Organizations, a jolly-looking middle-aged mar named Farley, stepped up to the stage. Much to everyone' relief, his speech was brief.

"And now, ladies and gentlemen, to assure you that you generosity is appreciated by the recipients, children from th Sisters of Benevolence's Home for Orphaned Children ar here to present a program of Christmas carols. The entire pro gram has been put together and will be conducted by Mis Polly MacNamara. Miss MacNamara is a dedicated voluntee at the orphanage."

Polite applause greeted Mr. Farley's announcement. Poll thought she heard Mr. Brundage's voice call out a hearty "Hear, hear!" but she wasn't sure.

She had been nervous before. Now, as she looked at th happy, shining faces of her darling singers, she decided sh had nothing to fear. These children needed her confidence, an by George, they were going to get it. James Drayton coul just—just—well, she wasn't sure what he could do, but sh resolved to give her best to her choir.

They'd only been through the songs with an orchestral ac companiment once, earlier that very evening, but everythin went beautifully. They sang "Silent Night" as purely an sweetly as she'd ever heard it sung. When their sophisticated audience joined in during "Jingle Bells," Polly knew her choir was a success.

To cries of "Encore," the little musicale came to an end. Polly wasn't sure what to do about an encore, so she did nothing. She did smile and curtsy at the end of their performance, as Mother Francis Mary had indicated was appropriate behavior. Then, just as she was about to follow her children into the back room and give them all a round of hugs, she discovered her hand being pulled on. Surprised, she turned to find Mr. Farley, a beatific smile on his ruddy face, beckoning to her.

"Ladies and gentlemen," Mr. Farley called, "I think we owe this lovely little lady another round of applause for all the work she's done and the time she's taken with those delightful children."

A cheer went up at Farley's suggestion.

Pleased and more than a little embarrassed by the approval of her audience, Polly allowed herself to be led back to the stage. Having practiced for hours in front of her mirror for just such an eventuality, she swept another graceful curtsy.

When she rose, however, her festive mood collapsed at the sight of Lady Midnight clinging to James Drayton's arm. The over-jeweled, underdressed floozy was slithering—Polly couldn't think of another word for it—her bosom against him. Polly just barely managed to stifle her offended gasp.

Turning impetuously, she beat a quick retreat into the room where the excited singers were being feted with punch and Christmas cake. She joined them, deciding that any one of them was worth a dozen James Draytons and positively hundreds of that awful Lady Midnight, whoever she was.

As soon as the orphans spotted her, they ran up and dragged her over to the table. Mother Francis Mary handed her a piece of cake and she picked up a glass of punch.

"Your choir was certainly a rousing success, my dear," the Mother Superior said.

"Yes, I should say so. They did a wonderful job."

"Mr. Drayton and his lady friend seemed impressed."

A quick, suspicious glance at Mother Francis Mary found the nun ladling out another glass of punch, an expression of consummate innocence on her wrinkled old face. Anger bubbled in Polly's breast and she was about to disabuse Mother Francis Mary of her assumption when Raymond Sing appeared at her side.

"Mr. Sing, what a pleasure to see you."

"Good evening, Miss MacNamara. I must say you did an admirable job with the children. You must be very proud of them."

"Indeed, I am."

Mother Francis Mary joined Polly and Raymond, and Polly was able to concentrate on the conversation with a fair degree of aplomb. The ballroom was visible from the door of the choir room. Out of the corner of her eye, the specter of James and That Woman haunted her, but she tried her best to ignore it.

James wanted to deck Cynthia Ingram. Of all the inconvenient women he'd ever met in his life, she topped the list. Right now, she was hanging on to him like a barnacle, poking him with her breasts until he wanted to yell at her. He knew Polly was angry with him, and he didn't blame her.

Taking a step away from Cynthia, he shook off her clinging arms. When she attempted to sneak them back up his chest, he took both of her hands in his.

"Will you please keep your hands to yourself, Cynthia? I don't enjoy being pawed in a ballroom."

Cynthia's laugh tinkled tinnily and James winced. He could almost see the brittle noise snaking into the choir room, circling Polly's head, shattering and sprinkling her with tiny poisoned spikes.

"You didn't used to mind, James, darling." Cynthia's coo had gone a little pouty.

"I know, Cynthia. But I mind now." Irritably, James added, "Didn't you come to this thing with Wilding? Where the hell is he?"

Cynthia's pretty mouth pursed into a moue of wounded vanity. "He's undoubtedly at the punch bowl. You're ever so much more amusing than he is, James. I don't know why you're being so silly tonight."

"Dammit, Cynthia, I thought we had all this out the other day. I've come to this function with Miss MacNamara, and I don't care to have you smothering me. Why, just imagine how she must feel."

"You didn't used to care about things like that, either, James," Cynthia announced in a much less purry voice. She sounded, in fact, downright catty when she glanced at Polly's back and observed, "That prim little thing? She doesn't seem quite in your style, James."

For several seconds James didn't answer Cynthia. When he did, he chose his words carefully. "She wasn't in the style of the man I was. I believe I've changed, Cynthia, and she is now. I intend to deserve her."

Cynthia scoffed, "You can't mean to tell me you've begun taking up with virgins, James. I can't quite believe it of you."

"Will you keep your voice down, Cynthia?" James cleared his throat and said aloud for the first time, without even testing it in private first, "I love her, Cynthia."

"My God." Cynthia stared at him for several seconds.

"Will you please go back to Wilding now?"

After another appraising look at Polly, who seemed to be in a deep discussion with Raymond Sing and Mother Francis Mary, Cynthia said, "My God," again. Then she said, "Oh, James, I had no idea. Well, I presume I am to wish you happiness. I certainly hope I didn't spoil anything." Then, with another glance at Polly and one more, "My God," Cynthia Ingram turned and slunk away.

Breathing a deep sigh of relief, James joined Polly's group. His relief was short-lived. Polly gave him the coldest look he'd ever received from her and did not even pause in her discourse. She was in the midst of explaining the fine art of child-raming to Raymond Sing.

"It's really not difficult. You merely have to remember that, while they are children, they are still human beings. I don't think most children respond as well to harshness as to kindness. There are, possibly, exceptions." She cast a speaking glance at James.

With an inward groan, James put on his best society smile and said lightly, "May I please remove the heroine of the

Emma Craig

evening from your company for a moment or two, Mother
Francis Mary and Raymond? I'm sure Polly must be ready for
some refreshment.''

"We've just had refreshments," Polly told him icily.

Oh, dear. "Why, you've only had cake and punch. Why
don't we see if we can't get you some oysters and a glass of
champagne?''

"I'm fine," Polly snapped, obviously ready for battle.

Only James heard her because the Mother Superior said, in
a louder voice than Polly's and at the same time, ''Why, what
a wonderful suggestion, Mr. Drayton. Our Polly deserves to
be refreshed after all she's done today.''

James could have kissed the wise old lady. He could tell
Polly was seething, but she managed a tolerably gracious.
"Well, all right then." Then she hesitated to put her hand on
his offered arm, a circumstance James took as a bad sign.

He nodded to Raymond and the little nun. Mother Francis
Mary's eyes had taken to twinkling like a couple of Christmas
candles and he felt a sudden lick of irritation. That old lady
seemed determined to laugh at him. He wasn't sure he appreciated it.

"Have a good time, you two." James heard her rusty
chuckle and bit back a frown.

As soon as they entered the refreshment area, Polly snatched
her hand from James's coat sleeve. The delicious warm spot
she'd made on his arm immediately chilled and he felt ridiculously bereft.

He said, "You were wonderful with those children, Polly."

She said, "Thank you."

He said, "I haven't heard many children's choirs, but yours
was definitely the best of the small lot.''

She said, "Thank you."

He said, "Would you like a plate of oysters, Polly?"

She said, "No, thank you."

James sighed, frustrated. Although he knew Polly didn'
want him to, he took her by the arm and began to walk toward
a small balcony. She balked, and he ended up nearly dragging
her out the door. As a precaution, he drew the drapes so they
wouldn't be spied on by the rest of the celebrants.

"Listen, Polly, we need to talk. I have to explain what happened in there."

She arched her brows haughtily. James hadn't ever seen her look haughty before. He hadn't known she had it in her, in fact, and was unhappy with the demonstration.

"You mean the spectacle you and that Lady Midnight character made of each other while the choir sang? Is that what you want to explain, James?"

She said *James* as though it were a curse word.

"Please, Polly. It's not the way it looked."

"No?" She turned her back on him and stared over the balcony.

Use of the ballroom had been donated by a wealthy San Francisco family, and Polly found herself staring at a vast lawn. She was pretty sure that if it had been daylight, she would have been treated to a view of tasteful gardens surrounding the grassy area. Since, however, it was full dark, she could see nothing beyond a small swath of green. The effect was eerie, and she tried to concentrate on the possibility of ghosts as a pleasant alternative to this conversation. She was mad as fire now.

"No. Please let me explain. Mrs. Ingram and I have—well, we've known each other for a long time."

"Have you?" Polly could hardly believe the acidic tone came from her mouth. She was proud of herself for a second time this evening.

"Yes. We—we're old friends."

She whirled around. "Old friends? Old friends, my eye, James Drayton!"

"Polly—"

Furious, she glowered at James. "Don't you 'Polly' me! How dare you invite me to come to this function and then spend the evening with that—that *creature* plastered to you. Why, I saw you!"

"Polly, please—"

"Please what? Please don't be angry? Please don't be offended? Please don't take exception?"

"Polly—"

"No! Just because I'm a mere typist doesn't mean I don't

287

Emma Craig

have feelings, James Drayton! I can't believe even *you* would
treat a lady this way!'' Polly recalled the kisses they'd shared
and wondered if she should be calling herself a lady. Well, it
didn't matter.

''You had no right to humiliate me in front of all those
people. You had no right!''

''Oh, God, Polly, please. I didn't mean to humiliate you.''

''Hah!'' Afraid she was going to cry in anger, Polly turned
her back on him again. She wanted to say more, but her throat
ached, and she couldn't.

''Please, Polly, listen to me. I tried to brush Cynthia off,
but she wouldn't be brushed. I finally told her to let me go,
to stop doing what she was doing. It was embarrassing to me
too.'' James paused.

Still not mollified, but having worked the ache in her throat
down to a manageable knot, Polly turned and uttered a contemptuous, ''Oh, really?''

Raking a hand through his brown curls, James said, ''Yes,
really.''

His eyes pleaded for understanding. Polly, not wishing to
appear easy, refused to give it to him. ''Well, now, isn't that
grand?'' She turned around again so as not to be tempted by
his whipped-puppy expression and her heart's inclination.
What she wanted to do was fling herself into his arms.

''Oh, God, Polly, please listen to me.'' He sounded pathetic.
She muttered a sour, ''I'm listening.''

''I—I had already told her I wouldn't be seeing her any
longer, that she and I would no longer be spending time together.''

''Apparently she didn't believe you.''

James's miserable huff of distress almost made Polly turn
around. She forced herself to hold her ground.

''Aw, Polly, give me a chance. I didn't want to make a
scene tonight.''

''Hah! You did make a scene, though, didn't you?''

''I didn't mean to.'' James sounded disgruntled. ''But it
won't ever happen again, Polly. I—I told Cynthia. I told her
the truth tonight.''

288

Christmas Pie

Suspiciously, Polly asked, "And just what is the truth, James?"

Polly heard his scraping breath. She held her shoulders rigid, not daring to hope she knew what James's truth was. Although she'd eschewed it as ridiculous not fifteen minutes earlier, she reached for her coin and clung to it like a magnet.

"I told her I love you, Polly."

Polly turned around and stared at him. She wasn't sure she believed him, and she searched his face to determine the truth of his declaration.

"I told her I love you. And now I'm telling you."

Polly opened her mouth but nothing came out. James spoke for her.

"I love you as I never expected to love anybody. Will you marry me, Polly? Please say you'll marry me."

He stood stiffly before her. Polly realized with awe that his stiffness was due to fear. Fear! He was afraid she'd refuse him. Good heavens.

"Oh, James." She didn't recognize her voice.

James's brows dipped a fraction. "Is that a yes or a no, Polly? Please say something soon. I'm going crazy, waiting."

All at once Polly's insides lit up as though a Fourth of July skyrocket had somehow managed to fly through the months to explode inside her this Christmas Eve. Slowly, she smiled and watched a similar smile spread across James's face. His eyes sparkled.

She said, "Yes, James. Oh, yes."

And then she was in his arms.

J. P. Drayton had waited all evening for this. His bark of laughter startled a group of people standing nearby and they looked at him. He crumpled the note in his fist and looked back, considered scowling at them for their impertinence, decided it wasn't worth the effort and laughed again.

"By damn, they did it!"

With a chortle more nearly jolly than any he'd given in years, he peered about the room.

Now all he had to do was find that blasted boy and his silly lady love.

His merry mood lasted through one sweep of the room wi
his piercing gaze. It diminished during a second sweep un
it teetered on the brink of wrath. J. P. scowled. Damned di
respectful puppy. If this wasn't just like him, to disappe
when J. P. wanted him.

In a towering grump, he stomped around the room, searc
ing for his son. He ripped a curtain back from a balcon
startling a young man and woman who had been on the ver
of a Christmas Eve kiss. The young woman screeched ar
J. P. yanked the curtain closed again after shooting her
scowl.

"No need for that," he barked, and strode on.

By the time he spotted Raymond Sing, J. P. was mad as he
and about to explode with thwarted purpose.

"You there!"

Raymond turned, surprised. "Me?" He pointed at his che:

J. P. snorted. "Of course, you! Who the hell else do y
think I mean?"

Raymond looked about uncertainly for a moment, the
walked over to where J. P. stood, glowering for all he w
worth.

"May I help you, Mr. Drayton?"

"Do you know where my damned son is?"

"No, sir."

"Why not? You're one of his damned associates, arer
you?"

Raymond gave the old man a wry grin. "Yes, sir, but I'
afraid I wasn't assigned to watch him this evening."

"Harumph!"

Unused to being frustrated and not liking it in the least, J.
stood still and seethed impotently for a moment or two. A
last he said, "Well, can you think where he might be?"

"No, sir. The last I saw of him, he and Miss MacNama
were heading toward the refreshment room."

"Well, they ain't there now," J. P. told him, as if Raymo
were a fool even to suggest it.

Raymond only shrugged. His grin got bigger.

"Damn it, I need him, boy!"

"The name is Sing, sir. Raymond Sing."

Hell and damnation. J. P. had never encountered so many eople who insisted on being disrespectful to him. First his retched son, then that absurd little girl and now this upstart Chinaman. J. P. did not approve.

"Well, Raymond Sing," he said nastily, "do you suppose ou can find him for me?"

Raymond eyed James's father with mounting distaste. "Well, now, sir, I expect if neither he nor Miss MacNamara re in this room, it's because they have other things to do. ogether. I don't know that I'd like to interrupt whatever those hings are, no."

"Hah! That's because you don't know what *I* know."

"And what might that be, sir?" Raymond inquired politely.

With a malevolent frown, J. P. considered Raymond Sing. hen he decided that, since James and Raymond knew each ther a hell of a lot better than James and J. P. did, Raymond ould be more apt to find him than he would.

"Can you keep a confidence, boy?" Recollecting Ray-mond's earlier objection to the word, J. P. muttered, "That is o say, Mr. Sing?"

Raymond—obviously a damned lawyer, thought J. P. ourly—equivocated. "Depends on the confidence, Mr. Dray-on."

J. P. glared at Raymond. Then he recalled his agent telling im that one Mr. Sing, a Chinese gentleman, had been in-uiring about the U.S.S. *China Seas*, and J. P.'s expression ghtened. He grinned. Then he smiled.

Then he leaned over and whispered something in Ray-ond's ear. He was not surprised when Raymond's eyebrows ot up. Nor was he surprised at his strangled, "My God!"

J. P. straightened and beamed like an enormous, grizzled, owerfully cantankerous Christmas elf.

"Well, will you keep my confidence now?"

Raymond, reeling with the news J. P. had just whispered to im, cried, "My God, sir! You can't keep this news secret! /e should shout it from the rooftops! You have no right to eep it from them!"

Idiot, fumed J. P. "For God's sake, I don't plan to keep it om them. What I plan to do is—" He broke off and cast a

surreptitious glance around the room. Then he leaned towar
Raymond and said, "What I plan to do is—" And he whis
pered into Raymond's ear once more.

When he drew away from Raymond, he could tell th
blasted boy still was not convinced. "Oh, for Pete's sake!"

He leaned over and whispered again. When Raymon
seemed inclined to pull away, J. P. grabbed him by the shou
der and whispered even more.

When Raymond straightened up again, his expression wa
one of reluctant appreciation.

J. P., unused to sharing confidences, felt uncomfortable.
lot was riding on this young Chinese boy's slender shoulder

"Well?" he demanded.

Raymond hesitated for another moment or two, the
squared those same slender shoulders.

"All right. I'll do it."

J. P. actually smiled at him.

"Not for you, mind you," Raymond hastened to assure him
"But for James's and Miss MacNamara's sakes, I'll do it. Th
is important to James, sir. And so are you, although I fail
see why, now that I've met you."

Before J. P. could do more than register an expression
incredulous fury, Raymond turned around and walked brisk
away.

J. P. fumed for a full minute before he, too, turned. As h
headed for the cloak room to pick up his top hat, cane, an
overcoat, he growled, "Youth of today. No manners at al
Wastrels! Idiots! They're all a passel of damned uncivil whip
persnappers!"

Chapter Twenty

"Oh, James, this is so beautiful. I never dreamed I'd actually live here one day. With you."

"Did you think you'd be living here with somebody else?"

Polly could tell he was teasing her. Although it seemed impossible, he sounded as happy as she felt.

"Of course not." She laughed and hugged his arm tighter. She couldn't remember ever feeling this effervescent, as though her veins were filled with champagne.

James led her through the elaborate double front doors and turned on the electric lighting.

"Electric lights! Oh, James!"

"Only the best for you, my fair Polly."

The floor of his home's foyer was laid with beautiful tiles. "I had them imported from Spain. Before the war, of course."

"Of course." In all her twenty-one years, Polly had never set foot on anything so exquisite. It seemed almost a sacrilege to walk on them.

"And here's the main hall." James ushered Polly into another room.

"The hall," she breathed. Mercy. It was bigger than the

whole first floor of her humble home. Rooms led from it, and James gestured to the one on his left.

"That's the music room. You can practice your piano playing in there. And I expect you to teach our children all the carols you taught those orphans, Polly."

He was teasing again, but she felt herself blush at the thought of herself and James having children together; and what led to the having of them.

"And over there's the breakfast room. The kitchen and pantry abut the breakfast room, and the big dining room is on the other side of the pantry. Straight in front of us is the large parlor.

Polly had already noted with approval that James had had the hall decorated for Christmas, but she was unprepared for the magnificence of his parlor.

"Oh, James."

A uniformed woman stood in front of the gigantic tree, a lighted taper in her hand.

"I just got the last candle lit, Mr. Drayton," she said with a smile. A ladder stood behind her; she must have used it light the uppermost candles.

"Wonderful." James took Polly by the hand and led her toward the woman. "Polly, let me introduce you to my housekeeper, Mrs. Pinkney. Mrs. Pinkney, you're the very first person to know that Miss Polly MacNamara here has done me the great honor of accepting my proposal of marriage. Very soon Polly will be Mrs. James Drayton."

"Mr. Drayton!" After her squeal, the woman turned to Polly and pumped her hand, as if she expected water to spurt from Polly's mouth.

"Oh, ma'am, I'm so very happy for the both of you. I've been telling Mr. Drayton these many years it's past time he found himself a wife. And you're perfect for him. I can tell, you're just perfect!"

James muttered something under his breath.

Polly, however, returned Mrs. Pinkney's enthusiastic greeting with warmth. She didn't think she could bear to have been met with disapproval.

"Thank you very much, Mrs. Pinkney. I shall certainly do my best to earn your approbation."

"I think you've already earned it," her beloved mumbled. To Mrs. Pinkney, he said, "Well, yes. So now that you two have met, why don't you go on to bed, Mrs. Pinkney. I'll show Polly around."

"Of course, Mr. Drayton." The housekeeper bobbed a curtsy, gave Polly one last big smile and left.

James pulled Polly into his arms in front of the Christmas tree. "Do you like it, Polly?"

"Oh, James, yes. I just love it." She turned into his embrace. "I love you."

This time, James didn't have to initiate the kiss. Polly slid her fingers into his hair, cupped his head and drew his lips to hers. James soft groan was music to her ears.

"Come upstairs with me, Polly. Let me show you our room. I have something there for you."

"You do?" Shivers thrilled through her. Although she wasn't sure she could negotiate the stairs because her legs had turned to rubber, she wanted more than anything else to see their room. Their room. Oh, mercy.

She needn't have worried about her rubbery limbs. James stooped, slipped one arm around her back and another behind her knees and lifted her. She clung to him as he carried her up the broad, curved stairs. Vaguely, Polly noticed that they were covered in thick burgundy carpeting—nothing akin to the threadbare runners on the stairs in her home. Her former home. She gave James a squeeze and he kissed her.

She closed her eyes right before James pushed the door to their room open. She wanted to be surprised.

"I hope you like it, Polly."

He wasn't even breathing heavily, a fact Polly noted with approval. Her James wasn't soft and out-of-shape like Lawrence Bullock. James was hard and strong and handsome. And hers.

When he lowered her onto the bed and she felt the soft feather mattress, Polly languidly lifted her eyelids. She didn't want to let go of James; she wanted him to join her, and

295

wondered if her desire was the sign of an abandoned soul. Then she decided she didn't care.

"Here, Polly, let me show you what I have for you."

Although she was disappointed when he left her alone on the magnificent bed, James's withdrawal allowed her to look at the room that would soon be hers. Hers and James's. Since James was no longer there to hug her, she hugged herself as she looked around.

It was a beautiful room, and Polly was pleased to see that no feminine hand had as yet touched it. Smugly, she thought of Lady Midnight, and decided that whatever sordid alliance she had once shared with James, her presence had left this room untainted.

The bed on which Polly sat was covered with a spread of green-and-gold Chinese brocade. An ebony headboard carried out the Chinese motif, as did the rest of the room's furniture. She liked it. The green carpeting and cream-colored curtains gave the room a restful feeling appropriate for a bedroom.

"Here, Polly. I want you to have this."

James's voice startled her out of her perusal of the room. Her hand trembling with excitement, she took a tiny box from his hand.

"I hope you like it."

He looked concerned, as though he was worried she might not appreciate whatever resided inside the box. As if he could ever give her anything she wouldn't like.

When she pressed the latch, the lid sprang open, revealing a ring: an exquisite creation featuring a single sparkling diamond mounted in a setting sprinkled with tiny rubies and emeralds.

"Oh, James. Oh, my goodness. It's beautiful."

"It was my mother's, Polly. I saved it, thinking that if I ever married, I'd give it to my wife. I'd begun to believe no one would ever wear it again until I met you. Here."

Kneeling, James took the ring out of its box and slipped it onto the ring finger of Polly's left hand, where it rested comfortably.

"This is the engagement ring, Polly. There's another ring— a plainer one—for the ceremony."

"Thank you so much. It's absolutely beautiful." Polly flung er arms around him and drew him onto the bed with her.

"Oh, Lord, Polly." James went with her willingly, raining isses on her cheeks, chin and throat.

Pressing her gently back into the soft mattress, James began) deliver a lesson Polly would never forget. Heat radiated rom everywhere he touched her. Gently, he slipped the Chi-ese silk shawl from her shoulders, and it drizzled to the floor ext to the bed. The next to go were her slippers. She nudged 1em off one by one and didn't even hear them land on the lush carpet.

Heedless of propriety, she grabbed the lapels of James's vening jacket and jerked it away from his shoulders. He hrugged it off and she began on his shirt buttons.

"Are you sure, Polly?"

James's voice sounded ragged, and it made Polly glad. She elt a little ragged herself.

"I'm sure, James. I've never been so sure."

Need spiraled within her. Everywhere he touched her, every :roke of his hand, every tender kiss, made sparks ignite in er body, heating it until she burned with passion.

She groaned. His hands had begun playing havoc with her reasts now, and her nipples had puckered into aching nubs.

"Please, James." Polly wished she lived in a more enlight-ned age so she'd know what to do now. She wasn't even sure hat to ask for.

Carefully James unbuttoned a million or so tiny pearl but-ons at the back of her dress. When the elegant creation finally elinquished its hold on her, Polly felt as though she'd been elieved of a terrible burden. She whisked off her gown and y before her beloved in her underpinnings.

Not to be outdone, James slipped out of his trousers and the irt Polly had thoughtfully unbuttoned for him. Since he was good-hearted young man, he helped Polly unfasten her cor-t, flung it aside, then wrapped her in a crushing embrace.

"Oh, James." This time, Polly's whisper was distinctly aaky.

"Polly, I love you so much. I love you more than life. I

swear, I didn't think I'd ever find you. Let me love you Polly.''

"Yes, please. If you don't, I'll never speak to you again.

Needing no further encouragement, James proceeded t adore Polly's body. Never in her born days had Polly eve guessed the delights a man and woman could give each othe James's gifted hands burned her sensitive flesh, from he throat to her belly, and lower. When his tongue flicked a rigi nipple, Polly almost screamed.

"James! Oh, Lord, James!''

"Do you like that, Polly?''

She thought his question absurd. Nevertheless, she manage to gasp, "Oh, yes. Oh, mercy, yes.''

"Good.''

His hand had taken to stroking up her leg, scorching a pat from her ankle to her knee and then higher, until he stroke her silky thigh. When his clever fingers found the petals o her womanhood and then the bud of her desire, Polly nearl came undone.

"Yes, Polly. Oh, yes. Open for me. You're so warm an wet. You're mine, Polly, and I'm yours. We'll be togethe forever, love. You and me. Forever.''

"Oh, yes, James.''

In truth, speech was difficult. It soon became impossible a he continued to touch her. As he stroked, first one finger, the two, dipped into her. Reason fled, replaced by feelings, wor derful feelings, feelings Polly didn't understand. Her body re acted for her, lifting to meet James's gentle probing, guidin her higher and higher. Suddenly Polly cried out in amazeme as James sent her into a place she'd never been before; special place sparkling with love and light.

Before she'd come to earth again, James kissed her ha and positioned himself over her. With a hard thrust and hoarse cry, he claimed her.

Polly knew this was supposed to hurt, but she was sti contracting with release and barely noticed the pain. What sh did notice was the feeling of fullness as he entered her. Sh loved the feeling. They were joined. They were one.

Polly felt a surge of pure joy as James, with a shout of completion, exploded inside her. When he collapsed next to her they were still joined. Polly lay on her back beside him, staring at the ceiling of her soon-to-be-bedroom and marveled at the goodness of life.

James turned to look at her. Polly saw him out of the corner of her eye, but felt too stunned to move. She was surprised when he looked worried. "Polly? Polly, are you all right. My God, I didn't mean to hurt you."

"Hurt me?" His odd interpretation of her blissful mood nudged Polly into stirring. She turned her head and stared at him. "Hurt me? Oh, my goodness, James. You didn't hurt me."

He looked relieved.

"I'm so happy." She heaved a huge, satisfied sigh. "I've never been so happy."

When they were finally able to stir themselves, James helped Polly dress, even going so far as to fasten her irritating corset. Polly thought she'd found perfect happiness when she sat on the cushioned ebony bench, stared at her reflection in the large mirror above his vanity table and watched James brush her hair.

She was glad she'd decided to dress her hair simply tonight. However much she loved him, she wasn't entirely sure she trusted James with her hair. She didn't expect he'd have much trouble with the two combs she'd borrowed from her mother, however.

"You hair is exquisite, Polly."

As he punctuated his brushes with kisses, Polly only sighed and smiled. She felt languid, relaxed, and oddly sleepy. She couldn't imagine ever sleeping again.

"I don't want to go home," she confessed when he put the last pin in her hair.

"I don't want you to, either. But soon this will be your home and you'll never leave it again."

She smiled, and was amazed at the Polly she saw reflected in the mirror. This was a Polly she'd never known before. Her

face held a mysterious aura of satisfaction. Must be love, s▌
decided.

"This house is big enough for your mother, Polly, so ▌
you're worried about her, please don't be."

She looked up quickly. "Thank you, James." She felt t▌
sting of tears behind her eyes. Oh, my, she loved him.

It was quite late when James drove Polly home. They we▌
in his Olds Curved Dash Runabout because his groom h▌
already stabled the two fine black horses with which he ▌
driven her to the ball.

When they pulled up to the sidewalk in front of t▌
MacNamara residence, it was two o'clock on Christmas mor▌
ing.

"My goodness, I've never seen so many lights on in t▌
house in my life," murmured Polly. "I hope Mother hasr▌
been up worrying about me."

"Me, too." James's guilty expression turned into one ▌
surprise as he looked about the darkened street. "Where ▌
earth did all these motorcars come from?"

Polly hadn't noticed before, but at James's comment, s▌
too glanced at the street. Sure enough, two other horsele▌
carriages were parked nearby. Good heavens. She'd never se▌
so many motorcars in one place in her life.

"Maybe the neighbors have visitors?" she offered unce▌
tainly.

Before he took Polly's arm, James paused in the glow ▌
the gas porch lamp to inspect her face. His smile told her s▌
passed inspection.

"Nobody will ever know," he assured her. Then, as thou▌
he couldn't help himself, he wrapped her in a huge embrac▌
"But they will soon."

They laughed as they walked up the steps. To Polly's su▌
prise, she didn't even have to dig in her handbag for her ke▌
because the door burst open as they approached.

"Raymond! What in God's name are you doing here?"

Polly, as startled as James to see Raymond Sing standi▌
at her front door, a big grin on his face, asked in alarm, "▌
anything the matter with Mother?"

She heard her mother's voice sing out from the parl▌

"There's nothing the matter with me, Polly. Nothing will ever be the matter again."

Puzzled, Polly looked at James.

"Everything's fine, James, Miss MacNamara. Come in. Come in." Raymond sounded as jolly as a Christmas elf.

"Get in the blasted house, you ridiculous runaways!"

James stopped in his tracks, horrified. *"Father?"*

J. P. Drayton charged out of the parlor. "Yes, it's your father, you damned insolent whelp. Get the hell in here!"

Too startled to take exception to J. P.'s profanity, Polly allowed James to grip her arm and lead her toward the parlor door. Raymond, chuckling and rubbing his hands together, followed them. This whole scenario was absurd; Polly couldn't understand any of it.

She and James exchanged a befuddled glance as they walked together into the parlor. Then Polly looked up, her gaze automatically going to the fireplace.

"Stephen!"

Later she would laugh when Stephen told her that her shriek probably woke up residents in the churchyard a block away.

Right then, though, Polly didn't think at all. She saw her brother—in his naval uniform and as handsome as she remembered him—grinning at her from in front of the fireplace, and she shot from James's side as though propelled by gunpowder. She raced straight into Stephen's arms.

Laughing and sobbing, she cried, "Stephen, Stephen, Stephen," until her brother finally pried her arms away from his shoulders.

"I'm a wounded man, Polly. Ease up a little." He had tears in his eyes, too.

"You're wounded?" Snatching away her arms as if afraid he'd shatter if she continued touching him, Polly dashed a hand across her eyes and peered up into his face.

"It's not bad," he said. His words were thick.

"Oh, Stephen!" There she went again, weeping onto his chest, clutching him as though she'd never let him go.

James stared in astonishment, unable to believe the man at the fireplace was truly Stephen MacNamara, who had been, the last James had heard, a sailor lost at sea. Quickly, he scanned the room. The faces he saw told him that his senses had not gone haywire; the man was, indeed, Polly's lost brother. As if to put the period to further doubt, James finally noticed the naval contingent: two uniformed brass, grim-faced and stiff, standing in a corner as though they didn't quite know what to do with themselves in the face of this much spontaneity.

All these people must account for the motorcars parked outside, James decided irrelevantly.

His eyes were the same color as Polly's, James realized when Stephen lifted his face and swept a glance around the room. It landed, with appropriate brotherly concern, on James. Stephen gave a little shrug, as though to ask, "What can one expect from a sister?" and James snapped out of his stupor.

"You're Polly's brother? I've been trying and trying to find you."

"Couldn't do it, though, could you, boy?"

James jerked around to stare, dumbfounded, at his father. He couldn't speak.

"Your father was the one who clamped the lid of secrecy on it, James," explained Raymond. "He sent a ship out to search for the missing vessel. His ship found the *China Seas'* crew stranded on an island in the Philippines. They'd managed to make it there before a storm kicked up and their boats floundered. He rescued them. Most of the men were saved, and only a few of them were so done in that they had to be hospitalized. Your father saved the day."

James's gaze shot from Raymond to his father. "*You* did it? *You?* You *helped* them?"

J. P. scowled, as though somebody'd just snatched away his favorite toy. "Yes, damn you, I helped them. For *free*," he added smugly.

With another glance, which took in Raymond, Polly and Stephen, and Lillian MacNamara, wiping her eyes as she watched her children, James swallowed hard. Then, feeling as though he were living a dream—one he didn't dare quite believe might have a happy ending—he walked to his father.

All sorts of words slammed through his brain; phrases of gratitude; questions; words of love. He was too confused to pick out an appropriate one and ultimately said simply, "Thank you, sir."

He stood in front of J. P. Drayton for a good minute or more, staring at his father, who stared back. J. P. looked nervous. James felt awkward. Then he tossed a lifetime's worth of old bitterness over his shoulder, reached out and hugged the old man. It was something he hadn't had the nerve to do since he was five years old.

After a shocked moment, J. P. swallowed audibly and hugged his son back. So softly that only James could hear, he mumbled, "I never meant to be a bad man, son. I just didn't know how not to be hard. I did it for you. I love you, James."

Afraid he was going to burst into tears and disgrace himself, James said, "I know that, sir. I think I understand now."

Thank God, he didn't cry.

All of a sudden James heard Polly's thin, shaky, "And we're going to be married!"

He let go of his father and turned around only to be careened into by his darling little Polly, her usual reserve obviously shattered beyond repair this evening. Laughing, he wrapped his arms around her and let her sob onto his lapel this time, since she'd apparently given up on Stephen's for the time being. James planted a kiss on her beautiful hair and lifted his head to face the room at large.

Mrs. MacNamara dabbed at her eyes with a hankie that looked as though it had already been through more than it was designed to bear. Raymond grinned from ear to ear. J. P. looked as though he'd expected something of the sort; his bushy brows plunged and he frowned. J. P.'s frown gave him the look of a man on the verge of a temper fit, but James realized for the first time in his life that this was only his father's way of dealing with life outside his world of business. James didn't suppose he'd ever like it, but he began to feel the vestiges of reluctant understanding.

Only Stephen appeared at all grim, and James would have liked him less if he hadn't exhibited such brotherly concern. In order to assuage Stephen, James walked over to the fireplace, dragging Polly along with him, and held out his hand.

"I'm James Drayton, Mr. MacNamara, and I'm in love with

your sister. I hope we can be friends, because we're going to belong to the same family soon.''

Lifting her head from James's soggy lapel, Polly sniffled and said in a sadly watery voice, ''This is the happiest Christmas of my life.''

Stephen grinned.

No one disagreed with her.

''I'll be damned,'' roared J. P. Drayton to no one in particular an hour or so later, ''if I'll allow these two idiots to have their engagement party in any home but mine!''

Silence greeted the old man's belligerent declaration. Everyone looked at everyone else. J. P. glowered at them all, his grizzled brows giving him the appearance of a huge, bad-tempered troll.

James couldn't believe it when he started to laugh. He'd never laughed at his father before in his entire life. All of a sudden, however, the old man's antics seemed magically to have lost all power to touch him with anything but amusement and the vague regret that old J. P. felt it necessary to intimidate the universe. Did the poor old soul actually fear the world *that* much?

J. P.'s hot glare only made James laugh harder. He wiped his eyes and held out his arms, palms up, toward his father, in a gesture meant to beg forgiveness for a weakness the sufferer couldn't control.

''I mean it.'' J. P.'s glare raked the assemblage, as if daring anyone else to do anything so inappropriate as laugh at him.

Polly opened her eyes wide and nodded. Then she ducked her head and hid her face against James's shoulder.

Stephen turned suddenly and pretended to pour some brandy into his already full glass.

Raymond studied the floor with apparent fascination.

Lillian said, ''I don't believe you'll hear an argument from anyone here, Mr. Drayton.'' Then she lifted her much-abused handkerchief to her mouth. Something sounding very much like muffled mirth sneaked out from behind the hankie.

The navy had left by this time. Undoubtedly the navy would not have laughed at J. P. Drayton.

When James could finally catch his breath, he gave Polly an extra squeeze and stammered, "I—I'm sorry, Father. Of course, we'll have our engagement party at your house. We'd be honored, sir."

James felt Polly wipe her eyes against his coat sleeve and decided a little more water couldn't hurt it. She lifted her head and said, "Of course. We—" She slapped her hand over her mouth, obviously to hold in her giggles. "We wouldn't dream of having it anywhere else."

It was the best she could do. Unable to stifle her laughter a single second longer, she dove back to the shelter of James's shoulder.

"Sounds like a great idea to me." Clearly the most disciplined of the lot—no doubt due to his naval training—Stephen was able to speak his entire sentence without chortling once. He did, however, turn back to the brandy decanter as soon as the words left his lips.

Raymond said not a syllable, but stared at the carpet, as if trying to memorize its pattern.

J. P. nodded, evidently choosing to ignore the amusement his demand had caused. "Good. New Year's Eve, then."

"The turn of the century," murmured Raymond.

Polly lifted her head. "My word, that's right. The year 1900. Goodness, it doesn't seem possible."

"A perfect time to begin, my love." It felt so good to be able to hold her and squeeze her any old time he wanted to that James did it again. He wanted to do it forever.

"Oh, my, yes," Polly breathed.

Chapter Twenty-one

The party was in full swing and everyone seemed to be having a grand time. Not only were the revelers celebrating James and Polly's upcoming nuptials, but the beginning of a brand-new century.

Polly had never been so happy. She fingered her medals and looked up at the sparkling sky. James stood at her side and held her close. They'd slipped away from the crowd and now graced the balcony of J. P. Drayton's grand mansion together.

"Wishing again, love?"

Polly glanced at his face and saw that he was looking at her with the most tender expression she'd ever hoped to see. Oh, my, she loved him.

"My wishes have all come true, James. I have nothing left to wish for."

"What about our happy future?"

"I already know we'll have that."

"Children?"

"I know we'll have children, too, James."

"You do?"

"Yes."

"Good. I want to make a family, Polly. I want a family like neither of us ever had."

He sounded very emotional as he wrapped her in his arms. Polly hugged him back and felt just wonderful.

They were quiet for a long time, loving one another in the soft winter night. Music drifted out to them from the ballroom. Happy laughter punctuated the air. Polly fancied she could see the gaiety drift up to the stars and weave around them, making their sparkles brighter.

At last she said quietly, "It *is* magic, James."

As she expected, he didn't have to ask what she meant. "You really think so?"

"Oh, yes."

"I'll be damned."

He picked up her hand, which still held her coin, and stared down at it.

"I have to give it back," she said after a minute or two of silence.

He kissed the coin in her hand. "Why is that, love?"

She didn't answer for a minute, then gave a tiny shrug. "I'm not sure. So some other lost soul can borrow it for a while, I guess." She looked up at him and smiled. "I only know I have to do it."

"Would you like to do it now?"

"Now?"

His smile made her breath catch. "Why not? Nobody'd miss us if we snuck away for a half-hour or so."

The idea captured Polly's fancy. "Can we take your Olds Runabout?"

He laughed. "I can't believe you actually want to ride in a horseless carriage, my fair Polly."

"It's a new century, James. I guess I just want to keep up with the times."

So, confiding only in Raymond Sing, Polly and James climbed into the Runabout, James cranked it up, and off they sped toward Chinatown.

"You know," Polly said when they were halfway there,

"that old lady's never been in the shop when I've gone back before."

"I bet she'll be there tonight."

"Really?"

Peering at him through the darkness speckled here and there with the amber glow of street lamps, Polly saw him nod. He was grinning.

"Sure. If it's a magic coin and you've used up your part, I expect she'll know it, won't she?"

Polly cocked her head quizzically. For somebody who used to claim not to believe in magic or the delights of Christmas or love, James certainly knew how to act as though he did.

"I believe you're right."

He was.

The street was busy tonight, with people out celebrating New Year's Eve. Musicians played Chinese tunes, masked dancers made their way from doorway to doorway, sprinkling luck on shopkeepers and their merchandise. Incense hung in the air along with smoke from celebratory firecrackers. A string of firecrackers popped nearby, making Polly jump and laugh. James hugged her tight as he opened the door to the small curio shop.

The bell tinkled, as it always did, and Polly had to blink several times to adjust to the shop's twilight atmosphere. When she could distinguish things against the darkness, she noticed the beaded curtain, hanging still and silent. Good old curtain. She loved that curtain.

"Good evening, lady."

Delighted, Polly turned toward the counter. "Oh, James, you were right."

There she sat, smiling, bobbing a nod at them both, the little old lady who had given Polly her coin. She held out her hand, palm up, as though she'd been expecting them and knew why they'd come.

"Here, Polly, let me."

James untied the red velvet ribbon and slid the coin from it. He held it in front of his eyes for a minute, staring at the beautiful, lustrous old thing. Then he gave it a quick kiss

308

fisted his hand around it once as if for luck and placed it gently into Polly's open palm.

Polly felt quite emotional when she wrapped her fingers around the coin and walked to the counter. She held the coin close to her breast for a moment, then quickly handed it to the old lady.

"Thank you," she murmured softly, afraid she was going to cry.

"It work good," the woman said. "It work real good for you."

"Yes. Oh, yes, it worked wonderfully."

"It work again." The little old face's thousand wrinkles creased into a happy smile. "Somebody else need soon."

"Of course." Then, on an impulse, Polly reached over and kissed the old woman's cheek. "Thank you," she said again. "Thank you so much."

The old head bobbed again. The tiny woman held up the coin, gripped between her thumb and forefinger. "Magic in you," she said, nodding at Polly. "Coin unlock."

With her hand pressed to her breast Polly whispered, "Really?"

"Oh, sure," the old lady said.

And with that, she hopped down from her stool and trotted through the beaded curtain. It clicked once or twice and stilled. In only a second or two, it was as if nobody but Polly and James had ever been in the shop that evening. Polly stared at the curtain for quite a few minutes, wishing she could talk to the old lady again.

Then, with a little laugh, she pressed her bare skin and said, "I guess I have nothing left to wish on."

She felt James behind her for a second before he slipped his arms around her waist and bent to kiss her on the side of her neck. "You have me, Polly. We have each other."

With another laugh, she turned into his embrace. "And we both have Dewey!" she declared, as though it were the final word on everything.

They were both laughing when they left the shop.

* * *

309

It was as James had predicted. Nobody had even noticed they were gone.

James sidled up to Raymond. "Any fussing?"

Raymond laughed. "Not a fuss to be found tonight, James."

"Good."

His left arm still around Polly's waist, James snagged a glass of champagne from a passing waiter.

"Here, love, let's share."

He tilted the glass to Polly's lips and watched her take a sip. Very carefully, he placed his lips over the spot where she'd drunk and took a sip of his own. Lord on high, he loved this woman. He sighed contentedly as they stood at the head of the five short steps leading down into the ballroom and surveyed the scene. Everybody sure looked happy. Good.

"Oh, James, look. There's still magic in the air."

"Mmmmm?"

"My goodness, yes. Why, just look over there. Look at your father and my mother chatting together."

James felt his eyes go wide with his astonishment. "My God, I've never seen the old man look happy before."

"And I haven't seen my mother actually stand up and walk with a wheelchair nowhere in sight for six years." She watched them for a moment or two and added, "And I haven't seen that look on her face since before my father died."

James heard Polly sniffle and knew she'd be asking for his handkerchief in an instant. He'd packed a second one just in case.

"And look over there, James."

He followed her finger and saw she was pointing to Raymond Sing, in deep and earnest conversation with a San Francisco businessman. They were obviously talking to each other as fellow businessmen and not as a Chinaman to an American.

"And, oh, James!" Polly cried.

James whipped out his spare handkerchief and quickly thrust it into Polly's extended hand.

"Thank you," she sniffed. "But look, James. Over there. Look at Stephen. Isn't he handsome?"

"He's handsome, all right," James acknowledged with a grin.

In truth, Stephen was handsome as the very devil. And the unattached ladies in the crowd thought so, too, if the looks on Constance's, Rose's, and Juliana's faces were anything by which to judge. If James were a betting man, he'd bet they were dragging the exciting details of Stephen's ordeal out of him right this minute. James and Stephen had become quite friendly in the week since Christmas Eve, and James was pretty sure Stephen couldn't wait until he could go back to being a plain sailor again. Stephen MacNamara was not one to glory in the past, his own or anybody else's.

"Oh, James, everything is so beautiful."

Then Polly uttered a little shriek, making James jump.

"Good God, Polly, what's the matter?" Frantically, he searched the crowd, trying to discover what foul creature had entered and caused his beloved Polly to become distressed. Had Lawrence Bullock broken out of jail and crashed the party? Was the punch bowl on fire? God knew, there was enough brandy in it.

When he saw what had startled Polly and realized she'd succumbed to gasps of laughter, he exhaled slowly, his panic subsiding.

"Oh, my God."

"You see, James, there still is magic in the air. If Dewey can crash a party and behave himself, you know there's still magic."

James began to laugh, too. "I guess you're right, love."

Dewey sat at J. P. Drayton's side, looking for all the world like the dignified, well-behaved, rarely seen Philippine Tapir Hound he was supposed to be. J. P. glowered around, as if daring anybody to object when he slipped the courteous hound another canapé. Lillian MacNamara only laughed at the two of them.

"How did he get here?"

"I have no idea. But it seems fitting somehow."

James squeezed Polly's shoulder. "Yes," he said, "it does."

* * *

Emma Craig

Polly and James were proud as punch as they wheeled the baby carriage down the crowded, narrow street toward the tiny curio shop in Chinatown. Throngs bustled around them. Sometimes a smiling pajama-clad man or woman would bob a greeting and exclaim over the contents of the buggy.

Such exclamations surprised neither parent. Their two-month-old daughter Stephanie was, after all, the most beautiful baby in the world. It wasn't just parental pride that made them say so, either. It was merely the truth. Anybody could tell.

Why, even Stephanie's grandfather doted on the girl. He had, however, objected strenuously when Polly took to calling him Uncle Ebenezer to his face. She compromised by only calling him that behind his back. Her mother didn't mind much, even though she and J. P. had become quite an item recently. There was even talk of marriage.

James, Polly, Raymond, and Stephen had spent an entire evening laughing uncontrollably at the thought of James's father and Polly's mother marrying.

"But I think it's wonderful!" Polly's throat ached from giggling, and she had to press her hands to her breast to hold down her bubbling laughter. "Truly, I do!"

"So do I," gasped Stephen, wiping his eyes.

James had to stand up and stamp, he was laughing so hard. "I've never seen the old man moonstruck before."

Raymond couldn't say a word. He was laughing too hard.

"He spoils Stephanie terribly," Polly said when the hilarity had calmed down slightly.

James shook his head. "Well, you know what he is. You'll never cure him. Claims it's his grandfatherly right and if anybody objects, they can go straight to hell."

The four friends got a good fifteen minutes' worth of amusement out of J. P.'s reported announcement.

Now, as they peered through the shop's window, Polly asked, "Do you think anybody's there, James?"

"Only one way to find out," he said, and boldly pushed the door open.

The bell tinkled right on cue. Polly loved this shop. The familiar scent of sandalwood caressed her nostrils and she smiled. It was just as she remembered. Same old beaded cur-

in. She fingered the beautifully embroidered cloth draped
ver the teakwood stand and sighed.

Yet there were differences, too. Of course, the ivory combs
w adorned her mother's lovely hair. Even J. P. said they
oked good in Lillian's hair.

And the old woman was nowhere in sight. Instead, to
olly's surprise, the beautiful young woman stood, still as a
atue, before the counter.

"Good morning," she said with her Mona Lisa smile.

"Good morning." Polly remembered the last time she'd
en the woman and realized she felt not a lick of jealousy
day. Her husband loved her; of that she had not a doubt in
e world.

The woman seemed to float over the floor when she ap-
oached them. She peered into the carriage, her expression
soft as eiderdown.

"Your baby is beautiful."

"Thank you."

James preened a little. Polly's insides lit up like fireworks.
I guess there's no need to ask if the old lady is here today,"
e said with a smile.

The woman shook her head. "But there's something for you
re." From her sleeve she drew out a long flat box fashioned
cinnabar and inlaid with carved ivory.

"Oh," Polly whispered, awed by the beauty of the box,
ow lovely."

The woman inclined her head. "Please to open it. It contain
ft for your beautiful children."

"Our children?" James looked puzzled and peered first at
e woman and then at Stephanie, who took that opportunity
yawn.

But Polly knew what the woman meant. She looked at the
oman for a moment, excitement dancing in her heart. "Re-
y?"

The woman inclined her head once more.

"Oh, how wonderful!"

Quickly, Polly opened the box. Four silver spoons lay on a
d of black velvet. Each spoon had a handle engraved with
inese patterns. Without understanding how, Polly knew

which was Stephanie's. She picked it up and looked inqu
ingly at the woman, whose graceful nod confirmed Polly
choice.

"The other three are for boys," Polly murmured, sure on
more without knowing how.

Again, the woman nodded.

"Oh, thank you!"

This time the other woman initiated the embrace.

Polly and James pushed their baby home through the cri
sunlight of a perfect December day, heading back to the
home on Russian Hill. If today was like most days, they wou
find J. P. there, prowling the grounds with Dewey at his hee
grumbling about the nerve of some people, to think they cou
take his granddaughter out of the house without consulti
him first. Undoubtedly Lillian would be sitting on the sto
bench, peacefully embroidering a new smock for Stephar
and telling J. P. that James and Polly would be home in
minute and not to fuss.

With luck, Stephen would pop by in the afternoon and
James and Polly would stroll out to the Japanese garden. Jam
and Stephen would argue about baseball while Polly walk
to the middle of the red lacquered bridge to throw bre
crumbs to the carp. Dewey, of course, would lope arou
chasing birds and squirrels. If their luck held, the clum
hound wouldn't fall in the pond this time.

Raymond and his new lady friend were joining them
dinner. Polly hoped Stephen would dine with them, too. J.
was actively recruiting Stephen to join his shipping conce
Stephen had also been keeping company with Constance P
a girl whom Polly had begun to consider both charming a
a true friend. She hoped Constance and Stephen would ma
soon; Polly had always wanted a sister.

Of course, J. P. and Lillian would be at the supper tab
Neither grandparent could bear to be away from Stephanie
too long at any given time.

Polly remembered a line from an old, old Christmas so
one she'd discovered in a book of venerable Yuletide ver
in the library. She never did find the music, but she loved

ancient words. She recited them to herself now, and smiled, thinking they fit her circumstances to the proverbial *T*.

> Without the door let sorrow lie,
> And if for cold it hap to die,
> We'll bury it in a Christmas pie,
> And ever more be merry.

She whispered, "Amen," and smiled when her husband looked at her quizzically.

Christmas means more than just puppy love.

"SHAKESPEARE AND THE THREE KINGS"
Victoria Alexander
Requiring a trainer for his three inherited dogs, Oliver Stanhope meets D. K. Lawrence, and is in for the Christmas surprise—and love—of his life.

"ATHENA'S CHRISTMAS TAIL" Nina Coombs
Mercy wants her marriage to be a match of the heart—and with the help of her very determined dog, Athena, she finds just the right magic of the holiday season.

"AWAY IN A SHELTER" Annie Kimberlin
A dedicated volunteer, Camille Campbell still doesn't want to be stuck in an animal shelter on Christmas Eve—especially with a handsome helper whose touch leaves her starry-eyed.

"MR. WRIGHT'S CHRISTMAS ANGEL"
Miriam Raftery
When Joy's daughter asks Santa for a father, she knows she' in trouble—until a trip to Alaska takes them on a journe into the arms of Nicholas Wright and his amazing dog.

___52235-7 $5.99 US/$6.99 CAI

THEIR FIRST NOEL

DON'T MISS THESE FOUR HISTORICAL ROMANCE STORIES THAT CELEBRATE THE JOY OF CHRISTMAS AND THE MIRACLE OF BIRTH.

LEIGH GREENWOOD
"Father Christmas"

Arizona Territory, 1880. Delivering a young widow's baby during the holiday season transforms the heart of a lonely drifter.

BOBBY HUTCHINSON
"Lantern In The Window"

Alberta, 1886. After losing his wife and infant son, a bereaved farmer vows not to love again—until a fiery beauty helps him bury the ghosts of Christmases past.

CONNIE MASON
"A Christmas Miracle"

New York, 1867. A Yuletide birth brings a wealthy businessman and a penniless immigrant the happiness they have always desired.

THERESA SCOTT
"The Treasure"

Washington Territory, 1825. A childless Indian couple receives the greatest gift of all: the son they never thought they'd have.

3865-X **(Four Christmas stories in one volume)**$5.99 US/$7.99 CAN

Dorchester Publishing Co., Inc.
P.O. Box 6640
Wayne, PA 19087-8640

Please add $1.75 for shipping and handling for the first book and $.50 for each book thereafter. NY, NYC, and PA residents, please add appropriate sales tax. No cash, stamps, or C.O.D.s. All orders shipped within 6 weeks via postal service book rate. Canadian orders require $2.00 extra postage and must be paid in U.S. dollars through a U.S. banking facility.

Name_____
Address_____
City_____State_____Zip_____
I have enclosed $_____ in payment for the checked book(s).
Payment <u>must</u> accompany all orders. ❏ Please send a free catalog.

IT'S A DOG'S LIFE ROMANCE

Stray Hearts by Annie Kimberlin. A busy veterinarian, Melissa is comfortable around her patients—but when it comes to men, too often her instincts have her barking up the wrong tree. So she's understandably wary when Peter Winthrop, who accidentally hits a Shetland sheepdog with his car, shows more than just a friendly interest in her. But as their relationship grows more intimate she finds herself hoping that he has room for one more lost soul in his home.
___52221-7 $5.50 US/$6.50 CAN

Rosamunda's Revenge by Emma Craig. At first, Tacita Grantham thinks that Jedediah Hardcastle is a big brute of a man with no manners whatsoever. But when she sees he'll do anything to protect her—even rescue her beloved Rosamunda—she knows his bark is worse than his bite. And when she first feels his kiss—she knows he is the only man who'll ever touch her heart.
___52213-6 $5.50 US/$6.50 CAN